WHERE COWARDS TREAD

A RAVENWOOD MYSTERY

SABRINA FLYNN

WWW.SABRINAFLYNN.COM

WHERE COWARDS TREAD

A Ravenwood Mystery

SABRINA FLYNN

Published by Ink & Sea Publishing

www.sabrinaflynn.com

ISBN 978-1-955207-14-0

eBook ISBN 978-1-955207-15-7

Cover Art by MerryBookRound
www.merrybookround.com

ALSO BY SABRINA FLYNN

Ravenwood Mysteries

From the Ashes

A Bitter Draught

Record of Blood

Conspiracy of Silence

The Devil's Teeth

Uncharted Waters

Where Cowards Tread

Beyond the Pale

Legends of Fyrsta

Untold Tales

A Thread in the Tangle

King's Folly

The Broken God

Bedlam

Windwalker

www.sabrinaflynn.com

To Gus Gus
eater of worlds

"Conscience doth make cowards of us all."
— William Shakespeare, Hamlet

DOMESTIC BLISS

Saturday, October 6, 1900

LEWIS J. FLETCHER DIDN'T WANT TO GO HOME. BUT THERE HE was. He slid his key into a lock. When it clicked he pressed the lever, but the door stuck. Even his key resisted the idea of home.

"Empty-headed…" he muttered.

He turned the key the other way, and this time the door opened. He stepped inside the cramped entryway and shed his hat and coat.

"Ella, you left the door unlocked!" he called.

What seemed a whole parade of running footsteps answered from downstairs.

Lewis clenched his jaw. He glanced in the hallway mirror and smoothed his black hair, then ran a finger over his chin. He'd need another shave before tonight.

An infant screamed from upstairs and a small child darted from the basement. The child wasn't wearing a scrap of clothing.

Lewis lunged for the child as he tried to bolt past. "Ella!" Lewis called. "Why is Bertie downstairs?"

The boy's face and hands were covered in honey.

"Dammit," Lewis swore, holding the child at arm's length.

"Is that you, Lewis?" a weak voice called from the second floor, fighting to be heard over the screaming infant.

"Yes, mother," he hollered back. "*Where* is Ella?"

"She's gone out. I'm not feeling well."

Lewis frowned at his blond-haired half brother. Nineteen years separated them, and a father. He carried the child into the kitchen. It was a mess like everything else in his life. Bertie had gotten into more than just the honey. Flour was strewn about like confetti.

Lewis set the child in the sink and turned on the taps. Bertie screamed with outrage. "It's your own fault. I should let the dog lick you clean."

Now there was an idea.

Lewis ordered his brother to stay put, and opened the back door. A mop of a dog came bounding in, its eyes covered over by a layer of hair. It was a wonder the mutt managed to get anywhere.

A shrill ring joined the infant's squalling and Bertie's whining. Lewis put a hand to his head. *What now?* He started towards the hallway telephone, then stopped, remembering the child. He hastened to get Bertie out of the sink, turned off the taps, and set the dripping, naked boy on the floor. The mop of a dog immediately got to work.

Lewis hurried to the telephone. "Hallo?"

"Lewis?"a voice came back.

"*Ella.*" His frustration with her came through the line. Younger by seven years, Ella was about as useful as Bertie at times. Why was she out so late? "Why aren't you at home? Bertie got into the kitchen, and the house is a mess."

"Didn't mother tell you?"

"I've only just arrived," Lewis said.

"You know mamma wants me to find work. I answered a wanted ad she showed me."

Lewis sighed as he leaned back to check on Bertie in the kitchen. Mop was doing her job admirably. Then he checked the time: a quarter after six. "Look, Ella, I have a board meeting at the Masonic Temple. Where are you?"

"I'm with Mr. Bennett at his house. His family are nice people, and so is he. They want me to start working for them right away. I'll be paid twenty dollars a month."

"Where's the house?"

Hesitation. Lewis pictured his younger sister trying to remember the address. She could be mindless at times. Eventually Ella dredged up the location, but as she did so, her voice trembled. With fear? Nervousness? Women were a mystery to Lewis.

"Hold the wire, I'll let mother know."

"I—"

Lewis didn't wait to hear what Ella had to say. He set down the earpiece and bounded up the stairs two at a time. The last thing he needed was to be late to the Board of Relief.

His mother was lying in bed with a washcloth draped over her forehead. The room was dark and an infant screamed in its cradle. Lewis plucked the babe from its bed and attempted to quiet him, as he relayed the information.

"Absolutely not," his mother said. "I don't know the family."

Lewis bit back a sharp remark. Then why had she sent Ella to interview for a position unchaperoned? "Is James hungry?" he asked instead.

"Colic." It was close to a moan.

Lewis awkwardly patted the infant's back, then gave him over to his mother. She took the babe, reluctantly. Lewis swore right then and there that he'd never marry.

Why his mother had married a second time after his father's death, he could not fathom. The only thing Daniel Spencer had done for his mother was to give her bruises and saddle her with two wailing, intolerable infants before promptly abandoning them.

But then Lewis had an inkling of why she'd remarried. Bertie had been 'premature.' Lewis loathed his mother's indiscretion.

"Tell Ella to come home *at once*. And to make sure to bring the groceries for tomorrow. That girl is the most absent creature in the world at times."

She got it from you, mother, Lewis bit back the words. Instead he fled the bedroom, and picked up the earpiece. "Mother wants you home at once."

"But the position—"

"We need you *here*." Lewis glanced towards the kitchen. The child was gone and so was the mop of a dog. "Come home now. Bring the groceries. If the Bennetts want to hire you, they'll understand you need to arrange your affairs."

Silence. And a faint, "I'll come home." *Click.* Lewis stared at the earpiece, then hung it on its hook. He checked the wall clock, swore silently, and went to find his honey-covered half brother.

2

WELCOME HOME

Monday, October 8, 1900

HOLDING A NEWSPAPER GROUNDED ISOBEL AMSEL RIOT FOR the first time in a week. It felt solid in her hands. Each crinkle of paper reminded her that the world kept turning and that she intended to rejoin it. Though sitting as she was on the window seat, with one bare leg dangling in the crisp air, she didn't appear to be in any hurry to leave her bedroom. *Their* bedroom.

Isobel lowered the paper a fraction and gazed at a large bed. Atticus Riot still slept, his raven hair mussed and boyish, the sharp grooves of his breastbone melding with muscles and scars, covered by a scattering of dark hair. Her eyes trailed appreciatively from his chest, to his ribs, over his stomach, and down to the line of hair that disappeared beneath the blankets.

She leaned her head against the wall, and took a drag on her cigarette. Smoke seeped out the open window, mingling with fog. The air was brisk and the logs in the fireplace smoldering. And contrary to what the newspaper was reporting, the weather wasn't warm in San Francisco. The Silver Mistress had her own ideas.

Isobel was tempted to slip back under the covers with Riot, but if that happened they'd never leave. She returned to her newspaper.

The war in the Philippines was still raging. President McKinley was up for reelection. Union strikes, baseball, an aeronaut whose balloon malfunctioned and parachute failed him, a dynamite explosion (she cringed remembering her own experience), a dead man found in an orchard—

Isobel sat up straight, her eyes narrowed on the short head-line. She was overtaken by a momentary twinge of *deja vu*. But, no—hadn't she read that very same headline at the asylum?

A soft scuff against wood, and Isobel looked up sharply. Riot hadn't moved. She leaned out of the window. A small girl was balancing on a bit of decoration, a rope ladder in her hand. Sao Jin, the younger of their adopted daughters, was dressed in a cap, sweater, and trousers. No shoes. Her long black hair was divided into two braids that hung down her back. Despite the scars that crisscrossed her face, some might describe her as 'adorable'. Isobel knew better.

Officially, in the Cantonese tradition of surname first and given name last, she was now Riot Sao Jin, but Sao Jin Riot would suit the pint-sized daredevil, too.

"Cigarettes are disgusting. They stain teeth yellow."

Isobel flashed her teeth. "I don't smoke often enough." She smashed the stub into her ashtray, which was mostly ash. "That rope ladder is only for emergencies."

"I am testing it for emergencies." Jin balanced along the decorative ledge, over thirty feet off the ground, as she held the ladder with one hand, pulling it around the corner.

Isobel had watched the girl climb too many trees to feel overly concerned. Still, there was an annoying twinge of fear that Jin would slip and fall. As wild as Isobel had been, she'd never forced her mother to watch any of her mountaineering feats.

"You've thoroughly tested it. Now climb back up."

"I must practice. If there is a fire, I might get confused by the smoke." On the surface, the argument was completely logical.

Jin reached out to hook her hand around the window frame. Isobel raised an eyebrow, wondering what the child would do with the ever stretching rope ladder.

"Don't think about coming in here. Riot isn't dressed."

Jin peeked around the window frame, and Isobel shooed her back with a raised newspaper. "Jin, I'm serious."

"I can never tell when you are lying."

"I never lie."

The girl stared at her.

"*Good morning*," Isobel said crisply. "How do you like your room?"

"I like it."

"Make a list of anything you need. Don't you have school today?"

"It is only six o'clock. Sarah says we have to help Miss Lily with breakfast, and then do chores. School starts at noon."

"Noon?"

"Did you expect Miss Dupree to wake up early?" Jin asked.

"I had hoped she would," Isobel muttered.

"You know she is a prostitute." The statement should've been shocking coming from a young girl. In another, better world, it would be, but Jin, like so many girls, had not had a perfect life. Jin's eyes were wise beyond her years and there was no going back.

"Are you excited to start school?"

"I would rather you teach me."

"I'm sure Miss Dupree will keep things interesting."

Jin looked dubious. "Are you coming down to breakfast?"

"I suppose." Isobel resisted the urge to glance back at Riot. *Sooner or later,* she added silently.

"What are you doing today?" Jin asked in her clipped tones. The girl had a personal grudge against contractions.

"We're headed to the agency. And no, you can't come."

Jin's shoulders deflated.

"So tell me, really, how was your visit with my mother and father?"

She and Riot had picked up the children Sunday morning, or tried to. Marcus Amsel had not let the new couple leave until they were fed stuffed to bursting with sausages and sauerkraut, and semi-intoxicated with beer. It had turned into an impromptu *Oktoberfest* when the local Amsel clan conveniently turned up at her parents' doorstep.

Isobel had sworn off food for the next week and Riot was currently sleeping off her father's schnapps. She had only a vague memory of sailing the *Pagan Lady* home that evening, and suspected Jin had done most of the piloting.

"I told you," Jin said. "I liked it."

Isobel's brows drew together. "Are you sure?"

"I like your mother and father."

Isobel gave a small shake of her head. "Amazing," she muttered.

"They took us swimming, but I jumped in the water and sank, and then Mr. Hop would not let me swim without a rope around my waist. Your father took us on walks, and showed us how to distill wine. We went sailing, to the theater, and Mr. Hop made me noodles and rice and pork buns, and *Avó* taught us how to make *sopas*." Avó, the Portuguese word for grandma.

"I'm glad you enjoyed yourselves."

Jin leaned forward, searching her eyes. "So tell me, *really*, how was your wedding trip?"

"It was relaxing."

"Are you *sure?*" Jin asked, doing a fair imitation of Isobel's earlier question. "Or did you discover that Din Gau is fat and lazy and smells bad?" Din Gau was what the criminal tongs called Riot: Rabid Dog.

"I can hear you, Jin." A deep voice came from the depths of the room. Riot's voice wasn't gruff. It was a smooth purr that made Isobel's toes curl.

Jin jerked in surprise, and Isobel grabbed the child's wrist before she teetered backwards.

"I am fine," Jin protested, wrenching her arm free.

"Think of it as a precaution."

Jin's eyes narrowed to a calculating slit. A moment of thought, and the child stepped backwards off the ledge. It was fortunate Isobel remembered the rope ladder, or she might have followed the child out the window in an attempt to save her.

Jin's left hand was solidly wrapped around the rope, and the child swung down and around the corner. The house shook with a bang.

"*Yiu!*"

The muffled curse reassured Isobel that Jin hadn't fallen. But Riot hadn't known about the rope ladder. He rushed to the window, and gripped the sill to peer down at the ground.

"She had your ladder," Isobel explained.

Riot swore under his breath, putting a hand to his bare chest. The rest of him was bare as well.

"Welcome home, Mr. Riot," Isobel said. She gave his flank a slap, and only narrowly ducked beneath his arms. But Riot was persistent. And quick. Isobel soon found herself back in the large bed by the fire, her laughter traveling through the open window.

3

HAPPY RETURNS

The kitchen in Ravenwood Manor looked like a somewhat courteous tornado had blown through. Dishes were stacked to one side, food wiped off, pots soaking, and even the crumbs were grouped into little piles waiting to be cleaned.

Mrs. Lily White ran a tight ship. She sat at the round kitchen table with her children: Grimm, Maddie, and Tobias. Sarah and Jin had joined the family, and Tim was leaning back in his chair with a mug in one hand and an unlit pipe in the other.

Watson sat on a stool, eyeing the remnants of bacon on a faraway plate. He had a calculating look in his feline eyes, and was measuring the distance with a wiggle of his rear end. No one was concerned that he would make the jump.

This was the lull in the storm—the quiet between breakfast and chores. "...he was covered in honey and flour, pale as a ghost, his eyes wide, and naked as the day he was born—"

"Ma!" Tobias tried to shush his mother, to no avail.

Lily didn't miss a beat. "I asked him what on earth he was doing. Do you know what he told me?"

Tobias put his face in his hands, and tried to melt under the table.

"He tells me, 'I can't figure out how white folks get the flour to stick.'"

Laughter filled the kitchen as Isobel wandered inside. Riot was right behind her, a wooden box tucked under his arm.

Maddie wiped the laughter from her eyes. "Toby had used up all the honey and flour, and we couldn't get more because the snow was waist deep. But all ma did was laugh herself to tears. I thought she'd gone crazy that day."

"A sure sign of someone cracked," Tim said, cackling.

"You mean Miss Lily didn't even scold him?" Sarah asked.

Riot joined Isobel by the counter. She handed him a cup of tea, then poured herself coffee.

Maddie was finding it hard to talk while she laughed. "No, ma'am. Ma put him in the stable with the sheep. They licked him clean."

"And that is why Tobias won't go near a sheep to this day," Lily said.

Tobias crossed his arms. "That wasn't right, Ma. That just wasn't right."

"Did they hurt you?" Lily asked.

"I was covered in drool! And they tried to eat—" Tobias cut off, ears near to burning.

"Bet you never did that again," Tim said. "That's cabin fever at its finest. Stranger things have happened, ain't that right, A.J.?"

Riot was leaning against the counter, blowing on his tea. "Are you referring to the time you and some other miners decided to put on a Parisian fashion show in the middle of winter in the Klondike?"

Tim beamed. "I won, too."

When the laughter died, Isobel asked, "Do you keep old newspapers, Miss Lily?"

"I do. Down near the boiler by the coal pile."

Without a word Isobel darted from the kitchen. Riot watched her leave, slightly puzzled. But then the woman was a constant puzzle.

Lily indicated an empty chair. "Have a seat, Mr. Riot."

"I'm afraid we're running late."

"Dam—darn straight," Tim hastily corrected, checking his watch. "We have an agency meeting."

"I do recall," Riot said.

"Yet you missed breakfast." Tim eyed him with a knowing glint.

Riot ignored the older man, and sipped his tea.

"What's in the box?" Sarah asked.

Riot had set the sleek wooden box on the counter. It had a red bow around it. "I'll let Bel explain," he said.

Tim pushed back his chair. "Thank you, Miss Lily. A fine breakfast as always." The old man plucked up his own plate and hers, and carried them to the sink. There was no place for formality in the family kitchen. Everyone helped themselves.

Isobel soon came rushing back with her satchel stuffed to brimming and bumping against her side. Her hair was unruly, neither long nor short, wisps stuck out in untamed directions. A smudge of coal was on her nose, and her blouse sleeves had similar stains. Riot found himself smiling at her.

"What?" she asked.

"You," he said softly.

Steely eyes narrowed on him, and he handed her the wooden box to distract her. Isobel turned to the table. "Here." She set the box in front of Jin.

"What is this?" Jin asked.

"It's a birthday present."

"It's Jin's birthday?" Sarah exclaimed. "I had no idea. How old are you?"

Jin frowned at the long wooden box tied with a bow. "I was born in the year of the Ox, but I do not remember the day."

"You're one step ahead of me," Riot said. He knew neither the day nor the year of his own birth. He figured he was either close to forty or a nudge past it, so he tended to make up an age on a whim. "We would have given you the gift yesterday, but that would have put it on the seventh."

"Why does that matter?" Sarah asked.

"Seven is considered unlucky. July is a 'ghost month' and..." He paused. "Regardless, many happy returns."

"I'll bake a cake for you tonight," Maddie offered.

"I do not like celebrations," Jin said, though she held the box with reverence.

"That's what we figured. You're safe for *this* year," Isobel said, giving the girl's braid a fond tug. Jin was too stunned to glare at her, or kick her shin.

"Open it!" Tobias ordered.

Jin scowled, but the other children took up the chant and Jin gave in. She set her gift on the table, removed the bow, and opened the box. Jin frowned down at the leather case inside, then picked up a card, and read it to herself. The girl swallowed. With eyes downcast, she snapped the lid shut, tucked the box under an arm and hurried from the kitchen.

"She didn't open it," Sarah said, dismayed.

"She didn't clear her plate," Tobias accused.

"Is she all right?" Maddie asked.

Isobel stared at a spot on the floorboards—a single water drop in the doorway. A tear. Without comment, Isobel handed her satchel to Riot and hurried after the child.

"She's likely overwhelmed," Riot explained. He nearly followed, but knew Jin had an easier time confiding in Isobel.

Grimm stood, his shoulders hunched. He always stood that way. The lanky young man either didn't know what to do with his height or he wanted to hide from the world. It was easy to forget he was there. Grimm quietly picked up Jin's plate, and set about doing the dishes.

Sarah sighed. "If anyone is wondering, my birthday is November seventeenth, and I *love* celebrations."

"Noted." Riot said.

"What did you get her?" Sarah asked.

"It's a surprise," Riot said. He placated the girl's arguments with a kiss on the top of her head. Sarah smiled up at him.

"We gonna need the hack?" Tim asked.

"We'll take the cable car," Riot said.

Lily pushed back her chair, and gave a look to the remaining children. They got to work without complaint.

Riot eyed the food, but his stomach hadn't recovered from the Amsel's feast. And his head was still throbbing from the effects of Marcus's liquor cabinet. Riot finished off his tea, and went with Tim to wait in the foyer.

ISOBEL CLIMBED THE STAIRS TO THE VERY TOP OF THE MANOR. She tried to imagine an old man and his housekeeper living in this house alone. How quiet it must have been. No clicking of heels, no drifting voices, no creaky stairs, and definitely no child bolting up four floors like a gust of wind. Was she growing old at twenty-one? Or had she never been exposed to the exuberance of youth?

Isobel paused at the attic door. There was another flight of stairs behind it. She tried the handle. It wasn't locked. Isobel poked her head inside. "Jin?" she called softly.

No answer.

Taking silence as an invitation, she climbed the last flight of stairs and gazed around the attic room. She would have loved the room as a child—private, with access to the roof and a rope ladder. Far away from parental supervision, and buffered by too many stairs. It was perfect.

Jin stood in front of the window, her body stiff and her shoulders set. Isobel knew by the severity of the child's spine that she was struggling with emotion. The box lay on a desk.

"This is why I never give anyone a present. It sends them running away," Isobel said lightly.

"I cannot accept it," Jin bit out.

Isobel walked slowly across the room to stand beside the girl. Jin turned slightly, so Isobel couldn't see her face.

"I knew we should have bought you a frilly dress."

Jin crossed her arms.

Humor wasn't helping. Isobel placed a hand on the girl's shoulder. "Jin, talk to me."

Jin took a step to the side. Her lips were set. Her cheeks dry. "I cannot accept the gift," she repeated.

Isobel considered her adopted daughter. One thing she had learned about the damaged child was to never back Jin into a corner, figuratively or literally. And most especially, emotionally.

"That's all right, then. But I'd like you to keep it safe for me. For a time."

A lash fluttered. "I might break it."

"It's been around the world at least twice. You're a tempest, but it's seen worse." Isobel touched the back of Jin's neck briefly. "I'll see you tonight."

She made to leave, but Jin broke. The girl turned and slipped her arms around Isobel's waist, burying her face against her blouse. Jin held on for a fierce moment. Isobel could feel the child trembling.

Isobel smoothed her hair, then placed a kiss on the top of her head. Deeply scarred, both mentally and physically, Jin had watched hatchet men butcher her parents, and then had spent years with a cruel woman. This wasn't something that would be fixed overnight. Words wouldn't heal the child, and so Isobel said nothing—only held her.

"I am a bad daughter," Jin said, her voice muffled. She turned her head, and rested it against Isobel's stomach.

"I'm a bad mother, but then we haven't been at this very long, have we?" Isobel placed her hands on Jin's shoulders and stepped back to catch the girl's eyes.

Jin's eyes flicked to the floorboards, and stayed there. Isobel studied the girl's face. Scars crisscrossed her cheeks. Some made with a knife. Others with fingernails. Jin was always difficult to read. She churned with emotion but kept it all hidden.

"Why do you think you're a bad daughter?"

The moment Isobel asked the question, she knew she'd get no reply. Jin had clammed up, and pressing her would only make her retreat farther.

Isobel sighed. She gave the girl another hug. Jin didn't resist. "Remember, I chose *you*," she whispered. "I won't be mad, Jin. Whatever is going on. I won't be mad with you. All right?"

Jin nodded.

Isobel waited. Hoping. But Jin only turned back to her window.

The old man rocked impatiently on his heels. "We could bring Jin with us."

"Bel and I considered it, but thought it best if she settled in here," Riot said, as he poked through the newspapers in Isobel's satchel. There was no rhyme or reason to them. Some of the dates were years old.

Tim was shaking his head. "I worry about that girl. I've seen soldiers with that same look in their eyes."

"So do I," Riot said.

"Either way, she's a bright one. Before she ran off to that asylum, she picked up everything I showed her like she was born to it."

Riot turned slightly. "What precisely did you teach her, Tim?"

Tim paused. He put on his "innocent" face. But before he could think of an answer, Isobel appeared at the top of the landing. Without breaking stride, she hopped up on the banister, slid down sidesaddle, and hopped off before reaching the end post. She landed easily on her feet, and took back her satchel.

Riot helped her into a coat. "Is everything all right?" he whispered over her shoulder.

He felt her sigh. "I don't know. Love can sting, I suppose."

It could. It pierced armor and defenses and went straight for the heart. "Should we keep her with us for the day?"

Isobel gave a slight shake of her head. "I think she needs some space to let things settle."

Riot nodded and got the door. Isobel and Tim headed through. As Riot turned to put his key in the lock, Isobel asked, "What was the other reason for Jin's birthday being on the eighth?"

"In Canontese the word 'seven' closely resembles a vulgar word for penis," Riot said.

Isobel laughed. "You'll have to teach me that one."

"Gawd, you have a mouth on you already, girl," Tim said.

"I can always use a larger vocabulary," she shot back.

"A big gun works best."

"Says the short old man."

"Who's still kicking."

The three strolled to Union Street, and crowded onto a cable car. Isobel stood on a runner just under Riot's arm, crushed between a woman draped in furs and a grizzled man whose girth threatened to get him sideswiped by street traffic.

Every time a wagon or cable car passed, the man had to suck in his gut.

Isobel seemed oblivious to the commotion of the city, her fingers drumming on the overstuffed satchel. She must have taken the entire burn pile.

They disembarked along Montgomery Street and followed Tim towards Washington Square, near where the new agency was located. Tim stopped in front of a run-down saloon-cum-whore house turned detective agency. Riot inspected the front, his stick clicking on the boardwalk as he walked along, eyeing the brick building.

"I know it don't look like much now," Tim said. "But work has been busy, and I don't have a whole lotta time on my hands."

"I didn't say a thing, Tim," Riot said.

Tim harrumphed. "But you was thinking it."

"Am I so transparent?"

"This girl here has ruined your cool hand."

Surprisingly, Isobel didn't take his bait. She was deep in thought and Riot knew better than to disturb his wife when she had that look on her face. Something was gnawing at her mind, and she'd only come to it when she was ready.

The windows were a threat—easy to shoot through—so Tim had bricked most of them in, leaving only the two in the front that were next to the door. But they were large and new, with bright gold letters on them.

But Isobel wasn't looking at the saloon-cum-detective agency. Her gaze was down the street on the whorehouses. "Can I borrow some money from you, Riot?"

"Everything I have is yours, Bel."

Isobel glanced at him, and held out her hand. He gave over his billfold and she marched off with the whole thing. Riot stood somewhere between amused and stunned.

Tim chortled. "What do you suppose..." The old man

trailed off as they watched Isobel corner a group of news boys. Riot couldn't make out her words, but she offered them each a cigarette, and flipped them a coin.

The group scattered.

Riot leaned on his walking stick, waiting for her to return. She handed him back his billfold. "You can take it out of my wages." Her eyes danced with amusement. Then she marched through the door, barely glanced at the room inside, and ignored the greeting of the ever cheerful Matthew Smith. Without further ado, She upended her satchel on the battered bar, and began sifting through her newspapers.

4

SHARP AS A KNIFE

SAO JIN SAT IN A CORNER CLUTCHING THE WOODEN BOX. SHE stared at the present. A gift for her, and her alone.

Jin had received a gift before—a wooden duck. It had happened in another lifetime.

She squeezed her eyes shut, and tried to melt into the wall at her back. The wood under her fingertips was familiar. Painfully so. But instead of a box, she felt the grain of her little wooden duck. She remembered joy. It was a distant thing—like a long forgotten language.

To calm herself, Jin counted to ten in English the way Isobel had taught her. Then she counted in Cantonese, Latin, Portuguese, and finally German.

A full minute passed. She opened her eyes.

The attic room was vast by her reckoning. The wooden walls had been whitewashed by Sarah and Tobias. A warm rug sat on the floor by her bed, and downy blankets covered a plush mattress. A desk, a wardrobe, and even a trunk that locked. All hers.

She could decorate the room anyway she pleased, but Jin didn't know what she wanted for herself. She had never had a room. She didn't even know who she was. For the past five years, she had simply lived for the sake of survival with a smoldering fury deep in her gut.

Fury had kept her alive.

And now she held a present in her hands. Jin stroked the wood, tracing the path of its life—the grooves and knots and smooth patches, like Jin's own skin.

Jin knew from experience that joy was fleeting. What if Isobel and Atticus were killed? She looked down at her present, but all she saw was a little wooden duck covered in blood.

Jin took a deep breath through a snotty nose. Annoyed that she had been crying, she opened the wooden box and stared at its contents.

She ignored the card for now. That was too painful.

Carefully, she picked up a battered leather case and slid out a sleek tube. Leather capped both ends. It was a spyglass made of brass and mahogany, she realized.

Jin removed the leather end caps, and extended the spyglass. She put it to her eye. Her whitewashed room jumped into high focus. She lowered it to study the wood. It was worn but well cared for. Many hands had held this spyglass. *V.S.* was etched in the grain.

Jin replaced the leather caps, and turned to the box. The note inside still stung. The words were like a dagger to her heart. Her throat tightened. She couldn't breathe.

She placed the box on the floor, and closed her eyes.

Eventually a soft something rubbed against the back of her hand. Softness was accompanied by a loud purr. Then a low growl. Jin opened her eyes. A giant orange and white head nudged her hand, then nibbled her.

"Ow. Get away from me, you stupid cat."

Watson fell on his side, rolled, and began batting the end of her braid. Jin snatched her braid away. The giant cat stretched, and extended his claws to grab her spyglass case. Jin hissed at him.

Watson narrowed his eyes. And sneezed. Twice. Then he rolled over, and with a flick of a tail sauntered over to her bed. For a large cat, he was surprisingly spry. One giant leap had him curled on her bedspread.

Jin set the box on her desk, and marched over to the feline.

"That is my bed. Leave. *Now*."

Watson purred at her.

Jin reached for the cat, and a split second later she leapt back with a bloody line across her hand. "*Yiu!*"

Watson squinted with contentment and began kneading the blanket, purring as if nothing at all out of the ordinary had happened.

"He's worried about you, is all," came a voice. Sarah stood on the attic steps, looking between the railing slats. She knocked on the wood, even though Jin was looking right at her. The southern white girl seemed unbothered by Jin's glare. "And before you say not to come in, I'm not inside your room."

"You *are* in my room."

"I'm on the stairs. Not my fault there's no door at the top."

"There is a hatch at the bottom," Jin pointed out.

"I knocked, but you didn't answer."

Jin was not about to get into an argument over door place-ment. "The cat is not worried about me. He attacked me." Jin brandished her bloody hand.

Sarah rolled her eyes. "Do you want him off your bed, or not?"

Jin hesitated. After a moment's thought, she gave a curt nod.

But instead of picking the cat up, Sarah sat beside it and began stroking its back. Watson's purr turned into a buzzing machine.

"Are you all right?" Sarah asked.

"I do not see how that question has anything to do with picking up a cat."

"You don't like your present?"

Jin looked away. "I do like it, but I am not worthy of it."

Sarah looked at her, puzzled. "Why would you say that?"

Jin bit her lip. Why, indeed, had she told Sarah anything at all? Jin instantly regretted the comment.

"Look, I won't beat around the bush. I know you don't like that sort of thing, so why are you crying?" Sarah asked.

Jin set her jaw. "You would not understand," she said through her teeth.

"'Course I wouldn't. I'm not you. You don't understand me either, I suppose."

"What is there to understand about you?"

Sarah sighed, but she let the comment roll right over her. Sarah Byrne was not easily provoked, as long as Jin left her art book alone. "I thought we had an all right time together with Isobel's parents. It was fun, don't you think?"

Jin lifted a shoulder.

"It helps to talk to people when something's bothering you," Sarah fished.

Jin crossed her arms in reply.

Sarah stood. "School starts at noon." She started towards the stairs.

"You did not take the cat."

Sarah looked back at her. A freckled face and large hazel eyes, curly black hair whipping out of a braid every which way. Sarah had a face of a young woman who had been loved. Trusting. Carefree. Naive. And yet... Jin shifted under her gaze. Sarah knew a lot of things. "I think you need Watson. He's trying to teach you how to be a friend."

Sarah left Jin alone with the fat cat on her bed. Jin frowned down at the creature, Sarah's words hanging in silence.

With a sigh, Jin turned to her desk, and stood over her gift. The note was open. Isobel's cramped script twisted her heart.

This has been in my family for generations. It's traveled the world twice over. It was my grandfather's and his father's before. And now it's yours. Welcome to the family.

The world blurred. Tears sprang to her eyes. She couldn't accept this treasure—this honor. Jin had plans. Bad ones.

5

LEAPS OF LOGIC

A GRUFF MAN WITH A DROOPING MUSTACHE LEANED BACK ON two legs of his chair. The legs were questionable, but he balanced with his boots on a table as he flipped through a notebook. Atticus Riot had spent a good number of years hoping Montgomery Johnson would flail backwards from a chair. A small, wistful part of Riot hoped it would knock some sense into the man. But he would never wager on it.

"Wilkinson case: cheating wife." Monty flipped to another page. "Brown case: cheating husband." Another page. "And the Donalds case: the wife was sneaking out to plan a surprise anniversary party to celebrate two years of marital bliss." Monty turned his head to propel a wad of tobacco towards a spittoon. A thick, brownish streak oozed down a side of the green patina.

Tim huffed around his pipe stem, a puff of smoke spewing from his lips. "I'm sure that went over well."

Monty inched back a centimeter and the chair creaked in protest, giving Riot hope. But not today. "When I told him, Donalds turned brick red and tried to wiggle out of paying us."

Riot braced himself for what was to come.

"Did you get the cash?" Tim asked.

"'Course I did."

"Not by force, I hope?" Riot asked.

"Well, I didn't have a fancy gentleman's stick to beat him with." Monty nodded towards the silver-knobbed walking stick resting against Riot's chair, then looked over to the bar, where Isobel had planted herself. A few minutes before, a newsboy had come barreling into the agency carrying another stack of newspapers in various states of decay. Now that delivery was scattered over the countertop and she was flipping through pages with an irritated air. When one newspaper disappointed her, she tossed it onto a stack and grabbed the next.

Monty shot Isobel a glare, then turned that glare on Riot. "I told Donalds if he didn't pay us that meant he broke contract and we weren't obligated to privacy laws. So I threatened to tell his wife he suspected she was cheating."

Riot nodded to the grizzled man. "Quick thinking, Monty." Another newspaper was flattened on the bar as Isobel bent to decipher its cramped script.

Tim scratched at his beard. "Huh." He was also watching Isobel's curious behavior.

"I solve three cases, and all I get is a 'huh'?" Monty growled.

Mack McCormick and Matthew Smith tore their eyes from Isobel. Riot had to admit, she was distracting.

Isobel hadn't acknowledged the other agents, she hadn't returned Mack's banter, and she hadn't looked up when Riot called them to order for a meeting. No one knew what she was looking for. And that included her husband.

Had she even noticed she was using a bar as a giant desk? The old saloon wasn't far along in renovations, but it was serviceable. Tim had framed in a consultation room, an office for files, and bricked up most of the windows. But the rest of the office still resembled a saloon and it would likely remain so because Riot had no intention of demolishing the bar. It made for a convenient workspace. Shelves that once held liquor provided storage for a small arsenal of weapons and ammunition, but more importantly the shelving was backed with iron plate. Riot was loath to tear down a bulletproof barrier.

"I'll see you get a bonus," Riot said to Monty. The offer appeased the grizzled agent. Monty clunked down on the floor, leaned forward, and extended a hand.

Riot eyed the dirty fingernails. "After you turn in your reports."

Monty leaned away, and spat a wad of tobacco on the floor.

Riot ignored the gesture, and turned the meeting over to Tim for a report.

"Mack and me traced that stolen racehorse," the old man said. "Idiot thieves covered half the thing in shoe polish, and was hiding with it in a shack down in Oakland. They took one look at Mack and ran for it."

Mack McCormick grinned, and cracked his knuckles. He was a useful agent. Both intelligent and intimidating—a rare thing for a tough—and he was devoted to Isobel. Perhaps a little too devoted.

"I couldn't catch 'em," Mack said.

Tim puffed angrily on his pipe. "We got the horse."

"A sick one," Mack growled.

Riot raised his brows in question.

Tim shifted, plucking the pipe from his lips. "Cussed fools didn't know shit about horses. They fed it bad oats."

"Will he recover?" Matthew Smith asked. Clean cut, his collar was crisp and he sat ramrod straight in his chair. There was compassion in his voice and kindness in his eyes. He hadn't cut it as a policeman, and Riot wasn't sure the young man would make it as a detective. Not for lack of intelligence, but for a large heart. There was worry in the man's voice. True worry—over an animal. What would a murder investigation do to that heart? Riot didn't want to find out, so he'd been assigning Matthew to simple cases.

Again, Riot glanced at Isobel, who was as young as Matthew in body, but not in mind. That same large heart beat in her breast, but it was surrounded by layers of iron plating.

Isobel Amsel was not callous. She just cared too much about things that mattered and that left very little patience for social niceties. She circled something in a newspaper, and set it on a smaller stack.

Tim shrugged. "We got paid. The rest is up to the owners."

"It's not like those race horses aren't run to ground, anyhow," Monty said, ever the cloud of gloom.

Matthew sighed.

"And your case?" Riot asked, looking to Matthew.

The young man already had his notepad in hand. He straightened even more, and flipped it open. "A Mrs. Stewart reported her necklace stolen. She was distraught, because it was a wedding gift from her husband, and they're set to celebrate their ten year anniversary. Her husband left on business two days before the theft and she was planning to attend some sort of charity dinner three days later. When she awoke on that third morning," Monty snorted at the agent's high words, "her lady's maid, Miss Grace, was gone. Supposedly to do errands. But Miss Grace never returned, and Mrs. Stewart discovered the necklace was missing that afternoon when she was getting herself ready. I tracked the maid down in Sacramento. She says she didn't steal the necklace."

"And you believed her?" Monty asked.

"I did, yes," Matthew answered. His gaze flicked to Riot, embarrassed.

"Why did you believe her?" Riot asked.

"She seemed sincere. She was really worried."

"What reason did she give for leaving?" There was no judgment in Riot's voice, only curiosity.

"She knew she'd be blamed."

"Let me guess," Monty said. "A wide-eyed cherry with heaving breasts."

Matthew blushed. "No, well yes. Not the bre... bosom." Matthew snapped his notepad shut. "Look, Miss Grace promised to stay at the hotel where I found her while I sorted things out."

"She'll be long gone, boy," Monty said.

"I don't think so." Matthew looked at the other detectives defiantly. "What else was I supposed to do? I searched her rooms and she didn't have the necklace. I can't very well rough her up without proof she's done something illegal, and I'm not about to risk a lady's reputation over circumstantial evidence. I genuinely believe her. She was scared."

"Of being caught," Monty said.

"Did you go around to the local pawn shops?" Tim asked. He was looking at the young man with a baleful eye.

"I did. The necklace is distinctive: a large sapphire nestled with tiny diamonds. Mrs. Stewart said two of the diamonds were missing. None of the pawn shops had seen it."

"What is your next step?" Riot asked.

"I don't know. But Mrs. Stewart wants that necklace back by next week. She's trying not to involve her husband in the matter. She said if Miss Grace returns the necklace, she's prepared to simply dismiss her without charges."

"Did anyone else have access to the room?" Riot asked.

"The cleaning maid. The butler, I suppose. But they're still there. I searched their rooms, too. Before Mrs. Stewart contacted the agency, she thought she might have just misplaced the necklace and so she turned over the whole house. It's not the first time she's misplaced something."

A newspaper ruffled loudly in the silence as Isobel folded it haphazardly and stuffed it on the larger pile.

"Why don't you send *Mrs.* Riot with him," Monty said loudly, though he was never soft spoken. "Or is she too good to do any work, like she's too good for our meetings?"

Monty was goading Riot. He always did. But this new dynamic of a woman—Riot's wife—working for the agency had complicated things. Riot had to be careful not to take sides. He glanced at Isobel, who seemed oblivious to the comment.

"Because Charlie's the boss's wife," Mack said in defense. "She can damn well do as she pleases."

"Yeah, she does as she pleases as long as she's screw—"

"Shut it," Tim snapped Monty short. There was something in that blue stare that made Monty click his mouth shut. Tim had no qualms about pulling a trigger. The old man was quite good at it.

"I do as I please no matter who I'm screwing," Isobel said without looking up.

Monty choked on his tobacco wad. Matthew turned a new, vibrant shade of red. And Mack started chuckling.

Riot adjusted his spectacles. "We have virgin ears here, Bel," he said gently.

She paused, then looked up to focus on Matthew. "Pardon my language," she said. "It's the husband."

Confusion passed over the men's faces. They looked at Riot with the same question in their eyes: Was she blaming her foul language on him?

Riot took a moment to think on her claim. "The husband?" he asked.

"Who else?" she countered.

"*Mr. Stewart?*" Matthew asked, perplexed.

"Yes, that's what I said. Did you think I meant Riot?"

"I'm sorry, Mrs. Riot—"

"Isobel will do," she said briskly. "Or Charlie, or whatever the hell you like."

"Bitch?" Monty asked.

The big Scotsman leapt to his feet, and Riot's hand twitched to pick up his walking stick and beat Montgomery Johnson senseless. Riot did stand, but only to place a hand on Mack's chest, stopping him short. He turned to Monty, staring down at the smug detective. "I'm only going to warn you once, Monty," Riot said, calmly.

"Or what?"

"He'll let me loose on you," Isobel said with a click of teeth.

Riot had no such intention, but he didn't press the issue.

Matthew shifted. "Why do you think Mr. Stewart would steal his wife's necklace? He wasn't even in town."

All eyes turned to Isobel, who looked particularly small standing at a bar piled with stacks of newspapers. Her black-dyed hair had faded over the summer, and golden hues were beginning to come through like sun breaking through fog. She still had the coal smudge on her nose from earlier.

Isobel focused on Matthew, who shifted in his chair.

Riot waited with the rest of the agents, though he wasn't as doubtful of her claim. She gave her answer in a perfunctory tone that barely allowed for breath.

"You said the husband left two days before. On business. And he was due back for their ten year wedding anniversary. Two days later, the lady's maid begins preparing Mrs. Stewart's clothing for the charity function. She discovers the necklace missing, knows she'll be blamed, and tells the household she's off to run errands. But she takes off for good. When she doesn't reappear, Mrs. Stewart begins dressing herself and finds the necklace missing.

"Three people had easy access: Mrs. Stewart, Mr. Stewart,

and the lady's maid. You say Miss Grace didn't steal the necklace, and I believe you."

"But why would *he* steal it?" Matthew asked.

"Mr. Stewart didn't steal it," she said impatiently. "He took it on his business trip to have the two missing diamonds restored for their anniversary. Tell Mrs. Stewart that you know where the necklace is, and you'll have it for her in a few days time. That way the husband can still surprise her. You can clear Miss Grace's reputation after that."

Silence.

Isobel had made grand assumptions and giant leaps of deduction wrapped in a perfectly logical bundle. The agents were trying to pluck at the threads to unravel her theory. But there were no loose ends.

Some might say it was a good guess, but Riot had worked with Zephaniah Ravenwood long enough to know that some people had an extraordinary knack for deduction. Isobel was one of those rare people.

"And that," he broke the silence, "is why Mrs. Riot does as she pleases."

Isobel turned her gaze on him, her eyes crinkling in a smile.

Monty got out his tobacco box, and stuffed another wad into his cheek. "You're guessing."

"I never guess," Isobel returned.

"The husband might have pawned it himself," Mack argued, grasping for threads.

"The Stewarts aren't at their rope's end. The wife hired our agency instead of contacting the police, which would have cost her nothing and would make sense if she wanted to collect insurance money. Therefore, the necklace clearly holds sentimental value for her, which makes it priceless."

"Maybe it's not insured," Monty countered.

Isobel arched a brow at Matthew, who flipped through his notes. "The necklace is insured," he confirmed.

"Could've been the butler, or anyone else," Monty said.

Tim nodded in agreement.

"I admit, matrimony has made me supremely optimistic," Isobel said crisply. "But I'm willing to wager a full week's pay. Are you, Montgomery?"

The man's jaw stopped working. He sucked in air between his teeth, leaned to the side, and spat into the spittoon. "I'll take your wager."

"I hope you have a nest egg. Anyone else?" Isobel searched the room for volunteers. No one else was willing to go up against her logic. She turned back to her newspapers.

"So whatcha doing, Charlie?" Mack ventured.

"Reading newspapers."

Monty cursed under his breath, and stood. "I need a drink." He grabbed hat and coat, and stomped for the door. He grabbed the handle and wrenched it open just as a man was about to knock. The newcomer arched his neck to look up at the grizzled man and took a hasty step back, nearly tripping down the steps. Monty bulled past the newcomer without apology.

Riot hurried to the door. With a glance he sized up the newcomer. Ruffled black hair, a thin mustache, and a stormy air. The man was in his early twenties, and the way he held his shoulders leant him a martial air. His eyes followed Monty, his jaw clenched in anger, but he held his tongue.

Riot nodded to the newcomer. "You'll have to excuse my agent. Some cases require rough edges."

The newcomer took in Riot's easy charm, scholarly spectacles, trim beard, and tailored suit. The muscles of his jaw unclenched, and the young man relaxed. "I can imagine. Is this the Ravenwood Agency?"

The letters on the windows apparently weren't convincing enough.

"It is. I'm Atticus Riot. Won't you come inside, Mr...?"

"Lewis J. Fletcher."

"These are..." Riot paused. Matthew and Mack had scattered. "My colleagues, Miss Amsel and Mr. Tim." Tim continued to lean against the bar and Isobel didn't glance up. "Forgive the mess. We've recently moved our offices and haven't had time to renovate."

"I don't need a wood worker. I need a detective," Lewis said.

Riot smoothly nudged the grimy spittoon under a nearby table with his boot, and took a seat, gesturing for Lewis to do the same. "How can I help you?"

Lewis's green eyes flicked to the woman behind the bar. "Actually, I was hoping to speak with Miss Amsel. To both of you."

Riot glanced over his shoulder, not surprised, but amused. Feeling eyes on her, Isobel stopped and glanced his way. She cocked her head in question, and he tilted his towards Mr. Fletcher.

"It's a matter of some delicacy," Mr. Fletcher said.

Isobel ran a cool, appraising gaze over the man. "Riot is far more delicate than I, but please go on."

"It's only that I read about you in the newspapers, Miss Amsel. That you found those missing boys in Napa. And I thought..." Lewis cut off. He cleared his throat gruffly.

"What has happened, Mr. Fletcher?" Riot asked.

"My younger sister. Ella. She's gone missing."

6

DARKNESS

MISSING. THERE WAS A DARKNESS IN THAT SINGLE WORD. Atticus Riot was familiar with that darkness. He had found what lay at the end of it too many times.

"How old is Ella?" It was a hard question. A beginning to a difficult path—the first step of responsibility.

"Fifteen."

Sensing Riot's shift in mood, Isobel abandoned her newspapers and pulled a chair over to the pair. Tim took out his notebook.

"My mother recently divorced our stepfather." There was distaste in Lewis's tone. "Times have been hard. Ella occasionally finds work minding children, but mother has been pressing her to find something more permanent."

Lewis reached inside his coat and withdrew a folded bit of newspaper, along with a letter. "This advertisement was in the morning paper on Friday."

Isobel leaned closer to Riot, and he held the slip at an angle so they could both read it.

WANTED—A young white girl to take charge of a child and do light housekeeping. Apply at Box 1520.

"Mother urged Ella to answer it, so she wrote a response," Lewis continued. "On Saturday, she received a reply." Lewis handed over the letter.

Isobel took the envelope and studied the front with an intensity that Riot could feel as a physical thing.

Elouise Spencer, 1747 Fulton Street. The return address was to *John Bennett, Box 1520.* San Francisco postmark. Isobel put the envelope to her nose, and inhaled.

Lewis's dark brows shot up in alarm.

"Cologne," Isobel said under her breath. She took out the slip of paper, noting how it was folded, and passed the envelope to Riot, who waved it under his own nose. He couldn't place the cologne.

The message was written in the same hand as the address:

If this letter does not reach you in time to call at the Popular Restaurant, 55 Geary Street, at 1 o'clock, call at 6 p.m. Ask at the restaurant for Mr. Bennett.

—JOHN BENNETT

Good spelling. Educated. Common paper. The kind bought at any general store. From the smooth ink lines, he'd wager it was written at a writing desk. But the lines were thick, and the slant severely to the right. Confident. Eager. Excited.

Riot nodded for Lewis to continue. "The letter was delivered too late for her to make the one o'clock appointment, so according to my mother, Ella set off shortly after five o'clock. I came home from work after six o'clock. I was in a hurry, and set to attend a meeting. Mother was ill, and the telephone rang. It was Ella. She told me about the advertisement, and that she had met Mr. Bennett and was at his house. His family, she said, were nice people, and they wanted her work straight away. She'd be paid twenty dollars a month. I asked her where the house was and she said 1500 Geary Street.

"I left her on hold to relay the message to our mother. Mother wanted her to come home immediately, and I agreed.

I told Ella and she said she'd come home. Then she hung up." Lewis smoothed his black mustache and closed his eyes briefly. "It was the last I heard from her. She never came home."

The last was a whisper. That creeping darkness had a hold of Lewis, and Riot well knew that it would never let him go. Two nights missing. Where was Ella? The imagination could be a cruel tormentor, but the rub, the true horror, was that generally imagination failed to live up to the truth. Truth was far more brutal.

"Why did Ella leave so early?" Isobel asked suddenly.

"I beg your pardon?"

"Your mother said Ella left at five o'clock. It can't take more than twenty minutes by cable car to get to the Popular. She could have started later and still had plenty of time to make the appointment. What was she doing for forty minutes?"

"I don't know." Lewis hesitated. "Maybe she didn't want to be late?"

"You said you came home from work after six. Do you remember the precise time of the telephone call?" Isobel asked.

Lewis thought a moment. "Six-fifteen. I'm sure of it."

"Are you sure it was her?" Isobel asked.

"I…" Lewis glanced at Riot, his brows knitting together with puzzlement. It was a slight expression, a mere twitch in an otherwise stoic face. "Yes, I'm sure it was my sister. Though…"

"Yes?" Isobel pressed.

"She sounded afraid. Or nervous. I'm not sure."

Isobel sat back, satisfied for now.

"What time did the call end?" Riot asked.

"It lasted maybe ten minutes at most. I was running late, you see. So without further thought on the matter, I ran out the door."

"To the the Board of Relief meeting at the Masonic Temple," Isobel stated.

Lewis started in surprise. "How did you know?"

Riot glanced at Isobel, who looked supremely pleased with herself. She caught Riot's eye and sobered. To the unobservant, Isobel's deduction was mystical, but Riot could follow the path of logic she had taken. Lewis sported a small Masonic square and compass pin on his left lapel. And it would only take someone who regularly read the newspapers to know that the Masonic Temple had a Board of Relief meeting on Saturday night at seven o'clock.

As impressive as it was, voicing her deduction interfered with Riot's observation of the young man—the telltale signs of a lie: nervousness, unease, fear. Surprise erased all of those. This would take some getting used to, Riot realized. He and Isobel had not worked as partners on an official case before. They had been more akin to rivals. And that was nearly a year ago.

Riot took a mental step back, giving Isobel the reins.

Isobel gestured to Lewis's lapel pin. "It was obvious."

Lewis glanced down at the pin, and nodded. "I see. Yes, I was set to attend the meeting."

"Had Ella answered other advertisements your mother showed her?" Riot asked.

"Yes, I think so. But they never panned out."

"What happened when you returned?" she asked.

"I arrived home at eleven o'clock and discovered my mother in a state of panic, which isn't uncommon. But Ella being out so late was. While she could be absentminded about time, she was never overly late. I immediately set out to 1500 Geary Street only to discover it was an empty lot."

Riot adjusted his spectacles.

"I began knocking on doors. No one knew of a family by the name of Bennett on the street. Frantic, I went to the

Popular Restaurant, but it was already closed. I hoped she'd be home, so I returned, but she wasn't." Lewis paled. "I thought she had perhaps disobeyed orders to come home and taken the job on the spot. But when we didn't hear from her on Sunday morning, I went to the restaurant. The staff said there was a man by the name of Bennett, who had come at both one o'clock and five o'clock, but he ate alone and no one saw Ella. Mother said she was wearing her golf cap and red capelet. It's hard to miss."

Riot rubbed a hand over his beard, glancing at the letter. "Have you reported this to the police?"

Lewis leaned forward. "Surely you see how this looks?" he asked in earnest.

Riot waited, watching the young man. He could feel Isobel vibrating with questions next to him. He discreetly touched her elbow. *Wait*, he silently urged, but it was too much for her.

"You think your sister ran away," she stated.

Lewis sighed. "I'm afraid so."

"Could she have gotten the address wrong? You said she was absentminded."

"She wouldn't get an *entire street* wrong. And besides that, she had money for groceries. This man Bennett—the staff said she never even met him at the restaurant. I think she made up a phony address and took off with a friend of hers."

"A friend?" Riot asked.

"Madge Ryan," Lewis said with a twist of lips. "She's a troubled girl. Wild and spirited. She ran from home some months ago."

Riot leaned back and crossed his legs. Suddenly the darkness wasn't so ominous. Then why was he still worried?

"My mother is frantic. She wants me to report it to the police, but if I involve the police, then the papers will find out about it. I worry about Ella's reputation. I came to your agency so you could find Ella. Discreetly. And bring her back."

"Why would Ella run away?" Isobel asked.

Lewis straightened his cuffs. "To escape her responsibilities and younger half brothers? I really don't have the faintest idea. But she's always been prone to wild imaginings. A few months ago she was set on becoming an actress, of all things."

"Did she pack a bag?" Isobel pressed.

"No, not that mother and I know of, but as I said she had the money for groceries."

Riot glanced at Isobel. She met his eyes. The gray in hers glistened like steel. She didn't like what she heard any more than he did.

Riot turned back to the young man. "Mr. Fletcher, before we accept your case we have one condition."

"I'll find a way to pay whatever fees you require," Lewis said. It was clear by his suit that he was not a wealthy man, but he tried to be presentable.

Riot gave a slight shake of his head. "Payment is a secondary concern. I'm worried for your sister. You need to report this to the police. At once."

"But she's only run off," Lewis insisted.

"And if you're wrong?" Riot's question hung there, bloated with suggestion and creeping danger. Isobel did not break that silence—it was near to a tangible thing.

Finally, Lewis slumped in his chair. "Yes. I'll go straightaway."

WHEN LEWIS FLETCHER FINISHED GIVING THEM A DESCRIPTION of his sister, he left for the police station. Riot nodded to Tim. Words didn't need to be spoken. The pair had been down this road before.

"I'll get my people on it," Tim said, and left with the usual spring in his step. He had an impressive network of informants that spanned the west coast.

"Every time I ran away, I packed a bag," Isobel said as she studied Lewis's business card. *Lewis J. Fletcher, Junior Clerk. Ford and Co., Real Estate*

"It's certainly suggestive," Riot said.

Isobel slipped the card in a pocket, and reached for her hat. "I'm surprised you asked for police involvement at all. Won't they muddy the waters?"

Before Riot could answer, a woman came prowling down the stairs into the main room. He would not have recognized her but for the wild look in her eyes and the rat sitting on her shoulder. Miss Lucky Off was halfway presentable. Aside from an obvious bath, her gray hair was free and wild, but it was straight, and she wore an array of colorful scarves over blouse and skirt. Riot thought she wasn't much older than himself— maybe by ten years—but an unforgiving life had etched deep lines in her face.

The woman flew at the bar with intent. She began muttering to herself as she snatched up Isobel's newspapers.

"Don't touch those," Isobel snapped.

Miss Off did not listen.

Isobel abandoned her hat, and darted across the room to snatch the papers from the woman's arms.

"You've made a mess," Miss Off snarled. "I work my fingers to the bone to keep this dump presentable and you and your lot go and make a mess of it."

"I need those papers left *exactly* as they are," Isobel said through clenched teeth. "Who are you?"

Riot cleared his throat. "This is Miss Lucky Off. Miss Off, this is Miss Isobel Amsel."

"Oh, so you're the shaney's fancy mistress?" Miss Off snickered.

"She's my wife," he corrected.

Isobel looked to Riot. "Why is she here?"

Riot tapped a finger on his walking stick. Faced with Isobel's sharp eyes, Riot considered blaming the hire on Tim for a moment. But it was a long, tempting moment. "I hired her as housekeeper for the agency."

"That he did. And I'm doing a fine job." Miss Off again made a lunge for the newspapers, but Isobel slid the entire stack down the bar and out of arm's reach.

Isobel drew herself up to her full five feet of height. "Leave my newspapers alone."

"Or you'll do what?" Miss Off shot back.

Isobel arched a brow. "I can't vouch for the safety of your rat."

Miss Off shrank back, holding a hand up over her pet, trying to shield his pink little ears from threat.

The telephone rang. Miss Off flicked it an irritated glance. She gave Isobel a crude gesture, then stalked over to the device.

"Ahoy!" she screamed down the line.

Riot winced.

Isobel picked up a brick from behind the bar and set it on her stack of newspapers.

"You could always bring them along if you're that worried," he offered, as he returned her hat and opened the door for her.

Isobel stopped, and tapped her lips twice. "Now that you mention it, isn't a husband supposed to carry things for his wife?"

Riot firmly shut the door behind them. "What's caught your interest in the articles?"

Isobel turned serious. "I'm not sure yet."

He cocked his head.

"I mean, I do know... I just..." Color rose to her cheeks. "It may be nothing," she admitted.

"When something catches your eye it's generally *something*." He gave the brim of his hat a smart tweak.

"Your ego hardly needs bolstering, Riot."

"Monty would agree with you. By the way, I *am* sorry about him."

She lifted a shoulder. "Don't be. I'm used to his type. Besides, he's a good agent."

"Maybe so," Riot admitted. "But I wonder if he's worth it."

"Did you hire him, or Tim?"

"Ravenwood did."

She raised her brows. "Interesting choice."

"Some might say that about me. Believe it or not, Monty worked well with Ravenwood. He respected him."

"And brothers rarely get along," Isobel mused.

"Why do you say that?" he asked.

"Ravenwood was like a father to you, Riot. Perhaps he was to Monty as well—but you were the favorite. Small wonder Monty doesn't listen to you."

Riot frowned in thought. She had a point.

"Speaking of hiring. Well chosen with Miss Off." Sarcasm dripped from her lips.

"I admit Miss Off needs some work. But don't we all? She *has* improved."

"*Lucky Off?*"

"The name she gave me was far too crude."

The edge of Isobel's lip twitched upwards.

"Shall we find this wayward girl?" he asked.

"I sincerely hope we do. Where to first?"

Riot stared down at her, bemused. "Aren't you going to take the lead?"

"I'm captain on the *Pagan Lady*. While this…" she gestured at the street. "…is your domain. And your agency. I don't mind being your first mate on land."

"*Love hath made thee a tame snake,*" Riot quoted the poet.

Isobel's eyes narrowed. "A tame snake can still bite," she warned. "Anyhow, I'm sure we're of like mind on this."

"Are we?" he wondered.

"I know precisely where I want to start. Do you?"

"I do."

"Right, then. We'll set off on three."

Riot gave a slight nod, and Isobel began the brief count. On three, they walked their separate ways.

7

THE POPULAR

THE POPULAR RESTAURANT LIVED UP TO ITS NAME. A HARRIED waitress was navigating the crowd with a grace that Isobel admired. With her brown hair in a neat bun, a starched apron, and a pencil tucked behind her ear, she balanced an over-loaded tray in one hand and easily lifted it over the heads of diners.

"I'll be right with you," she said. "Grab a table if you see one."

Their prospects didn't look promising.

Riot leaned close to speak in Isobel's ear. "I hadn't accounted for the lunch crowd," he said loudly over the din. They were just blocks away from the financial district and on a main street; the place was packed with suits and newspapers.

"You're just thinking with your stomach, Watson." But she well knew that wasn't the case. Riot was a tracker. He preferred to start at the beginning of a trail and widen his search, while Isobel preferred to anticipate, and jump ahead.

A glint of amusement shone in his eyes. "I'm still recov-ering from the Amsel family *Oktoberfest*. We can head to Ella's house and return later." Going to Ella's home had been Isobel's idea.

A booming laugh rose above the din of conversation. She winced slightly. "We're here now. Let's get it over with."

Riot wound his way upstairs, but the farther they moved into the restaurant the more oppressive the air became. Sound was hitting her like crashing waves—a loud, overwhelming jumble of noise all running together. Her mind did not have a switch. It dissected and processed everything at once in a rush of stimuli that left her drained.

Riot pulled out a chair for her, but Isobel didn't take the offered seat. Her heart was pounding and she was finding it hard to breathe.

"I NEED AIR," ISOBEL MURMURED. SHE TOUCHED HIS ARM briefly, then nearly collided with the waitress as she flew down the stairs.

Riot started to follow, but stopped. He searched the crowd for anyone who might have alarmed her, but decided it was simply the noise. As high-strung as Isobel was, he suspected she was always trying to pick apart every detail in a crowd.

"Is something the matter with your chair, sir?" an out-of-breath waitress asked. She was balancing a heavy tray on one hand.

"Nothing at all." He smiled easily, and took a seat, his back to the wall.

"Can I get something for you?"

"Tea, please. Is it always this busy?"

"For lunch, but the crowd will die down soon enough." The waitress smiled and turned on her heel in a neat pirouette to deposit a plate on a nearby table.

Riot checked his watch. Twelve forty-five. Lunch was

nearly over. He hoped Saturdays weren't as busy. It would be difficult for the staff to recall a specific patron in a crowd this size.

A few minutes later the waitress set down his tea. "Can I get you something to eat?" she asked, taking out a notepad and plucking the pencil from her ear.

"Just tea for now. But when you have a moment, I have some questions. It won't take long." Riot glanced to one side. A graying man with a stoop hurried over and touched the waitress's arm. The pair looked to another woman—a blonde with puffy red eyes, who was tying on an apron as she walked from the kitchens.

The first waitress sighed with relief. "I'm due for a break. Mr. Krone will help you." She gave Riot an apologetic smile before hurrying downstairs.

"Poor Miss Marshal's been on her feet all day. What can I get you, sir?" Mr. Krone asked.

Starched collar, tie, and suit, the graying man wasn't dressed for waiting tables and he didn't bother with a notepad. Not a clerk, then. Nor a new manager. "You're the proprietor of the Popular," Riot said instead.

"I am. Mr. Krone, sir."

"Atticus Riot." He produced his card. "I have a few questions for your staff. They have nothing to do with your establishment, but your answers may help save a girl's life."

The man softened immediately. It was clear from the way he'd allowed Miss Marshal a break that he had a heart. And Riot was playing to that heart.

"Of course. One moment." Mr. Krone went to speak with Miss Marshal's replacement, then returned and pulled up a chair. "I've been on my feet most of the day, too. But the rush is nearly over and the orders are in. It's nice to have an excuse to sit."

"Your restaurant certainly lives up to its name," Riot noted.

Mr. Krone chuckled, a dry bit of amusement. "Trust me. There were some nerve-wracking months that had me questioning what sort of fool I was for getting ahead of myself. But yes, it all worked out in the end. I suppose this is about that girl and Mr. Bennett?"

"You know him?"

"I know Mr. Bennett, but like I told Mr. Fletcher when he came by, I never saw his sister. On Saturday, Mr. Bennett came for lunch at one o'clock and then returned for supper at five. He told Miss Marshal to send up any callers, but no one came."

"How long have you known Mr. Bennett?"

Mr. Krone's gaze turned inward. He rubbed his chin as he thought. "Oh, for years now. But only on and off, mind you. I only learned his name three weeks ago."

Riot waited for an explanation. A statement like that begged for one, and Mr. Krone obliged.

"Years ago, Mr. Bennett was a regular for about three weeks. I remember, because I had only just opened and I was appreciative of the business—he ate lunch and dinner here every day, then he just up and disappeared. He started coming again last year, and he told me he had given up his job as a printer to become a minister. Had a clerical collar and all. He comes every few weeks or so."

"Do you know where he went when he left on Saturday? Where he lives?"

Krone shook his head. "I've always assumed he's from the country, coming to the city on business. He has that look about him. A great strong fellow. Maybe your age, thirty-five or so. Has a reddish-brown mustache and wears clerical clothes. But I didn't see him meet a girl. I'd have remembered that."

A NARROW HALLWAY CAUGHT ISOBEL'S EYE. SHE SHOT DOWN IT, walked past the noisy kitchen, and shoved opened a back door. She stepped into a narrow alley and took a deep breath.

The noise had hit her worse than usual. Far worse. Between jail, months at a country asylum, and a week of sailing with Riot, she'd not had a great deal of contact with the world.

Isobel leaned against a brick wall and continued to breathe. Her sense of smell came back first. Garbage. Rotting food. Mildew. She opened her eyes to find an army of alley cats perched on various surfaces, staring at her. They were all fat. There likely wasn't a rat left alive in the alley.

Minutes passed, with only a faint din of noise spilling out from the restaurant. Deep breaths, she reminded herself, as she counted to ten in every language she knew. Eventually, her heart rate slowed, then picked right back up again as she clenched her jaw in anger. With herself. It was her first official day on the job, and she'd fled a restaurant in front of her boss. Never mind he was her husband, too. That made it worse somehow. Riot couldn't even fire her.

Isobel squared her shoulders and prepared to reenter the fray. Then the back door opened and a burst of noise filled the alley. It cut off when the door slammed shut. A thin woman wearing a starched apron leaned against the closed door with a long sigh. It was the harried waitress from inside. The woman glanced to the side, surprised to find a diner studying her. She gave Isobel an uneasy smile, and moved over a bit to rest a foot on the brick wall.

Isobel offered her a cigarette, but the woman shook her head.

"Not keen on the gentleman you came with?" the waitress asked. Although she had voiced the question, she sounded doubtful.

"It was the noise in there."

The waitress reached down and started massaging her ankle through her boot. "Don't I know it. Always is, this time of day."

"I'm surprised you got a break," Isobel said, tucking away her cigarettes.

"It's already dying down, and Amanda finally came. I worked through most of lunch without her, and she can darn well do the rest."

"How's the crowd after lunch, around one o'clock?"

"It's a lot quieter."

That was telling to someone like Isobel. One o'clock was the time Mr. Bennett had arranged to meet Ella, which meant he was familiar with the Popular Restaurant. The lunch hour would hardly be the time to conduct an interview.

The waitress was staring at Isobel intently. "Do I know you?" she asked.

"Isobel Amsel."

The woman's eyes flew wide. "I've heard of you!" She caught herself and flushed, embarrassed by her outburst.

"And yet you're still standing here with me." Isobel gave the woman a wry smile.

"I loved that you didn't back down from that Kingston fellow. Putting up with that kind of slime isn't worth any money in the world. By the way, I'm Laura Marshal," she said, offering her hand.

Miss Marshal had an easy way of talking, confident and sure of herself, like someone who has grand plans for life. But then that could be said of most people in San Francisco. It was a city of dreams. All that wild ocean tended to inspire the heart.

"Is that fellow at the table Atticus Riot?"

"He is."

Laura beamed. "I'll have a story for the boarding house. Mr. Riot... he's your husband now, isn't he?" Isobel nodded. "I saw him fall into conversation with Mr. Krone. He's the owner. I was worried it was something I said. Gosh, the newspapers didn't lie about him."

Isobel had written a number of those articles; she'd kept up writing while she was serving time in the asylum. A little positive publicity never hurt a business. Unfortunately, it had inspired a number of women to seek him out.

"Most of the time papers do lie. But not in this case." Isobel studied Miss Marshal for a moment. She had the look of an eager amateur sleuth, so Isobel decided honesty would work best. "We're searching for a missing girl," she explained. "Her brother came by yesterday. Lewis Fletcher. Black hair, thin mustache, has a stormy look about him."

"I didn't talk with him, but Mr. Krone did."

"No one asked you about a fellow named John Bennett?"

Laura smirked at her. "Do men ever ask us women anything?"

Isobel laughed. "I don't suppose you saw the man? He would have been here Saturday, possibly for lunch and dinner."

Laura thought a moment. "I remember that fellow. Both times he asked me to direct any callers to his table. I've seen him before, too. Fair tipper. Polite. He always brings a book or newspaper to read. But I didn't know his name until now."

"Did anyone meet him?"

Laura shook her head. "He ate lunch and left. Then later on he came back for dinner. It did seem like he was expecting someone, though. I saw him pacing out in front of the restaurant after he finished his dinner."

"What time was that?"

Laura shrugged. "I'm sorry, I can't be certain. Just before six, maybe?"

"Does he ever dine with friends?"

Laura shook her head. "Not that I've seen. And I practically live here."

"What does he look like?"

Laura tilted back her head and looked at a slice of gray sky between buildings. "He's a great strong-looking fellow. Nice hands. I don't think he's ever done a day's hard work." Laura held out her own hands to study them. Cracked skin, callused palms, strong fingers and short nails. Much like Isobel's own.

"He has nice teeth. Brownish hair and a mustache, maybe on the black side. But there's a certain droop to his eye." She gestured to her right eye. "He was wearing a long topcoat, a dark cutaway coat, and trousers of the same cut. A black derby hat. I think he fancies himself a sharp dresser, but nothing like your husband up there. If you don't mind me noticing."

"Not at all." Riot wasn't vain, but he dressed the part of a gentleman—a childhood of deprivation made him appreciative of finer things.

"You said his name was Bennett?" Laura asked.

"As far as we know."

Miss Marshal dropped her foot from the wall, a glint of excitement in her eye. "He had a diamond ring, too. Not on his wedding finger. And a gold watch with a gold chain. Personally, I thought his chin was too long for his face. He could do with a beard to hide it."

The comment struck Isobel. Was that why Riot wore his? To hide some deficiency in his jaw? She tried to picture him without his beard, but failed. Black but peppered with gray, it was soft and trimmed, and felt like a caress against her skin. She rather liked it.

"Accent?" Isobel asked.

"Not anything unusual. With his book though, he looked a studious type."

"Did he talk with anyone on the sidewalk while he was pacing?"

Laura shook her head. "Not that I saw. Of course, I was busy with customers."

Isobel handed over an agency card. "If Mr. Bennett returns can you send me a telegram? Immediately. And if you're feeling daring try to discreetly get more information out of him. Such as an address."

Laura smiled. "Like a detective?"

"Yes, but please be careful about it. I can't vouch for his character."

Laura gazed at the Ravenwood Agency card. There was glee in her brown eyes. "Oh, I know my way around danger. You can't be too careful in this city. I only wish more young women understood just how dangerous it can be."

Many did, eventually. Too many. Usually far too late.

Isobel walked back into the restaurant. It was much quieter, but she wasn't there to eat. She headed out the front door, and paced the front of the restaurant, imagining John Bennett doing the same.

A cable car rattled past, dinged its bell and pulled to a stop. The Geary line ran along Market and connected with Fulton, the street where Ella's family lived.

Isobel took off towards the cable car, past a general store, a laundry, and a law firm, then stopped. A Western Union office sat in front of the cable car stop.

Had Ella really telephoned her brother from Mr. Bennett's home? Miss Marshal confirmed that Mr. Bennett hadn't met the girl inside the restaurant, and even if they'd met on the street, they'd hardly have had time to travel to his home. That meant Ella had lied to her brother.

A bell tinkled overhead as Isobel shoved open the door. Two people stood in line, and a third leaned against a paneled wall, shouting through the paid telephone line.

A telegraph agent, message in hand, turned from the counter and sat at a desk. Isobel stepped up to the counter, smiled at the first man in line, who appeared to have come straight from a ranch, and casually reached over the counter.

She turned the logbook towards her. Keeping one eye on the agent's back and another on the pages, she flipped through to Saturday and searched the history of telegrams for the names E. Spencer or J. Bennett.

"Miss!" The cry told her she hadn't kept an eye on the agent. He burst from his chair in alarm.

"Sorry, but you seemed so horribly busy," she said in a flighty voice. Isobel shifted her shoulders to seem unsure of herself.

"That's government property, Miss."

Isobel's eyes flew wide. "It is? But I didn't... I mean... You won't summon the police will you? I've heard such awful stories." She dabbed at her eyes with a handkerchief.

"He'd best not," muttered the cowhand.

An older lady behind him narrowed her eyes. "And just what *were* you doing, Miss?"

They all looked at her, save the man on the telephone. Leave it to a woman to see through her act.

"It's my friend. She was here on Saturday, you see, and was supposed to get a telegram from me. Only she said it never got here, but I didn't believe her. The Western Union is reliable, isn't it?" Isobel fluttered her lashes. "Surely it's a more respectable means of communication then that infernal device on the wall."

The old woman began nodding in agreement. The agent looked perplexed. There was nothing like challenging the integrity of a business to rile a professional. The agent walked to the logbook and opened it to Saturday.

"Bennett is my last name," Isobel lied, and leaned over the counter to look at the list. "E. Spencer is my friend. Ella's younger than me. Dark hair. She'd have been wearing a golf cap with a little bob on top and a red capelet." Isobel gestured over her own head.

Light entered the clerk's eyes. "She did come in. I thought

it too late for a young woman to be out alone. I'm afraid she didn't ask me about a telegram. She just used the telephone there."

"Was she alone?" Isobel asked.

"Yes," the agent said.

"Well, I hope her father came to fetch her. He did, didn't he?"

"No, she just left. Now, if you'll excuse me…"

Isobel moved to stand directly in front of the man on the telephone. She stood very close, and stared. Hard.

The man straightened from the wall. If there was one thing she appreciated about her mother—it was the Saavedra eyes. Cut from steel, that stare flayed a person to the bone.

The man quickly said goodbyes to his sweetheart and fled. Isobel plucked up the receiver and clicked the lever.

"How may I direct you?" came a pleasant voice over the line. Not so long ago, rude boys had been employed by the telephone agencies. They had all answered the telephone with a demanding 'Ahoy!' With the boys' social skills lacking, the telephone agencies had quickly turned to women. A small part of Isobel missed that foul-mouthed band of telephone operators.

"Who is this?" Isobel demanded, channeling her mother.

"Excuse me?"

"I'd like to know who my daughter was speaking with."

"I'm Miss Clark. A telephone operator."

"A what?"

"I connect telephone calls."

"Who did you connect my daughter to?"

"I beg your pardon?"

"My daughter, Ella, placed two telephone calls on Saturday. The first was to her brother at 1747 Fulton Street at around six o'clock."

"Ma'am, I'm not allowed to give out that information."

"This is precisely why I won't install a telephone line in our home. They're the work of the devil himself. My daughter is *fifteen*. I'm having a time with her. *Please*."

A moment's silence. "Yes, of course, let me check the toll ticket."

Isobel leaned against the wall and waited, while the elderly woman in line huffed at her.

"There was a call placed to that address at six fourteen. It lasted ten minutes. And then, directly after, another call was placed to Menke's Grocery at Central and Golden Gate Avenue."

"A grocery store?"

"Yes, ma'am."

"Did she speak to a man?"

"We don't listen to calls."

That was a blatant lie. Operators listened to make sure the connection held and checked on calls to see if they had ended. And when an operator was bored, she just outright listened.

"Of course not. But surely you heard who answered?"

"I can ask the operator who took the call."

"Thank you."

There was a pause, then, "She's not working today."

Isobel made a sound of frustration. "What is her name?"

"Ma'am, I can't give out that information. If I can have your address, or…"

"Which telephone exchange is this?" Isobel demanded.

The line went dead.

Isobel stared at the box. Maybe girls weren't much more courteous than the 'Ahoy' boys after all.

If this John Bennett left The Popular at six o'clock and Ella placed a call to her brother at six-fourteen, that left plenty of time for the two to have met on the street. But was this John Bennett involved, or had Ella Spencer simply used the opportunity to run away from home?

Isobel started for the cable car, but the moment her foot

touched the runner, she remembered she had a partner. Riot, of course. This would take some getting used to. But when she headed back to the Popular to fetch her husband and partner, she discovered he had already left. At least, she thought, in this they were of like mind.

8

MENKE'S GROCERY

A SCARECROW OF A MAN WEARING ROUND SPECTACLES AND A green apron was stacking apples on an overturned crate. He was meticulous about their placement. Isobel stopped in front of Menke's Grocery, and waited for the man to place the crown on his apple pyramid. Through the windows, she saw a young man inside sweeping the floor.

She'd wager everything in Riot's billfold that this was the proprietor. Only a German would place an apple with so much precision. "*Herr* Menke?"

The man straightened. His eyes narrowed as he looked at her before answering. "I am he. Do I know you, *Fräulein?*" His accent was thick and his words sounded like mush. Isobel switched to German to practice her Bavarian accent. His eyes lit up.

"Do you know Ella Spencer?" Isobel asked. Pleasantries were lost on Germans. They appreciated a blunt approach. Ask what you want; don't circle around it.

"I do."

"Does she come here regularly?"

His eyes narrowed. "Is something the matter?"

Ella's brother had asked for discretion, but that was difficult when asking after the whereabouts of a young girl. "She's missing."

Menke made a pained sound, giving Isobel his full attention. "*Missing?*"

Isobel nodded. "Did she come by Saturday?"

"I was not here. One moment." Menke hurried inside with the springy step of a man who defied his age.

A moment later, Menke came out with a stocky lad. Swarthy and black-haired, he had the look of a footballer. But instead of a ball, he clutched a broom.

"Answer her questions, Leo."

Leo gave Isobel an apologetic look. Clearly the young man thought his boss was on the rude side.

"Isobel Amsel." She thrust out her hand to the boy.

"Leo," he said quietly. A blush turned him red when he met her eyes.

"You were here Saturday?"

He nodded. "Did a girl around your own age come in? Ella Spencer. Dark hair. She'd have been wearing a golf cap and a red capelet."

The boy took a moment to sort through her words.

"He does not speak English so good," Menke said.

"I speak it fine," Leo said with a thick Italian accent. "Yes. I have seen her."

"She came Saturday?"

"Maybe five o'clock. Maybe five thirty. I do not remember exact time."

"What did she do?"

A customer rang the service bell from inside and *Herr* Menke excused himself, but not before instructing Leo to tell the *Fräulein* everything.

The boy shrugged. "A little girl came in with her. That is Ruby. The older girl... you say her name is Ella? I see her many times. She bought a few things, then went outside. There was a man there," he pointed to a spot on the sidewalk some ten feet away, "Ella gave the things to Ruby. Then they went away."

It was difficult to make sense of his words, but if she switched to Italian now, the boy would be insulted. "The little girl went with the man?"

Leo shook his head. "Ruby walked away down the street, then the man spoke with Ella some more. I don't know where they went. I had a customer."

"What did this man look like?"

"He had a long coat and a derby hat."

Leo was not as observant as she'd like. But still. What could one see from inside the grocery store?

"Did he have a mustache?"

Leo thought a moment. "No."

"You said you didn't know where they went. Did Ella start walking with the man?"

Leo spread his hands.

"Did Ella appear worried?"

Leo shook his head. "Happy, I think. I always see her here. But she and her friend never talk to me." The last was said sullenly, and Isobel could well imagine the shy young man casting eyes at a girl his own age.

"Her friend? Do you mean Ruby? The little girl?"

"No. Her friend has red hair. They are the same age, I think. They use the telephone. They are always whispering and giggling when I work."

"Do you know who they telephone?"

The boy shook his head

"Do you remember if the telephone rang on Saturday? Around six thirty."

Leo nodded. "The caller hang up when I answered it."

"No one else was here?"

"Only a few customers."

Isobel pressed him further, but she got nothing more out of the boy. Finally, she produced an agency card. "Thank you, Leo. If you think of anything at all, telephone my agency or send a telegram."

Isobel mulled over the facts as she walked towards Fulton Street. So, Ella stopped by Menke's Grocery on her way to the Popular, purchased candy and a bow for the little girl, then talked with a man in front of the store. A neighbor? It could be anyone. Isobel tucked the information away. She needed a more complete picture of Ella Spencer.

Wagons trundled past, and horses and bicycles. So many shops and homes. A sea of faces to disappear into. It was like searching for a cork in the ocean. Of all the times Isobel and Lotario had run away, how many times had they been tracked down? Once. After six months, when a detective finally saw through their false trail and tracked them to a circus. And that was only because Lotario had broken down and sent a note to their father letting him know they were alive.

Isobel turned onto Fulton Street and headed towards Ella's home. It was a scant three blocks from the grocery. A cable car rattled past. It had taken Isobel twenty-five minutes to ride the cable car from the Popular Restaurant. If Ella had left Menke's Grocery at five-thirty as Leo said, she would have had plenty of time to meet John Bennett at six o'clock as specified in the letter. Nearly twenty minutes between getting off the cable car and telephoning her brother. Had she met Bennett on the sidewalk, interviewed, accepted a job, and mistaken the address? Or had this John Bennett given her the wrong address on purpose and taken her somewhere else? As far as Isobel knew, no child ever ran away from home without a suitcase.

She'd need to track down that postal box—

Footsteps were keeping time with her own. Isobel spun. A

man tipped his fedora at her as he strode past. "Just enjoying the view, ma'am," he drawled.

Isobel uncurled her fist and glared at her husband's back. When she realized he wasn't stopping, she jogged to catch up. Riot glanced at her, a smile in his eyes. He switched his walking stick to the other side and caught up her hand, tucking it through his arm.

"It's a good thing I didn't bring my umbrella," she said, leaning into him.

He gave his stick a skillful twirl. "I always come prepared to meet you."

Isobel snorted. "More like, sneak up on me."

"We do have a way of finding each other."

"Where did you run off to?" she asked.

"*You* ran," he countered. "I only meandered out of the restaurant."

"I came back for you," she defended.

"I assumed you picked up a trail and forgot about me."

Isobel ignored the last comment. She'd neither confirm nor deny that assumption. "It didn't lead anywhere." Isobel told him the gist of what she had learned, and he relayed his own discoveries.

Isobel shook her head at Mr. Krone's claim of knowing Bennett. "What a difference between town and country. Country folk won't claim to know someone till they've met the whole clan and held your firstborn."

"I didn't realize I married a country gal," Riot said with a distinct drawl.

"All the way from Sausalito." She pronounced it as Sau-sa-leeetoe. "You know Laura didn't mention the clerical collar," Isobel mused.

Riot tapped a thoughtful finger on his walking stick. "It's interesting how the mind will fill in blanks. Or cover up inconvenient details."

Isobel well knew Riot's own troubles of the mind. His own had created void-like gaps in his memory. Although he'd managed to fill in most of the gaps, it had been a painstaking process, and Isobel suspected he did not entirely trust his mind after its betrayal.

She looked away from the streak of white at his temple. It slashed through his raven hair. There was a deep rut in his skull under that white hair. A mark of death, as Jin so eloquently called it.

"Mr. Krone noticed that Bennett usually crosses the street whenever he leaves the restaurant," Riot continued. "There are a number of boarding houses and hotels across the way, so I went around to them. A man answering to John Bennett was staying at the Graystone Hotel. He fit the description that Krone and Laura gave us. He was there for a few days but checked out on the fourth."

"Did you search the room?"

Riot nodded. "I didn't find anything. Someone else had taken up residence."

Isobel frowned. "That doesn't sound like a man with a small daughter needing care. Was he meeting women there?"

"According to the staff, Bennett never entertained a lady while he was staying." Riot sounded doubtful. Hotel staff were paid to be discreet.

"Miss Marshal said Bennett left at six o'clock and paced out front. If Ella got on the cable car straight away, she'd have arrived at the Popular at six."

"It's possible Bennett and Ella met on the sidewalk," Riot said. "Was anyone with her on the cable car? That other man from the grocers, perhaps?"

Isobel shook her head. "Neither the conductor nor the brakeman remembered her. They were both on duty Saturday."

"I'd like to find out who she talked to in front of Menke's," Riot said.

"But if our unknown man at the grocery had something to do with her disappearance, why did Ella take the Fulton line all the way down to the Popular only to place a telephone call at the Western Union? And why call Menke's grocery after talking with her brother?"

"Maybe Ella expected someone to pick up the line."

"Her redheaded friend?" Isobel suggested.

"Could be."

"Let's hope so," Isobel said.

He gave her hand a squeeze. "I don't like it either."

9

HIDDEN DEPTHS

A ROW OF SINGLE-STICKS LINED FULTON STREET. ISOBEL AND Riot stopped in front of Ella's home. Ten steps led up to the front door, and six steps led down to a basement. It was a classic design in San Francisco. Tall, narrow houses that looked cramped on the outside, but stretched back along the property —narrow but deep and nearly sharing a wall.

"Care to take the lead, since this was your first choice?" Riot asked, ever the gentleman.

Isobel did not trust that glint in his eye. "It occurs to me that this is my first official case, Riot. I'd like to see how it's done properly. From a master. Besides, distressed women find you reassuring."

"You could always practice your bedside manner."

Isobel snorted. "Hardly the time to practice."

Before he could answer, she took the stairs two at a time and rapped her knuckles on the door. A dog immediately began yapping. She thought it came from around back though.

Riot joined her on the doorstep, his hands casually folded over the knob of his gentleman's stick. For all his apparent ease, Isobel knew he rarely let down his guard. His body was a

spring always on the verge of leaping to action. Atticus Riot
was quick. Quicker than any man she had ever met. It was the
reason he was still alive, and she intended to keep him
that way.

Inevitably, Isobel grew impatient when no one answered
the door. She knocked again, hard enough to send the dog into
a frenzy, then she leaned over the railing to peer through the
front bay window. The curtains shifted, fluttering slightly from
movement.

Isobel stretched to knock on the window. This time the
door opened. She straightened and looked into empty
darkness.

"Hello there, young man," Riot said warmly. He crouched
by her side, and Isobel dropped her gaze. A jam-covered
toddler with a bulging diaper stood in the doorway. Bright
blond locks bounced around his innocent eyes. He grinned
widely, pulling back his lips to display two front teeth, and
waved a jam covered wooden spoon at Riot.

"Phurdy!" the toddler burst with excitement.

Riot shook the boy's spoon in greeting and Isobel recoiled.
"I'll take the mother," she said, then thrust her head into the
doorway. "Hello!"

The toddler hiccuped, then stared up at her and froze. One
blink later and he was all mouth, tears, and wailing. Isobel
ducked back outside, but the child did not go silent.

"Oh, hell," she muttered.

Riot didn't hesitate. He plucked the child up, jam and all,
and caught the child's eyes. "Is your mother home, Bertie?"

The child quieted, and pointed upstairs with his spoon

"How did you know his name?" Isobel asked.

"He told us."

Isobel gaped. Another faint wail came from upstairs.
Alarmed, Riot stepped inside and called, "Mrs. Spencer. I'm

Atticus Riot. A detective. Your son hired my agency to find Ella."

"I'm ill," came a weak reply from above. There was movement in the dim lamplight. These homes were deep and dark and residents tended to keep the gas lamps dim, because of the expense. "Have you found my daughter?"

Bertie buried his jam-covered hand in Riot's beard and squealed with delight. Riot didn't seem to mind, but Isobel inwardly cringed. Both of them would need a bath now.

"My partner and I have questions. May we enter your home?"

"Of course."

"There's no need to come down, Mrs. Spencer. I'll just clean this little fellow up first."

"Oh, Bertie, I…"

The woman trailed off and Isobel silently filled in the vacancy: *I forgot about him.* Isobel caught Riot's eye, then plunged into the foyer. Coats were scattered around a coat rack. The umbrella stand was overturned, and a trail of jam led down the hallway. A pale woman leaned on the banister above. Her eyes were sunken in a once plump face.

Isobel feared Mrs. Spencer would topple down the stairs. She raced up the steps, caught the woman under the arm, and propelled her back into a room that contained a screaming infant.

The bedroom was dark and cramped, full of unwashed clothes and an untouched tray of food that looked two days old. The source of the wailing came from a cradle by the bed —a red-faced bald creature with flailing arms and legs.

Isobel sat the woman down, then threw open the curtains and lifted the window. The rattling squeal turned the infant's scream into a frenzied howl.

Isobel stared at the baby. An unfamiliar feeling rose in her breast. Panic. "Mrs. Spencer," Isobel said sharply. "What are you supposed to do with… that?" Was it male or female? How old was it?

"James has colic," Mrs. Spencer said weakly. "Ella helps me." And from the smell emanating from the thing, it had a dirty diaper as well. Mention of her daughter turned into silent tears. They dripped down Mrs. Spencer's cheeks, splashing onto her sweat-stained nightgown. Isobel doubted she was even aware of the tears. Mrs. Spencer's eyes simply started leaking. "Have you found Ella?" It was a desperate, quivering question.

"No," Isobel said bluntly. She stepped forward, plumped the pillows, and helped Mrs. Spencer under the covers. "Have you seen a doctor? Has the child been examined?"

Mrs. Spencer looked to the bedside table, where an array of tinctures and vials sat. "It hasn't helped," she said, the tears still leaking. "He says I have melancholy."

Isobel looked from the mother to the infant. She could not take the screaming anymore. There was something pathetic and pleading in that cry. Isobel picked the baby up under the arms and held it at arm's length. Its head flopped back and she quickly caught it with a finger, propping the head up.

"What's wrong with it? It can't even hold its head up." Isobel placed the baby in the mother's arms. "Perhaps it's hungry?"

The suggestion stirred Mrs. Spencer. Moving weakly, she undid her robe, and exposed a breast. The child latched on immediately, and started sucking with a desperation that left it squirming, but its nose was clogged and it seemed to have trouble feeding and breathing at the same time.

Isobel picked up each tincture, reading their labels. They were prescribed by a Doctor Limon, and had names like 'Miracle Cure All' and 'Soothing Cure.' Isobel uncorked a vial and sniffed at it. Laudanum.

"I'll be right back," Isobel said softly.

Isobel found Riot in the kitchen. Bertie was splashing in a

pot of water on the floor. "Mrs. Spencer and her infant need help. She claims the doctor is treating her for melancholy, but from the looks of it the doctor is a snake oil salesman. She says the infant has colic. But it's so weak it can't even hold its head up."

Riot looked up at her. "How old is 'it'?"

Isobel stared, at a loss. "It's small. And bald."

"Babies can't hold their heads up, Bel. You have to support them."

"Good God, are you serious?" Had she ever been so helpless?

Riot handed Bertie the washcloth he had been using to clean the child. The boy promptly put it on his head and resumed splashing.

"Haven't you ever held one of your nieces or nephews?" Riot asked.

"I never paid them much attention."

Riot gave a small shake of his head, and removed his spectacles to dry on a handkerchief. "I'll telephone Doctor Wise."

Relief washed over her. "It needs changing too."

Riot showed his teeth. "You put me in charge of Bertie, here." The child waved the washcloth around, sending spirals of droplets around the room. "Phurdy!" He looked very proud of himself.

"I've only been here five minutes and I already want to run away," Isobel admitted.

Riot plucked Bertie out of the pot and wrapped him in a towel. "I'll see what I can do about the infant. In the meantime…"

An idea sparked in her mind. "I'll call the cavalry."

Isobel left Riot to look for a telephone. She plucked up the earpiece and ordered the connection.

"Ravenwood Manor," a cheerful voice answered.

"Miss Lily?" Isobel asked.

"No, this is Maddie, Miss Bel. Ma is out. Is that a baby in the background?"

It was. The baby had begun wailing again. Isobel slumped. "We're on a case and the mother is in a bad way. She claims the baby has colic. It also has a dirty diaper. Do you know anyone who..." Isobel searched for the correct term, but discovered that child-rearing was not in her realm of knowledge.

"Knows a thing or two about babies?" Maddie asked.

"Exactly."

"Well, they're easy, Miss Bel," Maddie claimed. She went on to list a number of remedies for colic.

"How do you know so much?" Isobel interrupted her.

"Ma was sick as a dog after Tobias. Of course, with all that happened—" Maddie cut herself short. "Anyway, me and Grimm were left to care for Tobias. That boy had colic something awful. Or so we thought. I think he was just loud, because he still won't be quiet."

Isobel wondered what Maddie had been about to say. What happened to the White family? It wasn't the time for that sort of question, though. Instead she asked, "How would you like to work for Ravenwood Agency?"

Maddie didn't hesitate. "What's the address? I'll come and get things sorted."

"You will?" Isobel nearly fainted with relief. "What about your schooling?"

"I'll make it up. Miss Dupree will understand. Will the ailing woman have negroes in her home?"

Isobel clenched her jaw. Not over the inquiry, but that it had to be asked at all. "I don't know, Maddie. I doubt she's in a state to notice. But if she won't, I'll brain her."

Isobel relayed the address and hung up. She stared at the telephone for a moment, marveling at the confidence that Maddie had displayed over the telephone. The girl had been so shy during the events leading up to Isobel's arrest, but had blossomed while she was incarcerated. Was it Miss Dupree's influence? Or was Maddie in her element here?

Riot walked in with Bertie in his arms. The boy wore a dish towel as a diaper.

"Maddie is on her way."

Riot looked relieved as he set Bertie down. "Excellent. I'll see what I can do about the baby."

Isobel glanced at the boy's makeshift diaper. "Where did you learn that?"

Riot paused on the stairs. His sleeves were rolled up, exposing a faint dragon tattoo curling along his muscled forearm. Riot had other tattoos, but only she was privy to those. And he still wore his shoulder holster with his No. 3 tucked securely inside. Hardly the picture of someone familiar with domestic duties. "The sensible thing for me to tell my wife would be that I had charge of an infant during a case, and Ravenwood was absolutely no help at all."

"And the foolish thing?" she asked.

"Where there's women, there's generally children about."

"Ah."

Riot left it there. And so did she. She hadn't asked Riot about other women. She knew of one who'd died years earlier. But she suspected there were quite a few more in his past. Not that she bore any jealously. Riot was double her age, after all. Still, she wasn't sure she wanted to know, so she left it at that.

Isobel stared down at the toddler in a dishtowel. She could hear Riot's voice, calm and sure, drifting from upstairs. Bertie stared back up at her, apparently struck with awe. Either that or he was plotting how to best claw her eyes out. She wasn't entirely sure.

"Show me Ella's room," she ordered the boy.

The child threw his arms up in the air. "Alleee!" He ran towards the stairwell at break-neck speed. Isobel hurried after as he climbed the stairs, agile as a monkey. At the top, he shoved his head between the railing slats along with half his body, and dangled over empty air from the waist while cackling madly.

Isobel's heart leapt in her throat, but before she could catch him, Bertie pulled away, and stomped down the hallway. A tall gate had been placed in a bedroom doorway, and there were toys scattered about a small bed. Clearly Bertie had a future as an escape artist.

The slapping feet paused long enough to ensure that Isobel was keeping up. Bertie gave her the maniacal grin of a jack-in-the-box, and darted into a room at the end of the hallway.

Mrs. Spencer's voice drifted through an open door. Isobel slowed to listen.

"...he left us. Took all our savings. Abandoned us in worse straights than we were already in. There's no money left for a doctor."

Riot was bent over the infant, deftly changing the flailing pink thing. "Dr. Wise is employed by my agency, Mrs. Spencer. It's already included in your fee."

Dr. Wise was not employed as such, nor were his services part of the agency's fees. Love swelled in her heart for Riot, even more than before. Something she didn't think possible. How much love could a heart bear?

Swallowing down her emotions, she walked past Mrs. Spencer's room to where Bertie had disappeared. The boy was spinning around on a carpet. Inevitably, he got dizzy and fell to the floor squealing with laughter.

Ella's room was clean and well-ordered. A white iron bedstead with a dainty pink quilt. Postcards of far-off places and dream landscapes, and a calendar of flowers. A beautifully bound bible sat on the girl's nightstand along with a hand-written piece of paper. Isobel read the flowery script.

I'll be your sweetheart/If you will be mine/All my life/I'll be your valentine/Bluebells I'll gather/Keep them and be true/When I'm a man, my plan/Will be to marry you.

Isobel could not go on. The rest was equally as stomach churning. It had the sound of a song or poem.

She thumbed through the bible. It was little used, the marker stuck somewhere in Psalms. An inscription on the inside read, *May this help you achieve your dreams. Love Mother.*

Out of the corner of her eye, Isobel saw Bertie crawl under the bed. If he expected her to play 'hide and seek,' he'd be hiding there a very long time.

Isobel shrugged out of her short coat, and laid it over a chair. Starting in one corner, she began carefully taking the tacks out of each postcard and reading the back. Most were blank. But one was from Port Arthur, China. 'As promised. Yours truly, M.A. Serebrenek.'

As Isobel opened the wardrobe, Bertie crawled out from under the bed clutching a stocking. He took one look at Isobel and bolted from the room. She watched him clamber over the gate to his own room. That child needed a locked cage.

A dress that was out of fashion hung in the wardrobe, along with two older skirts and three blouses. A pair of battered leather shoes. The underthings were cheap, as were the blouses. No books. No letters in the desk, just blank sheets of paper. She took the bottom sheet and laid it over the top sheet, then used a pencil to rub the page. Faint words took shape. The words to the nauseating song or poem on the nightstand.

Isobel sighed. She turned to the girl's bed, unscrewing the tops of the bed posts, then searching under the mattress and in the bedsheets. Finally, she tapped the floor for loose floorboards, but turned up nothing. There was nothing of substance in the room. It had the feel of a facade. Was it a result of Bertie's tendency to get into trouble or was it due to an overzealous older brother?

Where did Ella Spencer live her life?

"Anything?" a soft voice asked from the doorway.

"Nothing stands out." Isobel said as she scooted from under the bed. Riot offered a hand. His sleeves were still rolled up, and the muscles along his forearm flexed as he pulled her to her feet. Isobel dusted off her split skirt, and drew his attention to the postcard from China and the sheet of words. "Do you recognize this poem?"

Riot took the sheet from her and read the words. Aloud. "I'll be your sweetheart. If you will be mine. All my life." It was close to a whisper. Passionate. Deep. As he looked into her eyes, the words didn't seem half as silly. But then Riot's voice often stirred her baser instincts. She realized her lips were slightly parted.

"We already swore to that in front of a one-eyed judge and a motley crew," she said lightly, hoping her voice was steadier than it sounded to her own ears.

"And I'll swear it every day."

Isobel snatched the paper from him and replaced it. "I'm torn between laughing at you and kissing you. Though the jam smeared on your beard is a deterrent."

"I had hoped I got it all," he said, rubbing a hand over his trim beard. He took out a handkerchief, and Isobel took it to dab at a missed spot. "It's a song," he said. "Musicians aboard the steamer kept singing it on my Pacific crossing last year."

Isobel gave an inward groan. "Children and music. The list of subjects I'm ignorant of is growing." Though she did have a fondness for Vivaldi and Beethoven.

"I don't think I've ever seen you so terrified."

"I'd rather face a revolver than a baby," Isobel agreed.

"Didn't you ever have a puppy or a kitten as a child?"

"A what?" she asked.

"A puppy?" Riot asked.

"What does a puppy have to do with this?"

"Puppies and children are essentially the same, Bel."

Isobel stared at her husband as if he'd gone mad. Which he had. He'd married her after all. "You've put diapers on puppies?"

Riot tucked away his handkerchief. "Their temperaments and their needs. Same principle."

"I'll take your word for it." She placed a light kiss on his jam-free beard. "Did you question Mrs. Spencer?"

Riot shook his head. "Not overly much. I mostly let her talk. Her first husband, Lewis and Ella's father, reportedly died a few years ago. A James Fletcher. He was an engineer on the steamer Tal Wo along the China Coast. He disappeared one evening on the upper deck. He was never found, and he was declared dead. Supposedly drowned."

"And the second?"

"A charming man."

"I'm always wary of those," she said.

"And yet you married me." Riot flashed a smile of his own. He *was* charming.

"Small wonder I'm suspicious of you. Tell me the rest of the story so I can learn from her mistakes."

"Timothy Spencer wooed her. Got her with child, and they married. Bertie was born four months later. She didn't admit that last part, but it wasn't difficult to put together based on Bertie's age."

"I wonder what Lewis thought of that," Isobel mused.

"Mrs. Spencer said Lewis never got along with his stepfather. He had a right not to. Timothy started beating Lewis's mother, and he spent what little savings they had. She finally managed to divorce him this year, but she was already pregnant with James."

"Wait, she named her ex-husband's child after her first husband?"

"James is a common name," Riot said.

"So is Alex. But I'm sure you'd take note if I named our son Alex."

Riot raised his brows. "Did you forget to share some happy news with me, Bel?"

She gave him a look. "Careful, Riot. I may start bringing a bat to bed. That creature—"

"His name is James," he said.

"…is a stark reminder of consequences. And a strong deterrent, even against your charms."

"Too late for that, Bel." That voice. Those eyes. All the nights, afternoons, and mornings spent in his arms—on top of him, under him—rushed through her veins, heating her body. Isobel tried to say something. Anything, but her mind was muddled. She closed her eyes, and took a deliberate step backwards.

It took her a moment to find her train of thought. Maybe they should have stayed on the *Pagan Lady* another week.

Isobel steeled herself to meet his gaze. Riot was staring at her lips.

"Riot."

"Yes?"

"You're distracting."

"I was thinking the same of you."

"Where were we?"

"Consequences of carnal bliss."

Isobel paused long enough to slap her mind into action. "Where is the ex-husband now?" There, she'd put a coherent thought together, and silently applauded herself.

"Currently unknown."

"Could he have something to do with this? Maybe the man outside Menke's?"

"A possibility." Everything was at this point in the investigation, his tone said. "Based on Bertie and James, I'd say Spencer was on the fair-haired side. Hair can be dyed, however."

Isobel had done that very thing.

"And..." Riot paused for effect, waiting until he had her full attention. "Mrs. Spencer is convinced that her first husband is alive. And that he came to get Ella."

Isobel scrunched her brows together. "Really?"

"Yes."

She glanced at the postcard from China, from M.A. Serebrenek.

"Mrs. Spencer commented how alike her late husband's hair is to mine. She has his photograph in her bedroom. An older version of Lewis."

"It must have been a somewhat happy marriage if she keeps his photograph close?"

"Distance makes the heart grow fonder."

"I'll keep that in mind when I strike out for Shanghai on the *Lady*."

Riot didn't even blink at her threat. "You'd still have your galley cook for those cold ocean nights."

Isobel dared not look at him. "Maybe the man in front of Menke's was her long-lost father." Stranger things had happened.

"I hope so," he said, but he sounded doubtful.

"Can I question Mrs. Spencer?"

"She's in a fragile state, Bel. Go easy on her."

"I'm the epitome of tact."

Riot grunted. "That's why I telephoned Dr. Wise."

MRS. SPENCER CRADLED HER BABY LOOSELY IN HER ARMS. THE infant was wrapped in a blanket and sleeping, and so was the mother. Isobel picked up a photograph of Ella from the dresser. The girl wore her hair down, the edges of a bow peeking from behind her head. She had an oval face, thick brows, small eyes and full lips. Photographs were always difficult to judge, but Ella Spencer looked like an intelligent girl. She had opted for a simple photograph rather than the insipid gaze that most young women favored.

Beside the photograph was one of a handsome man who could only be Lewis's father, the supposedly dead James Fletcher. There was no photograph of Timothy Spencer, the father of Bertie and James Jr.

Mrs. Spencer stirred, her eyes fluttering open and slowly focusing. "Have you found Ella?" she asked. It was a threadbare whisper.

Isobel pulled a chair beside the bed and sat, while Riot remained standing at the end. "We hope to, with your answers." Isobel tried to keep her voice low and calm. "Did you draw attention to the advert or did Ella show it to you?"

Tears welled in the woman's eyes. "I know something horrible has happened to her. She would never leave me for so long."

"Did you show her the advert?" Isobel pressed.

"I don't recall."

Riot handed Mrs. Spencer a clean handkerchief from the nightstand. "The more information we have, the better chance we have of locating your daughter, Mrs. Spencer." His voice lacked judgment or accusation. It was filled with warmth and kindness. And concern. Isobel could see it in his eyes.

"Does Ella have any friends?" Isobel asked.

"A few. She's very active in the church. The Methodist Episcopal at California and Broderick. She wants to be a Sunday school teacher." There was a proud glint in Mrs. Spencer's sunken eyes. "There was—"

"Yes?" Isobel asked.

"A girl named Madge Ryan."

"A redhead?"

"Yes, how did you know?" Mrs. Spencer asked in surprise. "Does *that* girl have something to do with this?"

Isobel cocked her head at the woman's tone. "It's my business to know, Mrs. Spencer," Isobel said, carefully. "You don't care for Miss Ryan?"

"That girl is trouble. She's rude and rebellious, and she has a wild temper. I forbade Ella from seeing her."

"Where does Madge live?"

"I don't know."

"Did Ella meet her at school?"

Mrs. Spencer shook her head. "I don't know where they met. Ella hasn't been in school since James was born. We needed her at home."

"Why did you forbid Ella from seeing Madge?"

"A mother knows," Mrs. Spencer said with the air of a mystic. "She's Catholic. Red-haired. *And* Irish. I didn't like how that girl talked to Lewis when she came over."

"How was that?"

"She was *flirting* with him."

"I see," said Isobel. "The day Ella went missing, she stopped at Menke's grocery after she left the house. She met a small girl inside. As well as a man outside. Do you know who they might be?"

"That would be Ruby Grant, and likely her father, Oliver Grant. He's my attorney. Ella minded his daughter for a time, but…" The baby stirred, and Mrs. Spencer absently patted the creature's rump, rocking it slightly.

"You were saying, Mrs. Spencer. About Mr. Grant," Riot gently prodded.

"It's no concern. Ella wasn't fond of Mr. Grant. He came to the house intoxicated once. She wanted nothing more to do with him."

"Why would she be pleased to see him outside the grocery?" Isobel asked.

"Ella is very fond of Ruby."

"Does Ella have any other friends?"

Mrs. Spencer thought a moment. "A Miss Searlight. I'm sorry, I don't remember her first name. They met at Mr. Grant's office."

Isobel paused, glanced at Riot, and took a breath. The question had to be asked. "Does Ella have any male friends?"

Mrs. Spencer started in surprise. The sudden movement jerked the baby awake. It immediately started screaming. Tears welled in the exhausted woman's eyes. But again, Isobel doubted she even noticed. She started patting the baby anew with a kind of frantic motion that was far from comforting.

Riot reached for the infant, and the mother gave it up eagerly. He laid the bundle against his chest, patting its back with more force than Isobel would have thought it could bear.

"You're a saint, Mr. Riot," Mrs. Spencer said.

"I don't claim to be," he said easily. "But I thank you all the same." Riot put his nose to the infant's fuzz-covered head. Did he just smell the creature?

Isobel shook herself. "Back to my question, Mrs. Spencer. Does Ella have any male friends?"

"Why no, she does not, Miss Amsel. Ella is a good girl. I know what you're thinking—that she ran off with a sweetheart. But she loves this house and her family. She'd never abandon us willingly." It sounded more like a statement of faith than fact.

"Ella never went out at night." As if that were the only time romantic liaisons took place.

"Yes, but were there any men who were just friends? Even older ones. An uncle? A friend of Lewis's?"

"No, nothing of that sort. She was a shy girl who kept to herself. She loves books. Not the fiction variety, but the classics."

"Save for a bible, there isn't a single book in her room, Mrs. Spencer," Isobel pointed out.

"Exactly," Mrs. Spencer said, eyes brightening. "See, a good Christian girl. That's my Ella." The last was said with conviction. But that emotion seemed to drain her further.

Isobel shared a look with Riot. She wanted to press the woman, but Mrs. Spencer was unstable. Emotionally, physically, and possibly mentally. Riot gave a slight shake of his head.

A knock sounded downstairs. The infant immediately started fussing again, and Riot walked out of the room with it to give the mother some rest.

Isobel hesitated for a moment, then grabbed the photographs of Ella and her father James Spencer and followed Riot outside. He raised a brow at her theft.

"I'm going to return them," she defended, as she tucked the frames inside her satchel.

Riot opened the door to find Maddie standing outside. She looked nervous, but showed off her dimples as soon as she saw the fussy infant drooling on Riot's waistcoat.

"Thank you for coming," Isobel said with feeling.

Maddie shrugged out of her coat. "I don't mind at all, Miss Isobel. Tobias was near to fuming when I told him I was helping you with a case."

"Dr. Wise is coming, too," Riot explained. "You'll have reinforcements soon."

"Is Dr. Wise used to babies?"

"I believe so," Riot said.

Maddie nodded, taking the infant from Riot with a practiced hand. "Some doctors don't have a mind for babies at all." Instead of holding the baby to her shoulder, she folded its arms just so, and laid it along her arm like a football with its legs dangling on either side and its head tucked in. The baby immediately quieted.

"You clearly do," Riot noted.

The girl glanced down, lashes fluttering. "I want to be a physician...for children." She was embarrassed, sharing a piece of her soul.

"That's a fine goal, Miss Maddie." At Riot's sincerity, Maddie stood a little taller.

They introduced Maddie to Bertie, and then to Mrs. Spencer, who thanked her profusely and assured her that Ella would be back any moment to lend a hand.

When Isobel finally stepped outside into a crisp afternoon on the edge of night, she took a deep breath. "I feel like I've sailed through a storm," she said.

Riot looked nearly spotless in hat and coat, though a wet spot of drool stained the silk of his waistcoat. "Not keen on infants, Bel?"

She narrowed her eyes. "Apparently you are. That creature was besotted with you."

"Infants, horses, and women seem to respond to a calm nature."

"Did you just compare me to a horse?"

The edge of his lip quirked, and he wisely hurried down the steps.

"You've become positively rude since we married."

"I was aiming for disagreeable and slovenly," he said, wiping at the drool on his waistcoat.

"That was *my* plan, Riot. You can't steal my idea."

"A rude man would steal it."

"Precisely my point."

"But you don't disagree?"

"That you've become rude?" she asked.

"About my calm nature."

Isobel changed the subject. "I don't think Ella Spencer was on the lookout for a calm nature."

"Financial stability, perhaps?" Riot suggested.

"Or excitement. I don't think we can trust Mrs. Spencer's opinion of her daughter. Ella had ample opportunity to live a double life. Picking up groceries, minding other children... Those are precisely the kind of opportunities I took to do everything I wasn't supposed to be doing."

Riot looked at her, something close to horror in his eyes. "My God, *you* minded children?"

Isobel crossed her arms.

"Did they survive?"

"Riot."

"Yes, Miss Bel?"

"You *are* distracting."

"So you've told me. And yet..." He took her hand, brought it to his lips, and placed a kiss over her wedding ring. "...you said yes."

"Under extreme duress."

"Whittled down by Nature's tranquility," he said wistfully.

Isobel took back her hand and reached for her watch. "Oh, let's be honest, Riot. I was in an asylum. I clearly wasn't in my right mind when I accepted your marriage proposal."

Riot paused on the last stair, his walking stick on his shoulder, hat at a cocky angle, a thoughtful look in his eyes. "Madly. Deeply. *Fervently* in love. Is there any sanity in those words?"

Isobel stared at him for a moment. Then clicked her watch shut. "Are you going to stand here waxing poetic or are you coming with me to Oliver Grant's office? He may still be there."

Riot fell in step beside her. "You didn't answer my question."

She glanced at him. "Love *is* madness. It's terrifying and thrilling, and I wonder if I'll ever stop falling."

At her quiet words, Riot reached for her hand and tucked it inside his coat, warming her skin. "As long as we're falling together."

10

A BLIND EYE

THE OFFICES OF OLIVER GRANT, ATTORNEY AT LAW, WERE tucked in a residential block along with a cluster of shops—a haberdashery, a barber, and a photography studio. The rest were homes.

Riot and Isobel arrived just as the open sign was being turned in the window. Riot applied his stick to the door, careful to avoid the glass.

A silver-haired woman with rosy cheeks waved the 'closed' sign back at him. He knocked again. She hesitated, her cheery eyes flickering to his waist. Riot wore his revolver in a shoulder holster for that very reason. He never went unarmed, but most only checked a man's hips for a weapon.

Riot dipped his fingers into his breast pocket and pulled out a card, holding it up to the window.

The woman unlocked the door, and took Riot's card. She gave it a quick glance.

"I'm Atticus Riot. This is Miss Amsel. Is Mr. Grant still in his office?"

"I'm afraid we're closed for the day."

"A girl has gone missing. Mr. Grant may be able to help her."

Put like that, a person could hardly say no. "I'm Miss Potter, Mr. Grant's stenographer," she said.

Miss Potter closed and locked the door, lest more potential clients sneak in. "One moment."

Isobel surveyed the office as Miss Potter poked her head into an adjoining room. The stenographer's desk was free of clutter. A typewriter sat under its cover. File cabinets lined one wall. Miss Potter's purse, gloves, and two tickets waited on her desk.

A murmuring of voices could be heard from the interior office. Finally, a balding man with stooped shoulders came out. Although he had black hair—what little was left of it—no one in their right mind would describe Mr. Grant as a 'great strong-looking fellow'. He was bookish and pale, and looked like a man under a great deal of stress.

This was no Alex Kingston, attorney to the rich and famous.

"I'm Oliver Grant. I've heard of you, Mr. Riot, of course. And Miss Amsel." His voice was as even, careful and calculated as that of a businessman sizing up a potential client.

"Won't you come inside my office?"

"Miss Potter may be of help too," Riot said.

The woman huffed.

"We only have a few questions," Isobel said. "Plenty of time for you to make the theater."

The woman started in surprise. Isobel let her marvel. Surely Miss Potter would realize Isobel had seen the two theater tickets sitting by her handbag?

"Elouise Spencer has gone missing," Riot said.

Mr. Grant stood up straight. While alarmed, he did not seem particularly surprised by this statement.

"You're acquainted with her, I believe?" Riot asked.

"Ella watched my daughter, Ruby, from time to time."

"Watched?"

"Mrs. Whitney has charge of Ruby now."

Riot waited expectantly, and Mr. Grant hastened to explain. "I thought a more mature woman would be better suited to watch Ruby. What with her mother's—" He cut off, his gaze turning somewhere distant.

Perhaps Mr. Grant had been successful at one time, but grief, Isobel could see, had profoundly affected the man.

"I'm sorry for your loss, Mr. Grant," Riot said.

Mr. Grant fumbled for a handkerchief and dabbed his eyes. "It's been over two years."

Miss Potter looked on, sympathetic. "When did Ella vanish?" she asked.

"Saturday," Riot said.

"But that's impossible," Mr. Grant said. "I saw her Saturday evening. I walked Ruby to the grocery store, and Ella was there."

"It was shortly after that," Riot said.

"I'm sorry to hear."

"But not surprised," Riot noted.

The attorney hesitated. "No," he finally admitted. "Ella was… not a good influence on my daughter."

"How so?"

Mr. Grant glanced at his assistant. "I don't like to spread rumors. Most especially where a woman's reputation is concerned."

"Her disappearance trumps that, I should think."

"I saw her being… familiar with a young man. Flirting. While she was in charge of Ruby. It was her mannerisms, you see." He shifted, uncomfortable.

"When was this?"

"Oh, months ago. I found a more mature caretaker for Ruby shortly after."

"Do you know the young man's name?" Isobel asked.

Mr. Grant shook his head.

"Description?"

"Light hair. Colorful waistcoat. Clearly a rake. They were talking outside a theater. The Olympia. I don't know anymore."

"What did you discuss outside the store?" Riot asked.

"I asked after her mother, and Ella asked me how Ruby was getting along with Mrs. Whitney. She had bought her candies and such."

"Mrs. Spencer said that Ella had a friend—a Miss Searlight. She claimed they met here."

"Miss Searlight," Mr. Grant repeated absently.

"A client of yours," Miss Potter said suddenly. "Heather Searlight. She and Ella met in the office. I was there. They fell into easy conversation almost immediately."

"Where can we find Heather Searlight?" Riot asked.

"That's confidential. I'm not allowed to share any private information."

"A girl is missing, Mr. Grant." The gravity of the words settled in the room.

"No, I'm sorry, I can't. Can I see you in my office, Miss Potter?" Mr. Grant shared a look with his stenographer, and the two went into his office.

Isobel beat Riot to the file cabinet. She rifled through the names, and pulled out Searlight. A woman of her own age. She had been involved in an inheritance dispute. Isobel noted the address, and slipped the folder back into place.

As the cabinet slid shut, the office door opened and Mr. Grant and Miss Potter returned. The stenographer began gathering up her belongings while humming a show tune.

"We won't take any more of your time, Mr. Grant," Riot said, opening the door for the women.

Before Isobel stepped out, she paused. "Can I speak with Ruby tomorrow?"

"Why?" Mr. Grant asked.

"She may have overheard something that would help us find Ella."

"I don't want my daughter involved in whatever this is, Miss Amsel. I've done enough." He gave a pointed glance to the filing cabinets.

Riot and Isobel exited with Miss Potter, who walked briskly down the street towards the closest cable car line.

"Curious term of phrase, 'whatever this is,'" Riot repeated in a low voice.

"And he never asked for details."

Riot paused under a street lamp to consult his pocket watch. "Where does Miss Searlight live?"

"A boarding house across town on Mission. But that was over a year ago. I'm thinking we may have better luck at her place of employment: Hale's department store. The court didn't rule in her favor, so I assume she's still working there." Isobel shivered slightly. The sun had never broken through the fog, and now it had set. It was dark and cold, and she had left her long coat at the agency. A hollow pit in her stomach told her she had forgotten to eat, as well.

"We'll call at Hale's tomorrow." Riot started to remove his overcoat, but she shook her head.

"I'm the one who left my warm coat at the office."

He shrugged out of his coat anyway. "Humor my gallant nature."

"I'm not sure I want to encourage it." But she allowed him to place his coat on her shoulders. She hugged it to her, putting her nose to the collar. It smelled of Riot—sandalwood and myrrh, wool and silk, and a masculine scent that made her want to drag him home.

"Does it need laundering?"

Isobel glanced at him. "No."

A curious glint passed over his eyes. "Why are you smelling it?"

"Because it smells like you."

Riot gently swung his walking stick. "Missing me?"

"Terribly."

Riot tapped his brim up, and bent towards the curve of her neck. He took a deep breath, inhaling her scent. "I've wanted to kiss you all day." It was a purr, and it warmed her more than his coat.

"You did. Thoroughly. Just this morning. Have you forgotten already?"

"I've been trying *not* to think about it... or about last week," he admitted. "The male physique is hardly subtle."

Isobel kept her eyes straight ahead. If she looked at him now they'd never get anything done. She swallowed. "Shall we try Miss Searlight's boarding house tonight?"

"It's late, and I want to stop by the agency to check in with Tim. Maybe he's turned up something. We can check on the fate of your newspapers, too."

Her damn newspapers could wait, but she bit back the comment. "And if nothing turns up?" she asked instead.

Riot put a hand on the small of her back. Despite layers of wool and silk, his touch sent heat blossoming along her back. Her pulse quickened. All she could think of was firelight and his hands on her bare skin.

"I'm sure we'll think of something to do."

11

THE QUIET ONE

GRIMM LIKED HORSES. NO WORDS NEEDED SAYING. A HORSE sensed moods, and Grimm supposed he could sense theirs too. Mr. Tim called the oldest mare Nag, and called the others whatever came to mind. But Grimm had his own names for the horses—names that didn't need saying because the horses all knew who they were.

Grimm found most things didn't need saying.

Mr. Tim and his horse were like an old married couple, the mare showing her disapproval by trying to bite Mr. Tim on a regular basis. But she never tried to bite Grimm. Tim's mare preferred to be called Mrs. May. She was a wise old gal, and he reckoned she had been spirited in her youth. Grimm always brushed her down with respect, and she repaid him with a stately pose whenever he cared for her.

The painted gelding was younger, but ornery as heck. Except when Mr. Riot walked into the stable. Then the horse calmed and looked at him expectantly. Mr. Riot called him by his true name, Jack, though his full name was Jack-be-Nimble. That fit Jack just perfectly. He was tolerant of Grimm, but it was plain who he preferred. Grimm thought the pair of them, horse and rider, had seen too much.

The third and final horse in Ravenwood stables was calm as a still mountain lake. Sugar. He thought of her as a friend, and hoped she felt the same. Grimm was brushing her now. It was simple work—the quiet kind Grimm preferred.

Jack raised his head and turned his ears forward in alarm. It had turned dark, and there were shadows in the yard. Light spilled from the kitchen of Ravenwood Manor, where his mother was moving around, preparing dinner for the boarders. Without stilling his brush, Grimm turned slightly to look at what had caught Jack's attention.

A shadow moved down the side of the house, not in a menacing way but stealthy. It touched ground with a gentle step. Grimm blew out a breath in relief.

The small shadow hurried towards the stable, and a cap-wearing girl walked into the lantern light. Her braids were tucked beneath an oversized cap, and she wore a dark quilted jacket with wide sleeves and the loose trousers that were common in Chinatown. As Sao Jin hurried inside, her gaze darted to the kitchen window.

Whenever Grimm saw Tobias glance over his shoulder like that, he knew his little brother was up to no good, but it was hard to know with Jin—she was secretive by habit.

Grimm stayed still, watching. That's what he did best. For all his height, he tended to blend into the world, as long as it was dark and no one noticed the color of his skin. He stood by Sugar and watched the girl.

Jin passed the stall where he was standing, and stopped. She cocked her head, then spun around, eyes narrowing and hands curling into fists, ready for a fight. It took a second for her to spot him. Then she relaxed.

"Is Mr. Tim home?" she asked.

Grimm shook his head, and ran a calming hand down

Sugar. Jin glared at the horse, but Sugar was a deep well of calm and she only snorted softly in return, taking no offense. Jack on the other hand stomped his hoof and knocked against the gate. Animals sensed moods, and Jin was all over the place. Her insides were confused.

Jin frowned. "I need a knife. For whittling. Does he keep extra?"

Grimm gave Sugar one final pat, and eased himself out of the stall. He walked to the supply room and rifled through a box of tools, then placed the knives he found on the work bench, lining them up for her inspection.

Jin tested the balance of each. In the end, she selected a folding pocket knife and a sheathed hunting knife. "Whetstone?" she asked.

Grimm opened a drawer full of rectangular stones of varying sizes, then pointed to a leather strap tacked to the wall. He left her to her work. Soon the rasp of steel on stone scraped through the stable. It was methodical, but it sounded wrong. Grimm hurried over and saw she was running the stone along the blade.

He shook his head, and held out his hands.

Jin hesitated.

Grimm had long noted her suspicion, not just with him, but with the world in general. To Jin's mind everyone was either trying to hurt her or had the potential to. That was fine, if sad. Grimm understood. Instead of snatching the items from her, he waited. He was patient and gentle—a man couldn't raise his voice if he didn't use it.

Eventually, Jin handed over the whetstone and knife. Grimm poured some mineral oil over the flat stone, and with a gentle sweep, tip to back, and precisely angled, he showed her how to sharpen the blade.

Jin tried a few strokes, and he waited until she had it. His work was done in the stable, so he made up new work. He lifted a saddle from a rail and sat down to oil it. Jack raised his head. It was Mr. Riot's saddle—worn and well-traveled. Grimm wondered how many miles man and horse had put on this saddle. What had Jack seen in his lifetime? Where had they been? Probably more places than Grimm. Although the horses were exercised daily in Golden Gate Park, it was easy to see Jack expected something more from life. He wanted adventure.

The whisper of steel on stone stopped. Jin ran her finger over each blade. The test drew a thin line of red on her finger, but the girl didn't flinch. She stood and turned towards a post. With a flick of her wrist, she threw the pocket knife end over end. It bounced off. She tried it again with the fixed blade, and it sank in.

Grimm kept his head down, focusing on the saddle, but he watched her out of the corner of his eye. Again and again the girl threw, until she could sink each blade in nearly every time. When she was satisfied, she gathered the knives and left the stable.

But Sao Jin didn't climb back to her attic room. She walked down the lane.

Grimm's hand stilled. He stared at the leather saddle in his lap for a long moment. With a sigh, he set the saddle aside and followed.

A LONG, LONG NIGHT

RAVENWOOD AGENCY SAT ON THE BORDER OF TWO WORLDS, with one foot in the Barbary Coast and one in respectable territory. The Barbary Coast district lay a block to the north. It was lit at night with electric lights, and throngs of men milled through the streets, while just a block to the south businesses were closed up and homes glowed with warmth.

The agency's street was a mix of lodging houses, shops, and buildings where red light spilled out into the night and prostitutes were open for business.

Light shone from the agency as well. Half curtains were drawn over the lower part of the windows. Mack, Matthew, and Tim sat around a table. Mack nursed a bottle of whiskey. Tim smoked his pipe and cradled a flask, and Matthew quickly jumped to his feet when Isobel and Riot entered.

Miss Off cackled from her perch on the bar.

"Sir. Mrs. Riot. Erm..." The crisp-collared man nearly saluted. A snifter sat at his place on the table.

"At ease, Matt," Riot said with amusement. He helped Isobel out of her borrowed coat.

"You look frozen, Charlie," Mack said.

"Close to it," she returned. "Where'd you get off to while Riot and I were combing the city?"

"*Undercover* work." He gave her a wink.

"Only a blanket would let you blend in," Isobel quipped. Mack McCormick had bright red hair, the jowls of a mastiff, and nose that had been broken multiple times.

Tim snorted a laugh.

"As long as you're thinking of me under it." The words were out before he thought, which was likely the reason his nose resembled a mushroom. The Scotsman darted a quick look at Isobel's husband, but Riot pretended not to notice the comment.

"Any luck, Tim?" Riot asked.

"My eyes are all over the city and beyond, but I don't expect any word today."

"There's another girl we want you to look for—a Madge Ryan," Isobel said. "Ella may be in her company. A redhead of about the same age. Unfortunately, that's all we have on her."

"If Sarah is willing, we'll have sketches for you tomorrow," Riot said.

"That girl is useful," Tim agreed. "Small wonder you adopted her."

"Clearly that was the only reason," Riot said dryly.

Isobel walked behind the bar. Her newspapers were still securely under the brick. She nodded to Miss Off, who made a crude gesture with one hand and shielded her pet rat from Isobel with the other. Isobel retrieved two shot glasses. She tossed both to Riot, who deftly caught one in each hand, then set them on the table. Mack leaned forward to pour two glasses.

"How'd your case go, Matt?" Isobel asked. She hoped if she were informal the agent would stop calling her Mrs. Riot.

"Aren't you chipper," Tim said with a puff of smoke. "Talking now and everything."

"It's been a long day," Isobel admitted.

"That's 'cause you've been lounging around a resort for months," Mack said. "Then a honeymoon. You're getting soft, Charlie. You clearly should've married a Scotsman instead."

"Not as soft as you, Mack. Is that a new vest? Pop the buttons to your last?" Isobel grinned at him.

Mack leaned back and patted his gut. "This here is called Scottish padding. For winter. If you had a bit more meat on your bones you wouldn't need to rob a poor gentleman of his coat."

"A.J. never lends me his coat," Tim grumbled. "And I'm always shivering."

"I don't want it smelling like an ornery goat," Riot said.

"You'll have to send it to the launderers now that Charlie's wore it," Mack said.

"It'll need disinfecting, too," Miss Off hollered.

"I don't care where you send it, as long as I can eat first. I don't suppose you have an apple?" Isobel asked.

"I do not," Mack said.

It was likely a bad idea on an empty stomach, but she knocked back a shot glass of whiskey anyway. It burned down her throat and filled the pit of her stomach. She felt warmer already.

"There's some lettuce in the corner," Miss Off said.

"That's my fern, woman. Don't you touch it. I bought it to liven the joint up," Mack warned.

Isobel had wondered who'd brought it in. It sat in a corner. Happy and green, and defying the rest of the saloon-cum-detective agency.

"Your case, Matt?" Riot asked, putting the conversation back on track.

"Mrs. Riot was right," Matthew said, amazement plain in his voice. "The necklace was at a jewelers on Post Street, the same store where the husband originally bought it." Matthew gazed at Isobel with something close to awe in his eyes. "How did you—" Matthew Smith never got to ask his question. A window shattered, and a brick crashed on the floor. Tied to the brick was a stick of dynamite.

The wick was flaring.

———

IT WAS CURIOUS HOW THE MIND FOCUSED. HOW TIME SLOWED. It seemed that minutes passed as that stick of dynamite sat burning in the center of the room.

A number of things happened at once. Two more sticks of dynamite were hurled through the shattered glass along with a volley of gunshots. Glass shards sprayed into the room, and Riot's shot glass exploded in his hand as a bullet passed through.

Matthew and Mack threw themselves to the floor. Riot drew and fired his revolver, but he wasn't aiming out the window. His bullet sliced the wick of the flaring dynamite. Tim flung himself at stick number two, and pinched the fire out.

Isobel dove for the remaining stick. She snatched it up, and threw it at the shattered window. A puff of air, a bullet, snatched at her sleeve as her dynamite soared, only the fuse was short. An explosion blew out the front of the agency.

Isobel was thrown backwards and stopped when her head hit something hard. She watched as glass floated in the air and splinters of wood flew in gorgeous patterns. The world was silent, save for a loud ringing between her ears. Then the world rushed back in.

A hand grabbed her collar and pulled. Glass shrieked beneath her, accompanied by a far-off feeling of pain. A face swam into view. Riot. Concern was etched in his features. He held a revolver in one hand and patted her down with the other, searching for injury. His lips were moving. *Stay here.*

"You goddamned sonabitches best have an army!" Tim yelled out the broken window.

Tim's shout pierced her daze. She blinked. And a wave of chaos drowned out the ringing in her ears. The bark of guns. Shouts. White smoke drifting overhead. Then the mirror behind the bar exploded. Isobel curled into a ball and Riot flung himself over her as glass rained down. Riot had dragged her behind the iron-plated bar for cover.

When the glass stopped falling, he grabbed a rifle from one of the liquor shelves. "Cover!"

Gunshots rang out.

Riot popped up and tossed the rifle to Tim, who stood at the edge of a brick outer wall with a revolver.

"Matt, dim the lights," Riot ordered. He rose from behind the bar with a rifle of his own and started firing blindly. In the volley of covering fire, Matthew dashed for the gas lamps and hit the floor the moment the room fell dark.

"No one shoots at my home," Miss Off snarled. She grabbed a revolver from the shelves, and Isobel helped herself to one, too. It was loaded, five shots, one chamber empty for safety. She rotated the cylinder to a live round.

Miss Off started to stand, but Riot grabbed the woman and yanked her down. "You need to protect your rat."

Miss Off snarled at him and jerked away, but she listened and began to coo softly to her rodent.

Silence fell over the saloon.

"You think they're gone?" Matthew hissed.

Tim spat. "Nah."

Mack slithered towards the backdoor on his stomach. Another shot barked into the night.

"They're a twitchy bunch," Tim said.

Isobel had never been in a drawn-out firefight. She felt lost. No amount of intelligence could stop bullets from flying. She didn't even know who was shooting at them. Worse, her hands were trembling.

Riot crouched beside her, and calmly reloaded his weapons. She was clutching her own revolver so tightly her knuckles turned white.

"What do we do?" she asked.

"Just wait," he said softly. "We have all the time in the world."

Isobel didn't know about that. She had snatched a stick of dynamite and nearly blown them all to pieces. But his voice was so calm. So sure. She forced herself to relax. To think. But there wasn't much plotting to do. They were pinned.

"Matt, can you get up those stairs?" Riot whispered.

"Yes, sir."

"Keep your head down," Riot said, holstering his revolver and grabbing the rifle. "Go. Now." Riot popped over the bar, firing and cocking the lever with rapid speed as Tim joined the barrage. Matthew sprinted down the hallway, his footsteps flying up the stairs.

"I'll get help out the back," Mack called from the far hallway.

"No!" But Mack McCormick either didn't hear Riot's shout, or thought he knew best. The Scotsman threw open the back door and gunfire filled the saloon.

Riot dropped his rifle and bolted down the hallway. Bullets splintered wood in the front room, but Tim just sighted down his rifle and calmly squeezed the trigger. The bullets coming in were cut short.

Mack started cursing from the back. Isobel darted after Riot. She smelled blood and the sweet, lingering odor of dynamite, and saw the big Scotsman reeling on the floor.

"He used me for a goddamn shield!"

Isobel didn't slow to check on the cursing giant. She hopped over him. Harried footsteps receded down the alleyway. Isobel bolted after the wisp of a shadow, only to trip over a lump. Fear welled in her heart. She turned the body over, getting blood on her hands. Relief washed over her. It wasn't Riot.

She scrambled to her feet, and rounded the corner in time to hear a volley of shots. The brick at her ear exploded. Her arrival was the distraction Riot needed. He fired off a shot from his cover, pegging his assailant in the hand. A revolver plopped to the ground.

The would-be assassin hopped up from his cover and tried to bolt, but Riot fired off another shot. His bullet hit the assassin behind the knee. He lurched forward and fell, sliding in the alleyway muck. Still he tried to crawl away. Riot raced forward to kick him in the ribs.

The assassin grunted. The blow stunned him. Time enough for Riot to turn him over and pat him down. Riot tossed a knife and gun away, then straightened.

He cocked his revolver and pointed it at the man's head. "Who sent you?" The question wasn't a bark. It wasn't a demand. But a cool three words that sent a chill down Isobel's spine. She froze in the alleyway, relieved she couldn't see Riot's face just now, because she had a clear view of the assassin's. He had the look of a man staring death in the eye.

"You've got a price on your head," the man blurted through his teeth. "Ain't nothing personal." The assassin was young, maybe her own age, with a wispy pencil mustache. He wore a low-slung belt and holster. His knee was a bloody, blown out mess, and he clutched at it in agony.

"Who put the mark on me?" Riot asked.

"I didn't ask no questions for a thousand dollars." There was a frantic, pleading tone to the man's voice. It made Isobel sick.

Riot uncocked his revolver, and holstered it. "Is that all you were offered? I suppose you're too young to know who I am. Where did you hear about the hit?"

"We're supposed to be paid at the Morgue on Battle Row. That's all I know."

Riot tilted his head to the side. "Why don't we take a little walk, you and I." Riot bent and lifted the man to his feet. The assassin screamed, and Riot shoved him forward, back towards the agency.

MACK WAS SHOT. HE SAT SLUMPED IN A CHAIR, HOLDING HIS gut and drinking a copious amount of whiskey.

"That man of yours used me as a bloody shield," Mack muttered for the tenth time.

"He saved your life," Isobel said. Her voice was distant to her own ears. A bullet wound stained Mack's waistcoat, the hole in the thick of his stomach. There was no exit wound, but his color was good. Riot had simply seized an opportunity. It had worked.

"I've summoned an ambulance," Matthew announced, hanging up the telephone. "Should I try the police?" Not a single whistle had been blown. The street outside was empty.

"You can try," Riot said. His vest and shirt were splattered with blood. Aside from being hit by shards of glass, none of it was his own.

Riot took her hands to study, then searched her face. He didn't bother asking if she was injured. She wasn't sure she could answer. Deadpan, grim as a grave, Riot reached up to pluck a sliver of glass from her cheek. She didn't even feel it.

Tim brandished a stick of dynamite in front of the would-be assassin, a Mr. Mason, who was seated in the chair Riot had tossed him into. "I can tell you're no professional. Damn sloppy. If you're going to kill a man, do it right."

Isobel looked down at her hands. There was blood on them —her own and blood from the dead man lying out back. Why hadn't the police come? Her sluggish mind provided an answer. An uncomfortable one. The police on patrol had been bribed to look the other way.

Riot glanced at Tim. "Are you up for a drink at the Morgue, old man?"

Tim cackled and began arming himself.

Riot looked Isobel in the eye for the first time as he buckled on a belt and holster in addition to his shoulder harness. Blood splattered the lens of his spectacles. "Wait here for the ambulance," he told her.

The words were gentle, full of understanding. He might as well have kicked over a smoldering log. Sparks of anger shot through her veins, clearing her mind as she realized what he intended.

Isobel bristled. "I'm *not* waiting here."

"It's not a request." The gentleness was gone. His voice came across like steel as he cinched his belt.

"You'll distract him, girl," Tim said, resting a rifle on his shoulder. "A.J. doesn't care if I get shot."

Riot didn't say another word. He grabbed Mr. Mason up by the lapels and pulled him to his feet. The man screamed in pain, slipping in the blood pooled at his feet. "I thought I was gonna wait for the ambulance."

Riot dragged the man out the front door, and Tim slapped a hat on his head before following. Isobel ground her teeth together. What happened to being partners? *Damn him.*

Matthew picked up the telephone, and Miss Off took another drink. She was muttering under her breath. "Just so you know, I'm not touching those," the woman pointed at Isobel's stack of newspapers. They were covered in blood and glass. "You can clean your own damn mess." The old woman stomped down the hallway to get a broom.

Isobel checked on Mack, who had finished off the whiskey bottle. He was singing a Scottish dirge in a slurry voice.

"Hello, I need the police. There was an attack on Raven-wood Agency. On Kearney street, yes."

If Riot thought she'd wait here like a meek little wife, he was in for a surprise. Cursing his penchant for heroism, she raced to the upper room where they'd deposited their trunks and supplies. She grabbed out a rough coat and trousers, dressed quickly, and thrust her revolver in a pocket. On the way out, she grabbed Matthew's bowler.

"Hey!"

Isobel didn't stop. She sprinted towards the Barbary Coast —in over her head, terrified, and furious as hell.

13

THE MORGUE

"You really think that woman of yours is gonna stay behind?" Tim asked.

Riot sighed. Likely not. And there'd be hell to pay when he returned. *If* he returned.

Fog was thick and cool, and phantoms moved in the night. It was the sort of night where bad things happened.

"She handled herself well enough back there with the dynamite."

"And nearly got shot," Riot said with a click of his teeth.

"Shit happens, A.J."

"Not if I can help it."

"Cool that heart of yours, boy." Tim warned.

Riot didn't argue. Tim was right. It's what he needed just then—to slip back into his gunfighting ways. He took a breath and pushed aside thoughts of Isobel, of the live dynamite in her hand, of the bullets that sliced through her clothes. He wrapped himself in an old, familiar calm.

The pair walked down the middle of the street. Riot hadn't bothered with his coat. His revolvers were plain to see, and Tim had his rifle casually placed on a shoulder. The old man also had a revolver on his belt, a sawed-off shotgun tucked in his overcoat, and a bowie knife in easy reach.

"Where are you taking me?" Mr. Mason gasped. The man was stumbling, dragging his bloody leg behind him. He was only upright thanks to Riot, who was half-dragging the young man down the street.

"Quiet," Riot warned.

The only people they passed in the night were freezing whores, addicts, and drunks. Most with sense were indoors enjoying the district's delights, and those outside who spotted the trio quickly looked away and quickened their stride.

When Mr. Mason saw their destination, he tried to back away. "Wait now. You can't take me in there. If they know I ratted 'em out, they'll kill me."

"Will they?" Riot asked softly. He tightened his grip and marched the man towards a cavernous stairway on Battle Row. Two men straightened at the entrance. They wore thick coats and low caps, and had billy clubs in hand.

The shorter fellow reached behind his back, and Tim stepped forward to drive his rifle butt into the guard's face, then into his gut, and finally the back of his head. At the same instant, Riot shoved Mr. Mason towards the second guard. It was all the distraction he needed. He was right on the stumbling man's heels. One upper cut to the second guard's jaw stunned him. The billy club fell from his hand, and Riot caught it deftly and swung it against the larger man's knee. A crack. And then another. Both men dropped to the ground.

Riot divested them of their guns.

"Shall we, Mr. Mason?"

Riot shoved the man down the narrow lane. Shadows with hungry eyes were hunched along the walls, a row of misery and filth. Riot dragged Mr. Mason down an uneven, slick stairway, and shoved him through the door of the Morgue. The door crashed open. Light spilled outside, and Mr. Mason fell into a cramped barroom with filthy sawdust on the floor. It was dim and dank and sparsely furnished. The denizens ranged from wild-eyed executioners to men one breath away from the grave. Thieves, macks, and addicts, and every despicable criminal under the sun.

No one looked at Mr. Mason whimpering over his blown-out knee. They looked at the man in the doorway. Blood splattered his spectacles and his once snowy shirt.

Tim came in behind him, and moved to one side of the doorway, his rifle held loosely, both hands at his waist.

"I'd keep your hands where I can see them," Riot said easily. "I'm Atticus Riot, and I understand there's a thousand dollar bounty on my head. I'd like to know who's fronting the money."

The thugs didn't move. They were busy sizing him up. One of them, a grizzled old man with one eye and scars criss-crossing his face, started chuckling.

Riot nodded to the grizzled man. "Old timers like Max Savage there will tell you a thousand dollars isn't worth the trouble for me."

"Damn straight," Savage muttered. "I warned those green-horns they'd have difficulty beefing a curly wolf like you."

"Hobble your lip, Savage. You and this old maggot don't matter in this century no more. It's a new world. The likes of you are relics." This from a man who wore a silk tie and a brightly colored vest with a striped shirt. His blonde hair was slicked back with oils that gleamed in the light. He was flanked by two toughs.

"It *is* a new world," Riot agreed amiably. "A more civilized one. I encourage you to take a good look at Mr. Mason here and ask yourselves if it's worth it to play puppet to whichever swell is fronting the price for me."

"Money is money," the silk dandy said, studying his nails.

"Then shoot me here and now." Riot spread his hands.

"I'm an easy target, right here in your very own territory." The room went still, so tense that the air thickened.

Riot watched the men in the barroom. *All action is of the mind and the mirror of the mind is the face, its index the eyes.* Riot could read eyes like an open book. He knew who'd keep still and who would shoot. He knew who would draw first.

Isobel kept to the shadows along the street. She hung back, watching as Riot strode up to a pair of toughs in front of a dark lane. As a teenager, she had roamed these streets, visiting gambling halls and dives in male clothing, but even she had her limits. This was the kind of alleyway she instinctively knew to avoid in the Barbary Coast.

The denizens of the street paused too, some curious, fearful, and feigning disinterest while the wise quickened their pace and fled.

In a blink, Tim and Riot struck. So quick that it took a moment for her to register the attack. Two guards dropped to the ground, and Riot dragged his prisoner into the alley. Two shadows came out of the fog, running up to the unconscious pair. Others joined them, and fights broke out as thieves and whores rushed to relieve the men of their weapons, billfolds, and clothing. They were stripped bare in seconds.

Isobel hugged the filthy wall and slipped past the mob. Dim light came from the end. But the darkness was so complete it took a moment for her eyes to adjust. People were lined along the walls of the alleyway. Hunched, miserable, and no doubt crazed, they looked at her with hungry eyes. She glimpsed a limp arm with festering sores that ran like tracks up it. Needle marks? No, too thick. They were more like small bore holes along the veins. The arm was attached to a man, his eyes staring sightlessly into the fog. How long had he been dead?

Voices echoed against stone. Riot's.

"Money is money," a smooth voice drawled.

"Then shoot me here and now. I'm an easy target, right here in your very own territory."

Fear gripped her. Fear of losing the man she loved. Heedless of the danger, Isobel rushed down the steps. She shoved open the door and realized her mistake. Too late.

Riot's back was to her. He cocked his head at her entrance. A flinch of movement to the left, at his back—a man reached for his revolver and Isobel threw herself at him.

Gunshots filled the barroom.

———————

WOOD CREAKED AT RIOT'S BACK. HE COCKED HIS HEAD TO the side. The distraction was all the invitation the men needed. Riot drew. Shots roared in the cramped barroom, an explosion of noise that left ears ringing. A crash, groans, screams. The first man caught a bullet in his eye. His hand on a revolver. He slumped forward in his chair, dripping blood on the table. A second man fell off his bar stool, and wheezed for a few scant breaths. His revolver had cleared the holster. And the third choked on the blood bubbling from his ravaged throat. He dropped his gun on the floor, one round spent.

Quick as he drew, Riot holstered his gun. There was a slice in his waistcoat along his ribs. It seeped blood. Max Savage started laughing, a deranged rasp that accompanied the third man's dying gasps. He slapped his hand on the bar burbling with mirth.

Tim cursed under his breath, pulled the lever to his rifle and trained it on the remaining patrons.

Keeping one eye on the barroom, Riot turned slightly. A dead man lay behind him to the left. The top of his skull blown off by Tim's rifle. And then Riot saw her.

Isobel lay on top the dead man, her hands on the forearm that gripped a revolver. He hadn't cleared the holster when Tim fired. But Isobel had been there—in front of Tim's muzzle. That was why Tim had aimed high and sheared the top of the man's head clean off. It was fortunate Isobel was on the small side.

Pale, wide-eyed, and covered in gore. Isobel swallowed, looked down at the dead man, and quickly scrambled away.

She was alive. That was all that mattered. Riot shoved possibilities aside, and turned back to the room. "I'll ask again. Plainly. Who wants me dead?"

The slick mack licked his lips, and his two toughs decided to study their drinks on the table. It was the bartender who answered. "He gave no name, Mr. Riot. A man with a mustache is all. But I seen him with the Pinkertons once upon a time."

"I'll take my leave then." Riot fished out a few dollars from his billfold and tossed them on the counter. "For your troubles. If any more of your patrons want to come and collect on me, make sure they keep it personal, otherwise I'm liable to fall into old habits."

"And just what are those habits?" the pimp called.

Savage wheezed out a laugh as he drew a bowie knife and bent over one of the recently deceased.

"I'll let Mr. Savage fill you in."

Savage's wheeze turned to a mad cackle. The barflies watched as Savage sliced off the dead man's ear. He put the bloody organ in his pocket, and turned to Mr. Mason who was curled around his knee.

"I'm not dead!" Mr. Mason pleaded. "What the hell—" His words turned into a scream as Savage added another ear to his collection.

Isobel was numb. She could not look away from the man with the blown out brains, and worse she could not look at Riot. Somewhere distant, a grizzly bear of a man cackled his insanity while another screamed.

Riot's hand curled around her arm, but the gentlemanly gesture sparked anger, and she jerked away from his touch. He nodded towards the door, and she stumbled up the steps—the laughter following her out into the filthy lane, past the dead addict, and huddling misery.

Riot didn't speak. And neither did she. Isobel didn't trust herself to say a word. She walked in a daze, the taste of blood and gunpowder heavy in her throat.

The silence wasn't a comfortable one. Tim smoldered with anger. Every once in awhile, he turned and spat. It was far worse than a verbal dressing down.

To stave off the adrenaline drop, she reached for anger. It kept her walking.

A policeman waited outside the ravaged agency. He puffed into his hands as he stood guard over three dead bodies.

"Back away now," the patrolman said to Isobel.

Isobel stopped short and studied the dead trio from a distance. Two had been shot cleanly, and the other... Well, Isobel had a good throwing arm. The stick of dynamite she'd tossed outside rendered him to bits. With what remained, it would be difficult to identify the corpse. Bile rose in her throat.

"Bel," Riot said.

"No," she said sharply. It was a nonsensical word. But it stopped him short. Her fury boiled over. With herself. At their would-be assassins. And she flung it all at Riot. "At the first sign of danger you try to tuck me away. I admit I'm out of my depth here, but I thought this was a *partnership*. Not servitude. We've not been two weeks married, and I've been reduced to a *distraction*."

"Bel, you're not a—"

"God dammit, Riot!" Her shout echoed in the street.

The policeman took a step back.

Isobel couldn't face the police. She couldn't take the questions, the accusations, the mess of paperwork and disapproving gazes. She'd had enough of it in the past year, and she'd crack if she were trapped in another interrogation room just now. So she ran.

14

A TURBULENT SEA

RIOT WATCHED THE FOG SWALLOW HIS WIFE.

"Time and silence ain't gonna help that, boy," Tim muttered.

Riot tensed to go after her, but stopped short at his name. He turned to find a familiar face standing in the agency doorway (what was left of it). He hoped Detective Inspector Coleman hadn't seen Isobel, or worse, heard her heated words. Silver-haired and studious, Detective Coleman was one of the few honest policemen in San Francisco.

"We need to talk," Coleman said.

Riot swore under his breath. He was torn, but duty called. And it would give Isobel some time to cool down, or quietly smolder. Either way, he knew where she'd go: the *Pagan Lady*. She always took refuge in her cutter when she was shaken to the core.

When Riot entered the remains of his agency, Sergeant Price gave him a salute. He was a bull-like patrolman who had accompanied Riot on countless raids over the years. Price still took great pride in his handlebar mustache. "I see you got yourself into more trouble, A.J."

"It's a hard habit to break."

Matthew Smith stood at attention. "Mack was taken away in an ambulance, sir," he reported.

Miss Off was busy hitting at the other police officers in the saloon with her broom as she tried to clean up the mess. It seemed a hopeless task.

Coleman eyed Riot, taking note of his weapons, the blood on his face, the gash in his vest. Not much escaped him. "Smith says one of the gunmen survived."

Riot nodded. "He escaped."

Coleman pursed his lips. "Did he?"

"He did." Riot walked around the bar, and plucked a bottle of whiskey from an interior shelf. He uncorked it and took a swig. Warmth spread through his body. "I suppose you'd like a statement, Inspector."

"I would," Coleman said. "I'll need Mr. Von Poppin's statement, too. And Mrs. Riot's. I certainly hope we won't need to drag her to the station."

Matthew shifted on his feet.

"You won't have to. Mrs. Riot was very much disturbed by events, as you can imagine. She needed to go home."

"I'll expect her tomorrow at the station. Is there somewhere more private we can talk?"

Riot took the bottle with him as he led the way upstairs.

Sergeant Price stepped into the storage room first. He filled the cramped room, and searched the corners for any lurkers. The Inspector settled himself on a trunk. It was an informal gesture, and Riot relaxed some. This wasn't to be an interrogation after all. Feeling suddenly exhausted, Riot seated himself on a crate, and took another draught of whiskey.

"You're injured," Coleman gestured to Riot's side.

Riot looked down, and carefully probed the slice in his vest. "A small thing."

"What happened, Mr. Riot?" Coleman asked.

Riot relayed the night's events, starting with the dynamite thrown through the window. He stopped at Mr. Mason being dumped in a chair.

"What did you do with the gunman?"

Sergeant Price held his notepad and pencil at the ready.

Coleman had been present in the cemetery when Riot gunned down Ravenwood's murderer. He was well aware of the politics at play in San Francisco, and had testified at Isobel's trial. Coleman was by the book, but he was also practical, which was a rare thing.

Riot glanced at the notepad in Price's hand. "Is this an official interrogation, or a friendly discussion?"

Coleman frowned.

"I'll remind you, Inspector, that no whistle was blown when my agency was attacked. A stick of dynamite blew out the front off my office, and gunshots were exchanged. Either your officers on duty were attacked, bribed to look the other way, or they had orders. And I sure as hell can't be dragged into an inquest every time I defend myself. Not with the undercurrents at play in this city."

Coleman nodded to Price, who lowered his notepad and tucked away his pencil.

Riot studied Coleman for a moment. He was taking a risk confiding in an honest policeman, but he needed an ally. "I took Mr. Mason to the Morgue on Battle Row. He was supposed to collect the bounty on me there."

Coleman leaned forward. "Who put the price on your head?"

"The Morgue doesn't ask names. The bartender said 'a man with a mustache' offered a thousand dollars for my head. And that he'd seen the man with the Pinkertons."

"The Pinkertons?" Price asked.

"It may be a lie, or…" Riot stopped there.

"Or Alex Kingston is trying to get even," Coleman filled in the rest.

"Maybe so." Riot removed his spectacles and studied the blood pattern on the glass. "Alex isn't my only enemy. I have a host of them. I think the tongs, at least, would do the deed themselves." As he mused, he poured a bit of whiskey on a handkerchief and went about cleaning his spectacles. "Kate would certainly pay to have me brought in, but only so she could shoot me herself..."

"Kate?" Coleman asked.

"Spanish Kitty, at the Strassburg."

Coleman stiffened. "Is there any criminal in the Barbary Coast you haven't offended?"

It was, Riot realized, a joke of sorts. Riot gave the Inspector a rueful smile. "I seem to offend lawmen in equal measure."

Coleman chose his next words carefully. "Often times, as you know, the two are indistinguishable. But really, Mr. Riot. Why did you go to the Morgue? You wouldn't catch me in there without a squad of men."

"I needed to send a message."

"And what message was that?"

Riot looked the man square in the eye. "That a thousand dollars is not worth the risk. Four men drew on Tim and me in the Morgue. Though I'm sure you won't be called to clean up the mess we left behind."

"*Four* men?" Coleman asked.

"Inspector, I can't have my hands tied when there's a price on my head. They didn't just go after me, they targeted my agency. My men. And my *wife*." He stressed the last.

Coleman leaned back, thoughtful. "Smith only reached me because he telephoned my home. No one at the station seemed overly eager to come to your aid."

"Are you surprised?"

Coleman met his eyes. "No," he said simply, then considered his next words. "I'll be sure to mention the bounty on your head in my report. That should offer you some protection if you find yourself in front of a judge again. In the meantime, try not to leave a bloodbath in the wrong place."

"I'd like to question the policemen who were on patrol."

Coleman shook his head. "I'm afraid not. I plan on questioning them myself. I'll let you know what I discover."

It was something, at least.

"I'll also see that men I trust patrol this area."

"Are there any?"

"There are," Coleman said with a sigh. "We're few, but we're growing."

"Take care, Inspector. Helping me could make you a target as well."

Coleman gave him a tight smile. "I have plenty of enemies already. Inside the department, and outside. Don't worry about me."

Riot nodded. "Is that all, Inspector?"

"As long as Mrs. Riot comes by tomorrow and gives us a statement."

"I'll poke around too," Sergeant Price said. "I have a few contacts who might know who put the bounty on your head."

"I'd appreciate it. And one other thing while you're at it…"

"Name it," Sergeant Price said.

"Before the ambush, Bel and I were looking into the disappearance of a fifteen-year-old girl. Elouise Spencer. Her brother, Lewis Fletcher, was supposed to report it today, but who knows where the report landed."

"Don't I know it. I'll see what I can do."

"And a girl by the name of Madge Ryan. A redhead. She supposedly ran away months ago. I'd like to know if her parents reported her missing."

Price wrote the names down.

"Watch yourself, Mr. Riot." Coleman offered a hand and Riot shook it—the two men a small but determined force of justice in a sea of corruption.

AFTERDROP

Cold air seeped under her collar, cut right through the wool, and gripped her bones. Isobel welcomed it. She shook with anger. At least that's what she told herself as she walked up to the gate of a secured harbor.

Another gift from Lotario.

'My Lady requires a proper berth—not the dumps you moor her in,' her twin had said. The renovated cutter did deserve better than Isobel had given her. And Lotario had spared no expense. He'd paid for a berth at the yacht club. It also meant better guards. After being rammed by assassins and nearly drowning with Riot in the *Lady's* cabin, Isobel appreciated Lotario's generosity.

Isobel greeted the watchman with a curt name. He checked his list, and nodded her through the gate.

Lotario had rented the last berth, the farthest point on the docks and closest to the open sea. Isobel hurried along the floating dock, her footsteps hollow on the planks. Salt air soothed her, but she still shook. She stepped aboard the *Lady* and opened the hatch, then climbed down into darkness.

Feeling her way along, she struck a match and put it to the

hanging lantern. Light filled the cabin. Home. Her chest was tight. Her heart was somewhere in her throat and her ears rang, but she could almost breathe again.

As Isobel shed her borrowed hat and coat, something plopped onto the ground. She froze. A grayish-pink lump attached to a jagged bone lay on her cabin floor.

The night rushed back, starker in her mind than when it happened. The creak of a door. A standoff. Guns blazing. The split second when she'd thrown herself at a man drawing his gun. But Tim was quicker and the man had taken a header. Isobel stared down at the bit of brain attached to a skull fragment.

Bile rose in her throat.

She grabbed the galley bucket and retched. There was nothing in her stomach, but she kept at it until she was gripping the rim and shaking.

They were scarcely a week into their marriage, and after all they'd gone through and all his promises Riot had ordered her to stay behind in typical male fashion.

Isobel was not a woman to be coddled, and he damn well knew it. But she *had* been useless, a smaller voice argued. Her arrival had sparked a shoot out.

A distraction.

Blood on sawdust.

A dying gasp.

Another dry heave wracked her.

Isobel quickly shed her coat and checked her clothing. Other fragments clung to the coat. She looked in a bit of mirror hanging on the wall. Dried blood smeared her face and more pinkish-grey fragments clung to her collar.

Isobel swallowed. She grabbed the bit of brain from her cabin floor, climbed on deck, and chucked it into the water. Her skin was crawling.

Her heart thundered in her ears and clawed up her throat.

She needed to *move*. She stripped down to her skin, dumped her clothes on deck, and dove overboard. The shock of frigid water hit her. It cleared her mind of memory, and the sea washed her clean of grime. With every reckless stroke towards the seawall she left the night behind.

THE *PAGAN LADY* WAS IN HER BERTH. THAT WAS A GOOD SIGN. Warm light seeped from between shutters and a thin line of smoke joined the fog from the stack. A knot unwound in Riot's chest as he walked towards her in the dark, and climbed aboard. "Ahoy there," he called, his voice bouncing against the lap of water.

No answer.

The fog obscured the moon, the dark was absolute, so when his toe ran into something wet, he paused. He bent and felt the shadowy lump. Clothing.

Riot moved to the hatch, and opened it. He stuck his head inside and peered cautiously into the cabin.

Water spots spattered the companionway, and a trail of water led to a small copper hip tub and a scrub brush. Isobel stood near the tub. She held her robe closed with one hand and her other held a revolver. When recognition flashed over her eyes, she cursed softly and lowered the weapon.

Riot hesitated before walking into the tiger's den. But as Tim had said, time and silence wouldn't fix this. He steeled himself, and stepped down the companionway ladder, hands in the air. "Now's an excellent time to shoot me. You'll walk away with the house and my not so impressive fortune."

Wet hair, chattering teeth, she shivered violently. Her lips had a decidedly blue tint. And yet, there was steel in her eyes.

"Why the hell do you still have your hands up?"

"You still have a revolver in hand," he said softly.

It was a precaution. A lifetime of training, conditioning, and frightening innate reflexes meant that Riot's brain didn't always catch up to his instincts until after he pulled the trigger. If she was furious enough to fire, then so be it. He'd take a bullet. But he'd take no chances of triggering his own reactions with the woman he loved.

Isobel paled in realization, and quickly set the revolver on a shelf.

Riot lowered his hands. "Bel, I shouldn't have—"

"But you did." The words hung between them. She cinched her robe with a grudge, and turned to the Shipmate stove for warmth, hugging herself. Clothes on deck, slicked-back hair, a trail of water drops leading into the cabin. Riot surmised she likely dove overboard for a bracing swim.

He wanted to put his arms around her. Warm her. Keep her safe. But then perhaps that was the issue. The silence between them was vast.

"Talk to me, Bel," he urged. Scream at me, attack me, anything other than *this*, he thought.

She spun. "Talk to you? *Talk?* Like you talked with me before you left? You didn't even bother to tell me where you were headed. You *ordered* me to stay behind." Fury warmed her, and for the moment she stopped shivering.

Isobel snatched up the hip tub, pushed past him, and lugged it on deck. Water splashed as it was upended, and then silence.

At least she hadn't asked him to leave. Small victories.

The night hit him like a train. Drained and sore, Riot hung his hat on a hook and shed his coat. The movement sent fire up his side and unleashed a fresh gush of blood. Moving more carefully, he divested himself of belts, holsters, and revolvers.

Some men felt powerful when they had a gun strapped to their hips. Others felt reassurance. But for Riot, guns were simply tools of his trade, and like any professional he was happy to lay down his tools at the end of a long day. A weight lifted from his mind, and he relaxed, turning to the gash in his side.

Riot eased out of his waistcoat, and was peeling off his blood-soaked shirt when he heard a slight intake of breath. He looked up. Isobel stood at the bottom of the companionway ladder, a bucket in hand. She nearly dropped it.

"You're shot."

"Only a graze," he said.

Water sloshed over the rim, as she set the bucket down and hurried forward. Gunfighter number three had fired off a shot just as Riot's bullet hit him. The bullet went awry and grazed Riot's ribs, leaving a red trail along his side.

Isobel bent to study the wound. "It'll need stitches." She turned to retrieve her medical kit, but Riot caught her hand. Her skin felt like ice. Instead of pulling away, she stayed in place.

"You *are* my partner," he said.

"I didn't feel like it back there."

"I apologize. I shouldn't have ordered you. This is... all new for me too, Bel. I wouldn't have let Ravenwood go either."

"Maybe not, but you sure as hell would have discussed your plans."

"I was angry. I wasn't thinking clearly."

"Because *I* was threatened," she accused.

Riot didn't answer.

"Would you have asked Ravenwood to get the lights?" she pressed.

"Matt was closer."

Isobel arched a brow. "Really, Riot? That's the only reason?"

He squared his shoulders. "The explosion shook you. You were dazed and your hands were trembling. You were in no state to come with me."

Isobel bristled. Steely eyes flashed and she was set to unleash hell on him, but then she looked him in the eyes and saw the brutal truth of it—no amount of arguing would change the fear she'd felt in that moment.

Adrenaline and fury rushed out in a breath. "And yet I did," she said softly.

"You did," he said.

She searched his eyes. "Would those men have drawn on you if I hadn't provided a convenient distraction?"

Riot knew what she was asking. It was a hard question. But shielding her from the truth wouldn't do much good. "One man would have."

"How can you be so cocksure of that?" she demanded.

"Think, Bel. What did you see when you entered?"

"I saw a man draw on you, so I charged him."

Riot inwardly winced at the memory. Tim had fired his rifle from his hip. It was fortunate he was a crack shot and Isobel was short. "But there was a split second before that. What did you see?"

"My husband about to be shot."

He waited.

Isobel growled in frustration. She took a calming breath and closed her eyes. "There was the pimp with his two guards. The grizzly bear of a man, the bartender, three women, the man in the corner behind you, the one I tackled. A third man at the bar, one at a table with his side to you—" Isobel opened her eyes. "It was him. He would have fired. He was sitting at the table, with his right side facing you, but the bottle and tumbler were on his left side. He was left-handed."

Riot inclined his head. "He was slowly reaching for his revolver, thinking I wouldn't notice. The others weren't going to gamble with their lives, but your arrival gave them courage. They took advantage of a distraction, just like I took advantage of Mack's reckless charge out the back door."

She swallowed as the full implication settled on her shoulders. "I nearly got you killed."

Riot closed the distance, taking her face gently in his hands. "You nearly got yourself killed," he corrected.

Isobel deflated right into his arms. They clung to each other, her face tucked against his neck. He could feel her breath, feel her trembling. He held her close, willing warmth into her bones.

"I should have listened. I knew you were quick, but—" She stopped, unable or unwilling to voice the events of the night. Isobel was too practical to think him a monster. He knew that much. And he was too seasoned to feel even a twinge of regret for killing in self-defense. Still, he wagered that had been her first prolonged gunfight and duel, all in a single night.

Riot brushed her forehead with his lips. "For what it's worth, Tim and I didn't expect you to stay behind."

"For all the good it did. I was useless." Her voice was muffled against his skin.

Riot's hands dropped to her upper arms, and he gently eased her back to catch her eyes. "You threw a stick of dynamite back at an assassin."

"I blew up your agency."

The corner of Riot's lip raised. "Only partly."

She frowned at him.

"I have a proposal regarding our continued partnership," he said.

"I'm not jumping ship on our marriage just yet."

"I'm relieved to hear." He brushed his thumb lightly over a cut on her cheek. "Would you like to hear my proposal?"

"Are we really going to discuss this while you drip blood on my cabin floor?"

"I'm not positive I want to discuss this while you're armed with thread and needle."

"Sounds like perfect timing." Isobel left to fetch her kit.

Riot poured water from the bucket into the kettle, and set it on the Shipmate stove. While the cabin warmed, he stretched out on a settee, half propped up so his side was accessible. Isobel pressed a bottle of medicinal brandy into his hand while they waited for the water to boil.

It was a long slice. Isobel washed it, and then disinfected it with carbolic acid. Needle and thread in hand, her brows drew together as she bent over his wound, tugging thread through his skin with each pass.

"What do you propose, Mr. Riot?"

Riot took another fortifying draught of brandy.

"I'm not going to jab you," she said through her teeth.

He eyed her warily, but spoke anyway. "We're both new to this partnership, professionally and in life. I might have a lifetime of experience, but, in some areas, you far surpass me."

Isobel snorted. "I doubt that."

"You're captain of this ship," he pointed out.

"Boat," she corrected.

"My point exactly. So when we're on this boat, I'll defer to your experience. And in agency matters, I'll take the lead."

"That's hardly fair, Riot," she argued. "How often do we sail?"

"Hear me out," he said with a wince.

Isobel took a calming breath, and more care with the next pass of the needle.

"I'm a fair detective, as long as there's a trail. Tim has a knack with people. But you... You leap ahead to the end, Bel. You have superb instincts for detective work."

"My 'instincts are incomparable but my judgment is sorely lacking'?" she asked, quoting something Ravenwood had often said of Riot in his journals.

"I wouldn't say that about your judgment. Not anymore."

"Is it because I have a needle through your flesh? Because tonight proved otherwise."

He grunted. "You don't need to prove yourself, Bel. You survived the past year. That's proof enough. When I worked with Ravenwood, he led investigations and I handled anything dangerous that came along. That's all I ask. That when it comes to a gunfight, you follow my orders."

"Will you share your plans with me next time?"

"If there's time."

She raised her brows at him.

"Yes," he conceded.

"Will you include me in those plans?"

"When appropriate."

"Here's the issue, Riot."

"Only one?"

"You have a protective streak in you. But so do I." Isobel brandished the needle at him, causing her robe to slip off one shoulder. "I know if I agree to this you'll try to keep me safe like some princess locked away in a tower. Your proposal isn't fair to me. I don't need a knight protector."

"It's a logical proposal. I'm more experienced."

"Until you get yourself killed."

"I won't."

"Neither will I."

Riot opened his mouth, and clicked it shut. As needle passed through flesh, he mulled the matter over.

Isobel sat back to regard him. "I have a question."

He waited.

"If I'm captain of this boat and you're captain of the agency, who gets to pilot our marriage?"

"That's a trick question."

"Is it?"

"At the very least it's a loaded one."

"You never flinch in the face of a loaded gun." Her lip quirked. "You're not dodging this bullet."

Riot's gaze flickered downwards. "Your most exquisite

breasts pilot our marriage, Miss Bel." He raised a brow towards her open robe.

Isobel stared at him. Then snorted. And finally laughed. "They're not the most prominent captains."

"They get my attention every time."

With a roll of her eyes she got back to work, but didn't bother fastening her robe. The view distracted him from her work. "You didn't seem surprised by the attack tonight," she murmured.

It took a second for his brain to make sense of her statement. "Fishing, Bel?"

"I suspect my partner is withholding information from me."

"Not on purpose. I was warned during that business with the stolen eggs—a lady of the night told me I had a price on my head and Kate confirmed it."

"Ah."

"As a general rule, there's usually at least one bounty on my head. I suspect the tongs still have a *chun hung* on me, too."

"Well, someone tried to collect tonight. What would you have done if the entire Morgue had drawn on you?"

"Hope a few missed."

"I'm serious, Riot."

He met her glare. "I am, too."

Isobel made a sound of frustration in the back of her throat, and refocused on her sutures. "Would Ravenwood have stayed behind?"

"Without a doubt," Riot said. "He'd have sat behind the bar, told me to handle things, then pulled out a book."

"I don't believe it."

"He was British. He preferred to keep things 'civilized.'"

"And let the conquered natives handle the messy bits?"

"Precisely."

"That's not in my nature, Riot."

"I'm well aware."

"Not that I was any help. I've been shot at, knifed, beaten, but that—" She shivered. "That was a whole other beast."

She was right about that. Riot remembered his first gunfight. Pinned down and surrounded, his urge to do something, *anything* had been nearly overwhelming. Tim had just sat there calmly smoking his pipe, waiting for an opening. He made his shots count.

Riot had been that inexperienced greenhorn a lifetime ago. He knew the course he'd taken to get to where he was today, but the thought of Isobel following a path like that made breathing difficult.

"Riot?" Her voice brought him back to the present. "Do I need to take that bottle away?"

"Only lost in the past."

Isobel tied off the last stitch, and snipped the thread. "That's a dangerous thing." She doused the wound with carbolic acid again, then motioned for him to sit up. Riot tested his arm. The sutured skin stretched and the movement sent a fresh wave of pain. She turned to her supplies and slathered something on a bandage before laying it over the wound.

"What's that?"

"*Apis mellifera.*"

"Honey?" He narrowed his eyes. "What witchery is this?"

"I did have an old woman in Italy brandish her cross at me once."

"I'm not surprised." Riot poked at the bandage as she secured it with plaster. "Why honey?"

"My brother Fernando is an Egyptologist."

"That's right." Isobel had nine brothers. All of them older, save for her twin. Two of them were deceased. She had shot Curtis in self-defense, and Decker was reportedly lost at sea five years before.

"You'll meet them all eventually, I'm sure. Ancient Egyptians used honey on bandages. I tested it once, and it works. Bacteria can't grow in honey. But you'll have to take care not to reopen it."

"Yes, ma'am."

Isobel put her things away, wrapped herself in a blanket, then leaned against his uninjured side. Riot draped an arm around her. The Shipmate stove was glowing with heat, and the cabin was cozy. Her teeth had stopped chattering. She idly ran a hand through his hair and he closed his eyes, savoring her touch.

"What part of your past were you lost in?" she asked softly.

"A gunfight. My first. Not a duel, but a battle. Tim and I cornered an outlaw and his gang. Or so we thought. It was the opposite—we were cornered."

"You two have a long history together." There was a note of envy in her voice. Of sadness. Riot shifted slightly to look her in the eyes. He cupped her cheek, and caressed her ear with his thumb. Isobel had beautiful lines. She was a study in contrasts: sharp cheekbones, wide mouth and lips, a jawline cut from stone, and a long, graceful neck. But it was her eyes that drew him every time. Fiercely intelligent, proud, and glittering with steel.

The last thing Riot wanted to do was hurt her pride. But how to explain?

"Who do you want on deck with you when you sail into a storm?" he asked.

"An experienced sailor."

"Isn't every sailor inexperienced at some point?"

"Of course."

"How does a sailor bridge the gap from landlubber to sea dog? How did you do it?"

"I know my way around a boat, but I wouldn't call myself a sea dog."

"Humility is a true mark of experience."

Isobel thought for a moment. "I was foolhardy, in over my head, and had dumb luck. That's how I bridged the gap."

"It was the same for me. Consider tonight a christening in blood. Your first storm."

She met his eyes.

"I took a risk going to the Morgue, Bel. I needed someone at my back who knew the ropes. It wasn't your sex, your ability, or our relationship. Taking Tim was simply the best chance I had of surviving a storm."

"Why go at all?" she challenged.

"Things changed while I was away from San Francisco. Three years is a long time in the criminal underworld. There's fresh blood now, and a new power dynamic. I thought it time I left an impression on a new generation of thugs."

"Do you think it worked?" she asked.

"It'll weed out a few."

"And what remains?"

"The desperate and dangerous."

Isobel took a shaky breath. "It was Alex, wasn't it?" Her ex-husband had a bone to pick, and hiring killers was just his style.

"I don't honestly know," he admitted. "I don't have a shortage of enemies. I suspect my half sister was keeping hired guns at bay over the years."

White Blossom, or Siu Lui—Jesse as he called her—a notorious madam in Chinatown who had been the mastermind behind a secretive society. Riot and Isobel had exposed her criminal organization. Their conflict ended in a stalemate, and she agreed to leave for three years to repay a life debt she owed Riot.

"Say what you like about her, but she kept a kind of balance in the city, and chasing her away left a void. It's bound to tip one way or the other now."

"Siu Lui physically left, Riot. That doesn't mean she's withdrawn her hooks from the city."

As his only purported family, Riot was aware he had a weakness for Siu Lui. They'd grown up on the streets together. Survived. And then their paths diverged, but that connection was still there. He tried not to think about what would happen when she returned.

Instead, Riot told Isobel what the bartender said.

"A man with a mustache. Well, that narrows things down." Isobel took the bottle of brandy from him, stared at it a moment, then handed it back, and got up to root around her galley. "Do you think that bartender was telling the truth? That the man who put the mark on you was a Pinkerton?"

"Could be an ex-Pinkerton like myself."

"You and Ravenwood didn't leave the agency on good terms, did you?"

"We did not."

"Convenient that Monty wasn't there for the attack." She let the suggestion hang in the air.

"We've never got along," Riot admitted. "But I don't think he'd put a mark on me."

"I personally think he would, and I doubt he has two coins to rub together, which is motivation in itself," Isobel said. "Think about it, Riot. Monty has intimate knowledge of your habits. He could be an informant."

"The agency pays well," he defended. "If he needed money that much, why ruin his only job?"

"You said it yourself earlier today."

"I did?"

"Monty respected Ravenwood. He doesn't respect you."

The thought made Riot tired. But there it was. Out in the open now.

"There's no proof," she said hastily. "But we should

consider all possibilities." She returned with tea, a plate of cut apples, dried beef, and cheese and crackers.

"Thank you." They ate and sipped their tea in silence while Riot considered the possibility of Monty's betrayal. Finally, he came to a conclusion. "I don't think Monty hates me that much. Does he want to beat me to a pulp? Absolutely. But hire someone else to shoot me? No. He'd want me to know it was him pulling the trigger. I've been wrong before, though," he admitted. "Maybe I just don't like to think of him as a Judas in my midst."

Isobel snorted. "Not quite that, Riot. You can't even swim let alone walk on water."

"I'm making headway." Not much, he admitted to himself. He found Isobel absolutely captivating in the water. The only headway he'd made was his ability to distract her from teaching him anything.

"I intend to make a swimmer out of you yet."

"Whatever keeps you close."

Riot leaned back on the settee, gently gripped her wrist, and pulled her down beside him. She gladly came, laying her head on his chest, and molding herself to him. Riot ran a hand through her hair, and slowly, deliberately, began massaging the contours of her scalp before working down her neck. Her muscles were corded in knots, and he teased them loose with each stroke of his hand.

A soft sigh brushed his skin. "This isn't how I envisioned our first day back," Isobel whispered. She liked puzzles. She did not like being splattered with brains.

"We can always pack up and leave for England. Apparently I inherited an estate there."

"Do you have enemies in England?"

A pause, then, "I've had a few difficulties."

Isobel considered the option. "I'm not sure English society is ready for the Riot family. I'd have even less freedom there, and so would our daughters, but if things get too dangerous…" she let the rest hang in the air.

"It never hurts to have an exit at hand," he murmured.

"How can you be so calm?"

"The same way a captain pilots a ship through a squall. I've been in worse situations, Bel. You do what needs doing until you drop dead."

She shivered against him. "It's the dying part I worry about with you. I don't fancy being a widow, Riot."

"I'll get there one day," he whispered against her temple. "But not today."

He had a reason to wake up every morning. She was wrapped safely in his arms, and Riot intended to hold on to her for as long as he could.

"You best not go anywhere. I'll have to find a new masseuse."

Riot had unknotted the kinks in her shoulders. His hand was strong, his touch precise. He had worked down her spine, and now ran a finger up her protruding vertebrae with the same sensitive touch he used with his marked cards.

Isobel shivered again—this time with a soft moan. She raised her face to his. "What did I ever do without you?"

In answer, Riot kissed her. He couldn't resist, and had no reason to. But his kiss was like a match to tinder. The instant his lips touched hers, she answered with a hungry, near savage return.

Isobel never did anything halfway. All her energy, all her focus, was thrown into that act, until he could taste lust on her lips. Riot was overcome, gripped in her passion—a need to be reminded they were both alive. Of skin on skin, and a melding of bodies.

Never breaking the kiss, of tongues warring with tongues, of frantic need, Isobel rose and straddled him, letting her robe fall open. She tugged at his trouser buttons as his hands roamed her body, stoking desire, and then her lips fell, teeth scraping across his chest. His head swam, pulsing heat rushed to his groin, until hard instinct was the only thing driving him. Riot hissed as she teased, his hand tightening on her buttocks, urging her towards a primal connection.

But Isobel resisted his direction, taking advantage of his injury. She grabbed his hand, and pinned it over his head, her eyes full of mischief. "Oh no you don't, Mr. Riot. Remember, I'm the captain on this boat."

The only word he managed was a groan.

16

A FRESH START

THE SIREN SCENT OF COFFEE COAXED ISOBEL AWAKE. SHE inhaled, her senses coming alive, and stretched. A yawn cracked her jaw. She could feel Riot warm and relaxed beside her on their double bed. From the rhythm of his breathing, she surmised he was still sleeping. Drowsy, she turned towards him, intending to go back to sleep.

Wait. Coffee. Riot was sleeping. Then who—

Her eyes flew open, and she sat up.

A small, black-haired girl in a boy's suit and an oversized cap crouched on the floor. Her black eyes were focused on Riot's foot. He tended to kick off blankets, and his leg was hanging out into the boat's passageway. Thankfully, the more important parts were covered. Isobel hoped signs of the night's activities weren't too obvious.

Silver light streamed through the hatch overhead, and she could hear footsteps on deck. Isobel squinted groggily at her daughter.

Jin answered her unvoiced question. "Sarah, Tobias, and

Grimm. Sarah came down too, but she turned very red when she saw your clothes all over the cabin and you both in bed. She is on deck now. I would pretend that you do not know she came down here. I cleaned up the mess you made."

So much for that hope.

"That will teach you not to disturb us unannounced."

Jin frowned. "It is close to noon. You did not return last night."

Memories of the day before came flooding back. She blew out a harsh breath, and put a hand to her head, suddenly sick.

"Why does *bahba* have a pig and barrel on the top of his feet?" Jin asked.

"So I won't sink," Riot muttered. He stirred and shifted, wincing as he pushed himself upright to rest against the cabin wall. "It's a mariner's tradition."

"He really went all out on his single ocean voyage," Isobel explained.

"Har. Har," Riot rasped.

Jin's eyes narrowed on his bandage. "You were shot too?"

Belatedly, Riot realized his state of undress, and clutched the blanket to his chin. Jin was unfazed. She'd spent a year in a high-end brothel cleaning up rooms and readying prostitutes for their next client. Jin spoke about sex in the bluntest of terms.

"Too?" Isobel asked. She knew who else had been shot, but she was surprised Jin knew.

Jin tossed three newspapers onto the bed. *The Morning Call*, the *Examiner*, and the *San Francisco Bulletin*. Riot reached for his spectacles, but found the small shelf empty. Jin plucked his spectacles from her pocket, and handed them over. "They were stuffed between the cushions."

Riot cleared his throat, and threaded the wire over his ears one-handed, while he clutched the blanket to his bare chest.

Isobel grabbed the *Examiner*. "You're an excellent first mate, Jin."

"He is your first mate."

"No, Riot is my cook. You'll always be first mate," Isobel said, unfolding the newspaper.

Jin picked up a basket from the floor, and set it on their legs with a pointed look at Riot. "Your cook is slacking on his duties, so it is lucky Miss Lily sent breakfast. I will bring coffee and tea. Should I make him walk the plank afterwards?"

Riot was most definitely not slacking on his husbandly duties, but Isobel kept that thought to herself.

"No leniency for an injured crewman?" Riot asked.

"I suppose. This once," Jin said. "But I want to see if your pig and barrel work."

Isobel looked up from the article *Detectives Ambushed,* which described the shoot-out at Ravenwood Agency, told in the play-by-play style of a man accustomed to covering boxing matches. At least Mack was feeling well enough to write.

Isobel studied her small charge. Wisps of black hair had escaped her braid, her collar sagged, and her clothes were wrinkled. Dark circles ringed her eyes, making her look more severe than usual.

Isobel did not ask the question on the tip of her tongue: What did you get up to last night? Jin would never give her a straight answer. Instead, she asked another, "Why are you buttering us up?"

Jin sniffed. "You are *so* suspicious of me." The girl marched into the main cabin, and Isobel leaned over Riot to call down the passageway, "Wouldn't you be suspicious of you?"

"I am suspicious of everyone."

"That's my girl," Isobel called.

She felt Riot stiffen under her. Not in the usual morning manner, but an alarmed reflex. Isobel sat up. He had the

Morning Call in hand, and his bespectacled eyes were fixed on a headline: *Disreputable Detective Runs House of Ill Repute.*

"Now *that* is Alex's doing," she said with a sigh. She read along with him. The article claimed Atticus Riot lived under one roof with his mistress *and* a wife, and speculated on his relationship with his adoptive daughters. Each word sickened Isobel further. She placed a hand on his arm. "We'll file a libel suit."

But Riot shook his head. "No use. The damage is done. People will believe what they like."

"You can't just let this lie, Riot. It accuses you of running a whorehouse out of your home."

"If we file a libel suit it will open us up for an investigation by the police." He let the statement hang there.

Isobel clenched her jaw. She saw it. A police investigation by the very department that only last night had been bribed to look the other way. "Damn," she swore. "Still, there's information in here that only someone inside Ravenwood Manor would know."

"Likely one of the boarders," Riot agreed.

"The innocent boarders will be sure to leave now. No respectable person will taint themselves with our presence." Which put their finances in further danger. The boarders at Ravenwood Manor were needed to cover costs of the oversized house. And worse, would this affect the agency's reputation?

Riot tossed the paper on the floor. There was nothing for it.

Jin brought back two steaming mugs. A coffee for Isobel and tea for Riot. "Thank you, Jin," he said.

"Are you all right?" the girl asked. A bit of blood had seeped through his bandage.

"Just a scratch," he said.

Jin nodded. Then glared at the two of them. "You promised you would be safe." She thrust a finger at the newspaper headlines. "*That* is not safe."

Her anger was born from both worry and love. Jin had witnessed the murder of her parents. She didn't want to lose another set.

Riot gave Jin's shoulder a gentle squeeze. "You'll get no argument from me." And then quietly. "Are you sleeping all right? You look tired."

"I was reading late," Jin said.

Riot held her eyes for a breath, then nodded. But Isobel knew he didn't buy Jin's answer any more than she did. A truthful response from Jin would have been, 'It is none of your business.' Her excuse of reading stank of a prepared answer, and it also nudged Isobel's mind.

"Ella," Isobel whispered. With the ambush, she had all but forgotten the girl. She tossed off her blankets, slithered over Riot, grabbed a robe off the floor, and hurried to the cabin.

Jin had stoked the coals to life, and the cabin was warm, but Isobel paid it little mind. She headed straight for the coat hooks, and saw that Riot had brought her coat and satchel from the agency.

"Sarah?" she called.

Sarah's head appeared from the hatch. "Are you both decent?"

"Not exactly. Did you bring your sketchbook and pencils?"

Sarah looked offended. "Of course I did."

"Good. Would you do something for me?"

Sarah settled herself on the top of the companionway, sketchbook balanced on her knees.

"I need you to draw this girl. Make as many copies as you can. And... this man too." Isobel handed photographs from her satchel up to Sarah, then called for Grimm and Tobias.

Tobias's head came down in front of Sarah's, only it was upside down, since he was crouched atop the hatch. "Aye, Captain?"

"I'm going to write an article in response to the one in the *Morning Call*."

Tobias crinkled his nose. "Ma was fuming over it."

"We are too. That's why I'll need you to take it to a reporter named Cameron Fry at the *Bulletin*. Are you willing?"

"Yes, ma'am."

If there was one thing San Francisco loved, it was a newspaper war, and she'd be damned if she didn't start the fight first. It was time to remind the city that Alex Kingston influenced the *Morning Call*.

17

THE PRINCESS

MACK MCCORMICK WAS RESTING ON A CLOUD OF PILLOWS. *The Princess and the Pea* came to Isobel's mind. Her father had relished telling his twin son and daughter fairy tales. Then with a twinkle in his eyes he'd ask their opinion.

"I don't want to be a princess," Isobel had declared as only a four-year-old could.

"No?"

Isobel shook her head. "I want to be a pirate."

"And what would a pirate have done?"

"Throw the pea at the prince, drop all the mattresses out the window, jump on them, and run away." Isobel had an extreme grudge against peas, princes, and princesses.

Marcus's lips had twitched, and she suspected, now, that her mother had laughed. At the time, it sounded like a grunt of disapproval. Her father leaned in close. "But you *are* a princess, my little bird. A princess can be a pirate, too."

Isobel crossed her arms in doubt.

Marcus tapped her nose. "Do you know how?"

It was Lotario who answered. "The prince was wrong. A

princess can be strong. Why would a pea hurt her?" His lisp didn't diminish the wisdom in his words.

"Aaah," Marcus beamed at his son. "Never let anyone tell you how you should be. You are what you are." The twins had certainly taken that to heart.

Looking at Mack now, Isobel imagined the big Scotsman would like living in a castle and being waited on hand and foot. "I hope there's not a pea under there," Isobel said by way of greeting.

Mack shot her a confused look, but she felt Riot chuckle at her side. The Scotsman would make for one hairy princess.

"Aye, I got to pee. Stop lookin' so smug, Charlie," Mack grumbled. His broad chest was bare, unless one counted the sweep of red hair, and the padded bandage wrapped around his gut. He looked pale and drugged, but Isobel noted his eye kept wandering in the direction of an attractive nurse. Clearly, he would live.

"Were the surgeons able to remove the bullet?" Riot asked.

Mack grunted. "That itty-bitty piece of lead didn't get far into my Scottish musculature." He patted his ample gut, then winced.

"Is that what you call it?" Isobel asked.

"Layers upon layers of muscles. You're lucky I deflected it away from your scrawny husband there."

"I do appreciate it," Riot said.

Mack gave him a hard look. "I couldn't let them get at Charlie, now could I?"

All this male protectiveness was getting on Isobel's nerves. However, she was hardly going to chastise a man in a hospital bed. She sat down on the side of his bed and handed him the *Call* article. "Have you seen this?"

Mack read the headlines, then turned brick red with rage. "I didn't write this," he said.

"I know," she soothed.

Mack glanced at Riot. "I wrote the one in the *Examiner*. I thought it'd be fine."

"It was," Riot assured. "The attack on the agency was bound to get out. Your narrative was accurate and didn't do any harm."

Mack looked relieved. "This is bollocks, Charlie." He thumped the paper. "No one will believe it."

"I'm sure enough will. But I don't much care. What I do care about is you getting better."

Mack eyed her suspiciously. "And?" He drew out the single word.

"There's information in here that only someone within Ravenwood Manor would be privy to. We need you to trace this article back to the person who submitted it. I could ask Cara Sharpe, but…"

"You want to save up your favors?"

"No. Men tend to gossip more."

"We do not," he defended.

Isobel smiled pleasantly. She didn't want to upset an invalid.

Mack thrust a finger at Riot. "What about *him*. He hardly says anything."

Isobel patted Mack's hand. "That's why I married him."

Mack blew a breath past his mustache. "I knew it. I should have played the strong and silent type."

"It was that, and the beard."

Mack fingered the cleft on his bare chin. "Well, there goes that; I hate those things. But look… what does it matter who wrote this? You know how newspapers are. They publish everything from speculation to outright lies. How many articles did you make up while you were working as Charlotte Bonnie?"

Isobel raised her brows innocently. "Ladies don't tell, Mack."

"All the same, we'd appreciate it if you traced the article," Riot said. "When you're healed up."

"Sure. I'll start fishing around once I get out of this bed."

Isobel twisted around to study the nurse who had caught his eye—she was a plump, black-haired woman with a ready smile. "Good luck."

MASONS AND BRICKLAYERS WERE LABORING TO FINISH THE newly opened Hall of Justice. A stream of wagons and workers hauled in furniture and files as uniformed policemen buzzed around the stone-columned building.

The woman at Riot's side slowed and he matched her pace as they entered the building's shadow. A caged wagon was unlocked and opened, and a line of prisoners in chains climbed out, guarded by men with billy clubs and hard stares.

Isobel stiffened at his side, then her step faltered altogether. "We should come back." Her voice was tight.

Riot glanced at his wife. She was pale under the brim of her hat, the blood drained from her face. He touched her arm, and turned to face her, blocking her view of the policemen.

"I'm afraid that won't help, Bel. Detective Inspector Coleman needs your statement."

Her eyes were wide, staring. And her breath quick.

"Bel," he said firmly. Riot leaned forward, catching her eyes, and waited until she focused on him. "You won't be arrested. You had no part in events last night."

"I killed that man," she whispered.

"You rid us of a stick of dynamite. He was foolish enough to still be standing there after he threw it. That's self-defense."

"The police might not see it that way."

"Coleman will. Trust me."

"No, I..."

She seemed about to bolt, so he grabbed her gently by the arms. "Bel, *look* at me."

"I can't go back to jail, Riot."

His heart twisted. "I know." He held her eyes, until some of the panic left. And then nodded his head towards a faraway bench across the green. "Wait over there. I'll ask Coleman to come outside. Fair enough?"

Misty eyes flickered over his shoulder to the commotion. She took a breath, closed her eyes briefly, and shook her head. "No… I need to do this, don't I?"

Riot wanted to tell her no. The memory of her behind bars was burned into his heart—a caged tigress pacing her cell in near madness. And now she was entering that cage again, with all the familiar smells and sights.

"I'll stay with you." He kept a firm hold of her hand as he tucked it through his arm.

"Do you ever feel broken?" she whispered.

"You'll build up strength again."

"I'm not sure about that." Isobel shivered when they touched the first step, but she kept her chin up and didn't slow. Riot opened the door for her, and she marched into a chaotic station. Desks out of order, supplies dumped on the floor, police and workers running to and fro.

Riot flagged down a patrolman, and asked after Detective Inspector Coleman. He waved them down a hallway, and Riot was relieved to find a nameplate attached to what he hoped was the correct door.

Coleman answered the knock with a harsh, "Come!"

"Inspector Coleman," Riot greeted. "Mrs. Riot has come as promised, though it's a bit hectic in here…" Riot let the comment hang in the air, and directed a pointed look to his wife. Coleman took one look at the pale woman and quickly ushered them outside into gray sunlight.

Isobel sat on a bench, looking dazed. Riot shared a silent plea with the detective, who seemed to understand his message.

When it was over, Riot doubted Isobel remembered a word of the interview. To Coleman's credit, he didn't press for answers but simply took her statement. She looked so fragile. Still, she had ventured inside. To hell again. Willingly. A small step, but one taken nevertheless.

Coleman read through her statement, then flipped his notebook closed. Riot drew him a few steps away. "Any word on the patrolmen?"

Coleman smoothed his waistcoat. "They were arresting a group of drunks on the other side of the Barbary Coast. Twenty, to be exact."

The hairs on Riot's neck rose. He wasn't being hunted by just any predator, but a careful one. "Are any of the drunks still in custody?"

Coleman shook his head. "As soon as they paid their fine and sobered up, we set them free. Nothing out of the ordinary."

"What drew the patrolmen's attention?"

"Shouting, broken windows, and a fight that moved away from your agency. I'll let you know if I discover anything more. And Mr. Riot…"

Riot waited.

Coleman lowered his voice and leaned in close. "Did something happen to Mrs. Riot while she was in our custody?"

"Yes, she was kept in a cage."

THEY DID NOT TAKE A CABLE CAR, BUT WALKED. MOVING helped. It was some time before Isobel focused on anything beyond the reassurance of Riot's forearm under her hand. She looked at their surroundings for the first time.

"Heather's lodging house?" she asked.

Riot nodded. "We're nearly there."

She swallowed. Heat rose to her cheeks. "God, I feel like an idiot."

"It happens to the best of us." Riot was referring to his own lapses. And it was true. Isobel had been at his side when driving fear overcame him.

"A year ago, I would have turned up my nose at the slightest showing of weakness in someone. And now here I am."

"Older and wiser."

Isobel glanced at him. "It feels more like tired and weak."

Riot squeezed her hand. "I won't argue with that."

She sighed. "I suppose, at the very least, it gives me insight into seemingly sickly people, like Mrs. Spencer."

"Ravenwood didn't have an empathetic bone in his body. That was always his blind spot in an investigation. He knew it, and relied on me for that. Understanding weakness is not a bad thing, Bel. Be patient with yourself."

It sure felt like a bad thing.

The more distance they put between themselves and the Hall of Justice, the easier she breathed, and by the time they got to Heather Searlight's lodging home, Isobel felt like herself again.

As she'd suspected yesterday, Heather Searlight had moved a while ago from her lodging house of last year. But they were told she was still employed at Hale's, so that's where they headed next.

Sharp scents of perfume stung Isobel's nose. She detested department stores. They were sprawling mazes of fashion and noxious hair products and perfumes, filled with idle women looking for an escape from boorish routines. Everything about them made her skin crawl.

She voiced her opinion to Riot.

"That's a harsh assessment, Bel."

"How so?"

"Not all women detest a domestic life."

"And you know this how?"

"Your own twin loves to shop. Lotario has trunks of dresses. I'm sure he'd be lost in here for hours."

"He only wears *bespoke* clothing," she clarified. Lotario would be appalled to hear Riot mention a department store and his name in the same sentence.

"Sarah enjoys coming here."

She glanced at him. "You took her shopping?"

"Of course. She needed clothes."

"And we're *this* broke?"

Riot adjusted his spectacles. "We're better off than most."

"Hmm."

Heather Searlight worked at the perfume counter in Hale's. She was a woman of Isobel's own age, her brown hair had hints of amber, and her eyes sparkled under lavish lashes. Heather could easily have been a poster girl for a Gibson girl advert.

Heather greeted Isobel with a friendly smile, but her eyes had wandered to Riot. She picked up a spritz bottle. "Care for a sample?"

Before Isobel could answer, Heather squeezed the bulb, sending a mist of stinging scents flying in her face. Isobel coughed, her eyes watered, her throat seized, and she took a hasty step back before the woman could attack her again.

Riot smoothly stepped in, sliding a calling card across the counter. "A lovely scent. I'm Atticus Riot and this is Miss Amsel," he said.

Heather's eyes widened a fraction. Her breath caught in surprise, and she plucked the card up. Then offered her hand. "Heather Searlight."

Riot touched her hand briefly in a courtly manner, while

Heather ran the card lightly across her breasts. Her collar might be high, but her clothing was fitted. "You're not here for my perfume, are you?"

"I'm afraid not. We're here because of you. Are you friends with Elouise Spencer?"

Isobel's eyes stopped watering and her vision cleared as she watched her husband interact with the woman. He wasn't flirting, per se. But Heather certainly was. Riot was just being... himself, which tended to leave an impression on the opposite sex.

Whatever loosened tongues, Isobel thought. She left the questioning to Riot and picked up a vial to sniff at it. She jerked away at the sharp scent. Now why couldn't anyone bottle the ocean? She'd douse herself in that all day.

"Sure, I know Ella. We met earlier this year." Heather blinked her large doe eyes.

"Here, at your work?" Riot asked.

"No, at Mr. Grant's office. He's my attorney. Ella and I hit it off, as they say. Sometimes there's an instant connection between two people, wouldn't you say?" She looked at him through long lashes.

Isobel supposed the woman was trying to be demure.

"I can't disagree with that," Riot said. "Did Ella call on you at home?"

"I invited her to come here, and she dropped by to visit once in awhile. But I haven't seen her in... Oh, ages. Has something happened?"

"Ella didn't return home." Riot left the statement there in silence to be filled with whatever Miss Searlight made of it.

Heather's eyes widened. "She's been talking about leaving home since I met her. She wants to be an actress. That's why we hit it off, you see."

"You're an actress?"

She blushed. "We did an Amateur Night at the Olympia Music Hall. I was told I had real talent."

"By a number of gentlemen, no doubt."

"Why, yes. How did you know?" Heather asked.

"I'm familiar with the theater world. Did the men compliment Ella as well?"

"Not as many," Heather said with pride.

"Did you audition?"

"I did. I'm to be Aphrodite in an original production at the Eden. But don't tell anyone here."

Isobel recognized the theater. It wasn't known for its respectable society.

"My lips are sealed, Miss Searlight. Did Ella get a part, too?"

Heather sighed. "I got her a part, but Ella got scared and backed out of it. She told me a friend of hers at the *Olympia* warned her away and was going to fix her up with a *real* act. As far as I know it didn't pan out."

"Was the friend a man?" Riot asked.

Heather shook her head. "No, it was one of the fat ladies there. I didn't bother with her name. I haven't seen Ella in ages. The last time was with Mr. Grant in front of the *Call* building."

"When was this?"

"I don't know. A week or two ago? She wasn't in a mood to talk."

Isobel nearly snorted at the woman's idea of 'ages' ago.

"Was Ella angry?" Riot asked.

"No, more like irritated. I haven't been around as much. I've been busy rehearsing." Heather leaned in closer, toying with his card. "I have a ticket for opening night if you'd like to come."

Riot smiled. "I'm afraid the pleasure will have to wait until we find Ella."

"I doubt she wants to be found."

"Why's that?"

"She was miserable at home. I told her she ought to leave. From what I gather her mother's lazy and her older brother is a tyrant."

"Did he harm her?"

Heather shook her head. "Not that she told me. She said he was strict. Didn't like her going to theaters or to the resorts. She wasn't even allowed at Sutro Baths."

"Did she go anyway?"

Heather tapped a perfect nail on the counter. "Probably. She was always sneaking out. But don't tell her mother that. From the sound of it, the woman would keel over to know."

Riot waited for more, but Heather was immune to silence. She tapped her nail on the counter and gazed into his eyes.

"If I may say, Miss Searlight, Ella's friend was right to warn her away from the Eden Theater. I wouldn't want a daughter of mine setting foot in there."

"It's fortunate I'm not your daughter, Mr. Riot." The naivety vanished, replaced by a wanton invitation. She slipped her calling card into Riot's breast pocket.

When Riot turned to leave with a tip of his hat, Isobel squeezed the bulb of a sample vial, sending a cloud puffing into Miss Searlight's face. The woman smiled, pleasantly. "Are you interested in purchasing that, Miss Amsel?"

"It smells fake."

Heather looked smug. "At least it gets a man's attention."

Isobel resisted the urge to slip her arm through Riot's as they walked away. She could feel Heather's eyes glaring at her back. There was no point in gloating. Isobel had nothing to prove to the woman, but it was tempting.

"If we bottled whatever scent you're giving off we'd be millionaires," Isobel mused.

"I beg your pardon?"

"You're positively magnetic, Riot. Do all women go doe-eyed when you're around?"

"On occasion they try to shoot me. That would be a risky cologne to wear."

"*L'odeur du danger*," Isobel said in French. The scent of danger.

"How else did I convince you to marry me?"

Their first night together came instantly to mind, and Riot gave her a knowing smile.

"Oh, stop looking so smug."

"This is the face of a contented man. Nothing more."

Isobel checked her watch. "To the Olympia?"

18

SPIES AND FAT LADIES

THE OLYMPIA MUSIC HALL WAS A FIRST-CLASS VAUDEVILLE house—and the largest establishment of its kind. And if the adverts could be trusted, it was also "America's Most Beautiful Music Hall." Isobel stared at her program, and marveled that anyone would pay ten cents to listen to two men with high-pitched voices sing about a red school house while a baboon and a woman in sparkly tights turned a jump rope for a dog. The place was packed.

"Good God," she said.

"Not your cup of tea?" Riot asked.

"Yours?"

"Preferable to the shows in the Barbary Coast."

The woman in the sparkly mid-thigh leotard bent over to feed the dog a treat, and a section of men in the crowd began to hoot. Apparently high-class vaudeville shows attracted the same sort of crowd as the Barbary Coast dives.

Riot and Isobel stood near the back, lining the wall with a host of others who hadn't found seats. That suited Riot just fine. The thought of sitting in the middle of an audience made the scar on his temple twitch.

"There," Riot said. "Miss Searlight wasn't being insulting." Riot pointed out an act to her: The Fat Lady Quartet.

The crowd gave polite applause as the act ended. A few coins and bills were thrown on stage, then a very small man, in formal attire and with a hat that was nearly as tall as he was, waddled out to introduce the next act. "Straight from the ancient world, slayer of civilizations!" the small man paused, an arm held towards the entrance, as a drumroll built in intensity, "I present to you... Samson!"

The crowd thundered as a blond-haired man, rippling with muscles and wearing only a scant loin cloth, swaggered onto stage. A number of women in the audience whistled. A piano tune was struck up, and Samson began flexing his bulging physique. He even performed a neat backflip.

Riot bent to whisper in her ear. "You appear positively engaged, Bel."

"I'm simply admiring his musculature development. Shall we?"

"We can wait until the act is over, if you'd like to admire him some more."

"Jealous, Riot?"

"Not especially. I'm likely to reap the benefits of your study later on."

Isobel snorted. Together they made their way to the entrance hall. It *was* a beautiful building. It had palm fronds in giant urns, gilt on walls and ceiling, and the decorative touches of a grand opera house.

They stopped in front of an inconspicuous door with a peephole that was off to the side. There was no guard, but it was locked. Riot knocked, and a man in uniform opened it.

"We're here to see the Fa..." Riot hesitated. He was a gentleman down to his bones, and it went against his nature to say anything rude about a lady.

"The manager," Isobel cut in. "We have an act that he simply must see."

The bouncer crossed his arms and flexed. He wore a bowler and vest, and looked like the strongman's darker brother. "Come back at Amateur Night."

"We're not amateurs," Isobel said.

"What's your act then?" the bouncer asked.

Isobel nodded to her partner. "Show the man your act, Riot."

Riot glanced at her. For a moment, he was stunned. A rare thing for a man like him. But he recovered. "I pull people from the audience and Miss Amsel deduces things about them."

"What's so special about that?" the bouncer asked.

"It's akin to mind reading. Why don't you demonstrate, Bel?" Riot turned slightly, a glint in his eye. He had overturned that table.

Isobel sighed faintly, then studied the bouncer for a moment. "Can you step out into the light and turn around?"

The bouncer did as she asked. During his slow rotation, she grabbed Riot by the lapels, and dragged him through the door. On the other side, she threw the latch. The bouncer thudded against the door, banging an angry fist.

"Now that's a talent," Riot said, moving down the hallway.

"I thought you would do a card trick or start twirling your gun."

"I'm not a trick pony, Bel."

"I've been riding you all week."

The comment sparked desire, or memory, or some combination of lust and fantasy. Riot quickly adjusted his trousers, and tried to rein in his thoughts. But damn it, she made it hard.

"Let's find our lady," he said through his teeth.

No one seemed to care they were backstage. For a vaudeville show that ran all day and well into the night, there was hardly space for the performers to stand. A wave of noise slammed into Isobel. Costume racks, a mule, yapping dogs, two baboons and a bear in a tutu along with a motley array of people of all shapes, sizes, and costumes. The bouncer wouldn't be able to find Isobel and Riot if he tried.

Isobel stood beside Riot, agitated by the wash of bodies pressing in on her. The commotion was near to unbearable. Riot caught up her elbow and took the lead. He found a hallway stacked with costume racks that led deeper into the building. Soon, cobwebs and dust covered the detritus of shows long forgotten.

It was quieter here. Manageable. Isobel took a deep breath and sneezed.

Riot drew her to a stop, and looked into her eyes. There was concern there. "Are you all right, Bel? You look about to bolt like you did in the Popular."

She started to snap out 'I'm fine', but swallowed the words. This was Riot, he was already inside her walls, and there was no use putting up her defenses now. She gave him a rueful smile. "I was hoping you hadn't noticed."

"You shouldn't have married a detective," he said with gentle humor.

"Too late now. It's the noise, I think. It's been awhile since I was around so many people," she admitted.

Close to six months of quiet solitude in an asylum had nearly driven her insane. But it had also healed her after a fashion. The noise, press of bodies, and commotion of a city that never slept was threatening to drown her.

Any other well-meaning man might have suggested she stay there, but Riot was not such a man. He only nodded. "Search the quieter sections. I'll search the crowd."

Isobel didn't argue. She went off to look for a quartet of large women.

A MAN SAT IN HIS DINING ROOM, HIDING BEHIND A NEWSPAPER.
His wife, or maybe a sister, sawed into a red slab of steak with
a knife. A piece was pushed off the plate and fell to the floor,
where a little hairy thing scooped it up. Sao Jin was not sure if
the thing was a dog or a sentient mop.

She angled the spyglass back to the woman and turned the
scope, straining to make out details through the window. Was
the woman glaring? Was she crying? By the set of her shoulders Jin surmised she was furious. Probably a wife, then.

The couple were unaware of the spy to their domestic life.
The woman stood and lifted a bottle of wine, but instead of
refilling her companion's glass she poured it into his lap. Red
liquid splashed down the front of his shirt and onto his
trousers.

A newspaper flew in the air. The man leapt to his feet with
a bellow that Jin could hear from her rooftop perch. She
snickered.

The man raised his fist in anger, the yapping little mop
latched on to his ankle, and the dark-haired woman began
yelling at him and hitting him over the head with his own
sopping newspaper.

Eventually the man stormed off, and the woman sat back
down to calmly eat the rest of her supper. She gave her
husband's steak to the dog.

"You know it's not right to spy on people," a voice came
from behind her.

"You will fall off the edge," Jin said. She could imagine
Sarah paling at her warning, her freckles standing out stark on
her skin.

"I'm not climbing out there," Sarah said.

"Why are you in my room?" Jin asked. It wasn't said with
malice, but Sarah took everything Jin said the wrong way.

"I was only seeing if you wanted to come to a vaudeville

show with Mr. Lotario and me. He invited you, too." She could hear the hurt in the girl's voice.

"A vaudeville show?" Jin asked, keeping her eye on the spyglass. Nothing more exciting was happening with the couple, so Jin moved to another window. At this time of day, most maids had drawn the curtains, but sometimes a few were left open. She passed over an office with a telescope, and went straight to a neighboring house. She found another open curtain, where a man sat at a desk, writing. Blond-hair, aristocratic nose, his collar looked like it was choking him. She focused the lens, hoping for another show.

"It's…" Sarah searched for the words.

"An amusing way to spend an evening," a voice drawled from downstairs.

Jin turned at the sound of the man's voice. It was Lotario. Sarah hadn't worked up the nerve to climb out on the roof. Her head poked out of the hatch, and her hands were flat on the roof as if to brace herself in case the house lurched suddenly.

Instead of pale, she was an odd shade of green.

"Are you two coming?" Lotario asked from below, impatient.

Jin considered the question. "Where is the theater?"

"Why does that matter?" Sarah asked.

"Why doesn't it?" Lotario returned.

"Should it?" Sarah asked.

Jin made a frustrated sound.

"It's a surprise," Lotario said.

Jin frowned. She had plans tonight; still, there might be an opportunity to slip away from the pair. "Yes. I will come," she said, closing the spyglass.

Jin put on a wide-sleeved coat and some loose trousers, weaved her hair into a single braid that resembled a queue, and joined the pair downstairs. The three went out into the night.

Fog spilled over the hills to the west and swept through the city. The air was crisp and clean, and pools of gaslight offered little warmth as the trio stepped from a cable car. Lotario Amsel looked nothing like himself tonight, or what Jin had come to expect. He wore a plain wool suit and bowler, and the only flamboyant things about him were a pair of blue-tinted spectacles and a bright green waistcoat. He was letting his hair grow out and sported a pencil-thin blond mustache that Jin suspected was fake.

"How was your time with my parents?" Lotario asked as they strolled towards the theater district.

"We had a wonderful time," Sarah said.

Lotario glanced at Jin. "You, too? Good God. What is this world coming to? I suppose Bel and I wore them down for you. Small victories."

"You shouldn't talk bad about your parents," Sarah chided.

"They're *my* parents. I can say what I like, as long as I say it to their faces, and believe me, I have."

Sarah shook her head.

"You are lucky to have them," Jin said.

Lotario started to reply with something flippant, then looked at the scarred girl, and said it anyway. "I am. And so are you two. Otherwise I wouldn't be here, and you two ladies couldn't bask in my supreme presence."

Sarah giggled.

Jin rolled her eyes.

"Where do you live?" Sarah asked.

"Oh, here and there."

Sarah waited for more.

Lotario shot Jin a look. He suspected she suspected. This one was far too keen for her own good, he decided. But then growing up in a brothel tended to age one quickly.

"Are we going to your theater?" Sarah asked.

To explain his penchant for makeup and his reason for having female clothing in his cottage at Bright Waters, he had told the girls he was an actor. Which was one hundred percent true.

"Heavens no. I'm sick of that place. I thought we might go to the Olympia."

Sarah perked up. "I was hoping to go there. You'll love it, Jin. They have all sorts of variety acts. My gramma never let me go to the vaudeville shows."

"You're in for a treat. So tell me," Lotario said, as he gave his walking stick a casual twirl, "did you two wheedle any information out of your thrill-seeking parents?"

"We are not spies," Jin said.

Lotario laughed softly. He had a musical voice, no matter what it was he was saying.

"I think Isobel was frightened," Sarah said.

"*Sarah*," Jin growled.

"She was. You could tell even after. And that *horrid* article." Sarah balled up her fists. Jin stepped to the side. She knew the girl had a mean right hook.

"Oh, yes," Lotario mused softly. "What are they going to do about it?"

"You should ask them," Jin bit out.

"I *could*," he replied, drawing out the word. "But where's the fun in that. Any idea who wrote it?"

"Isobel had Grimm and Tobias run an article she wrote over to the *Bulletin*. I think she thinks it's Alex Kingston," Sarah said.

"Hmm." Lotario looked to Jin in question.

Jin huffed at him.

"And they think one of the boarders is a spy," Sarah added.

"Makes sense." He arched a brow down at them both. "You two should look into it."

Sarah blinked, then seemed to consider it for the very first time.

Jin narrowed her eyes. "There are nine boarders in the house. It could be any of them."

"Eight," Sarah corrected. "Mrs. Lane's son Frankie is younger than Tobias. He hardly counts."

"He is a boarder, and he can read and write," Jin argued.

"Never underestimate a child. They're always up to something," Lotario agreed. "Who do you think has something to gain from the article? It has to affect the lodgers' reputations as well."

"It must be a man," Sarah said. "Men don't have to worry about their reputations."

Lotario pointed the top of his walking stick at her. "That's perceptive."

"Or a woman who was planning to leave. Maybe she needs the money," Jin said.

Lotario spread his gloved hands. "And there you are, off to a splendid start. I'm sure the both of you will uncover the spy within the week."

"I will be busy with school work," Jin said.

"This is important, Jin," Sarah said. "I'll ask Tobias to help, too."

Lotario looked supremely pleased with himself. By the end of the night, the girls would think it had been their idea all along.

FOUR WOMEN WERE GATHERED AROUND A COSTUME TRUNK. One wore a viking helmet and a steel corset with a costume sword strapped to her side. Isobel doubted the armor would hold up to scrutiny or stop a bullet, but it looked real from a distance and pushed her ample bosom to new heights. The second woman, a redhead, was dressed in flowing scarves with bangles and finger cymbals. The third was a medieval princess with bodice and tall cone hat. And the fourth was dressed as a cowboy. Isobel suspected she knew how to use the rope she was currently coiling.

"Are you the Fat Lady Quartet?" Isobel asked.

"What gave us away?" the redhead asked.

"I figured I'd just look for someone who could crush me."

The women laughed as one. The redhead smiled. "Dearie, if you're looking to join, you'll need to eat a few more pastries."

"Only a few?" Isobel said.

Another round of girlish laughter. These women had a sense of humor, but one wouldn't survive in a vaudeville act called the Fat Lady Quartet without one. They were confident, proud, and comfortable in their skin. But above all, friendly. Just the sort of women a girl like Ella Spencer might be drawn to.

"I'm Isobel Amsel." She shook their hands. And got their names. The blonde viking, Hilde Wulf, had a thick Saxon accent. Edna was the princess and Myrtle the cowboy. Finally there was Estelle Baker, a belly dancer. "I'm a detective from Ravenwood Agency."

"Oh, we've heard of you," Edna said.

"You have?" Isobel asked with surprise.

"'Course we have. You were all over the newspapers," Estelle said.

"Still are," the cowboy said.

Isobel grimaced. "It's a good thing you don't seem the types to be driven away."

"No, ma'am," said Myrtle. "You can't control what people say about you, but you sure as hell can control how you react. Embrace it, we say."

The women nodded as one.

"Women like us are too busy doing what we please to be concerned with wagging tongues," Isobel said.

"Amen," said the princess with a broad smile. "If you're looking to join, we could use a sailor in the troupe."

"Say, there's an idea," Myrtle said, eyes distant, looking dreamy. "We could call it 'The Fat Lady Quartet and a Tumbleweed.'"

"I'm honored, but I'm here on business. Do any of you know a girl by the name of Elouise Spencer? She goes by Ella."

Three of the women looked to Estelle Baker.

Estelle clicked her finger cymbals together. "Oh, dear. What's that girl gone and done?"

"She's gone and went missing."

Estelle checked her watch. "I've got ten minutes." The woman led Isobel to a quiet hallway off the main dress floor. "What do you mean Ella's missing?"

Isobel gave her a brief overview, but kept the key details to herself. This early in an investigation, it was wise to keep your cards close. One could never be too careful.

Estelle swore under her breath. "Pardon my French," she muttered. "It's only that I warned Ella about a fellow she was seeing."

"What fellow?"

"I don't know his name. I saw him with her a few times, and he was much older. She introduced him as her 'dearest friend.'"

"What did he look like?"

Estelle tapped her finger cymbals together in thought. "Black hair. Scar over his eye. A peculiar nose. Sensuous mouth, imperious-like. When he spoke he shifted his shoulders back and tended to throw out his chest. A strong fellow, I'd say. And he didn't look like a city man. More like a slick country broker."

"Mustache?"

Estelle shook her head.

Mustaches could be shaved or added, easy enough to change. Hair color as well. And what some called black hair, others called brown. But both Miss Marshal from the Popular and Estelle mentioned a quirk about the eye. This fellow could very well be John Bennett from the Popular.

"Did he look anything like this?" Isobel pulled out the sketch that Sarah had drawn of Ella's missing father. "He'd be older now."

Estelle studied it, but shook her head. "I don't think so. But mind you, I only saw him once or twice. The nose is wrong, I think. The man I saw her with had a sharper one."

"What made you warn her away?"

Estelle raised a painted brow. "You and me are women of the world. We don't have blinders on. He wasn't looking at her with avuncular affection. He's likely thirty-five and I doubt she's even sixteen."

Estelle was right. Ella was fifteen and painfully naive, and that put her just under the age of consent in California—not that cribs and brothels paid any mind.

"How long have you known Ella?"

"About four months. The girls and I met her at Amateur Night. She was so nervous I took her under my wing. She's a clever girl, but lacks talent for this business. And sense." Estelle shook her head, bangled ears shifting with the movement. "A friend of hers, I forget the girl's name, tried to get her to join a vaudeville show in a cheap theater. The bawdy kind. I steered Ella away from that gig."

"Was Ella already acquainted with this man when you first met her?"

"I don't know. I live in some lodgings by Turk and Taylor. A few weeks ago I saw him and Ella walking towards Market. Heard him say something about going to 'that little place on Taylor street,' so I followed. When they got to the Saddle Rock

Restaurant, they stopped. Ella made to leave, and he caught her by the arm and took her into the restaurant. After I saw that, I warned her away. But she didn't like what I had to say. I haven't seen her since."

Isobel questioned her further, but Estelle had nothing more to add. Their friendship had consisted of Ella dropping by the music hall from time to time. She didn't even know where Ella lived.

Isobel found Riot conversing with a crowd of men—the small man in the tall hat, the door guard they had given the slip to, and three large bouncer-types. Riot was completely at ease.

When she approached, the door guard glared.

"How'd you like my trick?" she asked.

The three other bouncers smirked.

"This is Mr. Robert Saunders, the manager and announcer for the Olympia. Mr. Saunders, my wife, Miss Amsel."

Isobel suspected Riot found the contradiction of introducing her as such amusing. She bent slightly to shake Mr. Saunder's hand.

"A pleasure, Miss Amsel. I've been trying to convince your husband to try out for an act. We don't have a mind reader. I can see it now. You'd be draped in silk scarves and bangles. And he'd look devilish in a turban and robe. With his coloring, he could easily pass for an Arab."

Isobel could, in fact, imagine Riot with a bit of eyeliner and a sharply trimmed beard. "And a curved sword," she added.

Mr. Saunder's eyes lit up. "Superb. When can I expect you, then?"

"I'm afraid not," she said. "I've already been offered a role as a tumbleweed in the Fat Lady Quartet."

"Pah. We'll schedule it so you can do both." Mr. Saunders had a glint in his eye. He knew she was pulling his leg.

"That's kind of you, but we have a girl to find. If our detective business ever goes belly up, we'll consider it."

Mr. Saunders took her hand in both of his. He fixed her with a serious eye. "For the sake of this city, I hope it doesn't. And don't you give a thought to anything people say about you. I've heard it all. Trust me. And look where I am."

"Still close to the ground, but loving it?" she blurted before she thought better of it.

He beamed. "Absolutely."

They were escorted back to the entrance hall. The guard tipped his hat, then slammed the door behind them. "Well, I've made another enemy."

"I'm sure he won't hold it against you," Riot said.

A steady line of patrons came and went. One of the draws of the vaudeville was that there weren't strict rules like at theaters. It wasn't considered rude to come in late to a show, and no one blinked if you slipped out early.

Isobel told Riot about her conversation with Estelle Baker.

"Miss Baker's description could fit with the others. It sounds like Ella knew John Bennett."

Isobel nodded. "Which means she's probably holed up with him somewhere." It was a common enough ploy. A man seduced a naive girl, promising to marry her, and then never followed through on the commitment. Every girl thought they found their Mr. Darcy, while they really ended up running off with a Wickham.

"I hope that's the case." There was a shadow in Riot's eyes.

Isobel raised a brow. "You think he intends to pimp her out?"

"He may have handed her off to someone already."

"He hardly sounds like bait for a mack. One would expect a young, charming man. Not an old one with scars."

Riot brushed a hand over his temple, where a streak of

white slashed through his raven hair. It covered a deep scar in his skull. "An old man with scars caught you."

Isobel gave his tie a yank. Riot coughed, and quickly righted it.

"Speaking of young, charming men..." She was looking over his shoulder.

Riot turned to find a man arguing with one of the ticket takers outside the audience chamber. A bouncer stood next to them with his arms crossed. Sarah and Jin were with Lotario. Jin wasn't wearing her usual wool suit and cap but her quilted tunic and loose trousers instead. Her hair was pulled back into one long braid that could be mistaken for a queue with her forehead covered by the cap. In short, she looked very Chinese.

"That's *absurd*," Lotario was saying. "I paid for a private booth. She's my niece. I won't allow her to sit somewhere else."

"It's policy, sir."

"No, it's rude," Sarah said.

"No Chinese are allowed in the main audience," the bouncer recited. "There's a special section in the second gallery for their kind. She'll be more comfortable there."

"She's my sister," Sarah said.

"I do not mind sitting upstairs," Jin broke in.

Riot and Isobel made a beeline for their family, who were beginning to attract an audience of their own.

Lotario caught sight of them. "Oh, splendid," he said with a hint of excitement. Lotario loved a good show.

Isobel had a barrage of laws on the tip of her tongue, the fourteenth amendment at the top, but then she noted Jin's posture. Her shoulders were slouched and she seemed to be trying to melt into the carpet. The girl was mortified by the attention.

It was Riot who spoke. "Is there some sort of trouble?" he asked. He held the bouncer's eyes, steady and calm.

"Nothing that concerns you, sir." Being male in a bespoke

suit had its advantages, but then Riot had a certain way about him—that of a bored panther considering if it was worth the effort to swipe.

"As these are my daughters and brother-in-law, I'd say it does." Riot pulled a card from his pocket. "Your policy doesn't take into account mixed families. I suggest you consult your manager, who can then address this with my attorney. But I'm not sure the hassle we'll give you is worth the price of a booth."

The ticket taker glanced at the bouncer, who hesitated, then took Riot's calling card. He frowned at the embossed raven on the thick pasteboard. It always left an impression.

Lotario offered his arms to the girls. Sarah took one, but Jin blew out a breath, turned on her heel, and marched away. The crowd started murmuring.

Isobel shot after her.

"I do not want to see the vaudeville anymore," Jin said when Isobel caught up to her. The girl shoved open the door, and walked out into a burst of cool air.

"I don't either. Let's get something to eat."

Jin spun on her. "Where? At the Palace? They will not let me in there because I am Chinese."

"I was thinking Italian."

But Jin shook her head. "I want to walk. I will be back at home tonight." Before Isobel could catch her, Jin darted at a cable car full tilt. She expertly leapt and latched onto the back, where she clung, unknown to anyone but Isobel.

"Damn," Isobel muttered. But even if she managed to catch up and rip the child from the cable car, what would she do? Tie her up and drag her home? A familiar presence stopped at her side. "Did you see that?" she asked.

"At least she promised to return," Riot said.

They stood on the street, watching cable cars and theater-goers move in a kind of deadly dance. So easy to get lost in, where one wrong step could cost a life.

"God, I hate people."

"No, you don't," he said softly, touching her elbow. "You hate bullies and willful ignorance."

Isobel swallowed a flippant comment. She wasn't in the mood. The sun had never broken through the fog. It was dark and cold and late, and they were no closer to locating Ella Spencer. Another day gone, and the girl was still missing. And now her own daughter was alone in a predatory city.

"We have a start on the case, Bel," Riot said, sensing her mood. "And Jin's as competent as you."

She tried not to think of all the close calls she'd had as a child. It was a marvel she'd made it to adulthood. "I'm beginning to sympathize greatly with my mother," she admitted.

"It happens."

A door burst open and they turned to see the two bouncers remove Lotario and Sarah from the dance hall. The door slammed on their heels.

Lotario was wheezing with laughter, while Sarah appeared to be in a state of shock.

Isobel rushed over and grabbed Sarah's shoulder, turning the girl to face her. "What happened?"

"I don't know what got into me," Sarah whispered. "I gave that fellow what for, then kicked him straight in the shin."

"It runs in the family," Riot said. "Shall we head home and wait for Jin?"

A RIOTOUS EVENING

AT THE BACK ENTRANCE OF RAVENWOOD MANOR, ATTICUS
Riot held a door open for Sarah, Isobel, and Lotario. Sounds
of dishes and conversation filled the empty courtyard. Tim's
loud voice dominated, talking about a time when he cooked for
a wagon train.

Tim stood in an apron and was up to his elbows in dish
suds, while Tobias wielded a drying rag and Grimm put the
dishes away.

"He wouldn't take it. And you're in trouble," Tobias called
to Isobel over the clatter of kitchenware.

"Who wouldn't take what?" Isobel said, pulling off her
gloves.

"The reporter fellow."

Grimm whacked his brother with a dish rag before turning
to face the new arrivals. The tall young man searched the
group as they shed their hats and coats, and then frowned. It
looked like he wanted to say something, but Tim spoke up first.
"Don't interrupt your elders, boy."

"It's true, Mr. Tim," Tobias said. "Mr. A.J.'s in trouble
again. Hi there, Mr. Lotario."

Lotario waved a languid hand at the boy, and moved over to the oven. "What *is* that delectable smell?"

"Shepherd's pie. Ma makes it a special way."

Tim cast a baleful eye at Riot. "Where's Jin?"

"They wouldn't let her sit with us in the theater," Sarah answered, peeking inside the covered dishes. "So she left. We did, too. But we don't know where she went."

"I thought they'd let her sit in a booth with us," Lotario said. "What does your mother put in this?" He was hovering over the open crockery with a spoon, but Sarah batted him away.

Grimm handed his dry pot to Lotario, and took off out the back door. As that door closed, another opened. Pushing through the dining room door with her hips, Lily brought in a tray of dirty dishes. She stopped with a frown, and Riot hastily moved to take the tray from her. But when he did, his side burned with pain. He quickly set the tray in a clear space on the table.

Lily hurried over to the oven, removed a casserole dish topped with pie crust, and began setting a fresh tray. "Where's Grimm?"

"He left," Isobel said.

"Left? Again? Did you send a child of mine on *another* errand?" She included both Riot and Isobel in her over-the-shoulder gaze.

Riot cleared his throat. "No, ma'am, we didn't. Not this time. Grimm didn't give an explanation."

Lily blinked. "He just left? I'm short-handed as it is with Maddie gone." Another pointed look.

"Give 'em heck, Ma," Tobias cackled.

"Shush it, Tobias."

Sarah quickly donned an apron, and took the fresh tray from Lily's hands. There were eighteen people in the manor to feed, but Isobel Amsel didn't care one bit about domestic pressures. "Tobias," she said impatiently, "*What* didn't the reporter take? My article?"

"No, ma'am. I mean, yes. He didn't take the article you wrote. Said he had another one all ready."

"Written by whom?"

Tobias shrugged.

Isobel swore under her breath and left the kitchen.

"She never could take criticism." Lotario surveyed the mess, and delicately put his pot on a clear space. "Well, I don't want to be in the way. I'll just go meet your boarders and sample the delicacies." He swaggered into the dining room before anyone could rope him into kitchen duty.

Lily took a calming breath.

Tim had rinsed the suds from his arms, and jerked his head towards the back door.

"Hey! You're not done," Tobias said, as Riot followed Tim outside. Riot could hear the boy muttering up a storm until his mother told him to focus on his work.

Tim took out his pipe, and dug around pockets for his tobacco pouch.

The courtyard was dark, the moon obscured by fog, bringing the scent of the sea. Riot couldn't make much of Tim's expression. "What is it?" Riot asked with some trepidation.

"I went to check on Monty. I can't find him, A.J."

Riot frowned. "Bel thinks Monty might be behind the attack."

Tim shoved tobacco in his pipe and tamped. Then a match flared, highlighting a face like worn leather. Riot waited, sensing the man thinking.

Finally, Tim flicked the match to the ground. "A thousand dollars ain't much for you. But maybe he took half and found some idiots to give it a go for a thousand. A contractor of sorts."

"You really think he hates me that much?"

Tim chuckled. "Hate might not have anything to do with it, boy."

Riot couldn't disagree. Men had killed for less money. "Regardless, we need to find him."

Tim grunted. "Monty has a habit of disappearing."

"Maybe so. I'll check some old haunts and see what I can find out," Riot said, then told Tim about the disorderly drunks.

"Now there's a mind," Tim said thoughtfully.

"I intend to look into that, too."

"Want some company?"

Riot shook his head. "We need to rebuild the agency. Otherwise, we'll be selling Ravenwood Manor. But keep your ears to the ground."

Tim nodded. "I don't much like an enemy in the shadows. You watch yourself, A.J."

"Don't I always?"

Tim snorted. "'Bout the opposite way I reckon."

LURED BY HEAVENLY SCENTS, LOTARIO AMSEL WANDERED INTO the dining room. A table long enough for a banquet stretched down the impressive room. He tried to imagine a lone miser sitting at one end, with an elderly housekeeper standing at his side. Zephaniah Ravenwood must have been utterly boorish.

Tonight the room wasn't empty—a crowd of lodgers dined under a crystal chandelier. Lotario's gaze swept over each in turn, as he casually made his way to the buffet. A beautiful woman sat at one end, the two chairs closest to her empty. She could be an artist's muse, a lust-filled fantasy of man or woman, and looked more suited to the arm of a prince than a miser's dining room.

Tall, shapely, with delicate touches of makeup and a

sweeping neckline, Miss Annie Dupree was a carefully sculpted work of art. She also happened to be his nieces's school teacher.

Lotario helped himself to a plate, and glanced at Sarah, who was just bringing in a fresh tray. "Oh, do take off that silly apron and dine with me."

"But Miss Lily needs help," Sarah whispered.

Lotario waved a hand at the buffet table. "Does it appear our lodgers are on the verge of starving?"

"Maybe Mr. Hughes," she whispered, and then started, putting a hand over her mouth. "I didn't mean—"

Lotario chuckled. "The Amsel's have sharp tongues. We've already corrupted you."

"You didn't meet my gramma," Sarah said with a twist of her lips. But she didn't argue any further. She stuffed her apron under the table and went to join him next to Miss Dupree.

A number of the lodgers started in surprise. He gave the room a warm smile. "I know, the resemblance to my sister is shocking. Lotario Amsel," he spoke to the room, but directed his gaze to Miss Dupree. Her eyes sparkled like sapphires in the candlelight. "Is this seat taken, Miss...?"

"Dupree. Annie Dupree. And no, it's not." Pleasant, friendly, and completely indifferent to the not so subtle snub of her fellow lodgers.

A blond-haired man in the middle shot a glower at the pair, before returning to his meal, or attempting to. Lotario had other ideas.

"So many lodgers under my sister's roof. Is it always so somber?" Lotario directed the blunt question to the glowering man, who gave a nervous sort of laugh. "Sarah, won't you introduce me?" Lotario prodded.

Sarah obliged.

The glowering man turned out to be a Mr. Dougal. Amelia Lane was a proper sort of woman in a worn dress, who sat with her small son, Frankie. Harry Hughes was an older man with gray mutton chops, an expansive gut, and cufflinks that could pay his rent for a year. Mr. Löfgren was a cheerful man with hair so blond it was nearly white. Mrs. Bee Clarke was a plump, gray-haired older woman who sat at the far end of the table. David Knight, a studious man with short trimmed brown hair and a British accent. Miss Pierce was tall and slightly bowed of back, and Lotario imagined she spent most of the day hunched over a typewriter.

"What is it that you do, Mr. Amsel?" Miss Dupree asked.

"I'm an artist," he said. "Of wood. A boatbuilder."

"For the Saavedra shipyards?"

"I don't work *for* them, Miss Dupree. But they do allow me to tinker in a boathouse. I'm a free agent."

"Mr. Lotario built the *Pagan Lady*," Sarah offered. "He made it suitable for a family."

"How quaint," Miss Dupree said.

"I thought so. It's lovely to have my sister married off to a respectable man, and two nieces thrown into the happy day. Wouldn't you agree, Mrs. Clarke?"

The woman blinked. She had that severe look of a woman in a church pew trying to avoid the taint of the masses.

"Er, yes, Mr. Amsel. I like to see a young woman settled. Are you a married man yourself?"

"I'm afraid I haven't found my soulmate, though my mother certainly wishes I would."

"Don't do it," Mr. Knight said. "It's a trap. A ball and chain. That's all marriage is."

Harry Hughes rumbled a laugh, as he shoved a forkful into his mouth.

"Not with the right person, Mr. Knight." This last came from Amelia Lane. She was longish of face, and as pale as her hair. She had dark circles under her eyes, but they were keen and sharp. A gold band encircled her ring finger.

Lotario glanced at the boy by her side. He looked to be around six years old. "And did you find the right man, Mrs. Lane?"

"I did." She glanced fondly at her son. "Only God saw fit to take him from me."

"Selfish of him, wasn't it?"

Mr. Dougal harrumphed. "I never did buy into that argument from preachers."

This triggered Mrs. Clarke, who rose to defend her deity. Within seconds, the silence that had hung over the dining room vanished, leaving Lotario space to sit back and observe the social dynamics.

Mrs. Clarke warred for dominance with Mr. Dougal, while Mr. Knight looked down his regal nose at them both. Mrs. Lane looked tired of the arguing, Mr. Löfgren embarrassed, and Mr. Hughes chuckled like a fond father over unruly children. And then there were young Frankie and Miss Pierce, who seemed confused by the exchange.

When Mrs. Clarke started quoting scripture, Lotario leaned on his elbow to whisper in Miss Dupree's ear. "One thing is certain, I know you didn't write that article."

"Are you so sure?" Miss Dupree whispered.

Lotario smoothed his mustache in thought. "That article could potentially empty the house of unwanted boarders, but it also brings far too much attention on yourself."

"Do I strike you as a woman who minds attention?"

"Only under the right circumstances."

"And what are those circumstances, Mr. Amsel?"

He gave her a knowing smile. "Discretion and deep pockets."

"So you believe the article?"

"Of course not," Lotario said, feigning offense. "You're clearly a schoolteacher of some means, who can afford the best rooms in the house."

"Perhaps the article is true, then," she suggested. Luckily, her voice was too low for Sarah to hear.

Lotario considered that. "About you being his mistress? I'm sure you tried to seduce Atticus, but he's immune to charm."

There was a slight arch of her sculpted brow.

"And while my sister is a progressive woman open to new ideas, she doesn't share well. I know," he said dryly, "I tried to sleep with her favorite stuffed tiger once. She nearly killed me."

Miss Dupree laughed softly, her lashes fluttering just so. Not in an affected way like many women, but natural. Charm and innocence; seduction and intelligence. There was a fine balance to it. And she played the role perfectly.

"...I'm a better man since meeting my Mary," Mr. Löfgren insisted to the room. The conversation, it seemed, had shifted once again. "I cannot stop smiling."

"You were smiling before," Mr. Hughes said.

"I think your Mary is wonderful," Mrs. Lane remarked.

Lotario noticed that Miss Pierce hadn't said a word. A shy sort, he decided.

"Will your Mary be moving here after the wedding?" Lotario asked, reaching for his wine.

"Housing is so difficult to find in San Francisco. We had planned to, but..." Mr. Löfgren hesitated. "I'm not sure this would be the best situation for her."

"And why is that?" Lotario said.

"Certain rumors, true or not, can affect a woman's reputation."

"Like the newspaper article, you mean?" Lotario asked innocently.

One would think he'd tossed a severed head onto the table. Lotario blanched inwardly, remembering that a head once *had* been placed on this very table—the head of Zephaniah Ravenwood.

Lotario avoided looking at the center of the table. He wasn't at all sure the man himself wasn't still there.

"Yes," Mr. Löfgren said with distaste. "I have never read anything so full of lies and indecency."

"Oh come now, Mr. Löfgren," Mrs. Clarke said. "You're not the only one who saw Mr. Riot return from the theater with Miss Dupree on his arm on multiple occasions. And..." she cut off, glancing at Frankie. "Well, there it is. I'm sure all of you can fill in the rest."

Sarah glanced at Miss Dupree, not in shock, but surprise.

"Oh, rubbish," Mr. Knight said. "So what if the article *is* true. This isn't London society. God knows I came halfway around the world to escape it. One encounters former prostitutes, drunkards, and common thugs at every function in this city."

"Mr. Knight!" Mrs. Clarke said. "There are children present."

Mr. Knight brandished his fork at the boy across the table. "My point exactly. There's no society in San Francisco. Children shouldn't even be eating at our table."

"We do things differently here," Mrs. Lane said.

"Yes, look at how outspoken the women are," Mr. Dougal rumbled.

"Give me a woman with a sharp tongue over a grumbling man any day," Lotario said. "I *like* a good lashing."

Miss Dupree choked on her wine. To her credit, she hid her surprised snort well, and picked up a napkin to dab at her lips.

Mr. Knight shot Lotario a hard look.

Harry Hughes rose to refill his plate. "I, for one, find San Francisco refreshing. One can be at ease with both sexes. It's rather liberating."

"There's no room for proper society in San Francisco. The geographical location makes it near impossible to house everyone, what with the constant flow of immigrants and visitors and those traveling through. There just isn't room for propriety." Miss Pierce delivered her single statement in a perfunctory manner. It was the first time she had spoken, and she seemed embarrassed by her sudden outburst.

"That's very insightful," Lotario said. "What is it that you do, Miss Pierce?"

"I work in statistics at the Census Bureau. I'm a mathematician."

Mr. Hughes slapped his hand on the table. "There you have it! A progressive society for women."

"And the same immigrants and influx of female workers make it hard for men to find decent work," said Mr. Dougal.

"Is there such a thing as *indecent* work for men?" Miss Dupree asked.

"You should know," Mr. Dougal shot back.

"Do you enjoy your work?" Sarah asked Miss Pierce, trying to defuse Mr. Dougal's mounting anger.

Miss Pierce hesitated. "I'm happy for the work, but I'm paid a fourth of what my male counterparts are paid and reduced to little more than an errand boy."

"You're still stealing a job that could be staffed by an actual boy."

Miss Pierce shot a scathing look at Mr. Dougal.

Sarah's shoulders bowed slightly. Lotario could see a touch of hopelessness enter her eyes. Though whether it was with the futility of brokering peace between lodgers or her own future as a woman, Lotario couldn't be certain.

"Things are bound to change," Mr. Löfgren said, cheerfully.

"We can only hope," Mrs. Lane said. "It won't change the housing situation in San Francisco, though. Most lodging houses aren't tolerant of children or single women, and those that are always have a curfew. I'm thankful for this house. I don't know where Frankie and I would go otherwise. But now, with that article, my employment is at risk."

"Women should not be out at ungodly hours," Mrs. Clarke said.

"Not everyone's husband died under suspicious circumstances and left her a fortune," Mrs. Lane said.

"If I *had* a fortune I wouldn't be here!" Mrs. Clarke snapped.

Mrs. Lane took a deep breath, looking exhausted. "If you will all excuse us. I have to get my son to bed before heading to work."

Mrs. Clarke huffed. It signaled the end of dinner, and not long afterward Lotario found himself sitting alone with Miss Dupree and Sarah.

"Now that was entertaining," Lotario said.

"That was the most awkward dinner I've ever had," Sarah said, pushing food around her plate with a fork.

"You didn't find it enlightening?" Lotario asked.

"That we live under the same roof with people who are at each other's throats? No."

"And there you have it, my dear. Motive."

"For what?"

"The article."

Sarah blinked. "Is that why you stirred the pot? To discover who wrote that foul thing?"

Lotario clapped slowly. "She'll catch on eventually," he said to Miss Dupree.

"Sarah is an exceptionally bright pupil," Miss Dupree said.

Sarah was caught between insult and compliment. She blushed.

Lotario leaned forward, eager. "Now *think*, Sarah. Think about what you heard here and put the pieces together."

"You can't possibly know who wrote the article based on that conversation," Sarah accused.

"I do."

Sarah gaped.

Miss Dupree was intrigued. "Do you?"

Lotario flashed her a smile. "And I suspect you do, too."

Miss Dupree gave a small smile. "I can't say I know for sure, but I have my suspicions."

"So modest of you," Lotario said.

"And hardly any modesty in you."

"You have no idea, Miss Dupree."

"Oh, I believe I do." The tone was innocent enough that Sarah showed only a mild interest, but Annie's eyes said more.

Lotario brushed her hint aside. "San Francisco is a small city. As you know, Miss Dupree."

She inclined her head.

The subtleties of the interchange went over Sarah's head. She leaned forward in a conspiratorial matter. "Who wrote the article?"

Lotario's eyes twinkled with mischief. "That's for you, Jin, and Tobias to discover."

"Are you giving my pupils an assignment, Mr. Amsel?"

"Indeed I am."

"You'll just change your idea of who wrote it based on what we find," Sarah accused.

"I'll whisper the name to Atticus. And the two of you do the same. Fair?"

Sarah thought for a moment, then nodded.

"We can give names all day long. Without proof, it's only speculation," Miss Dupree said to Lotario.

"I have every confidence that the children will find that proof. Besides, I don't like to get my hands dirty. Now if you'll excuse me. Ladies." He rose and bowed, and went to find his sister and her delicious husband.

GRIMM HAD LONG LEGS, AND HE USED THEM TO HIS ADVANTAGE. Streets fell away under his feet as he hurried towards a ghostly glow in the fog. It was cold and wet, but then what else was San Francisco at night? Quiet, too. And sometimes dangerous.

Along with his nickname, Grimm had been called scarecrow more times than he could count. Tall, lanky, and somber, the color of his skin didn't help. He wasn't tan, or brown, or a lustrous mahogany like his mother and siblings; he was black as coal. It made people afraid.

He flipped his collar up and kept his cap down, hoping to melt into the night. Fear turned people into animals, and patrolmen were the worst of the lot.

Soon his feet took him to narrow streets lit with red lanterns and braziers. Men in wide hats and wide-sleeved coats stood around the fires, smoking and chatting in low voices, while louder voices drifted down from the high windows. Everything was close in Chinatown—some buildings stared at each other, some leaned on their neighbors, and others threatened to pull their neighbors down.

Grimm stopped to warm his hands alongside a trio of men. They stared at him with open curiosity. One of them asked a question, in a language that ran together, a sing-song of highs and lows that Grimm couldn't make sense of.

It didn't matter. He wouldn't have answered anyway. Grimm kept moving and searching, but stayed away from the darker lanes. He walked under lines of laundry and paper lanterns, past restaurants blazing with light, and under balconies adorned with green lanterns, where men of all colors came and went.

As Grimm walked past, he glanced into an open door. Warmth and light invited him in. It was filled with men and silk-clad women. An old man at the door beckoned him over, calling to him in a friendly voice.

Grimm noticed women more than he liked. It made him

restless to be living his own life, but that was difficult to do while he was in hiding. How was he supposed to find a wife when one stray word could put his whole family in danger? They didn't go to church, they didn't go to school. The White family kept to themselves for a reason.

With no strings attached, brothels were an inviting answer to his loneliness. And they were all over the city. Although he was sorely tempted, something about the establishments didn't seem right.

Stifling his curiosity, Grimm ducked his head and kept walking. He stopped at a corner, and sighed. Hands in his pockets, he surveyed the crossroads. Narrow lanes branched out every which way. Chinatown was a maze of pathways. From one of the lanes, he heard voices in that same sing-song dialect, only this time female. He saw three men in peacoats strolling under a string of lanterns. They walked past two men with wide hats and wider sleeves.

Grimm frowned. The night before, when he had followed Sao Jin, she'd stayed away from alleys like these. He'd followed her all through the Quarter until he was lost. As far as he knew, she was too.

Grimm turned away and kept to the wider street. Either by chance, or by God's good grace, he spotted a small shadow on the corner of an intersection. He kept his head down, slouched his shoulders, and drifted closer to two men who were walking by.

The street wasn't wide. There was barely enough room for two wagons to pass. Grimm kept an easy pace, and was rewarded. Though he couldn't see the child's face, he recognized her oversized cap.

Grimm stopped short of the intersection, and stepped to the side to wait. What was she staring at? Four streets converged. Farther down one of the roads, light from a theater lit the fog. He looked across to the dark buildings. Candle light seeped out of shutters, but he couldn't tell if the buildings at street level were shops or homes.

It didn't matter. He had found her.

Sao Jin edged one foot forward, then froze. She wasn't standing at ease, but more like a small piece of timber waiting for an axe. Grimm searched the street for what frightened her, but no one seemed to be paying her any mind.

He glanced at the windows, but the night was too cold for shutters to be open. Smells of cooking and chatter filled the crossroads and a man stood above her on a fire escape, smoking and watching people pass. But Jin wasn't looking up; she was looking straight ahead at a dark building.

There was a sign with Chinese lettering, but Grimm couldn't make heads or tails of the broad strokes. His brows knit together as he leaned back into the shadows to wait. Jin took one step, then another, until she seemed stuck in the middle of the intersection, staggering under an invisible weight.

Voices carried down the street. Grimm leaned around the corner. Three men walked down the middle of the road, smoking and joking, the flare of their cigarettes lighting up the darkness under their hats. From the sudden din of conversation, Grimm surmised that the theater had let out. The glow of lights gave the fog a reddish tint and faces were lost in the gloom.

Jin didn't move, and the three men didn't change course. They weren't interested in her, but one of the men knocked her aside. She bumped into a second, who shoved her down, and kept walking. The third kicked her and laughed as he stepped past.

Grimm held his breath, willing her to stay on the ground. They're not interested in you. They're not interested—

Jin leapt to her feet with a scream. Not of pain or fear, but of unbridled fury. Light caught a metallic surface. A knife. The third man spun to face her, and the child struck, slashing blindly.

He staggered back, clutching his leg, and the other men scattered. Jin was crouching, blade in hand, snarling at the men. One of them laughed, and pulled out a club from under his quilted coat. Grimm hoped she'd run, but she didn't. Jin charged. The club landed a glancing blow that sent her rolling to the side. The man stepped forward, and raised his billy club.

Grimm darted from hiding, a swift, silent shadow that no one saw coming. He barreled into the man. A tangle of limbs and confusion, of labored breath. The clubman came out on top and drove the butt of his weapon into Grimm's face.

Screams of fury rose behind him.

The club came up again. Grimm grabbed the weapon, and wrenched it from the man's hand. He used his feet to get up and under the man, and sent him flying over his head.

Whistles were blowing. People gazed down at the street fight from the safety of their balconies. Reeling, Grimm crouched, searching the street. Jin was swiping her knife at the three men, while spitting curses and insults.

They looked confused rather than angry.

Grimm lunged forward to grab the girl's collar. Her knife flashed, but he had anticipated it. The blade sunk into his stolen billy club. He gave Jin a shake by her collar.

Her eyes focused, and she blinked up at him in surprise. Grimm didn't wait for explanations. He pushed her towards a side street, as the three men staggered in another direction. The whistles were getting closer.

Jin took the lead through the streets. They ran until their lungs burned, until his side was a twisted mass of ache, until finally, in a tiny square of shrubs with a lone tree, Jin doubled over and began coughing in the dirt.

Grimm pressed a hand against the stitch in his side, and stared at the girl. Distant lights illuminated the night. Fog-shrouded buildings surrounded them, looming in the dark. It was eerie and solitary, and Grimm was glad they were alone. He wanted to see who was coming.

"What are you doing here?" Jin hissed. She was bent over double, hands on her knees, glaring at him from the side.

He became aware of a throbbing on his face. He probed the swollen skin under his eye, and sighed. His ma would kill him. And he wondered how to answer Jin's question. Grimm didn't know what he was doing there either.

"Answer me!" she growled.

Grimm let his hand fall and searched her face. Words were dangerous things. Killing things. And so Grimm didn't much care to speak. The two faced off—a silent young man and a defiant girl.

After a solid minute, Jin cursed. "*Yiu!* Stupid *Wuai daan!*" And more, a whole string of Cantonese and Portuguese curses that Grimm didn't understand.

Eventually, Jin ran out of curses. Or breath. She wiped the knife clean with a handful of leaves, then tucked it back up her wide sleeve.

Her entire body vibrated. "Do not say anything to anyone," she said, thrusting a finger at him.

Grimm raised an eyebrow.

Jin faltered at the amusement in his eyes. Her shoulders slumped, and she seemed to relax. "How come you do not talk?" she asked.

Grimm started to shrug, but stopped. Instead, he ran a finger over his swollen cheek, then pointed at the scars on hers, and finally, back to his own heart.

Jin frowned.

With a question in his eyes, he pointed at her, then gestured back towards Chinatown. A single lamppost lit the square. It cast more shadows than illuminated, but he saw that his question got through.

Why were you there?

"Why were *you* there?" she shot back.

Grimm pointed at her.

Jin glowered. "You are spying on me," she accused. "Did Isobel tell you to follow me?"

Grimm shook his head.

Jin glanced towards Chinatown. Her next words were so faint he barely caught them. "Are your people cruel to each other, too?"

By 'your people' Grimm assumed she meant negroes. He nodded.

"I do not understand it. Why fight with each other when there are larger enemies?"

He suspected it was an age old question, and the answer was equally as old: fear and power. But it was too complicated to communicate without words.

Jin turned to leave, and Grimm started to follow. She stopped, glaring. "I am going home."

Grimm nodded again.

This earned him another growl. But the girl didn't break into a run. As stated, she headed back to Ravenwood Manor, and Grimm followed on her heels. Silent, alert, and thoughtful.

Lotario knocked. Standing in the hallway, he surveyed the third level. Ravenwood Manor was expansive, with a main staircase circling upwards, and a long drop to the entryway below. Voices carried, but not overly much; it was spacious enough to allow for privacy. Most of the boarders occupied the second level, while Sarah, Mr. Hughes, and Mr. Löfgren had rooms with Atticus and Isobel on the third. Jin was on the fourth floor, in the attic.

"Yes?" a voice called.

"It's me."

Footsteps approached and the door unlocked. Atticus Riot opened it to find Lotario smiling at him. "Going somewhere?" Lotario asked as he invited himself inside.

Riot's hair was damp and tousled, and he was working a link through his cuff. "I thought I'd put my ear to the ground at the clubs." It was obvious by his snowy shirt that he wasn't intending to roam the dives of the Barbary Coast.

"I'm surprised Bel's not gluing on a mustache."

"She's waiting for Jin."

Lotario dusted a speck off his coat. "Care for some company? I'm not much good in a fight, but gossip is my forte."

Riot considered his proposal.

"And I find myself without anything to do. You know what they say about idle hands." Lotario waggled his brows at Riot.

"Are you sure you want to be seen with a marked man?"

"Entering a club together is hardly being seen together, Atticus. And I know who wrote that article."

"You do?"

Lotario nodded, and told him. But Riot wasn't so easily convinced. "Do you have proof?" he asked slowly.

Lotario waved a flippant hand. "I set your junior detectives on the case. I'm confident they will turn up something."

Riot waited for more.

"Oh, don't worry, it's not dangerous, and they needed *something* to do. Surely you understand the feeling of helplessness. Otherwise they're liable to start trolling the streets looking for who put a price on your head."

Lotario watched for a reaction, but Riot gave nothing away. He was a cool hand, and it was Lotario's new goal in life to get a rise out of the man. Without a word, Riot finished dressing, and the two struck out for a night on the town.

Isobel sat in darkness. A single candle flickered in a decorative lantern, casting shadows of mythical creatures onto the walls. A knot twisted in her heart born from helplessness. Of the unknown. It made it difficult to breathe. She shivered, then came back to herself, tugging a blanket closer about her shoulders.

Jin's attic room was drafty but bearable, as heat rose from the depths of the manor house to warm it. But Isobel's day had been long and she was tired.

Faint footsteps sounded overhead.

Isobel cocked an ear, listening. Barely a whisper of sound, then a hatch opened, letting in a blast of cold air.

Sao Jin climbed down the roof ladder, closing the hatch as her feet touched the floorboards.

Isobel sighed with relief. And Jin froze. Slowly, the girl turned towards the attic window where Isobel sat on the floor.

The two studied each other. Isobel searching for injuries. Jin bracing herself for a barrage of anger.

"You lost your cap," Isobel said.

Jin nodded, unsure what would come next. She had openly defied her adopted mother. In another lifetime, Jin would have been beaten into unconsciousness then forced into a cramped space under the floorboards to fester for days.

Violence had not broken her; it had only made her fight harder.

When Jin didn't speak, Isobel filled the silence. "I've been sitting here wondering... did my own mother ever sit in the dark waiting for me to return?"

"Why *are* you in the dark?" Jin finally asked.

Isobel rested her head against the wall. "I like the lantern. It reminds me of the nights we spent camping at Bright

Waters. You can't see much of the stars here, with all the fog and city lights."

Jin pressed her lips together. There was nothing casual about Isobel Amsel. Everything was calculated, and Jin recognized the comment for what it was—a reminder of their friendship.

"Am I in trouble?" Jin asked.

"You're alive. So, no. But if that ever changes, I'll be furious with you."

Relaxing some, Jin sat on the floor, keeping the window between them. Together they watched shadows dance around the room. She liked the lantern, too.

Isobel fished in a pocket, and tossed a silver coin at the girl. Jin snatched it from the air. "Penny for your thoughts?"

Jin looked at the coin, puzzled. "This is a dollar."

"I figure your thoughts cost more."

Jin turned the coin over, then very deliberately set it on the floor between them.

Isobel's jaw worked. "Have I done something?"

Jin shook her head.

"Feels like I did. You seem… far away just now."

Jin tucked her hands inside her sleeves, and started scratching at her forearms. Isobel shoved herself off the floor and turned on the gas. Light chased away the shadows and mythical beasts.

Isobel sucked in a breath. There was dried blood on Jin's face, and angry bruising around a gash on her temple. "What happened to you?"

Jin frowned up at her. She kept her lips tight. The girl wouldn't lie to her, but that didn't mean she was going to answer either.

Isobel crouched, and gently probed the injury. "It looks like a billy club," she murmured. "And given the sulfur smell on your clothes, I'd say you were roaming Chinatown."

Isobel didn't expect Jin to answer. She knew she was right anyway. Instead, Isobel set about filling a washbasin, cleaned the cut with a washcloth, and repeated the process until the wound was free of dirt and grime.

"I know better than to press you," Isobel said, tossing the washcloth into the basin. "But damn it, why go to Chinatown?"

Jin pulled away from her scrutiny. "Am I not allowed to?"

"Am I not allowed to worry about you?" Isobel countered.

"I can take care of myself."

"Do you want to?"

"Want to what?"

"Take care of yourself? Do you prefer that?" Isobel asked.

Jin started in surprise, then turned thoughtful. Isobel retrieved Mei's ointment jar from the desk. It held a green mixture that worked wonders for healing.

Isobel dabbed her fingers inside, and gently smeared it over the cut. "I'll get you some ice. Do you have a headache?"

Jin shrugged.

"Sensitivity to light?"

Jin shook her head.

"Let me know if you start vomiting."

Silence, and finally, "No."

Isobel rolled her eyes. "What do you have against letting me know if you vomit?"

"I mean *no*, I do not want to take care of myself."

Isobel sat back on her haunches. "Then let me help you with whatever's going on inside that head of yours."

Jin shook that head of hers. "You do not understand."

"Of course I don't. You're not talking to me."

Jin sprang to her feet. "I am tired."

Isobel didn't look at her. Instead, she busied herself with screwing on the top of the jar, then placed it on the desk. "I could use your help with an investigation tomorrow."

"I have school."

Isobel brushed a finger across the spyglass case. She wanted answers. She wanted to restrict the girl's activities, board up the hatch, take away the rope ladder, and forbid her from leaving her sight. All for Jin's own safety.

Isobel looked at her daughter: wise beyond her years, scarred, frightened and defiant. There was a selfish reason for wanting to keep her safe—Isobel wanted to pad her own heart against the pain of love.

"I'll bring up some ice, and Jin…"

"Yes?"

"My window is always open."

———

"Yes?"

"Hop, it's Isobel."

"I do remember the sound of your voice, *Wu Lei Ching*. It haunts my dreams."

She ignored the endearment. "Is mother awake?"

"Mrs. Amsel is sleeping at this ungodly hour."

"Then what are you doing up?"

"Answering this rude machine." Isobel's parents had had one installed some months ago, and Hop was not happy.

"Is that father singing in the background?" she asked.

"We are smoking opium and gambling away his fortune. Into my pockets."

"I suspected as much. Erm, would you…" she hesitated.

"Would you like to speak to your father?"

"No. I… tell my mother I'm sorry."

"Could you be more specific? Or is this a general apology for your eventful life?"

Isobel sighed. "A general one."

"Perhaps you should tell her."

Footsteps crackled over the line. "Has my son-in-law been hurt?" a sharp, familiar voice cut through the crackle. Catarina Saavedra Amsel could flay someone with her tongue alone.

"Mother, I was speaking to Hop."

"And I was sleeping until you caused this infernal device to wake me."

"Perhaps you should have installed it farther from your room, Mother."

"That would negate the reason for installing it."

"Which was?"

"To be informed when my daughter and son-in-law have been attacked, rather than having to read about it in the newspapers."

Isobel bit back a comment. Instead, she took a breath. "I wasn't injured seriously. Riot was grazed by a bullet. He's fine. I should have sent a telegram."

She could hear her mother take a breath across the Golden Gate. "I'm relieved to hear about Atticus. But I've buried *you* enough that I won't believe you dead until I can sink a knife in your cold body."

Isobel paused. She wasn't sure how to take that. Flattered that her mother was so confident in her ability to survive? Or... Isobel decided to err on the side of affection. "That's why I telephoned, actually. I..."

It seemed stupid now. Hearing her mother's sharp voice and indifference. But it had to be said, and Isobel would rather say it with an ocean channel separating them. "I wanted to say I'm sorry, Mother, for all the worry I caused you."

Not even a heartbeat passed. "Your apology is *not* accepted, but the sentiment is appreciated. This is about Jin, isn't it?"

Isobel gawked at the receiver for a moment. "*Appreciated*, Mother? Really?"

"I thought that generous. Considering."

Isobel sighed.

"Is my *neta* well? Has she run off again? Should I expect her?" Isobel found the hope in her mother's voice utterly perplexing.

"She's here. Tonight, anyway. I was wondering—" she cut off. This was ridiculous. A foolish, emotion-driven act that had her picking up the telephone to speak with her mother. "Never mind. I'm sorry I disturbed the household."

"*Isobel.*"

Isobel paused. "Yes?"

"Speak your mind."

So be it. She'd already opened herself up to whatever her mother would unleash. "I wondered when you stopped worrying about me, and did it help?"

Silence.

It stretched so long that Isobel feared the connection had died, but the crackle remained, and finally her mother's voice came over the line. "Learning to live with pain is different than not experiencing it. Love never stops worrying. And I've never stopped worrying about you, Isobel."

"I see." Though her sight was currently blurring.

"Jin is so much like you…" her mother whispered. "I tried to keep you safe—I restricted you, tried to control you, punished you, and it only drove you farther away. Don't make my mistake, Isobel."

"What would you have done differently?"

"Loved you."

"HOW ARE WE SUPPOSED TO FIGURE OUT WHO WROTE IT?" Tobias White whispered across the family table after Sarah had related the conversation at dinner. Although it turned out that Tobias had been listening at the door for most of the time.

The family table was in a nook in the kitchen—a scratched

and dented round table that fit the Riot and White families snugly. After dinner was over, the children had helped clean the kitchen, and now they sat alone, plotting.

Sarah tapped a pencil on her drawing pad. She itched to draw something. Anything. To help her think things through. "I don't know," she admitted.

"Say, why don't we go to that *Call* building, and just ask."

Sarah frowned. It wasn't a bad idea. But it was asking for more trouble. At least Sarah thought it would be. "I don't like reporters. If I show up asking them who submitted the article, I'll be sure to find myself in the morning edition."

Sarah had had enough of newspapers. She had found herself at the center of a murder investigation—her uncle's. Then at the center of a trial. The whole thing had twisted her stomach into knots, and if it hadn't been for Atticus keeping most of the vultures at bay, she'd have fainted dead away. She didn't know how he had done it, but he had kept her shielded from the brunt of the news frenzy.

"Maybe I could get a job as an elevator boy." Tobias got a faraway look on his face. Either he was thinking there was more glory involved in the job than anyone in his right mind would imagine, or he was calculating how much candy he could buy.

Sarah sighed, and started sketching. The lines soon materialized into a caricature of Mrs. Clarke, with a huge cross hanging from her neck on a chain—the gruesome kind, with a tortured Jesus bleeding all down the wood.

"I don't think it's her," Tobias said.

Sarah tapped her pencil on the pad. "Why not?"

Tobias shrugged.

"That's not an answer, Tobias."

He rolled his eyes. "She *can't* be the one who wrote it."

"Because she's old?"

"She's a church lady."

"Aren't most people?"

Tobias planted his elbow on the table, and rubbed at the back of his neck. He always did that when he was working through a problem. And then his tongue came sticking partway out of his mouth. Sarah had never seen him massage his brain into working condition before, and didn't hold out much hope now.

"Why do you think she did it?" Tobias tossed the ball into her court.

Sarah frowned down at the dour Mrs. Clarke. "I don't."

Tobias looked at her sharply. "Then why'd you question me?"

"It's called playing the devil's advocate."

Tobias gawked. "I'm pretty sure your gramma would skin you alive if you said you were playing the devil."

"Well, she's not here, now is she?"

"Who isn't here?" a pleasant voice asked.

Sarah and Tobias started. Lily stood at the kitchen counter, putting on a fresh pot of water for her tea. She had a book in hand.

"My gramma," Sarah said. "We're trying to figure out who wrote that article."

"What have you come up with?"

"I don't think Mrs. Clarke did it," Tobias announced. "Or Frankie."

Sarah snorted at the boy. That was an easy one. There's no way a six-year-old could write an article like that no matter what Mr. Lotario said. The boy still picked his nose. But so did Tobias. Maybe she shouldn't discount Frankie after all.

Lily took a seat beside her son. She had warm eyes and dimples that always made Sarah want to smile, just so she'd get a chance to see them again. "Why not?" Lily asked.

"That's what Sarah asked me."

"Work through it, Tobias. Like any math problem."

"I don't like math."

"Well... this has clearly caught your interest, so use that brain of yours."

Tobias wrinkled his nose, and rubbed at his neck again. The weight of thinking clearly made his head want to droop.

"All right," Tobias said. "Mrs. Clarke is a woman, and it seems to me that what was being said in that article wasn't proper."

"It wasn't proper at all," Lily agreed. There was no warmth in those words. No humor. They were flat and void of emotion. Sarah had never truly seen Miss Lily angry. She reckoned she was seeing it now. But there was a tiredness, too. Miss Lily looked resigned, and that was unsettling.

"But she's also old," Sarah said. "And old people get away with more, and they love pointing out everybody else's sins."

"I thought you didn't think it was her either?" Tobias accused.

"I don't. Well..." Sarah tapped her paper. "I suppose it could be."

"I think it's Mr. Dougal," Tobias said.

"He's disagreeable," Sarah agreed.

"What motive does he have?" Lily asked, interested in her son's answer.

Tobias counted off on his fingers. "He doesn't like women, he doesn't like children, and his reputation doesn't matter to him one jot."

"Let's back up a bit. What purpose could that article serve the author?"

Both children thought.

Tobias's eyes snapped open. "Say, Miss Pierce said it's hard to find lodging in the city. Is it really, Ma?"

Lily nodded. "Decent places that aren't flea infested."

Sarah felt the need to start scratching her arm. But she resisted. "So that's a motive. Maybe one of them has a friend who needs a place to stay. Have any of the lodgers given notice yet?"

"Not as yet, but I suspect Mr. Löfgren will. And Mrs. Lane. Her employment is at risk."

"That means they aren't the snitch."

"Unless Mrs. Lane is lying," Tobias said.

"That's a horrible thing to say," Sarah said.

"So was the article," he defended.

Their speculation was interrupted by a door opening. Grimm walked in quietly. His head was bowed and his shoulders hunched. Without looking up, he headed for the servant's staircase.

"Grimm," the sound of his mother's voice stopped him, but he didn't turn. "Your coat is torn and there's mud on your trousers."

He braced himself, and turned.

Sarah gasped. Miss Lily shot out of her chair and began fussing, and Tobias started snickering about how Grimm was in for it. Grimm's left eye was swollen shut, and that side of his face was puffy. Had his skin been lighter, Sarah was sure it would be showing all sorts of colors.

"What on earth happened?" Lily demanded. Grimm kept his eyes down, as she grabbed his chin to examine the bruises. "Can you see out of it?"

Grimm nodded.

"Did Mr. Riot or Mr. Tim send you somewhere?"

Grimm shook his head.

"You got into trouble all by yourself?"

Grimm nodded.

Lily huffed and went to break off some ice from the icebox. But no matter how much Miss Lily pressed, Grimm wouldn't communicate. Not that he spoke. He sat in stoic silence as his mother cleaned and ministered to his face.

Sarah frowned in thought. Grimm had taken off when he learned that Jin had fled the theater.

"You scrub yourself good. I'll have Mr. Tim look over the rest of you."

Grimm sighed, and shook his head.

"Don't get stubborn with me," she said. "Either it's Mr. Tim or me. Do you understand?"

Grimm looked down at her. He seemed about to say something, but only nodded in the end.

"I don't know what this house is coming to," Lily said, walking towards her rooms. She was so flustered that she forgot her book and her tea.

ROUND TWO

Wednesday, October 10, 1900

ISOBEL KNOCKED ON THE DOOR AND BRACED HERSELF FOR another encounter with the pint-sized escape artist, but instead of Bertie answering, Maddie opened it. Her cheeks dimpled into a smile.

"Hello, Miss Isobel." The young woman hugged her, and Isobel stiffened in surprise. Maddie took a hasty step back. "I'm sorry. It's only…"

"Don't be," Isobel said quickly. "I'm not accustomed to embracing."

"I know," Maddie admitted. "It's only I read the newspapers yesterday, and when you didn't come by… Are you all right? Of course you are."

Isobel stepped inside, and froze in the act of removing her gloves. The entryway was immaculate, the coats hung up, the floor mopped. The house smelled of lemon and beeswax, and, most shocking of all, it was quiet.

"What magic have you done?" Isobel whispered.

"Just rolled up my sleeves, is all," Maddie said.

Anyone could roll up their sleeves, but not many could transform a home. "Where's Bertie?" Isobel asked.

Maddie led the way upstairs. The boy's room was clean, the toys put away, and the gate gone. Bertie was sleeping on a rug with a blanket and the dog, who blinked wearily at the pair. Mop's tail thunked tiredly on the floor.

Isobel had a dozen questions, but Maddie motioned her downstairs. She led the way to the kitchen. "Can I get you something to eat or drink?"

"Is that how you did it, you drugged them?" Isobel asked.

Maddie laughed. "Tea or coffee?"

"I think I need a stiffer drink." Isobel noticed the kettle on the stove and Maddie's own mug of tea beside a book. "Tea is fine."

Even the kitchen was transformed. Isobel marveled at the White family's ability to restore order. She picked up the book. It was on physiology.

"And you even have time left over for some light reading."

"Dr. Wise let me borrow it," Maddie explained. "Bertie and Mop were just cooped up. I don't think anyone takes that boy out. I took him and Mop for a long walk over to a park, where he played 'catch me if you can' with some other children."

She set down a mug in front of Isobel, who gratefully warmed her hands.

"The boy tuckered himself out."

"I can see that." Isobel pondered this bit of information. "Which means… Ella likely just left Bertie behind the gate most of the time. Or tried to."

Maddie nodded. "I suspect as much. But who knows. Maybe she was run ragged trying to care for everyone at once."

"*You're* caring for everyone at once."

Maddie blushed. "I'm used to getting things done. No use dragging my feet."

Isobel could relate. "How are Mrs. Spencer and the baby?"

"Dr. Wise said it's a cycle. The baby isn't sleeping because he's not getting enough to eat, and Mrs. Spencer doesn't have enough milk because she's exhausted. She's not sleeping and she's worried over money issues. So I hid all her tinctures, and we're just giving the baby a bottle for a while to give Mrs. Spencer some rest."

"Do you agree with the doctor's assessment?"

Maddie looked surprised that Isobel had asked. "Yes, I do. Seems to be working, anyway. Oftentimes simple things work best. But Mrs. Spencer…" Maddie glanced at the door. "She's a bit demanding."

"Was she rude to you?" Isobel asked sharply.

"No, Miss Isobel. Not any more than most ladies of the house." Maddie stopped to give Isobel a pointed look, but a smile was playing at the corner of her eyes.

"I *am* rude. And crude," Isobel admitted.

This cracked Maddie's lips into a smile. "Don't we know it. But Mrs. Spencer is like that even with her family. I know she's tired, but she expects Mr. Fletcher to do everything. I can't understand it."

Of course not. Not with a mother like Lily White. Miss Lily wouldn't place that kind of responsibility on her sons any more than Isobel would lounge around Ravenwood Manor and expect Riot to provide every luxury for her. He'd do it, of course. But the very thought rankled her honor.

"Did Mr. Fletcher return last night?"

Maddie nodded. "I told him I was sent from the agency. He took one look at the house, and said thank you. But he was not pleased at all to see Dr. Wise. He didn't like the thought of a Chinese doctor."

A common thing in San Francisco.

"Dr. Wise handled it fine, though. I wager he's used to that sort of thing. He handed Mr. Fletcher a Ravenwood card, and told him to take it up with Mr. Riot. Mr. Fletcher didn't have much to say after that."

Isobel drummed her fingers on the table in thought. "Did you overhear anything between mother and son?"

Maddie told her everything, word for word. The gist of it centered around the Masonic Temple charity fund. Mr. Fletcher wasn't on the board; he was an applicant. His family was in dire straits and it was left to him to fix things, so he had turned to charity. Lewis struck her as a proud man. How desperate things must have seemed, and how bitter the solution. Alone, Isobel could not imagine a situation where she'd turn to such measures. But now, with a family... Well, she would likely resort to burglary before charity.

"Did you spot a journal? Anything of Ella's? Notes, receipts?"

Maddie shook her head. "I was careful to look. I gathered all the loose papers and put them on the writing desk in the sitting room, but nothing stood out."

"Thank you. You'd make an excellent agent. We were fortunate your mother let us hire you at all."

Maddie glanced down at the mug in her hands.

Isobel blew on her tea, watching the girl. "You had her permission, didn't you?"

Maddie shifted. "I left a note."

"You didn't get her permission?"

Maddie showed her dimples. "I think you're rubbing off on me."

Isobel raised a brow. "There are worse things," she said primly.

Maddie laughed.

"Well, she didn't seem overly angry."

"I telephoned her yesterday," Maddie said with a sigh. "Ma

calmed when I told her the situation here. She knows I want to be a doctor like my father."

Isobel could not remember any previous mention of Mr. White. "What happened to your father?"

"He died."

Two clipped words, and Maddie White withdrew.

Isobel returned to safer ground. "Your mother won't let you study to be a doctor?"

"It's... complicated, Miss Isobel. But Doctor Wise offered to let me work at his clinic."

"You'll do it, won't you?" Isobel asked.

The young woman lifted a shoulder. "We'll see."

There wasn't much hope in the usually optimistic girl.

"I don't see why not," Isobel said. "You wouldn't be in much danger at a clinic."

Maddie shook her head. "It's not that, Miss Isobel. I can't talk about it."

But oh, did she want to. Isobel could see it brimming in her bright eyes. Before Isobel could dig deeper, Maddie changed the subject. "Is Mr. Riot all right? The newspaper said an agent was shot."

"Riot's fine." At least she hoped so. He had gone off with Lotario to various social clubs, and hadn't returned home last night. Knowing Riot, he had spent the night playing cards. Or Lotario had drunk him under a table somewhere.

"Did you want to speak with Mrs. Spencer?" Maddie asked.

"Is she awake?"

"I need to wake her. She's been sleeping all morning, and the baby's bound to wake up soon."

Isobel explored the house while Maddie served Mrs. Spencer lunch on a tray and brought in the baby to nurse. Bertie woke up somewhere in that time, and Maddie easily took boy and dog with her, promising he could help finish feeding the baby with a bottle.

Bertie skipped right along, happy to be involved.

Isobel steeled herself for another emotional breakdown as she walked into Mrs. Spencer's room.

"That girl is a blessing."

"She is," Isobel agreed.

Though circles still lined her eyes, Mrs. Spencer looked far brighter than the day before.

"And that Chinese doctor… I wasn't sure, but Miss Maddie said he was the best. And she's so sensible. Like my Ella."

Isobel doubted that Ella was anything like Maddie, but kept that thought to herself. Mention of Ella made the woman's hands tremble. She set down her fork. "Have you found my Ella?"

"We're searching. The police are, too." Before Mrs. Spencer broke down in another fit, Isobel quickly offered a distraction. "There's a postcard in her room from a Mr. Serebrenck in Port Arthur. Do you know him?"

"He's a friend of my brother. He's a Russian employed in the Orient. He came last month on holiday bearing a letter of introduction, and Ella and I met him for lunch at the Palace. It's such a grand place—it was a real treat for us."

"Is he still in the city?"

"No, he was due to ship out on Saturday, to Peking."

Isobel made a mental note to check on that. "Does he have a scar near his eye?"

Mrs. Spencer looked at her, puzzled. "No. Why?"

"No matter. Are you sure you don't know anything more about Madge Ryan? Such as where she lived before she ran away?"

"I told you this the other day. Ella wouldn't run off with Madge. She'd never leave this house willingly."

Isobel made a noise of understanding. She knew better

than to contradict the woman on her beliefs about her daughter. Maybe Mrs. Spencer was right. But after her talk with Estelle Baker the night before, Isobel was convinced Ella had been living a double life before her disappearance.

"All the same, it's important we talk with Madge. She may have seen something."

"But I told Ella to stay away from that girl. Why aren't you out looking for Ella?"

Isobel took a patient breath. "A number of agents are searching for her, as well as the police department, Mrs. Spencer," she explained for the second time. "I only wondered if Ella might have confided in Madge about any suspicious people following her. That sort of thing."

"Oh, dear. I knew it. I *know* something bad has happened to her." Mrs. Spencer's 'knowing' seemed to border on a kind of twisted hope.

Isobel tried another line of questioning, but Mrs. Spencer was either blind to her daughter's activities or didn't want to voice what Ella had been up to. Before leaving, Isobel replaced the photographs, and was left wondering if *she* even knew what her own daughters were up to.

21

THE TAILORS

SAO JIN WAS BURNING AND SHIVERING ALL AT ONCE. HER stomach felt like it was twisted around a piece of coal. She walked in a daze, barely aware of her feet touching the ground.

In the early morning fog, the Quarter was transformed from festive and sinister to dreary gray. Men still warmed themselves around burning barrels as they had the night before, but most went about their business. Storefronts were thrown open, lumber wagons trundled up and down narrow streets, and laborers balanced heavy loads on their shoulders with poles, while children giggled with delight around a toy merchant. Chinatown was awake with scents of incense and too many bodies living together.

Jin balled her fists inside her pockets. She felt exposed in the light even though she wore a wool suit and a cap, stolen from Isobel. Her braids were concealed and her eyes were hidden by the brim of her cap pulled low. She had a newspaper bag slung over her shoulder, and to the casual glance she looked like any other newsboy roaming San Francisco.

Jin glanced over her shoulder. She had hitched a ride on a

wagon, ridden two different cable cars, and walked a good mile in a tangled pattern. She didn't see Grimm in the mass of people. He *should* stand out in the sea of queues and quilted coats, but Grimm was like a ghost haunting her every step. Why was he following her?

She clenched her teeth, and turned randomly down an alleyway. Brick and timber buildings and laundry-draped balconies blocked out the sky. The alley was crammed with people wearing wide hats and somber faces.

Jin stepped into a doorway to wait, watching as men passed by, searching for her ghost. But she didn't spot him. Worse, she'd begun to attract notice—a dangerous thing in the Quarter. Stepping from the doorway, she rejoined the flow, weaving her way through the crowd.

As she passed a dark opening, she spotted a group of men gathered at a dead end, their gazes trained on a brick wall plastered with posters. Angry at herself for running away the night before, she boldly stepped into the crowd to see what was happening.

No one stopped her. No one even seemed to notice her. Snippets of gossip touched her ears: whispers of plague, of white conspiracies, of murder.

As Jin read the notices on the wall, her stomach lurched. Some were challenges between hatchet men. Others were *Chun Hungs*—contracts for killing: assassination of tong members; of factory workers; of businessmen; the Consul General; white policemen. And one contract for *Din Gau*—Atticus Riot. For murder, theft, and destruction of property.

Jin's heart skipped, and then her eyes fell on another name: *Wu Lei Ching*. Fox Spirit. Isobel Amsel. Her crime: dishonor and humiliation of an honored man.

Fear was quickly replaced with rage. Her hands curled into fists. What lies, she thought. The *chun hungs* were issued by Hip Yee—the Temple of United Justice—the tong that had held

Mei and her captive. They dealt in slavery. The "theft" was most likely Mei and herself. But the bit about humiliation had her stumped.

Jin tugged on the tunic of an elderly man. "Sir, what does 'humiliation of an honorable man' mean?"

The man's dark eyes darted side to side, then he bent his already bent frame to speak softly. "The white woman cut off Big Queue's queue." The man seemed to like saying it, his eyes dancing with amusement.

Jin's eyes widened. She knew that name. Big Queue was a dangerous hatchet man, and cutting off a man's queue was akin to castration.

Feeling suddenly exposed, Jin slipped out of the alleyway and didn't breathe until she got to wider streets.

She set her sights on her goal—the same street where she had frozen the night before. Home. But her old home didn't conjure warmth. It made her tremble with memories.

Jin wasn't sure if she should call them memories. They were more like faded impressions: her father's cheerful voice as she rode on his shoulders, the whisper of a kiss on her unmarred cheeks, his smile when he'd bent to give her a balloon from a merchant. And her mother—her laugh, the scent of jasmine and honey, and her light feet and loving arms. There were her stories, too, of dragons and river spirits, but she could not remember the words, only the images they conjured.

Jin wandered through the wider streets, one knife tucked up her sleeve and the other pressed against her lower back. With the plague in remission, at least according to the newspapers, the tourists had returned.

Streetcar-like wagons, full of ladies and gentlemen, had come to gawk at "Celestials," paying guides to take them to opium dens, joss houses, and locales with exotic foods.

Jin wished she could return to the warmth of her family.

Or even see the Quarter through the eyes of white tourists, with wonder and excitement. When she looked up at the windows and balconies draped with lanterns, banners, and laundry, she wondered how many children, like her, were trapped in hell under a two-faced silk-clad woman with a ready whip.

Jin clenched her jaw and turned a corner. A few men watched her as they sat against a wall, smoking their pipes. She didn't know her way around these streets. The expanse between her birth parents and her adoptive parents seemed a lifetime. Years trapped behind doors, behind walls, in trunks, and under floorboards. That had been her life in Chinatown.

Jin tried to remember where her feet had taken her the previous night, the intersection where she'd spotted her home. Walking too quickly would draw attention. Hesitating would draw even more. So she walked with the purpose of a boy delivering a message, even though every step was full of uncertainty and fear.

A large building brought her up short. Three stories high, festooned with banners and lanterns, and with a three-tiered balcony on the front. The theater. Jin remembered that. Yes, this was where she'd started last night, and then she'd gone down the street. A snippet of memory added to her disorientation. Silk. Piles of it. A needle and thread.

Jin froze with realization. Her *bahba* and *mahma* had been tailors. They lived close. Had they made costumes for the theater?

She walked past the theater, a joss house, and a restaurant. Two doors farther down she stopped as she had the night before. Men bumped past her, their long queues nearly dragging on the ground.

The storefront was no longer a tailor, but an herbalist shop. In her mind's eye, she saw a little girl playing with a wooden duck in front of the store. And then her eyes were drawn to the door.

Jin turned and bolted, with no idea where she was going. Just away. Far away from the store and the ghost of a happy child.

22

MIDDLEMAN

SAN FRANCISCO WAS REACHING FOR THE SKY, AND AN ARMY OF human ants were climbing up its scaffolding. One laborer, somewhere between boy and man, had a board on his shoulders with a curve cut out for his neck. Some forty bricks lay stacked on the board as he carried them across the yard.

Riot flicked his gaze over the laborer noting calluses, rough hands, the way his neck bent slightly forward, and the musculature of a sixteen-year-old who carried stacks of bricks all day. A scarf was tied around the laborer's neck to prevent chaffing, and a cap was pulled low against the light. Dark circles ran under his eyes. He walked up to the scaffolding where another laborer began plucking the bricks off the tray and tossing them upwards to the next tier. One brick after another, trusting that his fellow worker would catch each missile.

When the tray was emptied the boy walked back towards a waiting wagon. Riot intercepted him there.

"Scottie Barnes?"

The boy eyed Riot sideways. "I'm busy."

"I can see that. And exhausted, by the look of you."

"Get off."

The boy turned, the tray snug around his neck, as a man in the wagon began loading more bricks onto the board. With every tier, the boy winced.

"I'm a persistent fellow. I think you'll want to talk to me alone."

"You a copper?"

"I'm a detective."

The man in the wagon faltered.

Riot glanced up at him. "You're not in trouble. Neither is your brickyard."

The man kept stacking.

"I don't have to talk to you," the boy said.

"No, but I've a mind to keep you company the rest of the day if you don't."

"And what if I drop this right here, and dirty those fancy duds of yours?"

"Considering the bruises you earned from your fight last night, I'd say that would be a bad idea."

The boy glared. "What do you want?"

Riot held up a silver dollar. "Information."

Silver glinted in the mist. The boy took over one more load of bricks, then announced he was due a break. Riot stood by as Scottie drank from a canteen. Then he held out his hand.

"After I get my information."

"I can only stall so long before the foreman starts screaming."

"Last night, a fight started and you were part of a group that was arrested for public drunkenness and disorderly conduct."

"What of it? Nothing wrong with it."

"Someone hired you and your friends to start a ruckus."

Scottie shrugged massive shoulders. "He paid our fines, too."

"Who hired you?"

"The fellow paid for our silence."

Riot wove the coin between his fingers. The boy watched, mesmerized. "Will he know who talked out of a group of twenty?"

Scottie spat on the ground, and took off his cap, running a hand through his hair. "I ain't no rat."

Riot turned his hand over. A second coin appeared, the two silver dollars sitting in the palm of his hand.

The boy reached for the coins, but Riot closed his hand.

"We were roaming the Barbary Coast well into the bottle, and some fella comes up and says he'll pay us to start a fight. So we did," Scottie said quickly.

"What did this fellow look like?"

"Had a mustache."

Riot waited.

"Look, that's what he had. A bowler hat, rough sort, long mustache, sideburns down to his cheeks, and a cigar. He looked like a boxer."

"Brown hair? Scarred knuckles?"

"That's him."

A muscle in Riot's jaw flexed. He handed the boy his coins.

That description could fit a number of men, but the coincidence was too much for Riot to swallow. His hand tightened around his walking stick, and he went off to search for Montgomery Johnson.

DEAD ENDS

ISOBEL ALWAYS EXPECTED TO GET STRUCK BY LIGHTNING WHEN she set foot inside a church. A side effect of having a Catholic mother who used God as a threat rather than a balm. Only it had backfired with Isobel and Lotario. The twins decided early on that they were doomed, so why not go out with a bang.

Logic laughed at Isobel, but still that lingering doubt remained, and she held her breath as she stepped over the threshold.

No strike of lightning. Just music. Isobel passed a sign that read *Ladies' Aid Social*. The pews were empty, so she followed the music to one of the large parlors. A small musical group was performing for the ladies—a flutist, a violinist, and a singer with more spirit than talent.

Isobel eyed a buffet table set with finger foods, and then the ladies in attendance. From the state of their clothing, a good many were there for aid.

A white-haired man in a clerical collar spotted her lingering near the food. He approached and whispered, "You're welcome to sit and eat." He motioned to an empty chair.

Isobel showed him her card, and nodded towards the back. He hastened from the room, likely looking for any excuse to escape the vocalist.

"Reverend West," he introduced, shaking hands in the universal way every priest and reverend does, one hand to shake, and the other to place warmly on top of the newcomer's hand. Do they learn that in seminary school, Isobel wondered.

"Isobel Amsel. I'm here about a girl who attends your church. Elouise Spencer."

The name brought recognition to his blue eyes. "Sweet girl. I'm surprised she's not here today."

That surprised Isobel. "Was she here often?"

"*Was?*" Concern entered his voice. He was a sharp man.

Isobel pondered her slip. Did she share Mrs. Spencer's worry deep down? She shook the feeling away. "Ella's gone missing. My agency was hired to find her."

"That's horrible news," West said.

"Do you know a man by the name of John Bennett? He claims to be a preacher of some sort."

"Here?" West asked in surprise.

"I don't know."

"Bennett. Bennett. Well, he's no minister here. I don't recall Ella mentioning him, but one of the ladies may know. I wondered why Ella wasn't at church on Sunday. I assumed Mrs. Spencer was ill again."

"She is ill," Isobel said. "The family seems to be in a bad way."

West nodded in agreement. "The congregation has been sending meals to the home, but... Mr. Fletcher said it was no longer needed."

"It *is* needed," Isobel said. "And more."

West frowned. "He is a proud young man, I'm afraid."

"And his mother is suffering because of it."

"I'll check on them today," West assured. "It's difficult to accept help at times." He glanced at those gathered. "So we offer it in a different guise."

"Does a girl by the name of Madge Ryan attend your church? She is a friend of Ella's."

Again, he shook his head. "I'm sorry. I don't recognize that name. Ella attends with her mother. And she comes for the literary meetings… a book club of sorts. She often chooses books from the public library."

The free food was likely a bonus for Ella, to what was mainly a chance to escape the house. "Did you ever see her with a man? He may have looked like this, but older."

West studied the sketch that Sarah had drawn of Ella's father. But West only shook his head. Another dead end.

It turned out Menke's Grocer had Madge Ryan's address. Mr. Menke indicated that the family had an unpaid tab, and wondered if Isobel could somehow get them to pay. She told him she'd try if he would give her the address. But as she stood in front of the run-down building with its patchwork of windows, she held out little hope.

A band of scruffy children loitered outside, and a group of leering men stood across the street with nothing but idleness in their eyes. She expected to be surrounded at any moment and jostled in a classic thievery ring. They had the look of hoodlums, some obscure mutation of the word "huddle 'em" which was a favored tactic of thugs of about a decade or so earlier. They would shout "huddle 'em" before surrounding a victim and robbing them in the confusion.

She hoped the practice had fallen out of style in the neighborhood.

Isobel walked up the creaking stairs and entered a tilted rookery. Some unidentifiable carpet crunched under her shoes.

It was dark and moldy and she was glad there hadn't been any gas laid. The whole tottering building would likely go up in flames.

Madge Ryan's family lived in a section of rooms. This wasn't compartmentalized living quarters with separate bathrooms like Isobel's *Sapphire House*, but a hodgepodge of flimsy wooden walls and fabric doorways. She thought this might have been a warehouse converted into apartments.

She walked to the second floor, and knocked on a door with a faded number five etched into dented wood.

The door was wrenched open, and a gust of gin and fury hit her full force. "You ungrateful—"

The woman cut off. Red hair framed a face lined with contempt and a cheek covered in bruises. A shawl was draped over the woman's shoulders and she wore a thin blouse that had seen better days.

"Isobel Amsel. Mrs. Ryan?"

"What'd you want?" the woman drew herself up and closed her shawl, smoothing the faded blue material. With every word a new gust of gin-infused air blew towards Isobel. Somewhere in the background an infant wailed.

"Who's that?" a man hollered from the background. "I told that landlord I'd pummel him next I saw him."

Mrs. Ryan turned slightly. "It's some high-and-mighty lady."

A man stomped into view. Tall, black-haired, with a pock-marked face and coal-stained clothes. His knuckles were bandaged. He smiled at Isobel, displaying tobacco-stained teeth. "Won't you come in, Miss."

Isobel glanced at Mrs. Ryan. The woman cursed under her breath, and walked away from the door, heading for a gin bottle. It was nearly empty.

The infant's cries went unanswered.

It was a single room. The squalling infant lay in a drawer;

its bedding, at least, was clean. The single bed was unmade, the pillow and blankets dingy with sweat. A small kerosene stove sat on a battered cupboard with tin plates and cups.

"What can we do fer you, Miss?" the man asked.

"I'm looking for your daughter, Madge Ryan." Isobel presented her card. The lady snatched it and squinted, but the man tore it from her hands. "As if you can read. Says she's a detective." The man looked her up and down, slowly. And laughed, elbowing Mrs. Ryan.

"Are you Mr. Ryan?" Isobel asked.

Mrs. Ryan drew herself up, proper-like. "Mr. Ryan died some years ago. This is my current husband, Eric Harrison."

"As if I'd marry a wretch like you." He thrust out his hand to Isobel, who eyed it, then gave a small twitch of her lips.

"What, you're too good for the likes of me? I'm too low to shake your hand?"

"By your own words, you're too good for Mrs. Ryan here, and it's her I've come to talk to."

"Oh, is it? Well, I pay the rent here. Not this waste."

Isobel looked to Mrs. Ryan. "Your daughter was acquainted with a girl. Ella Spencer. Do you know her?"

"I don't know. Madge ran away months ago."

"Don't tell her nothin'," Mr. Harrison growled.

"Should I be suspicious of you?" Isobel countered. She leveled her gaze on him. He curled his fists in response.

"We don't want no police snooping around."

"You invited me in," Isobel pointed out.

"And here you are. In *my* home. All alone."

"And about to take my leave." She backed up towards the door. "I've learned all I need from you both."

Harrison rushed forward and slapped a hand to the door, holding it fast. "Now then, no need to hurry. I'm a gentleman. How 'bout a drink?"

Isobel was eye level with the man's underarm. His shirt was

stained and yellow and smelled like it had never been washed, like the man who wore it. "No," Isobel said simply.

"No?"

"I don't want a drink." Isobel looked up at the sneering man.

"Now ain't you feisty."

"Your baby is crying, Mr. Harrison. You have other responsibilities."

"And I just found a new one."

Isobel rolled her eyes, then struck without preamble. The fist to his solar plexus caught him completely by surprise, but he was dulled by enough drink to lunge at her. Isobel ducked under his clumsy grab. She struck a quick blow to his underarm, then spun around him grabbing up and between his legs and ruthlessly twisting his testicles.

Wheezing in pain, he dropped, both hands clutching his groin. With luck, he wouldn't father any more children.

"I'll be taking my leave." She looked to Mrs. Ryan. "And if I were you, I'd do the same before he recovers. He'll likely take out his rage on you."

Isobel opened the door into the man's head, and slipped outside. Small wonder Madge Ryan ran away.

BREAKTHROUGH

"I DON'T KNOW, TOBIAS. I THINK THERE'S LAWS AGAINST THAT sort of thing."

The boy frowned at Sarah. "You're chicken."

The two children sat on the landing of the third floor with their heads pressed against the railing slats. The view down to the entryway was dizzying.

"I think we should just observe the lodgers for now. I'll go to dinner again, and you can bring in the trays."

Tobias snorted. "How 'bout I sit at the table and you bring the trays in?"

"You think I should do that 'cause I'm a girl?" she said, offended.

"Depends. Are you tellin' me to bring the trays in 'cause I'm a negro?"

Sarah opened her mouth to protest. But Tobias got a sly look in his eye and nudged her side with an elbow. "You know you turn red as a brick when you're embarrassed?"

She huffed at him. "It's not fair."

"You know what's not fair? You not helping me."

"We could get into trouble."

Both children eyed the lower level, looking across the stair-well to a door. It was Mr. Dougal's door. He seemed the like-liest suspect. He didn't like anyone. Not children, not Miss Dupree, not the White family. And he was strapped for cash.

"Jin will do it," Tobias said.

Sarah sighed. Her sister had vanished again.

"She'll pick that lock in no time," Tobias said.

"Your ma has the key," Sarah pointed out.

"You think I'm crazy?" Tobias whispered. "I'm not stealing a key from my ma."

"But you'll pick a lock to break into a lodger's room?"

"That's different. Mr. Dougal won't catch us. My ma catches everything I do."

"What about the maids? We could offer to help them when they come." Miss Lily did not clean the house or do laundry. She hired outside help to clean and sent the laundry out. Once a day for light cleaning, and once a week for a more thorough one, including the lodgers' rooms. She didn't let the hired staff in her kitchen, though.

Tobias gave Sarah an "are you daft?" look. "Ma hires those ladies 'cause she trusts them. They're gonna tell her I offered to help clean, and ma will be on me faster than a blink."

Sarah thought about that. It was true. If the two of them suddenly volunteered for chores, it would raise everyone's suspicions.

"What do you think Jin got up to?" Sarah asked instead.

Tobias shrugged. "Probably picked a fight with a mule."

"And Grimm? Did he say anything? Did they fight with each other?"

Tobias fiddled with a splinter in the railing slat. His legs dangled over the edge, but he couldn't fit his head through anymore. "Does he ever say anything?"

"Can't you make him write it down?" Sarah asked.

"My ma can't even get a thought out of him." The boy

shrugged. "We aren't trying to find out what Jin is up to. We need to figure out who wrote that article."

"I'm not going to break into every lodger's room to rifle through their drawers, Tobias."

"You got a better idea?"

The front door opened downstairs, and a soft murmur of voices traveled upwards. Sound carried in the entryway, amplifying it. She saw the top of Atticus's hat as he helped Isobel out of her coat.

"I do, actually."

Isobel could tell by the way Riot gripped his gentleman's walking stick that something weighed heavy on him. But then she felt the same way.

They had come from different directions on the street and she waited for him on the front porch. The closer he got, the more exhausted he looked and he climbed the stairs like a man twice his age. She doubted he'd had a wink of sleep last night.

"No luck?" he asked.

Riot could read her like an open book.

"Not really."

He opened the door for her, and she strode into the foyer. It was warm, and she gave a sigh. "I checked at the Saddle Rock Restaurant on Taylor. No one remembers Ella or Bennett, so I went by Ella's church. The pastor knows Ella, but he didn't know Bennett or Madge. He promised to check on the family, at least. I decided to double back to Menke's Grocery and discovered that a Mrs. Ryan has an unpaid tab there."

"Not good?"

"Madge's mother is fond of gin and living with a first-class brute."

Riot helped her out of her coat. She could feel his eyes on

her, searching for injury. "Your assessment or firsthand experience?"

"I doubt he'll be fathering any more children."

She turned slightly, and gave him a small smile. Riot looked amused.

"Did you see this morning's newspaper?" she asked.

"I did."

The *Bulletin* had run an exposé to remind the public of the *Kingston vs. Kingston* case. It included a letter attesting to Riot's good character from Donaldina Cameron, also signed by a number of other well-connected ladies. Which was all well and good, except that the *Bulletin's* reporter added that he "could personally vouch" for the goings-on at Ravenwood Manor and the chaste nature of Sarah Byrne.

Riot didn't appreciate Mr. Fry mentioning Sarah—no matter how well-intentioned.

A lodger passed by in the foyer. At least, Isobel assumed the woman lived in their house. She vowed to endure one buffet dinner so she could meet the other lodgers. For all she knew the woman could be a vagabond passing through.

Isobel started up the stairs, then stopped, turning to see Riot gazing at the long stretch of stairs. "Shall I carry you?" she asked.

"I'm wondering if I should eat before making the climb."

Isobel smiled, and held out a hand. "I'll bring you a tray."

They said nothing more until they were tucked in their shared bedroom.

"Out all night with your mistress?" she asked.

"As if I have enough energy for another woman."

She'd take the credit for that.

Isobel tossed her coat on the hook, dropped her satchel on the floor and flung herself in Ravenwood's chair to kick off her shoes and drape her legs over the armrest. She idly watched out of the

corner of her eye as Riot began divesting himself of male accou-
trements: hat hung on a hook, walking stick in its holder, then the
ritual shedding of his coat. The unbuckling of his shoulder
holster, and the clink of metal as he wound leather around
revolver to clean later. Collar and tie came next, then he dropped
his cufflinks and pocket watch on a dresser, along with his billfold.

Riot fell into the chair across from her. He reached down
and tugged at his shoes, then pulled up his right trouser leg to
reveal a thick wad of cash tucked in his sock garter.

Isobel raised a brow.

His left leg had a similar stash. He tossed both rolls on the
table between them, then at last sat back and closed his eyes
with a sigh.

Isobel plucked up one of the rolls, and flicked through the
bills. She whistled low. "Either you robbed a bank or Lotario
coaxed you into working at the *Narcissus* for a night. I'm told
they tip their dancers well."

Riot cracked an eye at her. "Lotario *was* with me, but I'm
afraid it was nothing so sensational."

"Ah, cards then?" she said with a sigh. "Do you cheat,
Riot?"

"Have you caught me cheating?"

Isobel narrowed her eyes at him. They had played a
handful of games with the girls and Tobias and Grimm (something Miss Lily should never discover), and Riot had been
suspiciously cleaned out of all his candy currency.

"No," she said slowly.

"There you have it."

Isobel snorted. And mused over the rolls of cash. "Riot,
earlier this week, when I took your billfold, you told me all that
you have is mine… Was that all the money you had then?
What was in your billfold?"

"Would you like a drink?"

Isobel blew out a breath, and quickly got to her feet. "I don't want you keeling over on the floor."

She poured two brandies, and pressed a glass into his hand. He raised it in gratitude and she took the opportunity to brush the hair back from his forehead. He didn't feel feverish. "Is this how you've lived most of your life?"

"Hmm?"

"With a wad of cash in your sock garter?"

Riot savored the brandy for a moment. "Old habits die hard. Though the stakes are higher now."

"Does that thrill you?"

"Are you asking if I'm a gambling addict?"

"I am."

"I wasn't just fleecing the lords of their currency. Lotario was busy robbing them of their secrets."

"He's good at that."

"And I need money to hold us over until Miss Lily can pull us out of the gutter."

"It's as bad as all that?"

Riot tipped his head at the cash. "Not anymore."

"What did my twin discover?"

"It seems Kingston has fallen from grace."

She perked up at this. "Has he?"

"He was ousted from the Pacific Union Club, and lost a significant number of wealthy clients who've been keeping him on retainer."

"In any other circumstance, I'd be pleased out of my mind, but… this makes him even more dangerous."

Riot pulled out his deck of cards. His collar was undone, his sleeves rolled up to his forearms, his suspenders hung from his waist. She liked Riot disheveled, and admired him as he told her about his conversation with the hired drunk ruffian.

He shuffled as he related the details. Smooth and sure, like the man himself. Riot didn't shuffle cards like a normal person.

He arched them from hand to hand, creating a blurring bridge. She had only ever seen him drop his cards once. Thanks to her efforts.

But she had no intention of distracting him today. Shuffling was a testament to his mind at work.

"You were right," he said at last. "I didn't want to believe it. Monty might be rough around the edges, but we've been through… things together."

"I'm sorry, Riot. Do you know where he is?"

Riot shook his head. "I tried a few places, but I'm spent for the day."

A part of her was glad for that.

A knock sounded at the door. Isobel rose to answer before Riot could. It was Sarah. "Do you know what Jin is up to?" Isobel asked as Sarah entered.

Sarah shook her head.

"I suppose I should go check in with her."

"She wasn't at school today. Neither was Grimm."

Isobel rubbed her temples.

Sarah glanced at Riot, then back to Isobel and hesitated. Isobel sensed she wanted to speak with Riot alone. "I'll get us a tray."

SARAH PERCHED ON RIOT'S ARMREST. HE SMILED UP AT HER. "How was your day?"

"It was fine. We're reading Hamlet."

"Ah."

"Did you see the newspaper article in the *Bulletin*?"

"I did."

"Do you think it will help?"

"Time will tell."

Sarah fidgeted with the fabric of her dress. She generally

had a pencil at hand. He noticed that she tended to chew the tops of them, leaving bite marks on all her pencils.

"So… erm," she trailed off.

Riot squared his deck and tucked it away. "What's on your mind?"

"About that article…the one before, in the *Call*." Sarah blushed. "Is it true? About you and Miss Dupree?" She was so red that her freckles had faded.

He sighed. "Do you think it's true?"

"This isn't some… house of ill repute. And we're not mistreated at all. So, no. I don't. But… Atticus, she *is* pretty. Even Tobias makes moon eyes at her during class and he thinks girls are gross."

"Miss Dupree is very handsome," he agreed, "And she has accompanied me to the theater on a number of occasions. I was trying to present a certain image while investigating Alex Kingston."

"Oh, so it is true. You kissed her, then?"

"A gentleman doesn't discuss such things, especially with young ladies."

"You'd best not tell Isobel."

The edge of his lip quirked. "Bel knows all my secrets."

"And Isobel didn't kick her out?"

"What does that tell you?"

Sarah thought a moment. Then brightened. "So you didn't kiss Miss Dupree."

He spread his hands. "There you have it."

Sarah narrowed her eyes, but didn't push the subject. "Me and Tobias are trying to figure out who wrote that article."

"Does it matter?"

"Of course it does! We can't have a gossiper in our home. What if I kiss someone and it ends up all over the newspapers?"

"Like Mr. Cameron Fry?"

Sarah flushed, not in embarrassment but anger. "I'm going to brain that boy."

He was glad to hear that. Although on second thought… Isobel had threatened him often enough.

"Who do you think wrote it?" she asked.

Thoroughly disconcerted, Riot answered with a distracted air. "Lotario believes Mr. Hughes is our culprit." Surely Sarah wasn't interested in young men yet? She was only twelve, nearly thirteen, he corrected.

The edges of Sarah's lips twitched in triumph, but fortunately Riot didn't notice. He was busy staring into the cold hearth with concern.

"Mr. Hughes?" she asked. "Why would Mr. Lotario think that?"

Riot started. "I beg your pardon?"

She repeated the question.

"I don't know, Sarah. I haven't even met all the lodgers under our roof."

Sarah proceeded to list them, including the rooms they occupied, and their occupations or lack thereof. At least, he thought, she was occupying herself with a puzzle instead of boys.

ISOBEL ITCHED TO DO SOMETHING. TO BE OUT KNOCKING ON doors, demanding to search every lodging house, brothel, hotel in the city. But that would be futile.

In a city of strangers, how did one go about finding a girl who for all intents and purposes, doesn't want to be found? Isobel couldn't even find her own daughter. Jin wasn't in her room. Again. And Grimm was nowhere to be found. She could only hope they were together.

As she carried a tray upstairs, her mind returned to a plaguing question: Why?

Isobel refused to believe that some random person had snatched Ella between the cable car and the Western Union. That meant this John Bennett was involved, but why post a wanted ad in a newspaper? Why didn't Ella meet him inside the Popular? She had dined with him before. If she had been in danger, why hadn't she told her brother on the telephone?

Isobel returned to their rooms to find Sarah and Riot discussing Hamlet.

"But he *did* love her. He had to act crazy," she was saying.

"And ruined his life and hers in the process," Riot said.

"But it's *tragically* romantic. She loved him so much it drove her mad." The girl made a sound that seemed to come straight from her heart. "What do you think, Isobel?" Sarah was looking for a tie-breaker.

"Don't drag me into the middle of this."

"You *always* have an opinion," Sarah said.

Riot laughed. "She has you pegged, Bel."

"Shouldn't every woman have an opinion?" she countered.

Sarah nodded in agreement.

Isobel set the tray down on a table in front of the fire and handed Riot his tea. Personally, she thought Ophelia an imbecile and Hamlet an emotional wreck. There were far better ways to simply kill a man. But as she served Riot his dinner, she pondered the girl sitting on the ottoman.

"Is tragedy romantic?" Isobel asked.

Sarah thought about it. "Not in actual life. No. But in fiction… it's thrilling. At least I think so, like *Jane Eyre* and *Wuthering Heights*."

"You're entitled to your opinion, Sarah. But so am I," Riot said, plucking up his fork. "I maintain that Hamlet was a cad."

Sarah rolled her eyes. "Gentlemen just don't understand

romance," she said with all the confidence of a world-wise twelve-year-old.

She bade them goodnight, hugged them both, then paused at the door. "Was Jin in her room?" Sarah asked.

Isobel shook her head. "No."

Sarah frowned. "Something's not right with her. More than usual."

With that, she left.

Isobel got a fire going in the hearth, then tucked her legs on the big chair and rested her chin on her hand. Why shouldn't Jin be drawn to Chinatown? It had been her home. The place she was raised, a place to belong, where she wouldn't be turned away because of the color of her skin.

They sat in silence. Riot delicately slicing meat off his chicken thigh. How he managed to eat roasted chicken off the bone with knife and fork, she couldn't fathom, but he was meticulous about it.

Isobel stared at the flames in thought. She was thinking of Jin, of Sarah's last words, and the romantic notions of young women.

"Do you think girls consider notes and secret correspondence romantic?" she asked suddenly.

Riot stopped chewing, and stared at her. He swallowed down his food, and took a sip of tea before answering. "Being neither young nor female, I'd think you'd be better suited to answer that."

Isobel gave him a look.

Riot wiped his hands on a napkin, and sat back. His deck appeared in hand, and he plucked a card from it. "Say whatever you like, but you're my queen, Bel." He turned the card her way: the Queen of Hearts.

"I didn't say anything."

The quirk of his lip said otherwise.

"I *am* a woman, and young," she admitted. "*But* I'm an unconventional one."

The card disappeared into his deck.

"Are you sure you don't do any magic tricks?" she asked.

Riot ignored her question. "Would you find a cipher from me romantic?"

"I'd find it intriguing. But only if it was interesting."

"I'm always interesting," he said.

"Let's assume Estelle was telling the absolute truth, and she's not prone to fanciful stories."

"Did she strike you as such?"

"Absolutely," she said. "Ella meets this Bennett around town. Maybe while she's watching Ruby, or at the theater. Perhaps he approached her after amateur night."

"Wearing a clerical collar," Riot added. "That's a sure way to win a woman's trust."

"Irene Adler wasn't fooled," Isobel said dryly. "And a clerical collar is hardly romantic."

Riot pointed a card at her. A jester. "See, you do have a mind of a normal young woman."

"Who married a gunfighter." It was meant lightly, but it conjured images of three dead men at Riot's feet and a splatter of brains from Tim's rifle.

Shaken, she pushed herself out of the chair towards the window. More to give herself some time to drive the casual spilling of blood from her mind. She thought of the man she'd killed that night, and of Curtis, whom she'd indirectly killed last year. How many lives had Riot taken in his lifetime? Did he ever think of those men?

Isobel unlatched the window and threw it open. Cool air soothed her. She sat on the parapet bench and drew her legs up. It was useless theorizing. Everything came back to one simple fact: they needed to find either Ella or Bennett. Or Madge Ryan.

"It worries me that she didn't meet Bennett in the restaurant," Riot said.

"Me, too. If the advert was a coded message, why did Ella leave him waiting? Unless the entire restaurant staff is lying."

"Or simply mistaken. The Popular *is* busy."

"The same could be said of the Western Union office. But that, at least, fits. Ella had to have made the telephone call from somewhere, and I confirmed that a call was placed between that office and the Spencer's home, then another to Menke's Grocery."

A whisper of shuffling cards filled the ensuing silence.

Finally, she growled. "There's a string of possibilities and no substance."

The cards stopped. "There is one fact. Ella is missing."

"And it's very likely that she doesn't want to be found."

"We don't know that."

"No, you're right. I keep putting myself in her shoes."

"Running off with an older man?"

Isobel glanced at him across the room. "Look how that turned out for me."

"Saddled with two children and a demanding lover."

"I thought I was the demanding one," Isobel said.

"We're of like mind."

"In that, at least."

Riot gave her a look, and turned back to the case. "Some cases don't leave trails, Bel. Sometimes it takes months of leg work, the public's help, or a chance encounter. Tim's eyes and ears around the city and beyond have been alerted. They'll eventually turn up something."

Something he said pricked her mind. A thought, just out of reach. "What did you say?"

"It may take time."

Isobel gave an impatient gesture. "No, word for word. What did you say?"

Riot tucked his deck away, and repeated himself, sounding both amused and expectant. It was the word 'trail' that had snagged her mind. She latched on it. Ella *had* left a trail.

"I'm daft. It's so obvious." Isobel burst to her feet to redress. "But of course, you weren't there…The waitress in the Popular said Bennett always had a book with him. Ella's mother said she was a great reader, but there weren't any books in her room. And today at the church, the pastor said Ella attended the literary meetings and always had a new book to recommend."

"The library."

"And there's only two free libraries in the city."

Riot checked his watch. "Which are closed."

"So?" Tobias White asked when Sarah returned. "What was your big plan?"

Sarah kept walking down the stairs. The boy followed on her heels, sliding down each stair instead of stepping. The result was a dull '*bump, bump, bump*' behind her.

"I tricked Atticus into telling me what Mr. Lotario said."

"That's cheating!" Tobias hissed.

Sarah stopped, and shushed the boy. She glanced over the railing to see if anyone was snooping downstairs. But then there were doors and ears everywhere here. "It's not cheating. We're investigating. It was the quickest way to get information. You're just upset you didn't think of it."

Tobias rolled his eyes. "I'm not a girl. I can't just flutter my eyelashes and get my way."

Sarah tilted her head. "I did *not* do that."

Tobias fluttered his eyelashes in mimicry.

Sarah stuck out her tongue, and kept walking.

"Why did Mr. Lotario think it was—"

Sarah hushed him before he could blurt out the man's name.

"*Him?*"

"I don't know."

"Mr. Lotario could be wrong, you know."

Sarah considered that. "It's a place to start."

"But why would it be *him*? That don't make no sense."

"*It doesn't make any sense*," Sarah corrected. With Maddie gone, there was no one to correct Tobias's grammar and it fell to her. When she remembered. "And I don't know. Maybe he needed the money."

Sarah passed the second floor landing.

"Aren't we going to watch *him*?" Tobias asked.

"I want to talk to Grimm."

"Good luck with that," Tobias snorted. "I'm going to spy on Mr… you know who."

Tobias left, and Sarah went off to search for Grimm, but he was still gone.

SARAH STARTED AWAKE, AND SHIVERED. SHE HAD LEFT THE window in her room open, and was sitting on the floor under it, waiting. She heard a familiar scuffing, and got up, or tried to. Her legs were asleep, and pins and needles sent her back down to the carpet. She yanked herself up by the sill and stretched her leg to the side, trying to work out the kinks as she looked out into the fog.

Jin's rope ladder went right up past her window. It was stretched sideways, around the corner towards the turret room where Atticus and Isobel stayed.

Sarah listened to the low murmur of voices.

"… at least stop going at night," it was Isobel's voice.

"I can go where I like," Jin shot back defiantly.

"True, you can," Atticus said. "But we're asking you not to. You know as well as anyone how dangerous those alleys are." He sounded exhausted.

"I know what to watch for."

"Jin," Isobel said. Sarah could hear the restraint in her voice. "Please. For us. Don't go there at night. Last time we went in there to search for you, Riot got pummeled close to death and tossed off a fire escape."

Silence.

"Then do not look for me," Jin finally growled.

"If you're bent on visiting the Quarter, at least tell us where you're headed and when to expect you back." Atticus's voice was deep and low, and Sarah had to strain her ears to hear this last bit. She should have felt ashamed for eavesdropping, but she didn't even feel a twinge.

"I will come back before dark," Jin finally agreed.

"We were about to turn the Quarter upside down tonight, Jin. If you're even ten minutes late, we will," Isobel said.

"Do not come looking for me!" The force of the words jerked Sarah backwards, even from around the corner and in a window.

"Why not?" Atticus asked softly.

Sarah held her breath, listening.

It was a long minute. Sarah imagined Atticus waiting patiently, holding Jin's eyes in that way he did while Isobel bit back the urge to demand answers. Atticus won out.

"There is a *chun hung* with your names on it."

"Isobel, too?" Atticus asked, surprised.

"For cutting off Big Queue's queue."

Isobel snorted. Clearly amused. But Sarah was not. Her stomach clenched with fear.

"Jin, I've had a *chun hung* on my head for quite some time," Riot said.

"Someone tried to kill you the other night," Jin said firmly.

"It wasn't the criminal tongs," he said.

"How do you know?"

"I know," he said. "We're not in much danger unless we go into the Quarter, but you are. You're our adopted daughter now."

"I will be careful."

"Why are you going there?" Isobel demanded. Her patience had run out.

"Why can I not go?" Jin returned. "It is the only place I can go to a theater and sit where I want. It is the only place I can walk into a shop and not be chased away."

Was it Sarah's imagination, or did she hear a deep breath? Atticus likely put up a calming hand.

"You have every right to visit. You're not a prisoner, Jin. But we do have rules. Don't go into the Quarter at night. Is that clear?"

"Yes," she bit out.

Scuffing, and then a shadow appeared around the corner. Sarah ducked back inside the window and pressed herself against the wall as Jin passed by to climb up to her attic room.

Sarah stood for a few minutes, considering. She was the last person on earth Jin would confide in. And if she wasn't confiding in Atticus and Isobel, then that meant trouble.

Finally, Sarah laced up her shoes, and shrugged on a coat.

Sarah found Grimm in the stables. He was sitting in the dark beside Sugar's stall. The horse was snuffling his ear. His eyes were hidden by his cap and his shoulders were hunched. He rested his elbows on his knees, hands hanging limply.

Sarah rushed forward. "Are you all right?"

Grimm looked up quickly, causing Sugar to start. He tensed, on the verge of running, but when his eyes focused on her, he relaxed.

Grimm started to stand.

"You don't have to get up for me," Sarah said.

But Grimm stood anyway. He removed his hat and held it in his hands. His left eye was swollen shut, and his face puffy with bruises.

Grimm turned to a lantern. While he lit it, Sarah stepped forward to scratch Sugar's nose. Sugar nuzzled her neck, knocking her a step to the side.

Grimm came closer, and Sugar sniffed at his coat, nibbling on a button, until he rested a calming hand on her forehead.

"You've been following Jin into Chinatown, haven't you?" Sarah asked.

Grimm didn't seem surprised that she had pieced it together. He nodded.

Sarah turned to look up at him. Lantern light played over his black skin. It glowed with a kind of luster, tracing his features. Noble forehead, broad nose, and defined cheekbones, he was tall and his shoulders slim. His eyes were disarming— close to amber in color. He was the strangest, most beautiful boy she had ever seen. There was something angelic about his appearance. But his usually calm eyes, currently just one, was full of sadness.

"What's she doing there?" Sarah asked.

Grimm shrugged.

"Did she punch you?" She pointed to his eye.

Grimm shook his head.

"Someone else did?"

He nodded.

"Why are you following her?"

Grimm started to reach for the notepad he kept in his inner pocket, but stopped. "She's in danger," he whispered, his voice a rasp.

Sarah stood stunned for a full minute. Her mind worked, and her mouth fell open. Grimm had spoken.

"You can talk!" Her squeak startled Sugar. The horse jerked backward with a snort.

Grimm sighed, shoulders slumping.

"I won't tell anyone," she said.

He shrugged.

"What happened? Who's after her?"

"Herself."

Sarah frowned. Well Grimm could talk, but he sure wasn't making much sense. She looked out of the stable and up to the attic window across the courtyard. "What should we do?"

Grimm shook his head. He didn't know what do to.

Sarah wanted to go straight to Atticus and Isobel and tell them, but the conversation she had overheard was fresh in her mind. It was dangerous for them to venture into the Quarter. Besides, they knew Jin was going there, and, short of locking her up, they couldn't stop her. What was Jin after?

It didn't matter.

"Grimm," Sarah said. He looked at her expectantly. "I have an idea. I… I know someone who might be able to help."

He looked at her in question.

"I can't tell you," she admitted. "But it's kind of you to watch out for her. Give me a day to contact my friend. He'll know what to do."

With a smile, Sarah left the beautiful boy to tie a black ribbon around a laundry sack that was waiting for the morning's pick up.

WHEN IN DOUBT

Thursday, October 11, 1900

ISOBEL STOPPED AT THE THRESHOLD TO THE LIBRARY, AND inhaled. It was so sudden that Riot nearly ran into her in the act of removing his hat. He took the opportunity to study her. He couldn't help it. He was finding it difficult to keep his mind on task when she was about.

And it wasn't just that he was a smitten new husband. Other men noticed too. Wisps of blondish hair escaped from her felt hat. No flowers, no decorations, only a simple band, but there was something about how she wore it—a flash of eyes from under the brim, a tilt of the head.

She tugged off her leather gloves, and surveyed the shelves like a queen surveying a newly conquered kingdom. She wore a simple blouse and tie and her customary split riding skirt with a neat jacket, and a stylish overcoat that came to her thighs. Although bespoke and nicely tailored, it wasn't the clothes that lent her a queenly air. It was her presence, Riot decided. A combination of confidence, curiosity, and arrogance. He tore his eyes from her and searched the room for any threats. Not many in a library, but still, old habits kept him alive. And they would keep Isobel alive too, if he could only stop staring at her.

Tables, chairs, and books. People sat reading in quiet. Every sneeze and sniffle amplified.

Riot held a swinging gate open for Isobel, and she gave him a small smile. He had worried over the events in the Morgue— that he had shattered her trust, that she would put up her armor and refuse to be catered to. But she had grown during the past year, in confidence and wisdom, and the danger of the situation had not been lost on her. At least he hoped. Isobel did like her prey relaxed before she pounced.

Isobel set her sights on a rosy-cheeked woman sitting at the librarian's desk. Riot took her hint, and made for the counter, where a sharp-nosed man opened one book after another, stamping each one, making notations on three different index cards, then setting the book aside. The stack of books nearly dwarfed him.

"Good day," Riot said.

"Sir, how may I assist you?" Splendid. British. By the book, no doubt. Riot didn't waste time with a story.

"I'm with Ravenwood Detective Agency." Riot slid his card across the counter. "Does a man by the name of John Bennett frequent your library?"

The man looked pointedly at the books. "Unless 'John Bennett' is the title to a book, I can't help you."

"This particular person may be a danger to your young female readers."

The man stared at him. "That's not my concern." He stamped another book.

"Do you know a girl named Elouise, or Ella Spencer?"

"If I did, I wouldn't tell you. *You* may very well be a danger to our young female readers." The man gave a pointed look at Isobel's back. "Don't think I didn't notice you admiring that young woman."

Clearing his throat, Riot adjusted his spectacles. "Do you keep records on people who check out books?"

"We do."

Riot looked to the wall of index card file drawers. "I'd appreciate it if you checked to see if there's any books entitled John Bennett." Riot slid a silver dollar across the counter.

The man slid it back. "No."

Riot snatched back his coin, and started towards the shelves.

"You'll need to fill out a form to check a book out."

Riot stopped, and turned as Mr. Stuffy pushed an index card at him.

⸻

Isobel had taken one look at the stiff-collared man at the counter, and left him to Riot. Who knew, maybe the man liked men. She smiled at the rosy-cheeked librarian who smiled back, and took a seat. "I'm Miss Amsel, pleased to meet you, Miss…" She said breezily, extending a hand.

"Jennings."

Isobel clutched the woman's hand. "I'm in *dire* need of a professional woman such as yourself. My friends recommended a book, and I can't for the world think of its name. Do you know Ella? Ella Spencer? Well, Elouise really, but she prefers it shortened."

"I do know Ella. Are you with her literary group at the church?"

"Why no, I know her through a friend. Madge Ryan."

The woman nodded. "Of course. I often see the pair of them here. What was the book about? Do you remember?"

Isobel made a pretense of thought. "It had a cat in it. And a pirate."

The librarian tapped her finger on the table. "A cat you say? *And* a pirate?"

Isobel was fairly sure there were no literary works of pirates with cats, but one couldn't be too sure, so she tossed in another twist. "I think she said it was a romantic story. Like Elizabeth Bennett and Mr. Darcy. Say, do you know her friend Mr. Bennett, too?"

The woman stared, trying to drag her mind out of books and onto the vibrant young woman hopping from one subject to the next in front of her.

"Mr. Bennett?"

"Well, I was thinking of Mr. Darcy and Miss Bennett from *Pride and Prejudice*. Do you know it?"

"I do."

"Doesn't everyone?" She cast her eyes towards Riot. "That fellow over there strikes me as a Mr. Darcy, don't you think?"

The woman blinked at Riot, and then color rose to her cheeks. "Well, I suppose he does. Severe, isn't he?"

"A touch. Now I don't think Mr. *John* Bennett was severe. Dark hair for sure, but Ella thinks him fun despite that scar on his eye."

The woman adjusted her pince-nez. "Do you mean Mr. *Hawkins*?"

"Does he have black hair and a scar near his eye? A mustache too?

"Yes."

"Well, that must be him. Silly me. I get names mixed up all the time."

"I understand. Easy enough to do," the librarian soothed.

"What was his first name?" Isobel asked.

"I can't recall. I only know because he checks out books here and I see him often enough."

"Drat," Isobel knocked softly on the desk. "This will keep me up at night now."

"Now that you mention it..." Miss Jennings placed her hands on the desk, and stood. "Come with me. I have an idea. We can see what book your friend checked out, and we'll find Mr. Hawkins' name, too."

———

RIOT WATCHED AS THE TWO WOMEN CAME OVER. ISOBEL WAS rambling on like a mindless young woman. It was startling to watch her don that mask. And where did she dredge up that giggle? He rarely thought about the twenty year gap in their ages, but just now it was hard to ignore.

The act seemed to be working. Whatever Isobel had managed, she wouldn't get far with Mr. Stuffy standing behind the counter.

"Williams, do you know Mr. Hawkins's first name?" the cheery woman asked as she joined him behind the counter.

Williams raised his eyes to the ceiling, and stamped another book. "I do not, Miss Jennings."

Miss Jennings huffed, and opened the drawers. She rifled through, muttering the alphabet under her breath, then pulled out two cards and placed them directly in front of Isobel.

Isobel leaned in with interest. Riot itched to do the same, instead, he continued filling out the required form to enter the library. "Mr. Williams, what do I put here?" he asked.

The man tore his eyes from the index cards. "Your address, sir."

"Carl *Bennett* Hawkins!" Isobel exclaimed. "Oh, yes, of course. See, I knew there was a Bennett somewhere in there. Funny how the mind plays tricks, isn't it?"

"Indeed."

"The Golden West Hotel. Well, why would he be there? I took him for a resident."

"Some men live in lodging houses, Miss."

"I suppose. Do you have a bit of paper and pencil? I'd like to write down these books. Ella and I always discuss everything we read. Don't you think it adds to the experience? Discussing with a group?"

"Of course. You know the library has a literary group too."

"Does it? What times?"

"Let me get a flyer."

"Before you do, can I look at Madge's book list?"

"Why, of course."

Miss Jennings rifled through the index cards again.

Noting that Mr. Williams was taking an interest, Riot leaned over the counter and plucked up his stamp. "What sort of device is this?"

Williams nearly had a heart attack. He snatched at his stamp like Watson after shrimp.

Isobel quickly wrote down the desired information. "I don't think any of these have a cat in them, do you?"

Miss Jennings leaned close. "Maybe you're mixing it up. *The Moonstone* here has a Doctor Candy. Or a Sergeant. Cuff. And there are pirates of a sort."

"You're a lifesaver, Miss Jennings. I'll just go get that book."

Isobel grasped the hands of Miss Jennings, then went off to search the stacks.

"It's so nice to meet enthusiastic readers," Miss Jennings said as she tucked the index cards back in place. She shot Mr. Williams a glare. "Some people have no appreciation for books."

Riot found Isobel at an empty table with a stack of books. She was flipping through the pages, searching each one.

"Look here, Riot," she said as he took a seat. "On the inside of each book is an index card with all the dates it was checked out, returned, and the names of the borrowers. C.B. Hawkins checked this one out, then E. Spencer. And Hawkins again."

"Do you think they met at this library?"

"Perhaps. But look here as well. Madge and Hawkins were doing the same for a full three months before it started with Ella."

Riot glanced at the address of the Globe West Hotel. "If Ella and Hawkins were meeting here, then why did they resort to a wanted ad in a newspaper?"

Isobel thumped the last book closed. "Someone noticed they were spending time together? Maybe they were passing notes back and forth in the books… In any event, her mother really had no idea what her daughter was up to—these are *not* classics."

Riot surveyed the titles. They were all of a romantic sort. Some tragic, some lighthearted. "Let's try this Globe West Hotel."

THE HERBALIST

WHY? THAT QUESTION PLAGUED SAO JIN. WHY DID MEN butcher her mother and father? For years, she'd lived in a fog. Mei had coaxed her into the light, and then memories began to assault her. She could not forget.

Jin wished her mind were still enveloped by that fog. Though these past few months had been the most peaceful in a very long time. Jin had not had to worry about food, shelter, or when her next beating would come, but it had also left her mind idle. And now a single question thudded to the forefront.

Why?

Jin stood across the street from a herbalist shop. Memories came in snatches. Her nostrils flared as she fought to control her breath. She would not run this time—no matter how bad her heart clawed at her throat.

The past came alive in her mind's eye and she seemed to watch from far above, like a bird, detached, as three men from the past walked down the sidewalk. A small child played with a wooden duck in front of the tailor's shop. The leader smiled at her. The second ruffled her hair as he walked past, and she smiled brightly at the third. So trusting.

The trio walked into the shop—her bahba and mahma's—and she followed, eager to meet them.

But her father's face had fallen. Words were spoken. Words that escaped Jin now. She remembered the moment the strangers pulled cleavers from their coats. Her mother screamed as her father threw himself in front of her and attacked the men with scissors.

The blades cut. Blood splattered fabric. A hand flew through the air. An ear. It was brutal. Efficient. And Jin still heard her mother's screams, night after night.

Blood had run rivers around Jin's feet as she stood, clutching her wooden duck, and watching the slaughter.

The first man turned to her, and grabbed her chin, lifting her toes off the bloody ground. Transfixed by a pencil thin mustache on his upper lip, she didn't move. He raised a knife and the blade dug into her cheek, carving a path from nose to chin. She didn't make a sound.

But the second man, who had ruffled her hair, grabbed his leader's arm. Quick words were exchanged. She strained to remember them, but could not. Whatever the man had said, it worked. Mustache man dropped her, and the trio walked out, laughing.

Her parents butchered, her childhood stolen.

Jin touched one of the scars on her cheeks. The deepest, the most painful, the one that marked her a coward. She hadn't even kicked the man.

Jin took a deep breath, and marched across the street. Before she could stop herself she shoved open the door. A bell chimed, and she walked to the center of the store. She was barely higher than the counter. The walls rose up around her, shelves of jars filled with twisted roots and animal parts, and labeled boxes. The shop smelled like the earth.

Jin stared at the worn floorboards, now scrubbed clean of blood. Had the wood forgotten its touch?

A voice brought her back, a kindly one that sounded vaguely familiar. Jin focused on the speaker, and stepped back in surprise. A woman with a face like a prune and missing teeth stood in front of her. The old woman asked another question.

Jin did not understand the words.

"She wants to know what ails you," another voice said in Cantonese.

Jin looked up sharply. She didn't like being surprised. But here she was, wandering into an unknown store like a simpleton.

A man behind the counter leaned forward, looking amused. He had short hair, a scruffy goatee, and he wore a dark blue changshan.

The old woman shuffled closer, and Jin took a hasty step backwards.

"She won't hurt you," the man said.

Jin was not good with ages. Everyone looked old to her. But she thought the man behind the counter was younger than Atticus and older than Isobel, which left a wide gap between.

The woman spoke again, and the man translated. "My honored mother says you are a ghost. I think she means you look about to keel over. Normally, I wouldn't agree with her, but in this case I have to." He smiled down at her, and a wave of nausea hit Jin full force.

She tensed to run, but swallowed down the urge. How would she get answers unless she persisted?

"I am not ill," Jin said.

The old woman reached for Jin's hand, but Jin pulled back again.

"She won't eat you, kid. She only wants to take your pulse and see your tongue."

Jin glared at the man, but let the woman take her wrist. Her touch was light and sensitive, her skin thin. The woman closed her eyes, and placed two fingers on the inside of Jin's wrist. She seemed to hum softly as she did so. She opened her eyes, and stuck her tongue out, indicating Jin should do the same.

Jin returned the favor, the woman studied it, and then said something. "You have too much heat in your heart," the man translated.

The old woman shuffled towards a drawer, and took out a pair of scales.

"I am not sick," Jin protested. But the woman kept weighing and grinding dried plants into a bowl.

"That won't stop my mother."

The mother spoke again to her son.

"She says you have a conflicted heart. You are unbalanced."

Jin eyed the woman warily. She couldn't argue with that. "I did not think women were doctors." Especially not Chinese women. Mei had wanted to be a physician. She had seen so much suffering among women. But women helped the family business, they did not strike off on their own. And now Mei was likely in China, or close to it. Back with her family and already married to a stranger as a second or third wife.

The man chuckled. "Funny, coming from a girl dressed as a boy."

Jin narrowed her eyes at the man. "How did you know?"

The man nodded to his mother. "Not much escapes my mother. She comes from generations of physicians; she even taught her husband the trade. She's not as limited with who she can treat in America as she was in China. Some people aren't as concerned with tradition here. I'm Lo Ka Ho and my honored mother is Lo Tan Ling. I prefer Sammy Lo."

"Why don't you have a queue?"

"Most polite young girls give a name in return," Sammy said.

"I am not polite."

"I can see that. I'll answer your question anyway." He smoothed the sides of his black hair. "I was born here. I'm American. And my short hair drives my mother crazy."

The edge of Jin's lip twitched upwards. There was something familiar about this man. His eyes, she thought, but she could not place the memory.

Tan Ling returned with a small package and pressed it into Jin's hands.

Jin started to argue, but decided that it would be rude, so she bowed deeply in gratitude.

"Steep it in tea twice a day. It will restore your *Qi* and calm your heart," Sammy said.

"My what?" Jin asked.

Sammy gave her a puzzled look. "Are you sure you're Chinese?"

Jin glared at the man. "I am like you."

"Only more decorative." He traced a line across his cheek.

Jin hissed. Tan Ling placed a soothing hand on her shoulder and patted it, all the while casting dark looks at her wayward son.

"You have no sense of humor," Sammy said.

"Easy for you to say."

Sammy came from behind the counter. He relied almost entirely on a cane, and had a pronounced limp that threatened to topple him with each step. His legs were misshapen, and his left foot was mangled so badly that he walked on the side of it. The foot was in a slipper rather than a shoe, too twisted to conform to anything more. "It is actually easy for me to say. Do you think it would distract people from my legs if I added a scar or two to my cheek?"

Jin felt her anger ebb. "No. People always see the flaw."

"Wise words for one so young."

His mother spoke. Jin assumed it was about money. She fished in her pocket and brought out a silver dollar, but the old woman shook her head.

Their kindness rankled her.

"It's a gift," Sammy explained. "She lost a daughter."

Jin hesitated, searching Tan Ling's face for any recognition. But no, this was not her mother. What a stupid thought. Her mother was dead. But Jin had not seen her parents' bodies. Not afterwards. She had just stood there. Frozen. And had a vague memory of a woman picking her up and carrying her away.

Could her mother have survived the attack? There had been so much blood. A river of it.

Tan Ling took Jin's hand between her own and began warming it.

"There's your ghost act again," Sammy said, leaning against the counter, a casual motion that took the weight off his bad foot.

If only this were the woman who had plucked Jin from the carnage, how different her life would have been.

Jin slipped her hand free. She didn't need to be coddled. Determined, she put to words her worst day. "My mother and father used to have a shop here."

"Did they?" Sammy asked. "We've been here about two years." He translated for his mother.

Jin's heart fell. "Who did you buy it from?"

A shadow passed over Tan Ling's eyes.

Jin seized on that look. "Did you know my parents?" she demanded.

The woman shook her head. "I heard the story. This shop was abandoned when we came. Before us it was a curio shop that catered to tourists." Sammy translated.

From tailor to curio shop to herbalist. "Do you know why my parents were killed?" Jin asked.

Tan Ling shook her head.

"Who killed them?"

Again, a shake.

Jin growled with frustration. "Where did the curio shop owners go?"

"Back to the mainland," Sammy said. "Look, the high-binders don't need a reason to kill. They come and collect protection money from everyone. The only reason we're still here is because my mother patches them up when they come."

"She shouldn't," Jin said.

Tan Ling gave a sad smile.

"A hatchet man killed her daughter. She heals them anyway," Sammy explained.

"Why?" Jin demanded.

The old woman spoke softly, placing a hand over her heart. "Because the highbinders have mothers, too," Sammy translated.

Jin thought the reasoning was foolish, and yet... She had helped Mei's brother, Wong Kau. He was a hatchet man and he had shot Atticus Riot in the head. She wanted life to be black and white. Right and wrong. But it was so muddled it made her sick. She hastily bowed, and fled the herbalist.

"Wait!" Sammy called.

Jin stopped and waited, as Sammy limped painfully to the doorway. He leaned against it heavily, and she walked back, not wanting him to fall down.

He glanced down the street, both ways, and eyed the few men standing across the way. How many times had Sammy been beaten and mocked for his lame foot?

"My mother asks that you visit us again."

"Maybe."

"She could teach you a lot about herbs."

Jin hesitated. She rarely passed up a chance to learn some-thing new. "I have things to do," she said.

Sammy stooped down, so his voice wouldn't carry. "You

need to leave this alone—this business about your parents. I'm sorry, but highbinders don't like people asking questions."

Jin looked him straight in the eye. "I will not be silent." She turned on her heel and left.

A DARK PATH

The Globe West Hotel wasn't a dump, but it wasn't the Palace either. A modest three-story hotel off Market with a red canopy and a doorman in uniform. Riot felt he was putting a shape to this Carl Bennett Hawkins, if that was his real name. A man who liked resorts and music halls, and fought his advancing age by setting his sights on young, vulnerable girls.

Riot had met men like that before. He had no use for them.

Riot nodded to the doorman, and stood aside to let Isobel enter first. But once inside, she dropped back. It was these subtle cues that made a partnership. They were both trying to see where they fit with each other during an investigation.

"We're here to see Carl Hawkins," Riot said without preamble.

The man at the desk consulted his logbook.

The hotel was older, but clean. Worn brass rails, and an adjoining parlor that looked like it had been a saloon in a previous life. It was the sort of place a businessman would stay, or a salesman new to the city.

"I'm sorry, sir. Mr. Hawkins checked out a week ago."

"A week? Did he leave a forwarding address? It's important I reach him."

The clerk glanced at Isobel. "I'm afraid not."

Isobel beamed, and slipped an arm through Riot's. "That's splendid, my dear. You won't be able to return the money you owe him. You can take me to the Palace now."

They turned to leave.

"Wait, sir. I may have it here."

———

2211 SUTTER STREET WAS A SINGLE STICK HOME THAT LOOKED nearly identical to the one Ella's family lived in. The homes were narrow, but stretched back like horse stalls, and the basement door could be reached by a stairwell below street level.

Riot knocked on the front door with his gentlemen's stick, and Isobel leaned over the railing to look in the front window. The curtains were drawn.

It was a sleepy street. A lone cat watched them, swishing its tail on a neighbor's step. Riot knocked again, louder.

Impatient, Isobel slipped down a narrow lane. The pathway to the back of the house was oppressive, her shoulders brushing the sides of two homes. Though dark and moldy, the pathway was at least free of rubbish.

A rickety staircase hugged the back of the house. It went as far as the second story. A patch of a dirt yard extended to a high fence that was propped up by beams to keep it from falling over. The yard was only four feet deep.

Isobel looked through a grimy window. The back room was empty. She tried the window, and was rewarded when it slid up. She leaned in and stretched to reach a key on the mudroom sink... Her fingers brushed it and it fell to the floor. Cursing her height, she pushed the window all the way up and just slithered through the opening to thud onto a dusty floor.

A gloved hand swam into her vision. She jerked back, heart in her throat, then looked up to find the eyes of her husband.

"Goddamn it, Riot," she whispered taking his hand. "How on earth are you so quiet?"

He pulled her up. "A convenient bang covered the click of my lock picks. I prefer doors. They're easier on my suits." He inclined his head to the back door, and tried the knob. It opened without the key.

She frowned, brushing the dust from her clothes.

Save for a basin, and that blasted key, the mudroom was empty. She put the key back on the lip of the sink, and moved into the kitchen, which was also empty. There wasn't even a chair.

Wood creaked under her feet. The house had a musty, stale smell and it was as cold as the street in shadow. Isobel creaked towards the front parlor, and Riot went to try the gas. Light seeped through the curtains, enough to see that the parlor was empty, too. Swept clean. But not quite. Business cards and adverts were laid out on the mantel: real estate agents, movers, furniture stores, and dry goods.

The flair of a match signaled Riot had got the gas lamp working. Light illuminated the shadows and a pile of similar adverts and business cards that had been pushed under the door. Along with letters.

Isobel bent to retrieve a letter. "It looks like we're too late," she said with a sigh. Either Mr. Hawkins never moved in or he had fled. The letter was addressed to Mrs. C.B. Hawkins. She held it up to the gas lamp, and squinted. It was a 'welcome to the neighborhood' letter.

"There are furniture marks over the wood here. And considering the dust…"

Isobel looked at the spot he was considering.

"Maybe two weeks old."

She'd take his word for it.

Riot looked over to the stairs. "I'll check the basement."

Isobel nodded. She didn't much care for cellars, not after being hog-tied and beaten in one. Riot knew this, of course.

She walked upstairs.

Room after room was hollow and empty, with the stale cold that marked an unused home. She itched to pull the curtains back, to let gray light filter in. By the time she reached the third floor, Isobel was pondering their next course of action. Discovering who owned the building seemed the next logical step. Had Hawkins rented it or had he bought it?

But her thoughts came to a standstill when she opened the last door in the very back of the narrow home. Shadows disturbed the emptiness. Isobel paused in the doorway. A shade had been drawn over the only window, but it didn't completely block the light. As her eyes adjusted, she saw the shapes for what they were, a bed and a chair.

There was something… wrong about the bed. Her mind took a moment to catch up with the uneasiness slithering down her spine. Isobel swallowed, wishing Riot would suddenly appear. She walked over to the window to give herself some time. It was closed tight. She lifted the shade, then the window, letting fresh air and light fill the room. Then she turned to the bed.

"Riot." She had meant to shout it. But it came out a harsh whisper. Isobel stepped up to the bed and stared down at a thin coverlet and the suggestive lump it was hiding underneath.

Steeling herself, she gently pulled the coverlet down, revealing a youthful face marred by mildew-like blotches. A line of crusted blood escaped from the girl's lips.

Isobel turned away. She focused on the chair, and the pile of clothes. On top was a familiar golf cap with a red fuzz ball.

They were too late.

Atticus Riot found Isobel in the topmost room, in the very back. She stood over a bed, hands curled into white-knuckled fists. He moved into the room, and touched her elbow, only sparing a cursory glance at what he knew she'd found. She looked at him, eyes misting, her lips a thin line of rage.

"What do you see, Bel?" he asked softly. Ravenwood had asked him that very thing as he'd stood over the mutilated remains of a girl some years before. Riot had thought him heartless. Now he understood. Focus on the details, and drag Justice kicking and screaming into the light.

To her credit, Isobel gave herself a shake. He saw a mask slip over her face, as she tucked feeling behind some inner wall. Her eyes glittered with steel.

She looked down at the girl. Ella stared back, sightless.

Riot carefully folded the coverlet back.

Ella Spencer was naked. She lay in a restful repose. A portion of the sheet, slightly stained with blood, was wrapped around her right hand. Her left hand rested on a blood-stained towel on her stomach. It was dried and crusted. Her legs were crossed at the ankles.

The room was cold. No insects buzzed around the corpse. She wasn't stiff, and bloat hadn't set in yet. Her skin was mottled and discolored. Riot bent to lift her left hand and check under the towel. He expected a wound, but her soft stomach was pale and unmarred.

He turned her slightly to the side. The skin along her back and buttocks was bluish-purple, blood pooling in the corpse from gravity.

"She wasn't moved," Isobel whispered.

"No." Ella had lain there for some time.

Riot uncrossed the corpse's legs.

"What are you looking for?" Isobel asked

Riot pulled back so she might look. "Blood, tears, trauma. Anything of the like."

"Signs of rape."

Riot nodded. "There's some blood, but nothing alarming. Definite signs of sexual activity, however."

Isobel averted her eyes, and turned to less intrusive areas. Though her voice wavered, she examined the girl with a detached air, checking the girl's upper half. "Minor tearing to her fingernails, some blood underneath, no apparent marks on her neck. But it's hard to tell with the skin discoloration."

Riot bent to pick up a flask. He put his nose to it. Brandy. Only a few drops remained. He took out a handkerchief and rubbed the white linen against the mouthpiece. It didn't leave a mark. He carefully set it back down, and looked under the bed. Swept clean.

Finding that Isobel had moved on to a pile of clothing, he repositioned the girl as they had found her and lifted the coverlet over her body.

"Cheaply made underwear, chemise, underskirt. Even her shoes have recently been half-soled," Isobel said. "But the black skirt and jacket are much better quality."

Riot crouched in front of a fireplace. There were ashes inside. He took out a knife and poked at them. A white handkerchief had been burned, but a fragment survived the fire. It had a simple border, no initials.

"There are cards in her purse, mostly blank," Isobel said.

Riot opened the closet door. It was empty, save for two unused candles. He turned to find Isobel standing still, holding a little leather purse in her hands. Dainty flowers decorated the outside.

"Was the window already open?" he asked.

The question shook her from her stupor. She shook her head.

"Put everything back the way you found it. We need to find a call box."

Slowly, Isobel set the purse down, and went to close the window. "I'll have to tell her mother," she said faintly. *That I failed.* She didn't say the words, but Riot knew she was thinking them.

DETECTIVE SERGEANT DILLION WAS A CLEAN-CUT MAN WHO looked promising, especially since he wasn't Inspector Geary. His collar was crisp, his attire neat, and his shoulders spoke of a detective who enjoyed physical exertion. He even shook Isobel's hand, and greeted Riot with respect. But all of Isobel's hopes were quickly dashed when they took him up to Ella Spencer's final resting place.

"Well, well, well," Dillion said. She and Riot stood against the wall, spectators to the detective's search. He had a patrolman with him, who leered down at the girl as Dillion removed the coverlet.

Isobel felt Riot stiffen next to her. She heard him take a breath, and could feel him forcibly relax.

Dillion flicked the coverlet back in place. "It's a shame, Daniels," he said. "Girls selling themselves, then ending it all."

"*What?*" Isobel blurted out.

Dillion gestured to the corpse. "It's clear as day, Mrs. Riot. To the well trained eye. I don't expect an amateur like yourself to pick up these kinds of details. Surely you'll agree, Mr. Riot. The girl killed herself."

The patrolman kicked the brandy flask on his way to rifle through the girl's underthings. Dillion plucked it from the floor, passing it under his nose with a flourish. "Laudanum-laced brandy. Perhaps it wasn't on purpose, but a miscalculation."

"Whores are always drinking that stuff," the patrolman

grumbled as he held up a pair of underwear, letting the rest of the clothing fall to the floor.

"When is the coroner expected?" Riot asked. His voice was flat. Calm. And he had his walking stick planted on the floor, hands folded over the silver knob.

"Soon, I suspect. The dead wagon may be a bit later coming."

Isobel bit back an urge to pummel the pair as she watched them blunder their way through Ella's personal belongings.

Clomping footsteps echoed downstairs, followed shortly by a man who looked like a penguin stuffed in a suit. Coroner Weston had hunched shoulders and an ample gut that stretched the confines of his waistcoat.

Weston glanced at Isobel and Riot, grunted, then conferred with Dillion, nodding the whole time, and finally turning to the flask. Next, Weston bent over the corpse, squinting at the blood crusting the corner of her mouth. With a huff of satisfaction, he took out his documents.

"We were notified, Mr. Riot, that your agency was looking for the girl. Good work," Dillion said.

"Have you decided on a cause of death, Coroner Weston?" Riot asked with a diplomat's restraint.

The man nodded, scribbling on his certificate. "I don't agree with Detective Sergeant Dillon's assessment, Mr. Riot." He finished the statement by signing the end with a flourish. "I believe she died of natural causes."

"You haven't even examined her!" Isobel growled.

Weston turned a bushy gray brow on her. "You, Miss, should not be here. This is no place for a woman."

Isobel clenched her jaw. With a look at Riot, she stalked down the stairs and out the door, bursting into fresh air. Her fists worked, her blood pumped, she wanted to thrash some-thing. *Anything*.

She stopped her furious pacing when she caught sight of a

corner store at the end of the block. In front of it were two pint-sized newsboys lounging against the brick, smoking. She hurried over to them.

"Say, you two."

"Whatcha want, Miss?" They eyed her with baby-faced glares.

She handed a quarter to each. "I need some runners. Spread the word as fast as you can to all the reporters you know. There's been a murder in that house there and the police detective is bungling it."

The boys looked at the coins in their hands, and darted off. Satisfied, Isobel stood and waited for the reporters who were sure to light a fire under the police.

A NOBLE HEART

"*Now cracks a noble heart. Good night, sweet prince. And flights of angels sing thee to thy rest.*" Miss Dupree fell silent, her clear voice hanging in the room. Her students sat, entranced. Grimm, Tobias, Sarah, and Jin. One chair was empty. Maddie was still gone.

"That is stupid," Jin declared. "I'm glad Hamlet died."

Miss Dupree raised an amused brow at the girl.

"Did people really talk like that?" Tobias asked. "I can't hardly make sense of any of it."

"To answer your question, Tobias: Yes and no. Shakespeare wrote plays for entertainment. Do we talk like the characters in Gilbert and Sullivan's plays?"

Everyone, including Grimm, shook their heads.

"It is possible to get an idea of how people spoke based on the plays. But I doubt it was so eloquent. Shakespeare's plays are famous. They're known for their drama, turn of phrase, and wit." Miss Dupree closed the book. "What did you think of Hamlet?"

"He talked too much," Tobias said. "Who says all that while they're dying?"

"Poor Ophelia," Sarah said.

"She was stupid, too," Jin stated. "Why fall in love with a man at all?"

"*Amor et melle et felle est fecundissimus*," Miss Dupree said. Beautiful and poised, and with a voice like honey, the governess turned prostitute turned school teacher never failed to catch a person's attention. Man, woman, or child. The children fell silent.

"Something about love," Sarah said. She had been diligent in her Latin terms.

Miss Dupree inclined her head. "*Love is rich with honey and venom.* Love is both an extraordinary agony and one of the most delightful states to dwell in."

"That is why I will not fall in love," Jin said.

"You can't choose who you fall in love with," Sarah said with a sigh.

"Hamlet treated Ophelia like trash. She was stupid to fall in love with him," Jin insisted.

"Hamlet had to pretend to be mad or he'd be killed too," Sarah said.

"He should have killed Claudius straight away," Jin said.

"Did he have the right to?" Miss Dupree said.

"Claudius killed his father," Jin said immediately.

"And did his eventual revenge fix anything?" Miss Dupree asked.

The children went silent with thought.

"It made it worse," Tobias said.

"Someone had to do it. Otherwise Claudius would have escaped justice," Jin said.

"But he wanted revenge more than love," Sarah argued. "That's no way to live."

Miss Dupree leaned forward a touch, and focused on the tall silent young man who was looking out a window. "What do you think, Grimm?"

Grimm focused on her, and to her astonishment, he spoke. "Hamlet was already poisoned at the beginning."

It took her a moment to find her voice. "How so?"

"Revenge doesn't leave room for love. It eats a man."

Tobias's mouth hung open. Sarah wasn't surprised, and Jin only glared with anger. But no one argued with Grimm. He stood to gather his books, then left as quietly as he had entered.

"He can talk!" Tobias squeaked. "He can talk!" His brows scrunched together. "Wait, my brother can *talk*?"

"It appears so," Miss Dupree said.

It took a moment for everyone to recover. Except Sarah, who was considering his words. She glanced at the wall clock and raised her hand.

"Yes, Sarah?"

"May I be excused early?"

"Why?"

"I…" Sarah hesitated on the words. The thought of lying made her sick, so when she answered she wasn't actually lying. "I don't feel well. My stomach is queasy." It was true. Now. She could hear her gramma rolling over in her grave.

Miss Dupree inclined her head. "Considering our recent revelation, we'll end early today, but I want a report on Hamlet by tomorrow."

Tobias groaned and clunked his head on the desk.

SARAH BYRNE RIOT CHECKED HER CHAIN WATCH FOR THE tenth time. She sat alone on a bench in Golden Gate Park with a clear view of the track. Well, as clear as the fog allowed. She had watched the gray mist spill over the hills like a slow wave before washing over her.

It was cold and lonely, and even the horseback riders and bicyclists had gone home. She really didn't want to be out here after dark. Sarah checked the cryptic note again. There were creases in it from her repeated consultation. She had followed the bizarre directions exactly as written. It had been an exhausting amount of boarding cable cars, riding a few blocks, disembarking, walking back to where she'd started, only to get on another cable car, then finally coming to Golden Gate Park, where'd she'd followed a winding path to this bench.

A few people still strolled the pathways. Couples out for an evening, maids walking dogs, and a man selling roasted peanuts.

Sarah watched as a portly man with gray whiskers and tinted spectacles meandered towards her. With a sigh of relief, he sat down on her bench, raised his hat to her, and wiped his forehead with a kerchief. He was out of breath.

"Are you all right, sir?" she asked.

His suit was stretched and worn, but he was dressed as a gentleman with walking stick and gold watch.

"I'm thankful to sit for a time. I hope you don't mind if I share your bench, Miss."

Sarah perked up at his accent. He drawled in a nasally way, and dropped his R's. "You're from Tennessee," she said.

The man started in surprise. "Why, yes. My people are from there, and I do say you are, too. What a happy coincidence!" He sat a little straighter, folding his gloved hands over the top of his cane.

Sarah smiled at him.

"And why is a pretty young lady waiting here all alone?"

"I was out for a walk like yourself, and thought I'd rest."

"Mason Kelly." He extended a gloved hand and she shook the tips of his fingers.

"Sarah Byrne Riot."

"Pleased to make your acquaintance, Miss Riot."

"Likewise."

Mr. Kelly consulted his watch. Then huffed. "Seems to me the fellow you're waiting for is late."

Sarah's eyes widened. "How did you—"

Mr. Kelly nudged his tinted spectacles down, showing off his eyes—long, narrow, and dark, there was a very familiar glint of humor shining from them.

"Mr. Sin!" she gasped. Sin Chi Man, pronounced See-in Chee-mahn, was a mysterious detective in Chinatown. He had saved her from her uncle's murderers, and she had stayed in his underground hideout for months while Atticus and Isobel sorted out the dangerous mess that had put her life in danger. At first she had been terrified of him, but he proved to be a perfect gentleman. He had taught her calligraphy and music, and all sorts of things. He was the man she was waiting for. The reason why she had tied a black ribbon around a laundry sack.

Sin dropped his drawl. "It's fortunate everyone is currently out of earshot."

Sarah blushed. "Sorry, but I… How…" she stammered. "Your accent was *very* good."

"Is it?" He seemed pleased.

She nodded.

"I spent months listening to you," he said.

"I don't talk *that* much."

Sin raised his brows.

"I was bored. You were the only one there."

"And when you left peace was restored to my humble abode."

"Good for you." She poked his stomach. "What are you using for padding?"

He swatted her hand away.

"Did you eat a pig?"

Sin ignored her teasing. "I have been most amused by the newspapers of late."

Sarah sighed. "I'm not."

"I failed to teach you discretion. You could go into hiding and erase your name from society like me."

"I don't think that'd do much good. There's a spy in our house."

"Did the spy make you kick the man at the theater?" He looked at her with curiosity.

Sarah frowned at him.

"I hope you didn't contact me to deal with some petty spy under your roof?" he asked.

"It's my sister. Jin."

"She's the spy?"

"No, she's in danger."

"From whom?"

"Herself," Sarah said. "Least that's what Grimm says. They both came back one night with bruises. He's been trying to protect her, I think. She's up to something in Chinatown and she won't tell anyone anything."

Mr. Sin looked off into the distance, his hands still folded over his cane. He was a tall, thin man, but it was difficult to picture him as such with his disguise. Even his chin was flabby. Having helped Mr. Lotario don a disguise, she knew he would be impressed.

"I heard a report that a negro man and a Chinese child robbed three men coming from the theater."

"Grimm would never rob anyone!" she insisted.

He looked at her sideways. "Can you say the same of your sister?"

Sarah ground her teeth together. "I won't vouch for Jin."

"It's rumored the child attacked a man and stabbed him with a knife."

"That sounds like her."

Sin considered this. "But you want to help her?"

"Of course. I just don't know what she's up to. It can't be

good, though. She won't tell Atticus and Isobel much. Did you know there's a bounty on them?"

Sin inclined his head. "I would be surprised if there wasn't. Considering."

"Can you… have someone take the posters down?"

Sin ignored that. "What do you know of your sister's life before?"

"I don't know anything. She won't tell me. But she has heaps of scars and I think her parents are dead. I'm not really sure."

"Did you ask?"

"She doesn't like me much."

"And yet you kicked a man in the shin for her."

Sarah shrugged. "Family has to stick together."

"You are family on paper only."

"It's the only sort I have, Mr. Sin."

Sin nodded, once. "I'll watch her. But…" He held up a long finger. "Tell this Grimm not to follow her anymore. He has attracted attention."

"All right. I'm not sure he'll listen to me since I can't tell him about you."

"Tell him you have found help," Sin said simply. "And you —you must not go into Chinatown."

"Not even to a restaurant?"

"You know what I mean, Miss Sarah," he said severely.

"What about the theater?"

He glanced at her, annoyance flaring. "Do not go looking for your sister. The tongs are fighting for dominance and the Quarter is a dangerous place right now."

She frowned.

"And you would find the theater boring, I think," he said.

"I was stuck with you for months. If I could survive that…"

"Insolent child." But he said it lightly. Without a word, he snatched the crumpled note from her hand, got up and left. She watched him disappear around a bend.

Sarah stood and frowned at the darkening trees. If she hurried, she could make it home before the sun winked out.

As she hurried towards the closest cable car terminal, she marveled at the life she'd landed herself in—a gunfighter for a father, a detective for a mother, a hellion for a sister, and here she was, meeting a mysterious Chinese man dressed as a Tennessee gentleman at dusk.

San Francisco was an odd sort of place.

A CLASH OF MINDS

Isobel watched a parade of reporters stream in and out of the Sutter Street house. Sergeant Detective Dillion was hungry for fame, so he had jumped on a chance to give a tour of his crime scene. Naked girl and all.

Riot was cool and distant beside her. "You shouldn't have alerted the press." His voice was tight.

"They didn't even *look* at her, except for that patrolman leering at her breasts. Dillion stomped around the room like he was Sherlock Holmes incarnate, making a show of examining things. He's an utter idiot."

Riot set his jaw.

"Weston won't be able to sweep this under a rug. You know exactly what he was doing. Death by 'natural cause' only requires a signature, but murder requires work from him. With as much press as this will generate, he won't be able to ignore it."

Riot leaned closer, holding her gaze. "Ravenwood Agency prides itself on discretion. We were hired for that very thing, and now you've broken that trust."

She raised a brow. "We were hired to find Ella. She's *dead*. And the man who murdered her is still out there."

"We don't know that, Bel."

"Do you really believe she died of *natural causes*? Or that she killed herself? Would death by suicide have comforted the family? Suicide brings scorn; murder brings sympathy and aid."

Riot squared his shoulders. He wasn't backing down, but his voice remained calm. "Are you certain she didn't kill herself?"

"It's obvious."

"What evidence do you have? What proof?"

"For God's sake, Riot. Surely you don't believe Hawkins was some innocent bystander in this?"

"You should have consulted with me first."

"Well, now we're even," she growled.

Riot held her eyes in silence. He would let her come to her own conclusion about her impulsive outburst. "This isn't easy, Bel. I know. I'm frustrated too. But those reporters will drag the Spencer family through the mud."

"The press would've caught wind of it eventually," she argued. "This is about finding Ella's killer, not her family. They're going to grieve regardless."

"You know I don't think like that."

"What would you have done?" she asked.

Riot adjusted his hat. "Searched for the murderer quietly. Reporters and police will only muddy the waters."

"They could also fluster Hawkins into making a mistake."

"Or drive him into hiding," he countered.

"Forcing the coroner to reassess the cause of death now will make it easier to convict this villain when we run him down."

"Will it?" The way he said it—so quiet and calm—sent a chill down her spine. Did Riot plan on turning this man over to authorities? How many victims had been let down by the so-called justice system? How many murderers had escaped a noose? A girl of no means from a family without connections, one that set their daughter loose to run around the city—it wouldn't make for a very sympathetic jury.

Truth is our aim, Riot had told her once. And as she studied her husband, she wondered, at what point would he pull the trigger himself?

"Let's inform the family before the press starts knocking on their door."

Mr. Lewis Fletcher opened the door. He must have seen the lump caught in Isobel's throat because his greeting died on his lips.

"You found her," Lewis said instead.

"We did," Riot said. "I'm afraid I have bad news, Mr. Fletcher."

Lewis let them inside. To stall the inevitable, he began to prattle. "Mother's doing much better, and the baby. And Reverend West arranged help from the church, so I sent Miss Maddie home."

"Lewis," Riot said.

The man stopped, and stiffened. "Surely you can convince the scoundrel she ran off with to marry her? We can—"

"Your sister is dead." It was blunt. And soft.

Isobel was glad Riot was there to deliver it. She supposed there was no delicate way to announce death. No way to soften something so final.

Lewis paused, then closed his eyes, and when he opened them something close to relief passed over his eyes. "I see. How?"

"We don't know yet. We found her in an empty house on

Sutter. No obvious signs of death. Regardless of your mother's feelings, I suggest you request a post-mortem."

Lewis stared at the floor, scrubbed clean, smelling of beeswax and lemon polish. His home was finally in order, but his life was crumbling around him. "I'll, uhm… Be sure to send me the bill for your services."

"We intend to keep investigating," Riot said. "I think your sister was lured to that house and murdered by a man she thought was a friend."

Lewis's head snapped up. "Mr. Riot, I beg you to leave it alone. I don't want my sister's reputation dragged through the dirt."

"You don't care whether your sister's murderer is brought to justice?" Isobel asked.

Lewis ran a hand through his hair. "It's not that. It's… I have worries enough about the living."

It clicked then. "The Masonic Temple," Isobel said. "You've applied for aid, and if your family is involved in a scandal, the Board of Relief may not help you."

Lewis flushed. Anger, shame, and defensiveness came out. "Please, leave. I thank you for your services. I suspect the police will be along…"

"Lewis, is that Ella?" a female voice called from the kitchen. Mrs. Spencer came out a moment later carrying a cup of tea in one hand. Some color had returned to her face, and her hands no longer shook.

That would all change in a blink.

The woman stopped. "You found my Ella, didn't you?" Mrs. Spencer whispered.

Lewis hurried over, but his mother shrugged away his attempts to seat her in the parlor. "Tell me," she demanded.

Riot told her.

The cup shattered when it hit the floor, and it was a long time before her wailing stopped.

30

THE LONE OUTLAW

TOBIAS WHITE WAS ABANDONED. SARAH HAD RUN OFF, JIN WAS moping in her attic room, and Grimm wasn't ever game for anything. That left the task to him.

The Lone Detective.

But doesn't every detective *have* to have a partner? He narrowed his eyes, mind working furiously.

The Lone Boy? No, he decided quickly. People would call him the Lonely Man when he got older. The Lone Pirate. He smiled to himself, but then frowned. Why would a pirate be alone? That would mean his boat was small.

Outlaw. That was it. The Lone Outlaw.

Having decided on a suitable name, he turned back to the task. He twitched a drape, and squinted through the gap at a door. Mr. Hughes's room was on the third floor, along with Sarah's, Mr. Löfgren's, and the big turret room. The other boarders lived on the second floor. Miss Dupree on the first. And Jin in the attic. And his family got the entire basement to themselves. It was a big house. Bigger than Tobias had ever known. And was easy to get lost in.

The stuffy grandfather clock in the entryway chimed five

times, and like clockwork Mr. Harry Hughes came out of his room, locked his door, and made his ponderous way downstairs. Dinner wasn't served till eight, but Mr. Hughes liked to read for three hours in the library. He mostly napped.

Tobias got on his belly and slithered towards the railing slats. He pressed his forehead to the gap, and looked over the dizzying edge, all the way down to a wood floor. Mr. Hughes came in and out of view as he wound his way down the staircase. A great iron chandelier hung from the ceiling over the empty space.

Tobias was not allowed to swing on the chandelier. His mother forbade him before he even got a chance to try, and for some reason she reminded him weekly.

Tobias waited for the library door to close, then darted over to Mr. Hughes's room. The door was locked as expected. He took out the ring of lock picks that Mr. Tim kept in the stable house. They looked like keys, but they weren't made for any single lock. More like possibilities of locks. With this kind of old lock, all Tobias had to do was find a similarly shaped key. And with as much time as Tobias had spent studying his ma's ring of keys, he already had a false key in mind.

To his own ears, he sounded like the rag and bone man clomping down the street. Palms sweating, he worked the pick in the keyhole and turned. It didn't work. Tobias swallowed, spared a furtive glance over his shoulder and quickly selected another.

Click.

It was like a chorus of angels started singing all at once. In his excitement, Tobias dropped the lock picks and they clattered to the ground like a cymbal burst. He snatched up the ring, put his back to the wall, and looked as innocent as he could be.

But no one came, except a large cat. Watson's tail waved sinuously in the air as the cat sauntered up the stairs.

Tobias blew out a breath. Before his mother appeared, the Lone Outlaw slipped into Mr. Hughes's room.

Only there was a flaw in his master plan. Now that he was inside the room, he didn't know what to do. Tobias stood with his back to the door. The curtains were open, but the sun was falling and it was dark in the cramped room. He let his eyes adjust.

The room smelled of pipe smoke and polish, and while it was clean, it was brimming with belongings. Hats, shoes, smoking jackets, an entire wall of little paintings in ornate frames: idyllic visions of countrysides, of flowers and horses and dogs.

A washbasin, a desk inhabited by porcelain figurines, and a bed were ensconced between stacks of newspapers. Tobias walked over to the desk. It was locked.

He fiddled with Mr. Tim's ring of thief keys. Why did Mr. Tim have these? And he wondered, not for the first time, why Mr. Hughes would write such a horrible newspaper article. The cheerful man didn't strike Tobias as a spy, but then maybe that was the purpose of spies.

Tobias lifted the top of the desk. A stack of paper, an ink vial, blotter, pen, receipts stuck on a spike, and... Tobias looked back at the receipts. There were an awful lot of them. What did Mr. Hughes even do for work? As far as Tobias could tell the man ate breakfast, sat in the conservatory, went for a walk, then headed to his room for a nap, and then down to the library where he napped some more until dinnertime. Every day.

Tobias looked through the receipt stack: brandy, pipes, tobacco, pharmacies, launderers. What was he expecting to find in here? That Mr. Hughes owed money to the newspaper?

Tobias abandoned the receipts and turned to a ledger. He knew what it was because his mother had the same kind. She tallied everything at the kitchen table nightly and had shown

Tobias how to manage his own accounts. She made him keep a running ledger of his money earned and his candy store trips.

He squinted at the numbers. It took him a bit to sort them out. His mind mixed things up at times. Then he frowned. Mr. Hughes's account book looked like Tobias's. Not in the expenditures, but the money going out.

Mr. Hughes spent a whole heap of money (more than Tobias), but there was never money coming in. None at all. Not even a balance.

Tobias shut the account book and closed the desk. Bored now, he poked around the room. He opened the wardrobe hoping to find a skeleton (there was none), then turned to the nightstand. An old-fashioned pistol lay on a stack of postcards. Distracted by the pistol, Tobias ignored the postcards and picked up the weapon. It was the kind pirates used. Newer maybe, and it had a pearl handle.

Tobias set it back down, and picked up a business card with some lady's name on it and flowers. He was about to turn over a postcard when a loud meow sounded from under the door, followed by scratching.

Tobias's heart leapt in his throat. He quickly closed the drawer. Stupid cat.

Watson's yowling got louder, and then footsteps came. Ponderous and labored, it could only be one person. Tobias started to scoot under the bed, but it was filled with boxes and books. He scrambled towards the wardrobe and closed himself inside.

Tobias made himself small and compact in a corner, and held his breath.

"I don't have any food for you in there," Mr. Hughes said. He was good-natured and cheerful, and talked to the cat like he was a friend. "Making me walk all the way up here again. Then you'll just want to go back out. What did I tell you about scratching on doors?"

The bedroom door opened, and soon Watson was meowing and pawing at the wardrobe. Tobias squeezed his eyes shut.

"Oh, stop that. Bad kitty." Mr. Hughes huffed. "I don't know why I put up with you. It's three hours until dinner. I'll tell you what, old fellow. You and I will walk down to the market and get a treat. The bakery for me, and the fish market for you."

Watson's purr pierced the wardrobe. And then it opened.

Tobias held his breath, and cracked an eye open, waiting for an outburst. Hangers scraped against the back of the wardrobe. Then Mr. Hughes tapped on wood. A soft whisper of wood, and Tobias was crushed between a wall that hadn't been there a moment before and the side of the wardrobe.

Through his cracked eye, he could see Watson staring at him, his tail waving lazily in contemplation. The cat seemed to be weighing his options: attack the boy or get shrimp. Shrimp won out.

Both doors closed without incident, and the Lone Outlaw just about pissed himself. He sat curled against the wardrobe wall, panting softly in darkness.

After what seemed like an hour, Tobias moved a foot, then an arm. He reached out and pushed the wardrobe door open. He squinted against the light, and quickly scooted out.

The room was empty.

He sighed with relief, then turned back to the wardrobe. Mr. Hughes had opened something in the back, pressing Tobias against the inside of the wardrobe. A false back?

Tobias moved the clothing aside, just as Mr. Hughes had done, and knocked softly on the back. It took some minutes before he spotted a scratch on the wood. Tobias picked at it with a fingernail, and a small rectangle of wood slid aside to expose a latch. Tobias pulled the little lever down.

The back of the wardrobe opened, revealing narrow shelves.

Tobias stared in shock. A bit of drool curled down the side of his face, and he quickly closed his mouth. Glancing over his shoulder, he reached out a tentative hand and picked up a stack of paper. Bank notes. They looked old. The top one read one hundred silver dollars, with a picture of James Monroe (it said below) on the left side and a little one hundred on the right. A giant red stamp in the center drove home to Tobias White that he was holding a one hundred dollar bill.

Tobias looked back at the shelves. There were enough bank notes in there to stuff a mattress.

"You did *what*?" Sarah asked.

"Shh," Tobias shushed her loudly. "That's what we planned."

"I did not tell you to break into Mr. Hughes—"

Tobias clamped a hand over her mouth. He glanced around the empty room. It was a dance hall. At least that's what he'd heard it was. It was downstairs, a vast empty space with wood floors and a fireplace. His ma made him polish those floors whenever he did something stupid. The room tended to echo.

"Let's go to my fort."

Sarah rolled her eyes, but followed. When they were hidden away in his fort, he told her what he found.

"How much do you reckon was in there?" Sarah asked. She sat on the makeshift bedroll that Jin used when she was feeling particularly ornery.

Tobias shrugged. "Loads. There were all sorts of bills. And he didn't keep a balance in his books. My ma says there's no use keeping an account book if you don't tally the balance."

"Unless he keeps it in his head," Sarah said.

"Who'd do that?"

"Maybe Mr. Hughes." Sarah blew out a breath. "If he has so much money, why would he sell an article to the *Call*?"

"We don't know he did," Tobias said.

"Mr. Lotario thinks so."

"No. We don't know that either. Mr. A.J. said that's what Mr. Lotario said."

"Why would Atticus lie to me?"

Tobias gave her a look. "'Cause he knew you were fishin'. Mr. A.J. ain't dumb."

Sarah blinked, shocked at the suggestion that Atticus might mislead her. But then hadn't she tried to trick him? Thinking on it, it seemed like the sort of thing he'd do. Her brows drew together. "Or Mr. Lotario is wrong," she suggested.

Tobias nodded at that too. "Or he knew you'd cheat and gave Mr. A.J. the wrong name."

Sarah fiddled with a spring Tobias had found under a house some months ago. "Maybe it wasn't for money. What other reasons are there for writing that article?"

Tobias shrugged.

"Why do you tell on Maddie?" she asked.

"Maddie? She doesn't do anything bad."

"All right. Why would you tell on Jin?"

"She'd kill me."

Sarah made a frustrated sound worthy of her sister.

"All right, let me think." Tobias rubbed his chin in imitation of Atticus, who sometimes stroked his beard in thought. "Maybe Mr. Hughes wanted to get Miss Dupree in trouble."

"Maybe. But it got all of us in trouble. Mr. Löfgren may not move in with his wife, and the other women in the house have their reputations to worry about."

"Do all women care about their reputation so much?"

Sarah gave him a patient look. "A woman *has* to, Tobias. Otherwise she can't find respectable work, or a husband."

"Miss Isobel don't seem to care about hers. And she found work *and* a husband."

"Isobel is…" Sarah faltered. "Special. Most women aren't. You heard Mrs. Lane, she's worried about her job. And Mrs. Clarke is a God-fearing woman. She doesn't want that kind of stain on her name."

"Miss Pierce has a job," Tobias pointed out.

"True," Sarah said slowly. "She didn't mention that her employment was at risk. Only that she got paid less…"

Tobias sucked in an excited breath. "Maybe it has something to do with Miss Dupree's rooms. They're the best in the house."

Sarah abandoned the spring. "Aside from the turret room."

Tobias shook his head. "That big ol' room is on the third floor. Miss Dupree's is on the first, *and* it has its own entrance. Mr. Hughes wouldn't have to walk up and down all those stairs. He could come and go as he pleased, and let Watson in and out all day."

Sarah was beginning to see why Lotario suspected him. "Maybe Mr. Hughes thought the article would force Atticus to evict Miss Dupree, so he could rent her rooms."

"My ma would be the one to do that. Mr. A.J. don't even know who's in his own house."

Sarah couldn't argue with that. Atticus was barely ever home, and when he was, he kept to his rooms or the family kitchen. "The article *might* make people move out. Then your ma would be forced to get new boarders, or maybe even lower the rent."

"She'd never do that."

"I don't know. I've heard Atticus talking with Isobel. From the sound of it there's not much money."

Tobias nodded. "I peeked at my ma's account books of Ravenwood estate. She breaks even every time."

"Was she planning on raising the rent?"

Tobias shrugged. "I don't know, but it still doesn't make sense. Mr. Hughes could buy his own place with that much cash. Why rent a room on the third floor?"

"Maybe he's lonely."

"I don't think so. He had lots of calling cards from ladies."

"I never see any of them visit."

"Maybe he calls on them."

Sarah thought a moment. "I think we should tell your ma what you found."

Tobias nearly choked. "Are you *crazy*? I'd die before I told her what I did."

"Fine, but we have to find out if any of the boarders asked to switch rooms, or for their rent to be lowered."

"Or if they had trouble paying."

Sarah nodded. "I still think we should tell someone about all that money."

"Maybe Mr. Tim?"

That seemed a good start. Mr. Tim would hardly get mad at Tobias for using the lock picks he had taught him to use.

"You found *what*?" Tim asked.

The boy fidgeted with his cap, while Sarah stood watching for Mr. Tim's reaction. "We were only trying to find the writer of that article, Mr. Tim."

The old man was sitting on a stool in front of a wood stove, mending a pair of boots. He had, as it turned out, worked as a cobbler at some point. "I don't care how you got there, boy. But come again on the other part."

"He has a whole bank in his wardrobe," Tobias said. "There's enough to stuff a mattress."

"A hundred dollar note, you say? With James Monroe and a giant red stamp in the middle? You sure?"

Tobias nodded. "There were other bills, too."

"What should we do, Mr. Tim?" Sarah asked.

He grunted. "I'd like a peek at them."

"You gonna break in too? Here's the pick that worked." Tobias showed him the key pick from the ring.

Tim snatched the lock pick ring. "You can't go borrowing these without asking."

"I figured you wouldn't let me do it if I asked first."

Tim pinned the boy with a crisp blue eye. "Now why the hell would I stop you when I was the one that taught you?"

Sarah turned red at the curse. Tobias's mouth worked. He finally settled on an answer. "'Cause you're old."

"Do most old folks teach you lock picking?" Tim asked, rubbing his beard in thought.

"Well, no," Tobias admitted.

Tim had a twinkle in his eye. "Why'd I teach you something if I didn't want you to use it?"

"I'm not sure you should encourage him, Mr. Tim," Sarah said.

The old man grunted. "Maybe not. But then I was never one for sense."

"What should we do?" Sarah asked again.

"The man has a stash of cash in his room. There's nothin' criminal about that. Most old people don't trust banks. Myself included."

Tim set down his boot and tools, and reached for a coat. "I reckon we should consult with Miss Lily."

"You can't tell my ma what I did!" Tobias said. "She'll skin me."

"Don't you worry, boy. I'm not going to get you in trouble."

Sarah glanced at Tobias. Her look said it all.

TIM WAS AN ODD MAN. SARAH'S GRAMMA WOULD'VE FOUND HIM crass and uncivilized. And a bad influence. Which meant she wouldn't have allowed Sarah near him. He was sly, crafty, and had likely tried out all the sins in the Good Book, but he had the largest heart Sarah had ever known. He *cared* about things. Most of all, people.

Tim as usual took extra care to wipe his feet and wash in the mudroom sink before setting foot in Miss Lily's kitchen. They found her downstairs, in front of a crackling hearth in what constituted the White family's sitting room. It was cozy and well used, but as clean as could be.

Tim greeted Lily with a polite 'Good evening.' She was mending clothes by the light of the fire and a small lamp.

"Evening, Mr. Tim. Tobias, Sarah." Her cheeks dimpled, her eyes warmed. "It's a cold night again."

"I'll check the furnace," Tim said.

"No rush, Mr. Tim. Can I get you some hot tea? Coffee?"

"No thank you. I told you before I can get my own." Tim did not like being waited on. As he had put it one day, "The second I stop moving is the day I die." He said plenty of things like that.

"You *can*," Lily said, a twinkle in her eye. "But I don't want you rummaging through my kitchen."

"Now look here, I washed all up and made myself presentable." Tim brandished his hands.

"I'm not sure all the hot water in San Francisco would do the job properly."

Tim huffed, and stuck a cold pipe in his lips. He knew better than to light it up in the main house, but Lily allowed him the comfort of it.

"Are you children hungry?" she asked.

"No, ma'am," Sarah said. She glanced at Tobias, who made a motioning gesture. In turn, Sarah looked to Tim, who seemed to take a moment to remember why he was there.

"What's on your minds?" Lily asked, without looking up from her stitch work.

"Does Mr. Hughes pay with cash every month?" Tim asked, bluntly.

"Yes, he does. He's never been late." She looked up. "Why do you ask?"

"I'd like to see the money he pays with."

Puzzled, Lily stood up and walked down a hallway.

Tobias leaned over to whisper into Sarah's ear. "She keeps a strongbox behind a loose panel in her room."

Ravenwood Manor was full of all sorts of nooks and crannies. The children kept searching for a secret door and staircase, but so far hadn't found one.

Lily came back with three bills. She handed them over to Tim.

He stretched one and held it close to the lamp, and shut one eye.

"Don't tell me they're counterfeit bills," she said.

"No, no," Tim said. "These are the real thing." The way he said it left a wide open space for a larger question.

Sarah blinked in surprise. "There's such a thing?" she asked.

Lily frowned, realizing she had exposed the children to a criminal enterprise.

"Indeed," Tim said. "Forgery is an art. You'd likely be good at it."

"Mr. Tim!" Lily said. "Don't be putting ideas into their heads."

Tim winked. "You said it, not me."

Lily shook her head, and returned to her seat.

"Mind if I hold on to one of these?"

"Are you going to spend it?"

"No, no. Just check on a few things."

"You can keep all three."

Tim stuffed the money into his pocket.

"Why the sudden interest in Mr. Hughes? Is this about that article?" Lily asked.

Tobias and Sarah sat on the hearth rug letting the fire toast their backs.

"Yes and no," Tim said. "The kids here think he wrote it."

"Now why would you suspect Mr. Hughes?" Lily asked. "I thought you were set on Mr. Dougal."

Sarah glanced at Tobias, who somehow managed to shake his head without moving it.

"Mr. Lotario thinks Mr. Hughes wrote it," Sarah said. "But we... I was wondering if Mr. Hughes has ever asked to move rooms? Or complained about any of the other boarders?"

Lily's fingers stilled over her mending. She looked up in thought. "I don't think Mr. Hughes has ever made such a request. Why would Mr. Lotario think he wrote it?"

"We don't know."

"Why do *you* think?"

"Well..." Sarah looked to Tobias.

"We think he wrote it so Miss Dupree would be kicked out. That way he'd get her room and wouldn't have to walk up all those stairs," Tobias blurted out.

"I see. Do you have proof?"

"No, but we need to start somewhere."

"Mr. Hughes pays his rent on time. Gets along with all the other boarders, and his doctor wants him to walk up all those stairs for his health."

Tobias wrinkled his nose. "Who do you think wrote it, Ma?"

"You finally thought to ask me," she said.

"*Ma.* Just tell us."

"Doesn't matter who I think wrote it. Not until there's proof."

"All the same," Sarah said. "You know the boarders best."

Lily went back to her stitching, and Mr. Tim, never one to sit idle, leaned forward to toss another log into the fire, and stoke it to life.

"You both know I don't gossip."

"This is hypothesthising…" Tobias stumbled over the word.

"Hypothesizing," Sarah corrected. "Like in science."

"Miss Pierce is having trouble paying her rent. She supports her mother and a number of younger siblings outside the City."

Sarah frowned. "But that article could damage her reputation. She might be let go from her job."

Lily tilted her head from side to side. "Perhaps. But she's a mathematician. Any woman making her own way in a male-dominated profession has a questionable reputation in the minds of those who concern themselves with such things." Miss Lily did not concern herself with such things. Her tone left no doubt of that.

"So you think it's Miss Pierce?" Sarah asked.

Lily shook her head. "I didn't say that. I only answered your question. Anyone in this house could have written that article. But I'm not convinced it was someone who lives in this house. The article hurt all of us."

Sarah cocked her head. "But there were details…"

"And people talk, Sarah. People gossip. It only takes one stray word to ruin someone."

31

JOSS HOUSE

Saturday, October 13, 1900

THE STREETS WERE BECOMING FAMILIAR—THE STORES, THE merchants, even the alleyways. Chinatown was no longer foreign to her. Sao Jin had lived her entire life in the Quarter, but she didn't much know it. She had spent most of that life behind doors.

She remembered walking with her father, tottering on the sidewalk, holding his hand. But she wasn't sure if that was imagined memory or real, as she watched a small child doing that very thing.

A man in silk, with a long queue and impeccable white cuffs, held the hand of his small daughter. She looked like a doll with her rosy cheeks. She squealed with delight, as her mother trailed slightly behind. The mother was dressed in robes, and wore small slippers that bound her feet. She walked slowly, holding the hand of her son, who was leading his smaller brother by letting him hold on to his queue.

The family talked and laughed, but she could see the father eyeing the narrow lanes where men with broad hats stood.

Jin watched the men at the alleyway too. They were a blight on Chinatown, a disease that festered in shadows. The criminal tongs ripped the joy from residents.

The family fell quiet as they passed the men. Ten feet later, the children started giggling again.

A passenger wagon stopped on the street. It was full of white tourists exclaiming over the adorable children and the robes of the parents. A man hopped off the driver's seat to open the back gate, folding down the step so the tourists could disembark. They flooded the street, gawking at red banners and lanterns and festooned balconies.

Hucksters came with wares dangling from wooden poles: puppets and trinkets and tea. Jin trotted forward with a broom in hand, sweeping the way for a frilly-dressed woman trying to keep her skirts out of the dirt.

"So exotic. Look at his braid." The woman reached for Jin to feel her hair. She bit back a snarl, and hurried to sweep the street lest she hit the woman with her broom. "Are those some kind of ritual scars?" the woman asked her guide.

The guide answered in broken English. "Look see. Here. Here." He smiled and bowed, and pointed towards a joss house.

As the woman strolled inside, Jin heard the guide swear lightly under his breath. She shared a look with him. "They bring the money," he said in Cantonese, and flipped Jin a coin.

Jin stared at the temple. Two stories high, with an ornate roof and red banners hanging from its balcony, the characters reading Tien Hau Temple. Mother Ancestor. Goddess of Heaven and the Sea.

She watched the white tourists gawking and exclaiming as they walked up the stairs into the dark opening. Curious, she set her broom against a brick wall, and followed.

Jin found herself gawking along with the tourists. Hundreds of red and gold lanterns hung from the ceiling. The air was thick with incense. A few white women giggled into the deep silence.

Jin wandered past the group, farther into the temple where men and women prayed at altars. Some shook canisters of sticks—*kau cim* sticks, her mind dredged the words from a shadow of memory. Fortunes. Others bowed in front of teak altars festooned with candles and ornate statues, burning incense and throwing half-moon-shaped objects on the ground. And in the middle of it all sat Tien Hau, serene in red and gold and surrounded by attendants. Bowls of fruit, flowers, cookies, and cakes were laid out in offering.

A monk approached Jin and bowed deeply, offering two candles and a bundle of three joss sticks. She glanced to the side, where another woman was accepting candles and incense and dropping a coin into the monk's hand.

"What is this for?" she asked.

The priest looked surprised. "For your prayers." He nodded towards the goddess statue. "Through the mother's power, the daughter is powerful."

"Who is that?" she asked.

Again, surprise. "Mazu. Mother Ancestor and Goddess of the Sea, protector of fishermen and sailors. She's very clever and remembers everything she reads. The two guardians beside her are a Thousand-mile-eye and Wind-to-the-ear. They help her find people in storms, along with her red lantern."

Jin felt like she was in a storm searching for people. She glanced at the tourists and the residents, feeling caught between two worlds. She should know how to do this, but she was as clueless as the tourists.

"I do not know what to do," she admitted.

The monk smiled. "I will show you, *mui mui*." Little sister.

Feeling awkward, Jin followed him through the temple, walking in a very specific pattern to visit each altar and deity.

He showed her how to light the two candles, hold the incense, and how to bow.

In spite of the monk's encouragement, Jin did not introduce herself or ask any questions. She only went through the motions, feeling lost at sea. These rituals meant nothing to her, and so when she finally stood in front of Mazu and her demon guardians, Jin only glared in defiance.

The monk left her alone, and Jin thrust her incense into the sand, then shook out a *kau cim* stick. She took the number to a wall of drawers and got her message from the Goddess: *The dead trees break into green once more; The woods are alive with buzzing life. The immortal peach tree gives forth its fruit, And all the lost find their way home.*

Jin snorted, crumbled up the paper, and stuffed it into a pocket before marching out. Her question had not been answered.

32

QUESTIONING THE DEAD

COLD DEATH. IT HAD A DISTINCT SMELL, A STENCH THAT clogged the back of her throat. Isobel wanted to vomit it out, to rid her body of it. She swallowed down the urge, and forced herself to breathe through her mouth, as she walked down the steps to the basement of the city morgue.

Isobel tried not to think of Ella Spencer laying on a hard slab exposed to the elements. The dead didn't feel, but the living did. And Isobel currently felt the sting of failure.

They hadn't found her in time.

Riot walked in front of her. As somber as his dark suit, with lines around his eyes and a shadow in them. How many dead children had he found in his career?

"Does it ever get easier?" she had asked in the privacy of their rooms.

Riot had given a slight shake of his head.

Should it get easier? Would she be worried if it did?

The stairwell opened to a sterile holding room: stark, cold, and filled with corpses. Two rows of waiting dead stretched to the far wall. At the very end, through an alcove, was an operating theater: a washbasin, and a slab with grooves, buckets, and scales.

Two men toiled inside. They were opposites in every way. One was pristine: thin and older, with muttonchops that extended to form a mustache over his upper lip. The second man was disheveled, with a complexion the color of codfish and ears that looked like they were melting.

The second man looked up. "Mr. and Mrs. Riot!" Mr. Sims exclaimed. "Settling into matrimony, I see. Splendid timing you have. Why, Ella's just given up her secrets, and I think she's happier for it. Fine job you did finding her. She didn't much care to be in that dark house for five whole days."

Mr. Sims was an odd man. He had a voice that could wake the dead, and wore a baking apron that stretched over his gut. His job, as he put it, was to haul bodies around. And he claimed they spoke to him. Whatever the case, he gleaned secrets from them with uncanny ease.

He shook hands with them both, and Isobel was glad to find him free of blood. For now, the large man blocked their view of Ella Spencer. That was until he moved aside, sweeping his arm out. "You'll want to talk to her. She's had quite the number of callers over the last few days. Family, of course, but others too. Why, she's barely had time to herself..."

His words faded into the background. What remained of Ella Spencer lay on the slab. Her eyes stared sightless; her body was exposed and discolored, with a long line of sutures that ran from collarbone to pubic bone, along with a square of sutures on her throat.

"Mr. Sims." A stern voice cut into the man's recitation of visitors. But Sims didn't immediately trail off—he got one last visitor out. "...a pleasant redheaded friend."

Riot looked at Sims. "Madge Ryan?"

"I didn't get her name. A stout girl, though. She didn't even wobble. The mother on the other—"

"Mr. Sims," the older man said again.

This time Sims fell silent.

Riot looked to the older man. "This is Isobel Amsel. Francis P. Wilson, Police Surgeon."

Isobel expected the man to huff and dismiss them. Instead, he set down his clipboard and extended his hand to her. "Miss Amsel." He didn't hesitate over having been offered her given name rather than her married one. "Excellent work in Calistoga over the summer. I'm told we have you to thank for this."

Isobel raised a brow. "For what?"

Wilson inclined his head towards Ella. "Weston and Detective Sergeant Dillion are idiots," he said bluntly. He gestured towards Ella, and they gathered around her corpse.

"Sims here spotted it first."

Sims had folded his hands behind his back, and was humming softly to himself.

Wilson forced an eyelid of the corpse closed, and traced his pen over tiny pinprick dots on the skin. "Petechiae. Hemorrhaging. The presence of petechiae doesn't prove strangulation, but you will note these marks." Wilson traced what looked like faint smudges on Ella's neck on either side of her larynx. "We laid her pharynx bare and found two bruises, one of which was about the size of a half-dollar piece. The killing was carefully done."

"May I?" Sims asked, a hint of near glee in his voice.

Wilson nodded to the man.

Sims moved to the other side and placed his hands carefully over Ella's throat. Thumb and forefinger placed just so on her larynx. His left hand covered her mouth. For all his eagerness, he demonstrated it with a kind of reverence. After he was sure Riot and Isobel got the point, he covered the cadaver with a thin sheet.

"The room she was in was cold and enclosed, so the body

is in better shape than it should be. With these considerations, we estimate time of death to be sometime Sunday morning."

The weight of failure lifted. Ella Spencer was murdered before her brother had hired Ravenwood Agency. That fact didn't help Ella any, but it would help Isobel sleep better at night.

"Any indication of rape?" Riot asked.

Wilson glanced at Isobel, then cleared his throat. "Hard to say. There were clear signs of recent sexual activity. Minor tearing, too." Again, throat clearing. "Along with the blood on the towel we found, er… semen. But the amount of blood and tearing was consistent with what you might find on, er…"

"A wedding night?" Isobel asked.

"Yes," Wilson said.

"Tearing doesn't always occur," Sims said. "Though we did note blood under her fingernails, and a few torn nails."

A significant detail. Isobel picked the cadaver's hand up and studied the nails. Short and clipped, the hands of a worker. And healthy. She could have been trying to fight off her attacker, or… she could have been running her fingers down the back of her lover. Isobel was sure she had added a scar or two to Riot's collection on his back.

"No signs of poison, or organ damage, and only a mild amount of alcohol in her blood," Wilson concluded.

"Were you able to get fingerprints off the skin on her neck?" Riot asked.

Wilson shook his head. "We tried."

Isobel stared down at the girl's glazed eyes. "Do you know if she was strangled during sex?"

"There's no way to be sure," Wilson said.

"Would that matter?" Riot asked. There was a hint of curiosity in his question.

"Some men enjoy choking women during sex. Not to kill, but for power and pleasure," she said it lightly, but Riot wasn't fooled. A muscle in his jaw twitched, and she instantly regretted her observation.

She quickly looked away. On the surface, Riot seemed calm, but that slight twitch in his jaw told her otherwise. If Alex Kingston, her ex-husband, had walked through the door in that moment she had no doubt Riot would have gunned him down.

"It may have been an accident," Sims agreed cheerfully. "And you know some men like to be choked. It raises the blood pressure. Most hanged men are buried stiff as a board. And by that, I mean…"

"Sims," Wilson said. "I don't see how that's important, Miss Amsel."

Isobel gestured at Ella. "None of this makes sense," she said quickly. "John Bennett, or Hawkins, courted her for months. Why arrange all of this only to kill her within hours? Everything points to John Bennett setting Ella up as his mistress."

The men were silent.

Finally, Riot spoke. "Some men find the act of killing far more stimulating than sex."

"But do they leave a forwarding address to the house they plan to kill a woman in?"

Riot looked thoughtful, while Sims continued humming quietly to himself.

"And that's why I'm not a detective," Wilson said. "I wish you luck in finding her murderer. Regardless of circumstances," he frowned down at the girl, "it never gets easier seeing a child under my scalpel."

The medical examiner turned back to his notes.

33

THE FALLEN

Monday, October 15, 1900

ELLA SPENCER WAS DEAD. ISOBEL HAD FAILED HER. NO MATTER how she tried to quiet her imagination, she couldn't stop picturing her own daughters in that empty house.

With shops and stores closed, it was near to impossible to investigate on Sunday, so they had taken the day off to spend with their daughters. Sailing had helped. Isobel needed that time to reassure herself that Jin and Sarah were alive and breathing.

Now, Monday morning, refreshed and rested, she focused on her task—finding C.B. Hawkins. She and Riot had divided forces. But she wasn't entirely on her own. Riot had sent Matthew Smith with her under the pretense that the agent needed experience. It felt more like being assigned a bodyguard.

After sifting through the business cards that had been left behind, and making some inquiries, they discovered that Ford and Co. Real Estate owned the house—the very same company that Lewis Fletcher worked for as a junior clerk. The office was large and orderly, and a few men worked at desks, but Lewis wasn't in that day.

There were no women present, so she let Matthew take the lead, curious to see how he would do. He was her own age—tall, blond, and handsome in an athletic way. She wondered if he played football in his off hours.

"I need information about a house your company owns at 2211 Sutter Street," Matthew said.

"You and every reporter," a burly clerk said.

"We're not reporters."

The clerk eyed him, then glanced at Isobel. "You're not police either."

"We were hired by the family of the girl who was found dead," Isobel said. "The sister of one of your employees."

Matthew took out his notepad, and made a notation.

The burly clerk licked his lips. "What are you writing?"

Matthew nodded to the nameplate on the desk. "Your name."

"Why?"

"In case you dodge my questions."

"You didn't ask any," the clerk defended.

"I'm about to." Matthew glanced down at him. "Who rented 2211 Sutter Street?"

The burly clerk's mouth worked, his eyes darting from the notepad in Matthew's hand to a file cabinet on the wall. "Wait here." He rose and returned with a little man in a neat suit, who introduced himself as Charles Lahanier.

"Nice work," Isobel whispered as they were led to Lahanier's office.

"It's easier to manage with a badge," Matthew said.

Confronted with Matthew's official air, Lahanier admitted that he had rented the house to a Carl Bennett Hawkins two weeks before. He described him as a middle-aged man of medium height, stout of build, and florid complexion, with a blond or reddish mustache.

Isobel frowned at this. But then it was easy enough to dye hair and glue on a fake mustache. How many personas did Hawkins have? Isobel was certainly no stranger to multiple personalities.

She unfolded a sketch that Sarah had made of the suspect. They had taken her around to Estelle Baker and Laura Marshal to get a description.

"Is this him?"

Lahanier frowned at the sketch. "That's him all right. He paid thirty dollars for the month, with a six month agreement. He gave his previous address as the Golden West Hotel. He said he planned to settle in the city. I sent a man out to check his references at the hotel, and they checked out."

"Who did you send?" Matthew asked.

"I don't remember. Priber maybe." He nodded towards a burly clerk at a nearby desk.

"I gave Hawkins the keys, but he came back the next day complaining about rubbish left in the house. So I sent a man—yes, it was Priber—down to inspect it and clean it up."

"Can you call Priber in here?" Isobel asked.

The burly clerk was duly summoned.

"Did you check on 2211 Sutter Street?" Matthew asked.

"I did."

"Was there rubbish?"

"There was."

"And did you remove the rubbish?"

"Not personally," Priber said. "I had some boys clean it out and sweep."

"Was Hawkins present?" Isobel asked.

Priber shook his head. "No. They cleaned up, and left it for him."

"Did he have any belongings? Clothing? Boxes? Furniture?" Matthew asked.

Priber shook his head. "The place was empty."

"Did they lock the backdoor?"

"I'm sure they did," Priber said, taking care not to look at his superior.

Isobel was sure the man didn't know.

They got nowhere else with their line of questioning. And they learned nothing more from the Golden West Hotel. San Francisco was transient. People came and went, some stayed and some didn't. What was one more man coming in from the countryside?

"We could check the *Call* to see who placed the wanted ad," Matthew said, as they stood on a street corner. The suggestion broke Isobel from her thoughts. She looked up, half surprised to find Matthew standing there instead of Riot.

"I mean… not you. I could go in." Color rose in his cheeks. "Sorry, Mrs. Riot, I forgot about that bad business there." He left the words hanging.

"Considering how I left, it might be amusing to walk back into the building." Bruised, battered, and about to be arrested. "But no… I wonder if any of Mack's friends visited him in recovery."

"I just saw him yesterday. And I'm sure others did before me," Matthew said. "The way he talks he was well liked at the *Call*."

The edge of her lip quirked. "Mack would claim a hangman loved him."

———

THE COUNTY HOSPITAL WAS OVERCROWDED, AS USUAL, SO Isobel didn't bother checking in. Matthew appeared flustered as she walked by the desk and headed for the recovery ward.

"Shouldn't we check in?" he asked, glancing over his shoulder.

"Why? They'll just send us to his bed."

"But the nurses. And what if a doctor notices us just wandering about?"

Isobel tossed an amused glance at the man. "Are you worried they'll hold you down and force a urinary catheter on you?"

Matthew's mouth worked. He had the most unforgiving color. Then he closed his mouth, and set his jaw in what Isobel was beginning to think of as his "patrolman's face." He wore a bowler and suit, but it seemed to transform into a uniform with the strength of his posture.

"Relax. I'll handle it."

Isobel led the way through twisting corridors to the recovery ward. The desk nurse on duty was busy with a patient, so Isobel walked past her to the bed where she had last seen Mack.

A man with a broken arm lay there. She spotted the black-haired nurse Mack had been making eyes at.

"Miss?"

The woman looked up from the bed she was changing. "Yes?"

"Your patient, Mack McCormick, did he go home?"

The woman's face fell. "Are you a relation?"

"Yes," she lied. "I'm his niece."

Matthew made a strangled noise behind her.

The rest was a blur—hushed voices, a white-coated doctor, words of condolences.

Blood sepsis.

Mack had not gone home.

For the second time in a week, Isobel found herself in a morgue. She stared down at the big Scotsman on the table. His crooked nose, his reddish hair, his face devoid of humor.

"Does he have family?" a voice asked.

Isobel shook herself from a daze. Matthew repeated the question.

"I don't know," she heard herself saying. "I don't even know where he lives... lived."

Mack had been fine last week.

Isobel turned to the nurse. "I don't understand. He was on the mend. He was up and talking and laughing—"

"Infection, Miss. I'm sorry."

"But I visited him on Tuesday. He was in recovery." There was a quiver in her voice.

"And I was here yesterday," Matthew said with an unsteady voice. "He was up and walking around and talking about being discharged."

The nurse spoke words of comfort, explanations about a weakened liver, but Isobel only half heard. She lifted the sheet to inspect his gunshot wound. Fluid seeped from it.

"He did seem fine," the nurse said. "But blood sepsis... I've seen it kill a man in half a day. It only takes a bit of cloth left in the wound. He was up and about, then he got fever and chills. Lost consciousness. If it helps... I don't think he suffered much."

"Was anyone with him?" Matthew asked.

"Why yes, just before he fell ill," the nurse smiled at Matthew. "An older woman came to visit—a reporter, he said, from the *Call*. Sharpe, I think. And then a black-haired man with a white streak at his temple came first thing this morning. He paid for his funeral and said he'd look for his next of kin."

Isobel looked up at the last. "Riot was here?"

"I think that was his name. He was a real gentleman."

Isobel sucked in a sharp breath. "Thank you." She touched Mack's cold hand for a moment, before hurrying towards fresh air.

"ARE YOU ALL RIGHT, MRS. RIOT?" MATTHEW ASKED AS SHE waved down a hack.

"Stop calling me that. Isobel will do."

"Doesn't change my question," he said.

"Riot was here. He saw Mack."

"And?" Matthew wore a look of utter confusion.

Isobel turned to her bodyguard. "Monty Johnson arranged the attack on the agency."

Matthew blinked. His mouth worked. "He wouldn't."

"Wouldn't he?"

"But *why*?"

"It doesn't matter. What matters is Riot knows, and I fear he'll do something rash now that Mack is dead."

Matthew hopped to open the carriage door for her. "Mr. Riot do something rash?" he asked climbing in after her. "I doubt that."

Isobel shot him a look. "You don't know my husband very well."

RAVENWOOD AGENCY LOOKED LIKE A CHARRED BRICK. THE windows were boarded up, the brick blasted by dynamite. Chunks were missing, and the door didn't hang quite right. There wasn't even a sign. The building mirrored Isobel's current mood—battered from all sides. It certainly sounded like it was being battered from the inside. A symphony of hammers played.

She pushed open the door, and it fell off the hinges. Matthew stepped up to right it, and she stood in the empty barroom, surprised. The debris was gone, the floor swept clean, and despite a patch of char, the office was relatively unscathed. A single table and two chairs had survived the attack, and Mack's fern. Lotario, as dapper as could be, sat at the table with Tim. The two men were supervising an army of workers, while sipping wine poured from an obscenely expensive bottle.

Miss Lucky Off sat on the bar by the telephone, her bare feet knocking on the side, as she smoked a pipe and let her rat drink from her wine glass.

The workers all looked like cousins of Lotario's bodyguard Bruno at the *Narcissus*. When Isobel entered, the hammering stopped, and the laborers paused to remove their caps.

"Well, if it ain't the hussy," Lucky said.

Isobel ignored the woman.

"What on earth are you doing here?" she asked her twin.

He raised a glass to her. "Celebrating. Why don't you gentlemen take a break."

"Yes, sir." The men filed out, lunch boxes in hand.

"Celebrating what?" she asked.

"My new business venture."

"And what is that?" she asked slowly, glancing at Tim.

The old man looked pleased with himself. And slightly tipsy.

"I bought into a detective agency," Lotario said. "Thirty percent, to be exact."

"We needed capital," Tim said.

"Not only is Mr. Amsel the better looking of the twins, he's also keener," Lucky noted.

Isobel's head hurt. "So you talked with Riot this morning? He came by?"

"Well, no," Tim said. "I didn't exactly run it by him, but…"

"I have an accountant," Lotario said.

"So no one has seen Riot today?" Isobel demanded.

Tim shook his head. There was something in her tone. "What's wrong?" he asked.

"Mack is dead," she said. "Sepsis."

Tim sucked in a breath. Lucky's smug face fell. And into the ensuing silence, Lotario set down his glass and went to her, his fingers brushing hers.

"I'm sorry to hear," he said.

Tim sighed. "It's a dangerous business."

"Do you know where Monty is?" Isobel asked.

Tim shook his head. "Haven't found him yet. He's gone from his lodging house. What are you thinking?"

"That Riot's looking for him."

The significance wasn't lost on Tim.

"Did you try his boxing club?" the question came from the woman on the bar. "I heard him ringing it up one day."

"Where is it?" Isobel asked.

Lucky glanced at her nails, and sniffed. "Well, now. Look who needs *my* help."

"Mack is dead because of Monty," Isobel said.

Lucky cut off. "The Den, down by the warehouses."

THE DEN

THE DAY BEGAN TO WEAR ON RIOT. HOURS HAD BLED AWAY, and a cool anger was the only thing that kept him going as he searched Monty's haunts.

Mack was dead. *His* agent. Gunned down like a dog for no good reason. Killed by one of their own.

Eventually, Riot found his agent at The Den—a boxing club in a run-down warehouse district of Mission Bay. The gymnasium was full of half-clad toughs with bloody fists, but Monty stood out for his height and build. He was stripped down to his suspenders and undershirt. The shirt was soaked with sweat, and he smoked a cigar as he unwound the wraps from his fists. An opponent still sat stunned and battered in the ring.

"You get lost on the way to that fancy fencing club of yours?" Monty asked as Riot approached.

"Only looking for my wayward agent."

Monty glanced up from his wraps, the leather dangling from his wrists. "I'm not your goddamn agent anymore."

"I wasn't aware you quit."

Monty plucked the cigar from his lips. "You're a detective. I knew you'd figure it out sooner or later. Now unless you're willing to get in that ring with me, I have better things to do."

Riot watched two men sparring in a practice ring. The coach stood nearby, hollering instructions as flesh pounded flesh. "I hear you joined the Pinkertons."

The Pinkertons were a quality detective service, but they were also in deep with the Big Four railroad tycoons. Pinkertons were strike-breakers, bodyguards, and lately, the personal detective agency of the railways. In some states they were regarded as little more than hired thugs. There were good and bad in the agency, and those in-between, just like in the police force.

Riot hadn't always agreed with their tactics. He was no saint himself, but shooting hard-working men trying to better their working conditions had never sat well with him.

"A man can move up there," Monty said. "And I don't have to answer to a smart-mouthed bitch."

"This has nothing to do with my wife."

"Funny how you assume I was referring to Mrs. Riot. Did she give you permission to be here, A.J.? Never thought I'd see you so whipped."

"Whatever this is… it's about you and me."

"You came all the way out here because I didn't show up to work?"

"The agency was attacked. Mack is dead."

"Sorry to hear that."

"Are you?"

"He was all right," Monty said, smiling around his cigar. "You accusing me of something, A.J.?"

"I think it coincidental that you took up with the Pinkertons the day Ravenwood Agency was attacked."

"Coincidence is a bitch. I needed the money without the hassle of scraping to that ball and chain of yours, and writing goddamn reports for you."

"I also think it interesting that a group of drunks were hired to start a fight three blocks away from the agency by a man who fits your description—a man who was seen with the Pinkertons."

Monty smirked. "Seems I have a twin."

"Alex Kingston has a grudge against Bel and me the size of Texas. He was once attorney to the Southern Pacific railroad, and the Pinkertons are in deep with them. I'd say that all adds up."

"Here's the thing, A.J." Monty sucked in a breath of his cigar, savoring the moment. "I don't work for you anymore. I don't have to listen or answer to your shit." He blew a cloud of smoke into Riot's face. It took Riot straight back to his boyhood, to a run-down room and the line of men reeking of tobacco who came to use his mother.

Riot snapped. He punched Monty square—a mean left hook that flung the cigar from his lips. Monty staggered, but kept his feet. Then he charged. There was no finesse, only pure rage. Riot was rammed against a punching bag, but it gave. He hit the ground, Monty on top, and quickly brought up the knob of his stick. It clipped Monty under the jaw. He fell back, stunned.

Riot got to his feet, ready for another charge.

"Hoy!" a gruff voice shouted as Monty rose in a crouch. "Take it into the ring."

Monty wiped blood from his mouth. "You going to shoot me, A.J.? Isn't that what you're good at. Too yellow to fight like a gentleman."

"A gentleman? You're one to talk, Monty. You were too cowardly to try and kill me yourself. Instead you hired a group of sloppy thugs."

The boxing coach got between them, hands spread. He pointed to Riot's shoulder holster. "Either leave now or get into that ring."

Every eye was on the pair.

Monty spat. "He doesn't have the balls to get into a ring with me."

Riot ripped off his spectacles, and tossed them onto a mat, before shrugging out of his coat. He unbuckled his holster, handed it to a gnarled old man, and rolled up his cuffs. He climbed into the ring with his ex-agent.

The moment Riot cleared the ropes, Monty struck. It was a ferocious volley, barefisted and brutal. Riot got his forearms up, dancing to the side, keeping clear of the corners. Riot stayed out of reach, but Monty didn't care about defense. He was on the attack.

Riot ducked under a punch, and drove his fist into the man's ribs. Quick on his feet, he was gone before Monty recovered, adding a second blow to the man's kidney.

Monty grunted. Riot danced forward, throwing two quick jabs. Monty absorbed the blows, and struck with a volley of his own. Riot deflected with his forearms, but there was power in those punches—power that shook Riot's bones.

They exchanged blows for a long three minutes. Ducking, dodging, slipping to the side, fists connecting with flesh, neither gaining the upper hand. Monty had all the advantage: size, reach, and speed. But Riot was quick and calculating, and calm. For every blow Monty landed, Riot landed three.

Sweat and blood dampened Riot's shirt. Monty was breathing hard, but Riot was only just winded. If he could just wear him down… Where was the bell? It was a distant thought, as Riot ducked under a massive fist.

Monty drove him towards the ropes with another volley, then abandoned all pretense of boxing and charged. The large man slammed Riot into the ropes, and drove his head down on his.

Riot heard a crack. Felt it down to his toes. His vision blurred, and spots danced across his eyes as a flurry of fists pounded his head, ribs and stomach. Riot tensed his muscles as he tried to slip free of the ropes.

There was no bell. No call to break it up. This was no match.

Numb to the beating now, Riot waited, grunting as a fist connected with his stomach, then came up towards his face. Riot struck, a quick jab that connected with Monty's under-arm. It shocked the man, enough for Riot to stagger away.

Dazed and stumbling, he coughed out a mouthful of blood, and tried to shake the spots from his eyes, blinking rapidly.

Monty swam into view. "That's all you got?" He didn't wait for Riot to answer. Monty threw a wild, powerful hook. Riot stepped into it, lessening the force, and drove a fist into Monty's sternum.

Monty's blow connected at the same time. It knocked Riot's head to the side, blood flew, but he kept his feet. Monty stumbled backwards, trying to catch his breath, and Riot shook himself, pressing the attack. Quick and light, he jabbed at face, stomach, ribs until Monty slumped against the ropes. Riot didn't back off. It was a mistake.

Monty abandoned all semblance of a fair fight. He caught Riot in a powerful bear hug that threatened to crush his ribs, and used his superior weight and height to slam Riot to the mat. It knocked the wind right out of him.

Lungs burning, Riot scrambled towards the opposite side and slithered under the ropes, falling to the floor. But when he tried to rise, a foot slammed into his ribs. Riot fell, gasping. Then a volley of blows came down on his face.

Every pounding fist came from far away. Numb. Riot seemed to watch from high above as some stranger was beaten to a pulp below. Finally, after what seemed an eternity, a bell dinged. Two men pulled Monty off Riot. Dazed and delirious, blinking frantically, he tried to stand, but his limbs weren't working. The room was a blur, spinning, tumbling, falling.

"Looking for these?" a voice asked.

Riot lay on his back, trying to focus on the man, but there were a multitude of him, all holding a pair of spectacles. A moment later, Monty dropped the spectacles and stomped his foot. Glass crunched.

The knob of Ravenwood's walking stick caught Riot under the chin, forcing his eyes up. Monty's battered face swam into view. "Your problem has always been that you don't know when to quit. You pissed off some powerful men, A.J. That's how this world works." Monty leaned closer, nearly whispering in his ear. "You ever stop to think that I might have been trying to save your arrogant ass?"

Riot coughed, blood spraying on Monty's face.

"You stay away from your betters, and keep away from me."

Monty's scarred knuckles were the last thing Riot saw.

ROCK BOTTOM

THEY FOUND RIOT IN A GUTTER.

Face down, stripped to his underwear and violently shivering, thieves had picked him clean. Isobel rushed to him. She slid slightly in the muck as she tried to turn him over. The instant she touched him, he groaned and tried to struggle, but fell back down, his limbs stiff and unnatural, his forehead pressed against the ground.

Isobel must have made a sound, because he turned his head to search for her. The single eye that wasn't swollen shut rolled in its socket.

"Good God," Lotario whispered.

"Easy," Tim warned.

Matthew helped turn him over, but the new position on his back made him heave. It was violent, incoherent, and agonizing. Riot collapsed on his side, and Isobel steadied his head in her lap, bending over him. "You've certainly looked better, Riot."

He tried to talk, but his jaw wasn't working.

The night had a bite to it, and the closest lamppost was down the street, but she could see the uneven shadows of his face, smell the blood and feel it on her hands. She quickly shrugged off her coat and bundled him as best she could.

"Lotario, run and get a hack. Matt, fetch Dr. Wise. Bring him straight to the house," Tim ordered.

While the two darted off, Isobel sat and smoothed Riot's hair, whispering softly to him. "I'm here. It'll be all right." His spectacles were clenched in a swollen hand. The glass shattered, the frame mangled beyond repair.

Tim crouched, and struck a match, running it over Riot, who flinched at the light. Isobel sucked in a sharp breath.

"Worse than it looks," Riot slurred. The words were painfully slow. It was likely the very first thing he had tried to say, only delayed.

"A'yup. That's Monty's handiwork, alright," Tim said. "Of all the stupid, pea-brained, hell-bent ideas you've had, boy… this one takes the cake."

"Tim!" Isobel cried. "Wait until he's coherent to chew him out. He won't remember a word of it now." It was said lightly, but inside she was breaking. She didn't care what had brought Riot to this point. For now, he was alive. And no longer alone.

They had gone straight to the boxing club. A wrinkled old man with a broom had confided to Tim that Riot picked a fight outside the ring, so he was tossed to the curb after. The old man returned Riot's holster and gun, and pointed them down an alleyway where he'd been dragged by some locals. She feared they'd killed him. But no. He was breathing, if painfully.

When a hack pulled up at the alleyway entrance, Lotario hopped down, and trotted over to help move him. The three of them managed to half drag, half carry him to the hack, but when they loaded him in, the shift in movement made him retch again.

The rest of the evening was a blur. Rather than haul him up three flights of stairs with a house full of watching eyes, they took him to Tim's rooms in the stable house. He was a swollen mess—skin split, bruised and bleeding. Isobel focused on the gash on his side. "You've ruined my sutures, Riot," she said.

It took him a full minute to respond. "Sorry," he slurred.

"You can be sorry later," she said. "I hope you left Monty in a similar state."

"Fairly."

"Small victories." But inside she was close to tears. Lotario stood behind her, a hand on her shoulder. Light seemed to cause Riot pain, so they kept the room dim while they waited for the doctor.

Riot placed a swollen hand over hers. His knuckles were shredded.

It seemed a lifetime before Doctor Wise arrived with his medical bags. He took one look at his patient, and sighed. "What did I tell you about blocking punches." He looked to Isobel. "Do you want to stay?"

She nodded.

"Good. Someone get water boiling and bring clean towels."

"I'll tell Miss Lily." Lotario trotted away.

Tim leaned against the doorpost of his room, smoking a pipe.

"Mr. Tim, put a kettle on. You know how to steep this, I believe. And put that pipe out." Wise handed a paper packet off, and Tim left.

"Ice?" she asked.

Dr. Wise shook his head as he bent over Riot to examine him. "That will only delay healing. Our bodies flow with *Qi*, or energy along pathways. Injury causes blockages in those pathways. I'll help restore balance so his body can heal itself."

Isobel didn't know about all that, but she trusted Dr. Wise enough not to question his expertise. So she stood back and watched.

"I'm fine," Riot slurred slowly, and tried to rise—a clumsy jerk of movement. "Brandy."

Dr. Wise snorted. "I'm no Dr. Watson." He turned to his bag and unrolled a leather scroll-like bundle bristling with thin needles. He selected one, and with expert precision, inserted the needle at a point between Riot's eyebrows.

That sliver of a needle seemed to pin Riot to his pillow.

When hot water and towels were brought, Isobel helped strip him down to clean away the blood and muck. Angry bruises decorated his torso that reminded her of Ella's decomposing corpse. It made her sick.

Dr. Wise spent the next ten minutes turning Riot's feet, hands, and ankles into pin cushions. By the time Wise sat back, Riot resembled a hedgehog. Skin was sutured, salves applied, and finally the doctor added a few carefully placed needles on Riot's scalp.

Satisfied, Wise laid a thin blanket over Riot, needles and all. He sat back and peeled off his spectacles. "I have more work to do on him. I'll sit with him tonight," Wise said.

Isobel recognized the unspoken dismissal. "I can't sleep," she argued.

Dr. Wise reached into his bag, and handed her a paper packet of herbs. "Drink this then. He's severely concussed, I need to watch him."

"Prognosis?" she asked, bracing herself.

"We need to wait," Wise said, unwilling to voice his concerns. "He's speaking though. That's a good sign, but I'd rather be here in case anything… worsens. His nose is broken, his jaw may be too. I'll know for sure when the swelling goes down. One broken rib, maybe two, I think. It's fortunate he's a trained fencer and boxer. The muscle conditioning saved his life."

"Bel," Lotario said softly. "You can't do anything more."

"I can be here if he wakes up."

"*When*," Wise corrected. He smiled in understanding. "My people have a long history of training in the martial arts. We are very good at causing injury, and we are very good at putting people back together. I find Chinese medicine more useful in these cases than American medicine. Another physician would likely cut off his hair, give him brandy, leech his face, put ice on his head and hot water bottles at his feet. And then leave it up to time."

You On Chung, or Ewan Wise, was a University-trained physician who combined ancient arts with modern ones in an effective combination. Riot was in good hands. Quite possibly the very best. And he had brought Riot back from near death before, nearly four years ago.

"You have daughters. Go check on them."

"They know something happened," Lotario said. "It's impossible to hide anything from them. You need to tell them."

Isobel sighed. She leaned over, and placed a soft kiss on Riot's forehead. "If anything changes…"

"I'll let you know immediately."

A LONG ROAD

FOR NEARLY TWO DAYS ISOBEL WAS GLUED TO RIOT'S BEDSIDE. He mostly slept, and slowly, with Wise's treatments, he regained more of himself. He could recall his name, where he was, and sit up without toppling over. Recovery also brought out a stubborn streak and a short temper.

"I'm fine," he insisted. His face was still a lumpy mass of bruises, and his jaw was stiff. Dr. Wise had gently worked the dislocation back into position.

"Of course, you are. I've spent night and day treating you. As if I have nothing better to do," Wise said. "You need to rest. And by rest, I mean inactivity."

"I will." Riot slid his feet onto the floor. He looked around with one eye, his other still swollen shut. "Spectacles?"

"They were crushed," Isobel explained. "Your spare won't fit until the swelling goes down."

His shoulders sagged. "Clothes?"

"After the men at the boxing club dragged you outside, you

were robbed," Isobel explained. "The cleaner at the club gave back your revolver, though."

Pocket watch, billfold, and Ravenwood's walking stick were all gone. To say nothing of his hat and bespoke suit.

Riot fended off Wise's attempts to keep him in bed. Finally the doctor threw up his hands. Riot pushed himself off the bed, and stood. His blanket fell off.

"Well, at least the important parts are intact," a voice drawled from the doorway.

"Ari, go find him some clothes," Isobel growled at her twin. "Riot, where are you going?"

He swayed on his feet for a moment. "To my *own* bed and my *own* bathroom. Do you have any idea what it's like sleeping in Tim's bed?"

Isobel glanced at Wise, who caved in with a lift of his brows.

"Fine, but if you collapse on the stairwell, I'm leaving you there."

Riot managed shirt and trousers on his own, but he finally gave up on buttons and shoes and let Isobel help him. She rolled her eyes when he asked for a hat. "Absolutely not. You're more likely to run off if you have a hat."

Riot leveled a single blood shot eye at her. He was not amused.

Isobel slipped her arm through his, and, with Dr. Wise and Lotario hovering nearby in case he collapsed, she walked him into the main house.

For the past few days, they had managed to keep the children away, but Isobel was questioning her decision when they entered the main house for the first time and she witnessed their reactions: Sarah burst into tears and rushed forward, but before she could topple Riot with love, she drew up short in favor of a more gingerly display of affection.

"It looks worse than it is," he said.

"Can you even see?" Sarah asked.

She had a point.

Jin did not say a word, just walked to his other side and lent her shoulder as support in the guise of a hug. She stayed with him the entire walk up the stairs.

When Riot finally collapsed onto his bed, Isobel sighed with relief.

"Keep giving him these. I will return tomorrow," Dr. Wise said, placing a number of vials and herbal packets on the bedside table. "Let me know if anything new develops."

Sarah was busy fluffing his pillows and Jin was tugging off his shoes.

"I will. At least we have plenty of nurses," she said with a smile. "Thank you, Doctor."

Wise bowed slightly. "No strenuous activities, *of any sort*, for at least two weeks."

Riot grumbled in return.

"And move faster next time, Atticus," Dr. Wise crooned.

It was fortunate the girls were present and Riot's fingers were swollen, or she was sure he'd have replied with a silent gesture.

When Wise left, Lotario turned to her. "What more can I do, sister dear?"

"I don't know," she admitted. "Nothing else matters much right now."

He gave her a small smile. "I'll bring up a tray, then get out of the way."

Food did help. As she picked at her plate, she watched Sarah and Jin forcing chicken broth on Riot. Apparently having his brain smashed against the inside of his skull made him irritable. The girls weren't deterred in the least. At one point, Jin threatened to pry his mouth open if he didn't sip his soup.

Finally, Riot closed his eyes to sleep. The girls lingered at his bedside for half an hour, but eventually got bored watching him and left.

Alone at last, Isobel slipped under the covers, and rested her forehead against his shoulder. His fingers found her own. As she suspected, he had been feigning sleep in self-defense.

"Say it," he murmured.

"What the hell were you thinking?"

"I've known Monty for years. I wanted to give him a chance to explain himself."

"Did he?"

"I can't currently recall."

Despite herself, she laughed. "What *do* you recall?"

"He blew a cloud of smoke in my face. I don't remember much after that."

Ah. That explained everything. The action had been as good as a trigger for him. Isobel hugged his forearm to her. But even that was bruised and swollen.

"I'm sorry about Mack," he said. His words were still slow, and seemed to require careful forming.

"I am, too." She was quiet for a time, listening to his breath. "Was it always like this? For you, here in San Francisco?"

"Not always. But for a good many years."

"I can see why you wanted to retire."

"Do you want to?" He turned his head slightly, but it wasn't as if he could see much. Still, she raised herself on an elbow to look into his bloodshot eye.

"I can't let Ella down. And there's too many more like her."

"It never ends," he whispered before drifting off to sleep.

A CLUE

ISOBEL TOSSED A NEWSPAPER TO THE FLOOR.

Sarah stopped her sketching and turned the newspaper around to look at the front page. "What a horrible picture."

The *Morning Call* featured a sketch of a man choking Ella Spencer in her bed precisely the way Sims had demonstrated. The look of terror on Ella's face was haunting.

"It's a good sketch though…" Sarah admitted.

The three of them lounged in front of a crackling fire, Sarah lying on the floor with her sketchpad and Riot sitting in a chair across from Isobel. He was dozing. Even that seemed to exhaust him.

"Do you think they'll find this Hawkins?" Sarah asked.

"I don't know."

"I can't imagine what her family is going through."

There was a detailed article about how Mrs. Spencer had collapsed on top of the body of her daughter, after insisting on identifying her. The press had latched onto the case like vultures on a carcass. Ravenwood Agency and the police had been flooded with supposed sightings and offers from people claiming to have information: a man with a trunk whose contents could pinpoint the location of the killer, a host of clairvoyants in communication with Ella's ghost, and even an armchair detective claiming to be Sherlock Holmes reincarnated.

"Riot was right," she muttered.

"Of course I was," he said.

Sarah started in surprise.

Some of the swelling had gone down, enough to put on his spare spectacles, but he didn't reach for the glasses. He was still sensitive to light.

"And you're not going to let me forget it, are you?" Isobel asked.

His lips moved in an attempted smile, but the bruising made it difficult. "I'll have Sarah write down today's date and time for my records. I know *you* keep tabs."

"*I* don't need pen and paper to remember." Isobel tapped her head.

"That's a low blow."

Isobel stuck her tongue out at him. "You'll get no more sympathy from me. I ran out of that yesterday."

"What's the score?" he asked.

Sarah rolled her eyes. "If you keep a tally both of you will lose. And I won't write it down."

"I suppose he'll just have to forget this one," Isobel said, pleased.

Riot snorted, but instantly winced. It hurt to breathe, it hurt to move, it hurt to sleep. Dr. Wise was due back for another treatment today. He slowly reached for a mug, and with effort brought it to his cut lips, though half dripped down his beard. He grimaced at the taste of the medicinal concoction.

"Did you hear my twin is now a thirty percent partner in

your agency," Isobel said.

Riot coughed, spraying tea all over.

Sarah handed him a napkin.

"Did you wait until I was incapacitated to arrange that?"

"I had nothing to do with it," Isobel defended. "Tim made the deal before you were beaten to a pulp."

"He didn't consult me."

"Are you sure?"

"*Yes*," Riot said testily.

"Well, Ari is tickled to death over the idea. He's brought capital to the venture."

"What does Mr. Lotario do for a living?" Sarah asked.

Isobel waved a hand. "This and that." Before the girl could ask for specifics, she changed the subject. "Do you have any idea where Jin is today?"

Sarah looked back, innocent.

Isobel leaned forward to study the child.

"She's probably in Chinatown again," Sarah finally said.

"Doing what?"

Sarah paled under her gaze. "Don't look at me like that," she pleaded. She stood to plump Riot's pillow.

"Don't go to him for help," Isobel said.

"I'd like to know, too," Riot said.

"You mean you don't know?" Sarah asked.

"So you *do* know what she's up to?" Isobel accused.

"I don't know for sure. I... Grimm was following her. There's a rumor going around Chinatown that a girl and a negro robbed three men. I guess she stabbed one of them. I'm not sure what she was doing, but Grimm helped her out. That's why he had that bruised eye."

"She *stabbed* someone?" Isobel asked, stunned. "And you didn't think to tell us?"

"You've both been on the busy side," Sarah defended,

looking pointedly at Riot. "I forgot all about it. And anyhow, I took care of it."

"How? What did you do?" Isobel pressed.

"I contacted Mr. Sin, and he said he'd watch her. As far as I know he has been."

Isobel blinked, impressed. When had Sarah done all that? But then the girl was right—they had been distracted. "Thank you, Sarah. That was wise of you."

Sarah shrugged. "I still don't know why she keeps going into Chinatown."

Isobel and Riot shared a look. With Jin, it could be anything. Isobel wouldn't put bank robbery past the child.

There was a knock at the door.

"Come," Isobel called.

The knock came again.

Sarah hopped up to answer it.

Matthew Smith stood in the doorway, hat in hand, practically standing at attention. "Miss Sarah," he said. "I'm here to speak with Mrs. Riot."

"Isobel," she growled. "Stop standing there, and come in."

Matthew moved tentatively into the room, his gaze stuck on Riot's face.

"Mr. Riot," he said, with a nod. Then he turned to her. "Mrs. Riot…"

Isobel raised a brow at him.

"Isobel," he corrected.

"What is it, Matt?" Riot asked. "This isn't a mourning party."

Matthew cleared his throat. "I've been following up on every tip and sighting, but nothing's turned up, so I checked the business cards left at the house and managed to track down the stores where the furniture was purchased." He got out his notepad and recited a litany of facts. Nothing new, except…

"The deliveryman said when he carried in the mattress, he saw Hawkin's hands shaking. And there was ink on them."

"Why would that matter?" Sarah asked.

"I don't know." Matthew closed his notebook. "I went around to the *Call* again, but the advertisement people still couldn't find any receipt or log of the ad being placed. There was no record of it."

"Is that uncommon?" she asked.

Matthew considered her question. "Uncommon enough that the manager was upset, but that could be because it's part of a big story."

Isobel idly toyed with a chess piece as she stared into the fire. She must have been staring for some time, because Sarah had to call her name loudly.

She looked back at Matthew. "Where was the ink on Hawkins's hands?"

Matthew stared blankly for a moment until she made an impatient gesture at him. "I'm sorry, I didn't ask."

Isobel shot to her feet, and shrugged off her dressing gown, exchanging it for a coat. "Sarah, stay with Riot. Shoot him in the foot if he tries to leave."

Sarah gaped.

"Matt, come with me."

"Watch yourself, Bel," Riot warned.

She paused at the door. "I'll do my best. Besides, I have Matt with me. What could possibly go wrong?"

Matthew looked helplessly at Riot before hurrying to catch up to her. Sarah sighed, and got up to close the door. "It's a good thing she didn't leave those orders with Jin."

38

CHINESE THEATER

SAO JIN SAT IN A QUIET THEATER. NO ONE CLAPPED OR cheered the way they did in white theaters. The audience sat, respectful. Contemplative. She watched the play unfold, the brilliant costumes and masks, the makeup and sets, the dancing and singing. A feast for the eyes.

But she was puzzled by all the tourists on stage. White men and women, seated in a semicircle, watching the play. Some looked self-conscious, others imperious. She wouldn't want to sit up there on display. But those seats were the best in the house, and guides were there to whisper translations or explanations of what was happening. But she couldn't decide whether the white people had been given the best seats in the house, or if they'd been put on display for the audience. Was the audience around her interested in white people's reactions to the play?

Jin felt adrift in her own culture, so she focused on the story. It reminded her of *Hamlet*, only far more complicated. It was about a woman who falls asleep by a peony pavilion, and dreams of a scholar she has never met. But she can't find the man, so she dies of a broken heart. Currently the woman was on stage trying to convince the *Infernal Judge* to send her back to the land of the living.

Yet another story about a woman pining after a man. Jin rolled her eyes. But she wasn't there for cultural art. She was searching faces in the crowd. Searching for someone familiar.

The play went on and on. Tiring of it, Jin left the main auditorium. On a whim, she walked through a side door in the foyer. There must be a way onto the stage…

No one stopped her. And she found herself standing backstage with actors and actresses rushing around silently donning costumes. The back rooms looked like a giant wardrobe.

Jin wandered towards piles of silks. A woman sat in a chair with needle and thread, mending some tear in the fabric. It was delicate work, and the movement of thread and needle was mesmerizing. Jin drifted closer, until she could hear a soft tune on the woman's lips as she worked. The woman looked up, startled.

"I didn't see you there, child." She smiled. She was older, but her face was smooth and untouched by the sun, though her shoulders were hunched. She wore spectacles.

"I am sorry to disturb your work," Jin said.

The woman squinted at her. "You do not belong back here."

"No," Jin admitted.

The woman looked over her shoulder, on the verge of summoning someone to escort her out.

"Wait," Jin blurted out. "I am looking for someone."

"Who?"

"My parents were killed. Four years ago." The words came out in a rasp. "They were tailors. They had a shop down the street from here. I do not remember the name…"

"What is yours?"

"Sao Jin."

Sadness passed over the woman's eyes. "Your parents were known to me."

"You knew them?"

The woman shook her head. "I knew *of* them."

"Is there anyone here who knew them?"

"There is."

The woman hesitated, then stood and set down her work. She led Jin to a back room lined with costumes on racks. A small man sat on a cushion, legs crossed, sketching in a book. One shoulder was higher than the other, and his face was as wrinkly as a prune.

The woman bowed deeply. "Shi Bingwen, I have brought the child of an old friend."

The man did not look up. He continued his sketching.

"Sao Gan and Ah Lam."

The man's hand stopped. His head jerked upwards, and sharp eyes focused on Jin. But Jin forgot to breathe. The woman had said the names of her parents. Before today, she could not remember them. Her lip quivered. She wanted to run. She wanted to find Isobel. She did not want to continue alone. But she had to.

Bingwen gestured with a grunt, and the woman bowed again, backing up before leaving Jin alone with the man. He returned to his sketching.

Jin waited patiently.

He was drawing an elaborate costume. A dragon. Making notations and focusing in on details. "Sao Gan and Ah Lam used to help me craft costumes. They were master tailors," he said without looking up.

"Why were they butchered?" she asked.

He took a deep breath. "Do hatchet men need a reason?"

"*I* need a reason," Jin said.

Bingwen's pencil stopped. "Why?"

"Would you not want to know? I loved my parents. I want to know why they were killed."

"Knowledge can be dangerous here."

"I do not care."

He huffed. "So like your father. Do you know the saying about the reed, child?"

She shook her head.

"*The green reed which bends in the wind is stronger than the mighty oak which breaks in a storm,*" he said.

"What does that have to do with my parents?"

"Everything."

"Who said it?"

"Confucius."

"I do not know that man," she said.

He tapped his pencil against paper. "How can't you? He's a great philosopher."

Jin ground her teeth together. "I was a house slave for four years. After my parents were killed, a woman took me, then I was passed to another. And another," she bit out.

Bingwen ran eyes over her scarred cheeks. "I looked for you. I did. I thought…" He trailed off. "I thought the hatchet men had taken you for a brothel." He shook his head. "I am sorry I did not find you."

"I am here now."

"Yes." He smiled, sadly. "Your father was not a reed; he was an oak. Bold, fearless, he would not bend under Gee Sin Seer's threats. Some called him brave. I call him a fool."

"Do not speak of my father like that!" she hissed.

The artist spread his hands. "Yet he is dead. And so is your mother. Sao Gan defied the criminal tongs. He reported crimes to the Consul and identified hatchet men to the police force. He and your mother rescued slave girls and helped them escape. They hid them and took them to the mission for safety. That's why they were killed."

"Gee Sin Seer killed them?" Jin said.

Bingwen inclined his head. "They have no regard for human life. Killing to them is no more than swatting a fly. That is what we are to them. Flies."

"Because you do not fight!" Jin said.

"We survive. As you have."

Her nostrils flared. "Which hatchet men killed my parents?"

"I do not know."

Jin lifted her chin. "Chinatown has many ears. There are always rumors."

Bingwen dipped his head. "Rumor says it was Maa Min and Niu Tou."

Jin frowned. They were not normal names, but words with meaning. "Horse-face and Ox-head?" she asked, puzzled.

Bingwen sighed. "You don't know that story either, do you?"

Jin shook her head.

"Horse-face and Ox-head are the two guardians of Hell. They escort the newly dead into the Underworld and drag them in front of the courts of Hell."

Jin shivered. "What about the third man?"

"Nobody of note."

"He is noteworthy to me."

"Nin Sam, I think. He killed Niu Tou some years later during an argument."

Jin snorted. Hatchet men couldn't even work together without turning on each other. "And Maa Min?"

Bingwen put down his pencil, and leaned forward, touching the back of her hand lightly. "Are you alone?"

Jin shook her head.

"You have a home?"

"I do."

"Are they kind to you?"

"Atticus and Isobel—Din Gau and Wu Lei Ching—adopted me."

Bingwen's eyes widened a fraction. "I see. But they are white. You have a family here at the theater, Jin. A *Chinese* family. You will never truly be a part of Din Gau's family."

Hands curled into fists. "My bahba would never have stopped looking for me, and neither would Din Gau." She left the old man with his pretty costumes and philosophies.

39

THE CALL

FROM THE MOMENT ISOBEL ENTERED THE *CALL* BUILDING, SHE attracted stares. Trailing behind her was a six-foot-tall blond agent who oozed 'police.' That definitely helped. She marched straight to the lift, and the three men in the lift moved to the opposite side, directing glares her way.

Matthew leaned down to whisper in her ear. "What did you do?"

Isobel raised a shoulder and ignored the men, but she received the same cool response when she entered the bullpen. Conversation fell to a hush as she marched through the desks.

"You're not welcome here," a harsh voice said.

More voices joined the discord.

"The sooner I get answers the quicker I'll leave," she said offhandedly, walking down an adjoining hallway to the Sob Sisters's office.

As she had hoped, Cara Sharpe was sitting there, along with Jo Kelly and Rose, the pair who had ratted her out before her trial.

Jo Kelly got to her feet. "You have a lot of nerve coming here."

Confronted with open hostility from a woman, Matthew stopped in his tracks and actually took a step backwards. Some bodyguard.

"I'm not here to banter with you," Isobel said.

"You got Mack killed!" the redhead accused. Young, attractive, and spirited. It wasn't hard to imagine Mack being more than "just friends" with Jo Kelly.

Isobel faltered. Had she got him killed? Maybe so. Still, Isobel wasn't about to admit it to Jo Kelly. "*This* newspaper fired him. He needed a job. Unfortunately, the detective business is a dangerous one. He knew the risks." That's what she told herself, at any rate. Riot's frantic call for him to stay put still echoed in her ears. But Mack had... what, panicked? Thought himself invincible? Had he been trying to protect her?

"He was fired because of *you*," Kelly said.

Isobel took a breath. "You're right. And I'm sorry, but I can't change what happened."

Jo Kelly stepped forward and slapped her. Flesh on flesh echoed in the office. She didn't even feel the sting on her cheek. It was deserved.

Jo gathered her belongings and stormed out, and Rose followed suit, but more quietly and with a muttered apology. Cara still hadn't acknowledged her. The older woman was bent over her typewriter.

Isobel sighed faintly, and unfolded one of Sarah's sketches. "I'm sure you've heard of the Ella Spencer murder. You've been here longest, Cara. I think the wanted ad was placed from *within* the *Call* building, either by the murderer himself or a contact. I'll give you an exclusive if you give me his name." She placed the sketch face down on Cara's desk.

Cara punched the period on the typewriter, then took her time removing the paper and reading over her page. Finally, she placed it on top of a stack.

Isobel stood patiently as the steel-haired woman lit a cigarette and gazed out of the window. "You could have argued that when Jo and Rose exposed your cover, they set in motion the events that led to Mack's death."

"I could have."

"You could have also argued that a reporter's job is a dangerous one, too. That Mack chased the wrong story or that his principles got him killed."

Matthew cleared his throat, and wiped at an eye. Cara turned to the man. "What do you think?"

Matthew started. "Me?"

Cara nodded. She was a heavyset woman with steel gray hair, and had the look of a confident tabby that could turn dangerous at any moment.

Matthew composed himself. "I only worked with Mack for a few months, but... he was a good man. Honest. Brave. He hated bullies. He died fighting a fight he wanted to be in."

Cara raised her brows. "Well now. That's a noble sort of speech." Cara pointed her cigarette at Matthew. "I have a nose for truth. And that was the truth. Make sure you remember that, Bonnie."

It was easy to say; harder to believe.

Cara turned over the sketch, and studied it. She tapped her finger on the man's nose in thought, spreading ash over the page. "He's familiar."

Isobel perked up. Her theory had been a long shot, but the pieces fit. Ella had been seen in front of the *Call* building with a man who Heather Searlight thought was Oliver Grant. But how close to the two of them had Heather been? Why was Ella irritated with a family attorney? What was Ella doing downtown? There weren't any clubs or resorts. Then the ad placed with no record of payment. Someone inside the building, familiar with the ins and outs of the newspaper could easily slip an ad into the mix. Finally, the ink on Hawkins's hands.

His disappearances, his comings and goings into the city, his disguises and the false names. All of that came natural for a reporter.

"Hadley," Cara said suddenly.

"He's here? In this building?"

Cara shook her head. "He used to work here as a reporter. Then he got injured—that drooping eye—and moved on. That was well over a decade ago."

"The owner at the Popular said he returned last year."

Cara stood. "Can I take this and show it to Griful?"

"As long as you don't let him get his grubby hands on it. A girl was murdered, Cara. I'm not doing this for a story. Do we have a deal?" Isobel held out her hand.

Cara shook it. "I'd leave the building if I were you. Everyone blames you for Mack's death. I'll meet you at the coffee shop across the street."

"Can we trust her?" Matthew asked as they waited at a table. He had ordered a sandwich for himself that was so big Isobel doubted she could have gotten her mouth around it. Matthew was having no issues.

Isobel took a sip of her coffee and watched the front of the *Call* building. "Cara is a woman of her word," she finally said. "She's also dangerous, sly, and has dubious motives. Not unlike Tim."

Matthew gulped down a bite, and swallowed before speaking. "I'm not entirely sure Mr. Tim shouldn't be in prison."

Isobel snorted. "I'm afraid that applies to most of us, Matt."

He grimaced. "Do you ever…" he hesitated.

She arched a brow.

"Feel like a hypocrite? Not just you…" he blurted out. "But

here we are tracking down criminals and it seems like we're not much better than them at times. I mean... I understand why people kill and thieve. Some motives make sense to me, and I think I'd likely do the same in their shoes."

"*We're not lawmen; we're detectives. Truth is our aim,*" she quoted.

"Mr. Riot told me that."

"And Ravenwood told him. I think it's good advice."

Matthew nodded, slowly. "What do we do with that truth, though?"

Isobel met his eyes. They were blue and bright, so honest and open. "We do what's right, and pray we can live with ourselves afterwards."

Cara Sharpe kept them waiting for the better part of two hours. After an ashtray of cigarettes and enough coffee to power Isobel for a week, the newswoman finally arrived.

"Charles B. Hadley came back all right. He asked for his old job, but Griful wasn't impressed. I found a friend of his in the ad department who he regularly visits. He got him a job at the *Examiner* as a bookkeeper. But the fellow doesn't know where Hadley lives."

Isobel sprang from her seat. She had the villain now.

BUT THEN ISOBEL DIDN'T HAVE HER VILLAIN. CHARLES B. Hadley had not come into work at the *Examiner* since the eleventh—the day after Ella's body was discovered.

Cara threw her seniority around in the reporting world and got the address Hadley gave when he was hired. A house off Mission Street.

The woman who answered the door was in her thirties. A harsh woman with golden hair piled high and rings decorating every finger. Miss Jessica King. "He up and left a week ago Friday. Went into the bathroom with a newspaper, then came out, tossed all his things in a bag, and took off without a word."

"Do you know where he went?" Isobel asked.

"If I did, I'd have followed him and shot him."

"Can I search his belongings?"

The woman snorted. "I burned the lot of it. I'm done with him."

Isobel wanted to choke the woman.

"Did he have friends?" Matthew asked. "Correspondence? Family?"

"He wouldn't introduce me to anyone. Wouldn't even marry me. We've been together for close to six years, but he came and went as he pleased." She dabbed at her eyes.

"I'm sorry," Matthew said. "I truly am."

Isobel looked back from a series of photographs of a familiar coastline on the wall. "Are you a photographer?"

The woman shook her head. "Charles took them. He's a reporter—so he claimed."

"Did he ever speak of Monterey?"

"He always promised to take me there. Said his uncle had a place. But said it was too run-down for me to stay. He promised we'd spend a weekend at the Del Monte one day." She snorted. "Fat chance of that, the bastard."

40

THE DEL MONTE

Saturday, October 19, 1900

"You are *not* coming Riot." Isobel insisted.

He had managed to drag his suitcase from the wardrobe. "I'm not letting you track down a murderer alone."

"I'm taking Tim."

Stubbornly, he placed a shirt inside. Before he could make any more progress, she dumped the contents on the bed, and stuffed his case on the highest shelf.

"Bel!" he growled.

"Don't make me call Dr. Wise. You can barely stand."

"I'll be sitting on a train."

"I'm not taking a train. I'm sailing."

"In winter?"

He had caught her. It would take two days to sail to Monterey, and likely triple that to sail back without a steam engine. The train was more practical, though not as exciting.

Isobel took a breath. "Riot," she said softly. "*Please.* You're in no shape to walk down the stairs by yourself, let alone travel. It's barely been five days. Be patient with yourself."

He sat on the bed. Tired.

Isobel ran a gentle hand over his bruised face, and he looked up into her eyes. "I'm twenty years older than you, Bel. At some point, this… caretaking will be permanent."

Isobel nudged his legs open and moved closer, taking his face in her hands. "I'm positive you will get yourself killed before it comes to that."

He raised a sutured brow, then winced. "Is that your plan?"

"Or maybe I'll just hire a nurse—an unattractive one, with a horrid enough disposition to make me seem warm and caring."

A corner of his swollen lip quirked. "Go find your murderer."

She kissed the top of his head, and he hugged her tightly, his face buried between her breasts. "Heal," she urged. "Rest, for my sake."

"I will," came his muffled promise.

"Besides," she leaned back to tug on his beard, "two weeks of no strenuous activity… It's best if I'm gone."

He grunted.

When she opened the door, Sarah and Jin were waiting outside. "I am coming too," Jin stated.

"Me, too," Sarah said.

"I am not taking the two of you to hunt down a *child murderer*." She glanced back into the room. "Besides, someone has to watch Riot."

The girls looked inside.

Riot slowly sank back to the pillows. "I feel faint," he moaned.

Isobel laughed, but the girls were not amused.

She bent down and lowered her voice. "I'm serious," she said. "He suffered a severe concussion. If he overdoes it…" She swallowed. "It could be bad. Aside from Dr. Wise's bullying, you are the only two who can persuade him to rest."

Sarah straightened her shoulders, and nodded.

Jin looked on the verge of tears. "I want to go with you," she whispered. There was something in those dark eyes, a strong emotion, a pleading that tore at Isobel's heart. She dropped her bag and knelt. "What's going on, Jin?"

Jin shook her head.

Isobel pulled her into a tight embrace. The girl resisted for a moment, then relented, melting into her. "I can't help you unless you tell me," she whispered in her ear.

Again, a head shake.

Isobel held her at arm's length. She directed the full force of the Saavedra gaze on her, but Jin was resolute. And confusing. The girl seemed torn, too.

"I need someone to protect, Riot. Understand?"

Jin nodded.

"I don't know why you're going into Chinatown, but I want you to stop stabbing people. Is that clear?"

Jin's eyes widened, she glanced at Sarah, who had gone suddenly pale. "Oh, stop looking at her. I have my own informants," Isobel lied through her teeth. "Were those men after you?"

"No. One of them pushed me down."

"And attacked you?"

Jin hesitated. "One kicked me, so I stabbed him."

"Fine, don't stab people unless absolutely necessary."

Jin sighed.

Isobel pulled her into another hug, then did the same to Sarah, and left a very disgruntled family.

———

THE *DEL MONTE* WAS RHYTHMIC. A STEADY CLINK OF RAILWAY wheels, the sounds of steam and whistles, and gentle rocking.

All this fell to the background as Isobel stared out the window. Tim was strangely quiet at her side.

"What are we going to do about Monty?" she finally asked.

"What about him?"

"He thrashed Riot near to death."

"If Monty wanted A.J. dead, he would've finished him."

"Monty dragged him outside and left him to thieves."

"That's what generally happens when you sucker punch someone in a boxing club, girl."

She bristled.

A woman opposite eyed the old man warily. Isobel lowered her voice as much as she could with the clanking engine. "He likely hired those men to kill us, Tim."

"Maybe so, but we don't have proof enough for the police."

"The only reason Monty didn't kill Riot then and there was because there were witnesses."

"Here's the thing." Tim leaned in close. "If someone hired Monty like you think, then those same people are mighty displeased that he fouled up the job."

Isobel studied his craggy features. Despite the severity of his words, he had an impish glint in his eyes that reminded her of a devious leprechaun. Tim flashed her a smile, showing off his gold teeth, as if to convince her he was one.

"You're counting on someone snipping off a loose end."

Tim inclined his head.

"That doesn't help Mack any," she muttered. "And we don't know who hired him."

"You want to take it to the police?" he countered. "Maybe we'll have A.J. go in and explain what happened to the men who attacked us, or better yet, he can tell the noble lawmen what transpired in the Morgue."

Isobel opened her mouth, then clicked it shut.

"One day, I hope to God the police can be relied on, but

out here—in the West—civilization's toehold is in a heaping pile of shit."

The Wild West. Tim had lived through it, helped shape it. Survived. And now, though the era was waning, the west was still wild. Tim was born in a time when men took the law into their own hands. No patrolmen, no whistles, no call boxes. A time when shopkeepers and family men took up arms to hunt down criminals.

Tim referred to his informants as Vigilance Boys. In the fifties, San Francisco had rallied to fight a gang called the Sydney Ducks. Ordinary men founded a Committee of Vigilance, a vigilante group that was surprisingly orderly. When the threat had been dealt with the committee laid down their weapons and went on with their lives, and when calls came again they took up arms as needed.

"I'm content to wait," Tim announced.

The whole situation put her on edge—an unknown threat. She was fairly sure Alex Kingston was behind it, but… there were other forces at work. Rich and powerful men and criminal organizations. It was a constant worry in the back of her mind that she'd return home to find Riot dead.

"So what's the plan? Tim asked.

Isobel reined in her thoughts. Focusing on one murderer at a time seemed simpler. "From what we learned about Hawkins, or Hadley, he favors resorts. Everyone I interviewed seemed to think he was a country man who spent time outdoors, but I never got the impression he was a laborer, so I suspect hunting, fishing, or sailing. He may have spent the last few years as a reporter covering sports in Monterey. I'll check on that, but… my gut tells me that he's more con man than reporter.

"The Hotel Del Monte is a perfect place to prey on tourists. I think he wears a clerical collar to gain trust. What better way to get money or handouts from tourists than to masquerade as a vacationing parishman. I doubt he'll have a mustache. I think it's a fake. He left San Francisco after Ella was found. That was smart. He was waiting to see what the police would make of her death. And he would have been in the clear if we hadn't interfered. So we know he's a cool hand.

"If it were me, I'd bide my time in Monterey to see how the investigation goes. It's a port city. Shipments of abalone and sardines leave for Japan and China every week. It's an ideal place to make a quick escape. You take the harbors, I'll take the Hotel Del Monte. Look for a preacher with a sailing or fishing boat, and try to find that cabin his lady friend mentioned."

Tim grunted.

"What? You don't agree?"

He chuckled, shaking his head. "No, it's only... you sound like Zeph."

Isobel started. "What?"

"Zeph used to do that sort of thing all the time. He'd pinpoint a criminal from his armchair and me and A.J. would go pick him up."

"You can congratulate me when I'm right."

"There's a cafe, *Sally's*, on Ocean View Avenue. I'll meet you there tomorrow for breakfast, or leave a note."

Tim took his hat and rucksack and walked down the aisle. He'd likely make friends with the stokers and end up driving the train before the journey was finished.

———

CHARLES CROCKER HAD A VISION. THE RAILROAD BARON BUILT a resort in the sleepy seaside town of Monterey, and the world took note. Newspapers called it Crocker's Folly. But the newspapers were wrong. In the first six weeks, the hotel had been forced to turn down three thousand reservation requests.

The world fell in love with the deep blue bay. It was difficult not to—bracing air and bottomless waters that teemed with life: kelp forests, sea otters, whales, clouds of sardines. Monterey was where sea monsters played and a lone cypress defied a wild ocean.

Isobel stood in front of the Hotel Del Monte with its gothic spires and trellised archways. A steady stream of carriages, buggies, horses, and even a motorcar flowed past, on their way to begin the 17-Mile Drive. On the hotel grounds guests strolled through carefully cultivated gardens to take in the salt air.

Isobel turned her back on it and made for the ocean. How could she resist?

That blue. So deep. It quickened her pulse to find a bobbing bay of masts and Monterey clippers. To watch otters playing in kelp beds and swimming between boats. She followed her heart to a sandy shore strewn with dried kelp and sat on the rocks, listening to the wash of surf. Children played in the tide pools, screaming with delight, while others walked barefoot in the sand, women unconcerned with trailing hems.

Out beyond the breakers, men in white linen dove into the icy waters. Japanese abalone divers. Americans didn't know what to do with the strange shellfish, but the Japanese treated them like gold, hauling in boatloads and shipping them directly to Japan and China.

Sails billowed in the distance. Isobel ached to be on the water. A romantic novelist would have had her sailing down the coastline and docking in Monterey to search for a murderer. But by sea it would have taken at least two days. By train it had taken three and a half hours.

Modern conveniences spoiled the romance of adventure.

Isobel turned back to Hotel Del Monte. She had a murderer to catch, and it was time to play the socialite.

One did not walk into the Hotel Del Monte and request a room. It was world-renowned and reservations were a must. And rooms came at a hefty price that would punch a hole through her family's dwindling funds. Instead she found a little inn by the sea, set down her things, freshened up, and struck out on a mission.

Isobel set her sights on 17-Mile Drive. Special touring wagons traveled the road with five rows of benches in the bed to accommodate tourists. She chose a spot just out of town, and started limping along the road. It didn't take long for a touring wagon to come along. She waved it down.

"Hello there!"

The driver reined in the horses. "Might I get a lift back to the hotel? My group went off and left me. Can you imagine? Why yes, I just walked over to the water's edge and turned my ankle in a tide pool. Thank you."

She was helped up onto a seat by an older gentleman with a distinct German accent. Perfect.

"You poor dear," his wife said.

"It's fortunate you came along," she said breathlessly. "I dreaded that walk back with this ankle."

"We'll get you some help at the hotel. Are you staying long?"

"A few days," Isobel said switching to German.

The couple's eyes lit up, and the thirst for one's mother tongue provided needed kindling for a fast friendship. By the time the wagon pulled up to the Hotel Del Monte, Isobel knew their entire family history, the names of their sons and daughters, and those of their grandchildren. She also had an invite for dinner. In the company of her new friends (they might as well be family) no one would question her presence in the hotel now.

41

CAT BURGLAR

Tuesday, October 23, 1900

"WHAT ARE YOU DOING DOWN HERE?" TOBIAS ASKED SLEEPILY.

Jin glared at the boy. "It is not your business."

Tobias yawned. "These are our rooms."

"I was looking for Watson."

Tobias wrinkled his nose. "This early? In a hallway?"

There wasn't much in the hallway. A carpet runner, a potted plant, and a mirror. As well as a bright painting of the sea to liven up the corridor. And doors. Tobias had just stepped out of the bathroom, and caught her in the hallway. He looked to the locked door behind her. It was the storage room—the one that Riot had had them load all the attic supplies into a few months back.

Jin sighed. "Fine. I am practicing." She slipped out a lock pick.

That seemed closer to the truth. "Don't suppose we could play with the sword…"

"No. Go back to sleep."

"Where are you going?" he asked.

"I have work."

With that, Jin walked off. Curious, Tobias followed her to the entryway, then stopped to watch her stomp back up to her attic room.

Frowning, he shrugged, and went to the kitchen to sneak some pie before his mother woke up.

But Jin didn't remain in her room. She climbed out onto the roof, and then down her ladder. She stopped on the ledge and shimmied around the corner. Her feet were so sure that she didn't feel she needed the rope, but kept hold of it just in case.

She paused at the turret room window, and peeked inside. The window was open. Atticus liked fresh air, and it was early yet. He was sleeping in his bed and she knew he had taken a sedative. She had given him a double dose for pain late last night.

Still, Jin hesitated. She hadn't wanted to resort to this, but she had no choice. The storeroom hadn't had what she needed.

Hooking her rope ladder on a nail, she slipped inside. Two empty chairs sat by a smoldering hearth. Bookshelves lined one wall, two wardrobes, hooks with hats, and a settee. It was a large room that accommodated two people just fine.

Jin moved across the room on light feet. She wore simple clothing: wide-sleeved jacket, loose blouse, and trousers with slippers. The bland gray material was perfect for blending in with fog.

Glancing over her shoulder, she eased Atticus's wardrobe open. Having helped care for him the past few days, she knew the room like her own. Crouching, she moved a pair of his shoes aside, and shimmied a large box closer to the edge of the wardrobe. It wasn't locked. She opened it and stared at its contents.

This was wrong.

Jin froze at the feeling. She knew it was true, with every

fiber of her body. Atticus and Isobel trusted her. And now she would betray their trust.

But she needed to do this.

Jin reached inside, and selected one of Atticus's revolvers. He had a number of them, and she doubted one would be missed, especially while he was recovering from his injuries.

The one she chose was worn, but polished and cared for, as was the case with all his weapons. But this gun was different from the one he carried in his holster. That one was sitting on his bedside table. This looked older, and bore numerous notches on its battered grip. The marks looked deliberate, like the scars on Jin's arm. It seemed fitting.

Determined, she stuffed a box of cartridges in her pocket along with the revolver, and put the rest back the way she found it.

Jin hastened back to the window, and paused. Atticus had shifted, pushing away his covers with a pained sound. Setting her jaw, she tiptoed to his bedside and stared down at his battered features. The bruises had turned black, and his face was etched with pain. Even sleeping hurt.

Feeling a tug on her heart, Jin pulled the blanket back up to his chin so he wouldn't get cold.

"Goodbye, *bahba*," she whispered. Then left.

THE HUNT

AFTER TWO DAYS OF CHATTING, WALKING, DINING, AND MAKING generally dull conversation with tourists, Isobel hadn't caught a hint of Hadley. She couldn't find any preachers who were busy making friends or photographers or artists lurking around the grounds preying on foreign travelers.

Worried she had been wrong, she plopped herself onto a chair in *Sally's*, and ordered a coffee. Charles B. Hadley could be halfway to Hawaii by now. Or in Mexico. If she'd been running from the law, she'd have struck out for Europe by way of India by now.

Tim hadn't arrived yet, but Sally, an old woman with cheery eyes, several missing teeth, and a pipe, came up to the table. She and Tim were old friends.

Sally slipped her a note along with her coffee. Isobel opened it, read the scrawl, and quickly tossed down some coins.

ISOBEL LOOPED THE REINS OF HER HORSE OVER A LOW LIMB, gave the mare a pat, and ducked into a forest that bordered a single track. Mist clung to the ground, twining through Monterey pines. Soft moss cushioned her footfalls, and as she walked through the lush forest, she couldn't help but think of Jin—the girl would love it here.

A pang stabbed her heart. Those eyes. Why hadn't she taken her along? The answer was obvious. Isobel wasn't there for pleasure; she was there to track down a man who had murdered a girl.

She found Tim leaning against a tree, smoking a pipe. He tipped his hat, and turned his eyes towards a lone cabin set in a clearing.

"See, I *was* wrong," she said.

Tim shook his head. "Hadley is known around here. Keeps a boat in the harbor, used to charter it, then he started posing as a preacher till the hotel caught on. I reckon that's why he headed back to the City."

"A confidence man?"

Tim tilted his hand. "There's nothing illegal about charitable donations to a preacher down on his luck."

"But he's not one, is he?"

Tim snorted. "Half the preachers in the West are outlaws that put on a clerical collar."

Point taken. "What's he been doing?"

"Keeping a low profile. I only found out about him 'cause his uncle visited a saloon and mentioned it to a patron who happened to be a friend of a friend of mine who has strong feelings about preachers."

Isobel considered the cabin. The land around it was cleared. An outhouse, a shed, and a corral. A thin trail of smoke rose from a chimney to mingle with the mist. "Have you seen him?" Isobel asked.

Tim shook his head. "Came over as soon as I got the tip

and left a message for you. A gray-haired fellow came out to tend the horses. I hear that's his uncle."

It was early yet, and Hadley seemed the type to sleep till noon. "What should we do?" Isobel asked.

Tim puffed out a cloud of smoke. "You're running this show, girl."

She arched a brow. Normally she'd agree, but lately she had discovered the value of experience. "I've wised up, Tim," she said. "I don't have anything to prove anymore, and I'm keen on staying alive."

Tim eyed her. "Humor me, then. What would you do?"

Isobel thought about it, her gaze flickering down to the rifle at his side. "Do you think his uncle will be an issue?"

"He's a sturdy fellow."

"We could plug the chimney and smoke them out. But that would put them on alert." She considered the cabin door. She hadn't changed into shirt and trousers, and was still dressed in a riding outfit—hat, blouse, split skirts and boots. "Or I could just go knock on the door."

"A.J. wouldn't like that."

"Well, he went and got his plow cleaned, so he doesn't have a say in it."

Tim grunted, then nodded. "See if you can lure one of them away. I'll keep on Hadley."

"Try not to shoot him, Tim."

"Yes, ma'am."

Isobel adjusted her hat, slipped off her wedding ring, and marched up to the cabin. "Hello there! Anyone home?" she called in a melodic voice. Instead of knocking on the front door, she knocked on a post. "Hello?"

The door opened. A fit, gray-haired man in a plaid shirt and Levi's with suspenders filled the doorway.

Isobel took a hasty step back. "I'm so sorry, sir. My horse threw me, and I seem to be lost. I'm from the Hotel Del

Monte. I started walking, you see and…" Isobel stumbled over her own feet and fell back with a thud.

The man rushed out. "Are you all right, ma'am?" he asked.

Isobel blabbered on about her clumsiness, and clutched her ankle.

"Charlie, get out here."

"I'm so horribly clumsy. It's not hard to imagine how I got turned around, I'm sure." She tried to get up, but the man wouldn't have it.

Charles Hadley soon came out. Tall and broad of shoulder, he was as fit as his uncle, but two decades younger. Dark brown hair, with a scar on his right eye that lent him a rakish air. While his uncle wore practical clothes for working, Hadley wore something more suited to a gentlemanly hunt.

"What's happened?" He had a pleasant voice.

"I'm afraid I startled her," the uncle said. "She's from the Hotel Del Monte. Lost her way."

The two men shared a look, and Hadley bent to examine Isobel's ankle.

"I'm sure it's just a turn." She offered her hand, and Hadley pulled her carefully to her feet. His hands—large, strong, and gentle—steadied her around the waist.

"Thank you," she said breathlessly, looking into his eyes.

The uncle bent to retrieve her hat, and dusted it off.

"Are you sure you can walk?" Hadley asked.

Isobel tested her weight on the foot. "Yes, I believe so. I'm so sorry to disturb you both. If you could just point me towards the hotel, I won't bother you further."

Hadley smiled. It even reached his eyes. "It's no bother. I'm Charles Hadley. This is my uncle William."

"Mary Read."

In short order, the men got her situated on a stool on the porch and pressed a glass of lemonade into her hand. Charles was all charm without pressing her. Interested in her without being intrusive. He listened, and his eyes, a deep blue, were attentive and curious. Small wonder Ella had been seduced by him.

Isobel had expected a man who oozed seduction like strong cologne. But he was the opposite. Genuine. Rugged, yet cultured. And he was also interested in her family. Where did she live? Napa. What did they do for work? Wine merchants from Germany. With each baited answer, Charles Hadley was hooked through the cheeks. Only he thought he was baiting her. And that's precisely what Isobel wanted.

"I'll just get the horse saddled," William said.

"There's no need. I can walk..." But her protests fell on deaf ears. William insisted, and soon came back leading a dappled gelding. The horse nuzzled her ear and she squeaked in surprise.

Charles laughed. "Honey wouldn't hurt a fly," he said. "Gentlest horse you've ever met."

"The horse I got from the Del Monte stables could use a few lessons on that."

"We'll find her." Charles put a foot in the stirrup and swung into the saddle with ease. With a smile on his lips, he offered a hand.

Suppressing a shudder, Isobel reached for his hand and settled herself behind him. She wrapped an arm around his waist expecting a lecherous touch, but he didn't pat her hand or make any suggestive comments.

Again, not what she expected.

Honey knew the pathway and walked at a leisurely pace. The trees closed in and mist wound its way through lush ferns as birds sang their hearts out.

"Have you lived here long?" Isobel asked.

"I used to visit my uncle when I was younger, before the hotel came around."

"Are you glad it did?"

He thought a moment. "Sure, I'm glad. Or I wouldn't have met you."

"We've only just met, Mr. Hadley."

"But Honey likes you. That's special."

"You said Honey likes everyone."

He chuckled, a soft rumble. "I suppose you caught me. Can I show you around Monterey, Miss Read?"

"I've already done the 17-Mile Drive."

"That's for tourists. There are places only locals like me know."

"I'm not sure... We've only just met."

"That's all right. I understand. How about lunch? Your choice."

No pressure. No coaxing. How many months had he courted Ella before gaining her trust? This was a patient man, in the most dangerous sense.

"I'd like that," she said.

They talked of her interests, of sailing and reading, and hiking, anything to lure him farther away from the cabin and into a state of relaxation. But the moment the pathway curved around a tree, the foliage opened just so, giving Charles Hadley his first glimpse of Isobel's horse and the reins tied to a tree.

Isobel felt Hadley stiffen and Honey stopped, sensitive to his rider's emotion.

"Someone must have found her!" Isobel exclaimed. But even as she said it, she knew the excuse was too late. No one "found a horse" and tied it to a tree.

Where *was* Tim? Had he been trailing them through the forest or was he hiding by the horse? Good God, she hoped dynamite wouldn't be involved.

Isobel tensed to slide off, but Charles grabbed her left wrist in a vice-like grip and dug his heels into Honey's sides. The horse surged forward.

"Mr. Hadley!" She twisted her arm, trying to break free while keeping her precarious seat.

She glimpsed white as Tim stepped out from behind a tree and raised his rifle. Hadley veered sharply, and Honey crashed into the forest. Branches whipped her clothing and she glued herself to Hadley as he ducked under a low branch.

Her skin crawled with the thought of Tim's rifle aimed at her back. Would he take a chance? Tim was a good shot, but there were too many variables.

"What are you playing at?" Hadley hollered.

"I don't know what you mean!" Best to play innocent.

Hadley jumped Honey over a log and broke through a wall of branches, thundering onto the road. A touring wagon veered to the side, nearly toppling as the wagon's giant horse struggled with its footing.

Honey shot off down the road.

"That old man must have found my horse, Mr. Hadley! Please, let me down."

His fingers were strong. Painfully so. "You think I don't see that line on your ring finger?"

Damn, he was good.

Dropping all pretense of the helpless female, Isobel punched the side of his head with her right hand, only the angle was awkward and he got his arm up to block the blow.

Isobel continued pounding at him as the ground blurred below, but Hadley was an accomplished rider on a familiar horse, and he didn't need the reins to control his steed. Honey sped up with a simple 'yup yup'. Solid in the saddle, Hadley had all the control, while Isobel bounced and slid behind him without stirrups.

She jabbed a fist into his kidneys. He grunted, but when she tried it again, he yanked her left arm, pulling her off-balance. She nearly slid off the saddle.

They were coming up to a bend.

Isobel abandoned her punching and tried to reach for a knife in her boot. Hadley drove his elbow back. The blow knocked the wind right out of her.

Isobel struggled for long seconds, then gulped in air as they rounded the bend. It curved sharply to the right. Honey slowed slightly, and Isobel gathered her strength. She threw her right arm round Hadley's neck, and he reached up to pry her arm free, but she was counting on that. As the horse curved around the road to the right, Isobel threw all her weight to the left. Both hands occupied, Hadley's weight shifted. It was enough to topple him. Both riders slipped from the saddle.

Isobel hit the ground, and bounced. Dirt and gravel bit into her skin, and she slid for some feet before coming to a stop. Groaning, she blinked past the grit in her eyes, and coughed as a cloud of dirt hit her full force.

Hadley's foot was caught in a stirrup.

Another rider thundered past. Tim's hat had blown off and the old man rode like a jockey, low in the saddle, milking every ounce of speed from the sedate hotel mare.

Tim came alongside Honey, hooked his foot on a strap and leaned over to catch the bridle. He pulled horse and its former rider to a stop, cinching the reins over his own saddle horn, before maneuvering around Honey to point a rifle at Hadley's head.

"I wouldn't move if I were you."

Hadley's foot was still caught in the stirrup. He didn't seem inclined to do much of anything.

"You all right, Miss Bel?" Tim yelled over his shoulder.

Isobel put weight on her arms. Found them sore but working, and spat a mouthful of dirt from her lips. "Well enough," she croaked.

"You're damn crazy!" Tim hollered. "Git off your ass and hog-tie this fellow."

Isobel staggered to her feet to do as ordered. She was moving. That was good. But she'd feel the fall tomorrow.

"What is this?" Hadley demanded as she tied him up. It wasn't quite a hog-tie but she used good, solid sailor's knots. Their captive was bruised and battered, and his clothes torn, but nothing seemed broken.

A pity, she thought.

"You know what this is," Isobel said, cinching a knot. "You killed Ella Spencer."

"I didn't!"

Tim spat from his saddle.

Isobel grabbed Hadley's collar and looked him straight in the eye. He looked so sincere, so honest, but then that was the game of a confidence man. She wanted to punch him.

"I *swear*," Hadley whispered. "It's true, I set her up in a house, then went out for food. When I came back she was dead."

"You left her to rot!" Isobel growled. She dropped him, letting his head thud against the ground.

"I left her like she was sleeping. Peaceful like. I folded her hands. I...I put a sheet over her! I knew how it would look. I *had* to run." Hadley was getting frantic, struggling against his bonds.

"Stay still," Tim ordered. "I got a twitchy finger."

"What's it matter? I'll hang anyway." Hadley looked on the verge of crying.

"You should have thought about that before you seduced a fifteen-year-old girl. At the very least, you're guilty of corrupting a minor."

"She was sixteen. I waited for her to turn sixteen."

Isobel resisted the urge to kick him, but Tim had no such qualms. He climbed right down from his horse and drove a boot into Hadley's side.

RECKONING

"THERE HE IS," THE BOY NEXT TO HER WAS WISE ENOUGH NOT to nod at the three men turning down a muddy lane.

Jin crouched in the dirt at the mouth of the lane with three other scruffy boys. She rolled her wooden dice, and barely noticed the boys' shouts of excitement.

A few coins and some whispered questions, it hadn't been hard to locate Maa Min. He was notorious. And feared. And he had added a goatee to his chin. Other than that, his face hadn't changed from the one she saw in her nightmares. He still wore a wide-brimmed hat, had a queue that hung to his waist, and was slim of build. His hands were lost in wide sleeves, and he was flanked by two men as they walked into a barber shop in the lane.

Fury blinded her. It made her cold. Someone hit her on the shoulder, and Jin lashed out with a fist. It connected with a boy's nose. He squeaked, and groaned, and the other two fell silent, watching her warily. Blood seeped from the boy's nose.

"It's your turn," one of them said weakly.

Jin snatched up her winnings and entered the lane. Keeping her pace even, she wandered past the barber shop.

There was only a small window, grimy and impossible to see through.

She had to catch Maa Min alone. So far, she had been careful. Never trailing him directly, but learning his habits. Watching. Waiting. And yet every time she caught sight of the murderer, she shivered with cold.

He sometimes visited gambling houses, but usually he disappeared down guarded alleyways. She took care not to follow him into those.

Jin could feel the revolver in her pocket and the knives resting at the small of her back. They burned against her skin.

The lane was clogged with people walking along planks. She stepped off into the mud, and sat on her hunches, keeping her back to the brick and an eye on the barber shop.

A man in rags shook a tin cup at her. He smelled like urine, and had a rag tied around his eyes. His forehead was bald and filthy and his queue undone like a wild man.

Jin dropped her dice winnings into his cup.

"Thank you," he croaked. With a shaking hand he pulled a trinket from a pocket and handed it to her. It was a small disc with a character carved into the wood. "For good luck," the beggar said.

She ran her finger over the lines. "I will need it."

"So much anger," the beggar said.

Jin looked at him sharply. "I am not angry."

He tapped an ear. "My eyes are gone, but I can hear it in your breath."

Jin did not answer. Maybe if she remained silent, he would think she was gone.

Maa Min's companions exited the barbershop. One headed out of the lane and the other stopped to light a cigarette. He flicked the match at the beggar.

Jin waited, ignoring the beggar's rattling tin cup. Maa Min did not come out. She tensed. Here was her chance.

Jin glanced at the poor blind beggar. She slipped a gold coin from her pocket and pressed it into his hand.

"What is this?" he whispered.

"I do not need it where I am going."

"Where is that?"

"To kill the Guardian of Hell."

Jin stood, or tried to. The beggar's cane got tangled in her feet. She stumbled forward and fell in a most anticlimactic way. It drew the attention of the smoking hatchet man.

Face first in the mud, she looked up to see him coming their way. Jin scrambled back against the wall. The hatchet man snatched the tin cup from the beggar. "Protection money," he said, emptying the meager coins into his palm. He pocketed the coins. Then looked down at Jin.

She stared defiantly back. "Give the coins back," she growled.

The hatchet man stared at her, stunned. Then he started to laugh. But like lightning, he changed from humor to brutality. The hatchet man slammed the tin cup into the beggar's head and the force knocked the beggar aside.

Jin did not hesitate. She would not let herself. Not ever again. No matter the circumstance. She pulled her knife out and drove it through the hatchet man's foot.

The man howled a curse. He tried to kick her, but she grabbed the handle, still stuck in his foot, and wrenched it to the side. His kick went wide, the blade came out, and she rolled under his legs delivering another strike to the back of his knee. The hatchet man went down.

The boys playing dice scattered in fear, and Jin sprang to her feet, darting after them as a gunshot rang out in the lane. Brick sprayed over her head. She rounded a corner as one angry shout joined another.

The boys bounded up a scaffolding, and Jin followed. They knew these streets better than she did. A board stretched between two roofs. The boys balanced across it, but before Jin could follow, one of the boys yanked the board away, onto his roof.

She skidded to a stop at the edge. "What are you doing?"

"You're crazy!" the boy said. "Do not follow us!" He turned, and bolted after his friends.

Jin growled under her breath. She ran back to the scaffolding to peer down into the lane. A hatchet man was climbing up while another waited below. The one below tilted back his head, staring straight at her. He had the remnants of shaving cream on his face. Maa Min.

The man she had stabbed was clutching his leg on the boards below. The beggar was gone.

There was nowhere to hide. No trapdoor. The hatchet men were coming. Jin did not look down again. She ran straight across the roof, towards the edge, and leapt. She caught the edge of the opposite building under her arms. Feet scraping against the brick, she hoisted herself up. A spray of air zipped past her leg, followed by the bark of a shot.

Jin ran towards a sloped roof. Up the tiles, she threw herself over the other side, sliding down. But it was steep. Very steep. She twisted on the clay tiles, and as her body dropped over the edge, she grabbed an iron spout. Her revolver fell from a pocket, plopping into the ichor below.

Desperate, she searched for escape. A boarded-up window. She shimmied to the side, then swung out and back, banging her feet against the boards. She bounced off and returned with more strength. If she could just kick it open—

A hand grabbed her wrist from above. Jin swung, and yanked downward the same instant her feet hit the boards. Wood broke. But her moment of triumph was short-lived. The hand came forward, followed by an arm, and then a man.

The hatchet man who had grabbed her from above lost balance. He fell forward, and took Jin down with him.

Pop! THE SOUND SHOOK HER. THEN CAME PAIN. AGONY climbed up her shoulder. Jin couldn't breathe. Her world was dark. And it smelled.

She reeled backwards. The ground held her for a moment, then she broke free with a sucking pop. She was in the alley below, buried in mud and refuse. The hatchet man who had fallen beside her lay unmoving on the ground, his neck bent at an odd angle. She could not work her left shoulder or hand.

Jin tried to stand, but pain pushed her towards blackness.

A figure walked down the alley. He stopped over the dead hatchet man, and cursed softly as Jin tried to stand. She managed to get up to her knees.

"Who paid you?" a voice demanded.

Jin tried to focus on the face. Thin mustache, goatee, dead eyes. Maa Min. Jin spat out blood at his feet. He lunged forward and seized her by the collar. She was lifted out of the mud, off the ground. Her feet dangled and darkness closed in, but she focused on Maa Min's face. The face that haunted her dreams.

"Are you Hip Yee?" he demanded. There was a cigarette hanging from his lips, casually burning. "Are they so desperate that they're sending children after me?"

Jin wanted to spit on him. She wanted to scream at him. Instead, she dangled in his grip. "They said I could be Hip Yee if I killed you."

Maa Min raised his brows, the cigarette between his lips moving upwards with his amusement. "I like your spirit." He flicked the scar on her cheek, and dropped her to the ground. Pain flared up her left side. Jin scrambled backwards in the mud as Maa Min reached inside his coat.

"Tell you what, kid. You kill a Hip Yee, and you can join Gee Sin Seer."

Jin's right hand curled around a grip. "Who do I have to kill?" Her left hand useless, she pulled the revolver to her, and held it against her body as she cocked it with one hand.

"Any of them will do. Does it matter?"

Jin glanced over her shoulder. Maa Min had a cleaver in hand. He was tossing it end over end and catching it by the handle.

"It matters to me." She turned, gun in hand, and aimed at his chest.

She wanted to see fear in his eyes. But Maa Min started shaking with mirth. "You're going to shoot me? How much are they paying you, kid?"

Jin growled. "You killed my parents!" she screamed.

Maa Min spat his cigarette on the ground. "Did I?" He looked again at the scar, and took a step forward.

Jin blinked away pain. The gun was heavy, her hand shook badly as she fought to keep it steady. "Sao Gan and Sao Ah Lam."

Maa Min knocked the brim of his hat up with his cleaver. She could see recognition in his eyes. "The tailors." He ran the blade along his cheek lightly. "I marked you, didn't I? I'd recognize my work anywhere. I shouldn't have let Sammy talk me out of killing you. But then... I doubt you'll pull that trigger."

Jin pulled the trigger. The recoil knocked her off her feet. Her bullet hit him square in the chest and Maa Min stumbled back a step, then surged forward. Flat on her back, with only one working hand, Jin couldn't cock the hammer for a second shot. He was on her in a blink, hand reaching for her throat.

Maa Min picked her up, and slammed her against a brick wall until the revolver fell useless from her hand. She could not breathe. Could not scream. Fingers dug into her throat, his face inches from hers.

Dimly, through the fog of approaching death, she could feel the metal under his clothing. Chain mail. He was wearing armor. "I will send you back to your parents a piece at a time," he hissed. Maa Min raised his cleaver, then jerked. His hand spasmed and he opened his mouth to scream, but two hands grabbed his head and twisted.

Snap!

Maa Min crumpled

Jin fell to the ground, gasping for air. Blinking away confusion, she watched as a figure in rags picked up her revolver. Maa Min lay nearby, his neck broken, blood seeping from his back.

Police whistles filled the alley. Arms lifted her. She smelled urine and filth. Jin looked up into the face of a blind man.

"Sarah sent me," he whispered. "Trust me now."

They did not go far. The beggar turned down an alleyway, and sat in a crumbling doorway. He set her down and she swayed. "You are sick. Do not speak," he warned.

It wasn't difficult. Blackness crept at the edges of her vision as she huddled against the beggar. Soon policemen flooded the alleyway.

The beggar shook his tin cup at them. "Sick boy. Please," he begged in broken English. "Help."

A pair of patrolmen backed away.

"*Please*," the beggar said.

"Did you see anything?" a patrolman asked in a loud voice.

"He's blind," the second patrolman said.

The first man stepped forward and nudged Jin's face up with his billy club. She hadn't landed in mud, but a cesspool, and she was covered in human waste. The patrolman wrinkled his nose and stepped back.

"Did you hear anything, old man?" the patrolman demanded.

"Fight. Men fight," the beggar said. "Voices." He pointed up. "Barking gun. Please help child."

"Get out of here. The both of you." The patrolman goaded the beggar with a billyclub.

The beggar stumbled to his feet, and pulled Jin up by her right arm. Her legs gave out, but he kept her up, navigating with his cane as the patrolmen sent them out of the alley.

"Who are you?" she whispered.

"Justice."

JUSTICE

Sao Jin was familiar with pain. She had endured most forms of it during her short life. But when Justice took her to the very shop where her parents were murdered to pop her dislocated shoulder back in place, she passed out.

When she came to, he was gone.

Tan Ling was kneeling by her mat. The old woman smiled kindly, and patted her arm.

Jin's hands, ankles and feet bristled with thin needles. She froze, too scared to move. Her feet were hot and so were her hands.

Tan Ling said something, gesturing along with her words to demonstrate. Jin tested the woman's suggestion, lifting her uninjured arm. The needles didn't cause pain when she moved, though they sent twinges up her neck. She settled back down on the pillow.

Tan Ling held up another needle. Her eyes asked permission, and Jin nodded. With a mere pinch of feeling, Tan Ling inserted the needle between Jin's brows. The sliver of metal seemed to pin her head to the pillow. She crossed her eyes, trying to look at it, then the strangest thing happened—the tension in her head began to unwind.

Tan Ling carefully placed a round bit of incense on one of the needles. She struck a match, and lit it. Jin watched as it burned, the aroma musky and sweet all at once. Heat spread through her body, but it didn't burn.

"Where is the man who brought me here?" Jin asked.

Tan Ling shook her head.

Bit by bit the incense burned, and as Tan Ling lit more, Sao Jin's anger and fear bled away with the twining smoke. It should have frightened her, but it didn't.

JIN AWOKE WITH A GASP. SHE SAT UP, TENSE, HER NOSTRILS flaring, searching for a threat. She was lying on a strange mat in a crowded little room. The room smelled of herbs and spices, and incense smoke hung in the air.

She was alone. Her shoulder ached, but it didn't hurt anymore. It was bandaged so tightly she couldn't lift her arm. She left it for now, and looked down at her feet. The needles were gone, and she felt surprisingly… rested.

She wore rough cotton clothing—loose trousers and shirt. Her own clothes, she remembered, were coated in filth. Her shoes, brushed and cleaned, sat on the floor beside her along with her knives and revolver. A pang of guilt clutched her, but it was overshadowed by questions: Who was Justice? And how did Sarah know him?

Clearly, the beggar was not blind, that much she knew for certain. Careful of her shoulder, she eased her slippers on, and checked the revolver chambers. She had four live rounds left. Jin rotated the cylinder to an empty chamber for safety as Isobel had taught her, then bundled up her weapons into an empty sack.

Cradling her bundle, she sat and thought for long minutes. Finally, she went off to search for Tan Ling and her son.

It was dark outside. Jin cringed, knowing she had disobeyed Atticus and Isobel, but then Isobel was gone and Atticus was too injured to notice her missing. And the time really didn't matter; Atticus and Isobel would not want her back after today.

She found the old woman in a small kitchen. Spices, fish, and vegetables were sizzling in a giant pan. Sammy stood over the pan, flipping its contents into the air with a flourish as flames rose and fell.

Tan Ling smiled at Jin, and beckoned her closer. The woman looked at her appraisingly, gently patted her shoulders, then said something that sounded approving.

"She says you look better," Sammy said.

"I feel better."

"We were wondering what happened."

Tan Ling looked at her, expectant.

Jin considered Sammy's back. "I found one of the hatchet men who killed my parents."

Sammy stilled, then translated.

Tan Ling shook her head, disappointment in her eyes.

"You're lucky that beggar came along. He wouldn't even take food in return."

"Yes, I am. But there is still one more man out there."

Tan Ling glanced at Sammy, but he shook his head. He transferred the pan's contents into three bowls, then added a bowl of rice to the center of the little table. Tan Ling reached up to pat the man's cheek affectionately.

Without looking at Jin, Sammy sat down on a stool.

Tan Ling nodded towards Jin's bowl. "Eat."

Jin's hand slipped into her bundle. "The third man's name is Nin Sam."

Tan Ling froze at the name, and Sammy paused, chopsticks

in hand. The twitch in his eye told her everything. "Do you know what the fellow looks like?"

"I do now."

He set down his chopsticks.

Tan Ling looked from Jin to Sammy, a man who was like a son to her, and finally to the bundle in Jin's arms.

Jin rotated the cylinder once, then eased back the hammer.

Tan Ling placed a hand on Sammy's shoulder, and then began to speak, a pleading in her tone.

"Quiet," Jin hissed. "You knew. You *knew* he was one of them."

Sammy's eyes turned dark, even as he put a comforting hand on Tan Ling. "Do not speak to her with disrespect. She knows, yes. I was one of the three men who came into your shop that day."

"You patted my head like a dog before you butchered my parents," she hissed. "Keep your hands where I can see them, Sammy."

Tears seeped from Tan Ling's eyes. She got to her knees on the hard floor, and put her hands together, bowing from the waist, pleading.

"Please, *mui mui*," Sammy said, holding up a hand. *Little sister*. "You may kill me, but do not shoot me in front of Tan Ling. I beg you. Let me explain."

"There is nothing to explain!"

Tan Ling started speaking in a rush. Her hands beseeching. Sammy hung his head in shame.

The dialect sounded like nonsense to Jin. Was it Mandarin? Or some other province? Sammy translated without prompt.

"She wants me to tell you that I also killed her daughter."

Jin sucked in a breath. Her eyes wide with shock. Her finger twitched on the trigger.

"I joined Gee Sin Seer after my father, a simple laborer, was hog-tied by a group of white men and then trampled by horses for their amusement. I burned with hate for all white people. I wanted vengeance."

Jin was on the verge of telling him to be quiet. She wanted to march him outside and take her own vengeance. But something stopped her—a tug on her heart, a whisper in the back of her mind, a feeling in her gut.

"Gee Sin Seer took me in. They fed me. They clothed me. They trained me. And I became like a brother to Maa Min and Niu Tou." Sammy raised his eyes to her. "The tailors, your parents, were to be my initiation in blood."

Memories came and went in flashes. Blood. A smiling man and a pat on the head, and Nin Sam, this same man, had stopped Maa Min from killing her. Had he actually swung a weapon?

"I could not do it. It was one thing to kill rival hatchet men, but another to slaughter my own people."

No, Sammy hadn't struck her parents, but he didn't stop them either.

Tan Ling nodded to Sammy, who took a deep breath and continued. "I was caught between love for my new brothers, my family, and my own conscience. I was a skilled fighter, so they laughed and called me weak-willed, but they didn't push me to kill innocents again. Until we came to Tan Ling's shop. Her husband had just died of pneumonia. She could no longer afford the rent, so she moved the practice here. This time, Maa Min and Niu Tou tasked me with extracting the money. Only she had none. For payment, Maa Min and Niu Tou decided to take her daughter."

He sighed with regret.

"I joined a tong so I could avenge my father. Not kill my own people. We were worse than the men who murdered my father. So I shot Niu Tou, and in the firefight, a bullet hit Tan Ling's daughter."

Silence settled in the little kitchen as Sammy struggled with his demons. He swallowed, his voice a rasp of pain.

"Maa Min stood and laughed while Tan Ling's daughter bled on the floor and Niu Tou took his last breath. Then Maa Min dragged me away. I thought he'd kill me. I hoped he would, but instead he made an example of me." Sammy stretched his legs out, and pulled up the hem of his pants. It wasn't just his foot that was mangled; his legs were twisted and uneven, bent at odd angles. "The members of Gee Sin Seer tied me up and each took a turn swinging a sledgehammer at my legs. Then they tossed me out on the street to die."

Jin looked to the old woman. "And you *saved* him? After he killed your daughter?"

Sammy bowed his head.

"*Why?*" Jin demanded.

Tan Ling gripped the table and made to rise. Sammy moved to help the old woman, but Jin hissed him to be still. With creaky knees, the woman gestured towards a small shrine on the far wall. There were statues of three bearded men sitting in a row, one white-haired and the other two black-haired, an incense holder, two candles, and a little lamp. An offering of fruit sat on the shrine.

Tan Ling approached the shrine, linked her hands together in a complicated knot, and bowed deeply to the three men. She lit three joss sticks, brought them briefly to her forehead, and said "Sao Jin." She repeated the ritual three times before placing the incense in its holder. She took a half step back, knotted her hands, and gave a half bow, bringing her linked hands to her forehead then down to her chest.

Then she smiled at Jin. "The Three Treasures, or Purities," Sammy translated gesturing at the altar. "Compassion, moderation, and humility." Tan Ling put a fist to her stomach. "Hate poisons the hater, not the hated."

Jin swallowed. Maa Min was dead. Niu Tou was dead. And

still she burned with hate and emptiness. Maybe the healer was right.

"I don't know why Tan Ling helped me," Sammy said. "But because of her, I don't hate anymore, and what is left of my life belongs to her." He got down to his knees and touched his forehead to the ground. "I am so sorry, mui mui. Please do what you wish with me, but don't make her watch."

Jin eased back the hammer, its weight heavy in the sack. Without a word she left.

THE BEGGAR WAS WAITING FOR HER OUTSIDE. BY WAITING, HE happened to be sitting on the corner where she crossed. Down the road braziers burned, and the lights of the theater blazed. She stopped in front of him.

"You knew, didn't you?" she accused.

Still blindfolded, he tilted his head to the side. She wasn't fooled by his blind act. He had tripped her with his cane on purpose. "Yes, I knew you dislocated your shoulder."

"You know who I am."

"I told you as much, child. Your sister sent me." Their voices were low. Not quite whispers, but low enough that she had to strain to hear his reply.

"Who are you?" she asked again.

"I told you."

"Did you know my parents?"

"I know of many things, but I don't know anyone."

Jin frowned.

"I hear every whisper in this Quarter."

"Then you know Sammy was there when my parents were killed. He used to be a hatchet man."

Justice nodded.

"If you are truly Justice, what will you do with him?"

"I was not the one wronged. His fate was left for you to decide."

"I nearly shot him."

"Then you would have shot him."

"And I would have left Tan Ling grief-stricken."

"Death has that effect. Justice doesn't discriminate."

Jin sighed. "I let him live." She could barely believe her own words. She felt as though she had failed her mother and father.

"Then justice has been honored."

Jin wanted to scream at the beggar. He answered questions with more questions. Nothing he said made any sense. She was a storm of emotion, of pain, and there was only one thing to do. Jin stalked off into the night.

———

THE HEARTH GLOWED WITH HEAT, AS RIOT HALF DOZED IN A chair. That was all he had been doing of late. Drifting in and out of a daze, answering questions for the sake of answering them, but struggling to understand the words and meaning. But the fog was beginning to part. Slowly.

Today was better than the last. Grimm had hitched up the hack and driven him to a barbershop. He felt human again.

A knock sounded, softly.

Riot blinked against the dim light, and got to his feet with glacial care. His head throbbed, his jaw ached, his ribs burned, every step felt like a victory or a glimpse into his future.

He could have simply said, 'come in,' but this gave him something to do. The knock, a mere scratching, sounded again. "Yes?" he asked.

"It is me," a faint voice answered.

"Jin?" She rarely came through a door. He opened it to find her standing in the hallway. Circles ringed her eyes. She looked stark in the gas light, her cheekbones severe, her eyes panicked. Her shoulder was in a sling, and bruises blossomed on her neck. The mark of a hand. She hugged a sack to her chest. "What on earth happened to you?" He reached out for her, but she rushed past him.

When he turned, she sank to the floor on her knees, and placed the sack between them. She pressed her forehead to the rug. "I stole your gun," she blurted out. "I stayed out past nightfall. I stabbed one man and shot another, but Justice killed him. And I nearly murdered a good man."

Riot took a moment to sort through her words, but whether it was from disbelief or his head trauma, he wasn't sure. He knelt down to touch her back. "Yes, but are you all right?"

Jin lifted her head to look at him. "I disobeyed you and Isobel."

"You do that frequently," he said.

"But this time I tried to kill a man. I am ready for my punishment."

Riot gave her back a quick pat. "Good, help me up."

She did so, and he closed the door before limping to his chair by the fire. Jin picked up the sack, and hurried over. She carefully unwrapped his revolver and held it out.

Riot took it from her hands. "Have a seat."

Jin sat on the ottoman at his feet while Riot inspected the revolver. It was filthy—caked in mud and hastily wiped clean. One round spent.

Riot glanced at Jin, who looked on the verge of collapsing, screaming, crying, or possibly attacking him. He emptied the chambers, paused, then pocketed the cartridges and set the revolver aside. He hoisted himself out of his chair, and dragged a blanket from Ravenwood's chair and laid it on the girl's shoulders before heading to his drink cabinet.

Ignoring Dr. Wise's orders, he defiantly poured two very

small portions of brandy. He handed the second to Jin, who sniffed at it warily.

"Am I allowed to drink this?" she asked.

"Probably not." He sipped his own glass, watching as Jin sampled the alcohol. Her eyes flared open and she started coughing in surprise. Color returned to her face.

"Now, start at the beginning. Speak slowly. My head hurts and it's hard to make sense of things."

"Isobel always says that too," Jin noted.

"Just so." He raised his glass to her.

Sao Jin told him everything. She watched him carefully for a reaction, but Riot betrayed nothing, until she came to the part about Maa Min, and dangling off a roof top, falling, and nearly being choked to death. At that point, he poured himself another glass of brandy. A generous one.

And finally she came to Sammy.

"I let him live. I could not shoot him. I failed my parents." Jin fell silent. She clutched her hands, nails biting into the skin, and hung her head in shame.

Riot leaned forward and took her hands in his. The edges of his vision narrowed and a wave of dizzying pain hit him, but he managed to keep upright. "Jin," he said softly. "How did you feel after Maa Min was killed by the beggar?"

Jin looked up at him. "Relieved. Empty. Angry. I do not know... My parents are *still* dead." Tears spilled from her eyes. She bit them back, but before she could swallow them down, Riot pulled her closer and then up onto his chair. She fit beside him, under his arm, and buried her face against his waistcoat, her tears soaking the wool as he stroked her hair.

How many people had failed this girl? The police. The community. The justice system. Small wonder she had taken the law into her own hands. He knew what it was like to be utterly alone and invisible in a harsh world. He should have seen it; he should have realized what she'd do.

"I know what it's like growing up in... less than ideal circumstances. Of fending for yourself. Of wanting revenge. Of getting it. But you're not alone anymore. You don't have to carry the weight by yourself."

Jin pulled back to look up at him. "But I am a coward."

"*Thus conscience doth make cowards of us all.*"

She wiped her nose on a sleeve. "Hamlet."

"What did vengeance cost Hamlet?"

"Everything."

"But he got it," Riot said.

"So did you. You killed the man who killed Ravenwood."

Riot nodded. "But before that... I killed people who I *thought* killed him."

"The tongs. Hatchet men," she nearly spat the word. "I heard about the attack when I was a house slave. The merchants threw a celebration in your honor."

"Still, I have to live with that."

"But they were *bad*. Boo how doy cause terror and misery in Chinatown. Everyone is afraid of them."

"Not everyone," he said. "Your father wasn't. Justice isn't. But hatchet men have families, too. I made widows and orphans that day. How do you suppose their sons and daughters view me? How many will grow up and come gunning for me one day?"

Jin was quiet for a time, but she was relaxed by his side, safe under his arm. *Alive.* Riot closed his eyes briefly. He owed Sin Chi Man three debts he could never repay. For saving his own life, for saving Sarah's, and now Jin's.

"It is a cycle," she whispered.

"And you broke it when you let Sammy go free—you saw past blind rage, listened to your conscience for what was right, and you *broke* that cycle."

"Maa Min is dead because of me."

"One could argue that Justice saw to that."

Jin twisted to meet his eyes. "So you think I was right to go after him?"

"No," Riot said, firmly. "I do not think an eleven-year-old daughter of mine should have gone off to assassinate a notorious killer, *by herself.*"

Jin pulled back as much as possible in the close confines.

"Do you have any idea how dangerous that was?"

"Like Hamlet, I did not expect to live."

"And how do you think your death would have made Bel and me feel?"

"Glad to be rid of me?" she asked slowly.

"Heart-broken," he said in clipped tones. "Shattered."

"And then you would have avenged me and killed Maa Min," she accused.

Riot opened his mouth to deny it, but... "I'm trying to work on that."

Jin scrutinized him. "Is that why you were beaten so badly? You tried to kill the man who killed your agent?"

"No, I tried to *talk* with him," Riot said dryly. Two decades ago, the man he was would have simply shot Monty and been done with it. Civilization would be the death of him.

"Talking didn't work out so well."

This talk was not going in the direction he wished either. So he changed it. Riot was not the one to give lectures on vengeance. "As for your punishment..."

Jin stiffened.

Riot pointed to the bookshelf. "See that tattered book there. The book by the green one. Bring it over, please."

Resigned, Jin dutifully walked over to the shelf. She hesitated over the indicated volume. "This one here is thicker. Would that not be better to beat me with?"

"Jin," he said firmly. "I want you to *read* the book to me."

"What?"

"For your punishment. Read me the book."

"Why?" She picked up the leather bound book.

Riot lay his head back on the chair and closed his eyes. "I currently can't read for more than ten minutes before my head feels on the verge of bursting."

He felt her settle back beside him. "*Pride and Prejudice* by Jane Austen?" Pages rustled. "I would rather read you the *Adventures of Sherlock Holmes.*"

"This is not up for debate."

"You do not like Sherlock Holmes?"

"Holmes is an ass," Riot muttered. "Watson's a good chap, though."

She fell silent at this. Then after a time she confided in a threadbare whisper, "I... hated the man, Sammy, for sparing my life almost as much as I hated them all for killing my parents. He should have let me die."

Riot put an arm around her. "There's times I've felt that way. Things would've been easier for certain."

Jin looked up at him, surprised. "But I would not know you. My life would be even worse."

"Likewise. And if I had died, I wouldn't have met Bel or Sarah or you. That's a terrifying thought. I suppose we're all responsible for each other, in all sorts of little ways."

"I want to visit Tan Ling, but I do not know if I can forgive Sammy."

"No one's asking you to."

"Tan Ling said that 'hate poisons the hater, not the hated.' Do you think she is right?"

Riot considered the girl looking up at him. He answered truthfully. "I do. But I don't think all men deserve forgiveness. I do believe in redemption, however."

"What is that?"

"Making amends for all the wrongs I've done."

"What is right and wrong?"

Riot raised his brows. "I'm no philosopher, and I'm definitely not a preacher. I don't have those kinds of answers, Jin."

She considered this for a moment. "You are a good man," she stated with certainty. "I do not think you have much to make right."

"I wasn't always."

Jin looked at him in a new light. "Just like Sammy."

"I can't vouch for him, but I believe men, and women, can change for the better."

"Then I will help Sammy with his redemption."

Riot blinked. "I didn't say that."

"No, but I will do it. It feels right."

"Jin, I'm not comfortable with you visiting him."

"Why not?"

Riot found himself backed into a corner of his own making. "I don't want you going alone. At least until I meet him."

"You should not go into Chinatown."

"Your safety means more to me. It's not up for debate."

To his surprise, Jin didn't argue. She looked relieved. "I will not go without you."

"I'll hold you to that. Now, for your own redemption…" He gestured at the book.

"*It is a truth universally acknowledged, that a single man in possession of a good fortune must be in want of a wife.*" Jin stopped reading. "Is this a *romance*?"

"It's my favorite book. I find it soothing."

She made a sound of disgust.

"It's part of your punishment," he reminded.

"What is my other punishment?"

"You have to do the voices for the dialogue."

"I would rather be whipped…" Jin muttered under her breath. But she began to read, voices and all.

INTERROGATION

Wednesday, October 24, 1900

THE LOCAL SHERIFF OFFERED AN ESCORT, BUT TIM DIDN'T LIKE the idea of handing their captive over to the law. They'd manage just fine, he said.

And they did.

All the while Tim coached her on the finer points of escorting a prisoner. What to watch for, what to expect, and the tricks prisoners played to escape.

At least they didn't have to worry about a gang trying to break him free.

They were in a private compartment, a first-class one stripped down to transport prisoners. Isobel sat across from Hadley. He wore iron on his wrists and ankles and looked resigned to his fate.

Something was nagging on her mind. He seemed sincere. Adamant that he hadn't killed Ella. But who else could have?

Once they arrived in San Francisco, she'd likely never get a chance to interview him, so she considered her approach. Blunt confrontation and demands might not work here.

"You met Ella at the library, didn't you?" she asked, breaking the silence.

Hadley looked up. "I'm not talking to you without a lawyer."

She smiled. "If you're telling the truth about Ella, I'm your best chance, Charles."

"Who are you? You're obviously not Mary Read."

"Isobel Amsel with Ravenwood Detective Agency."

His eyes widened a fraction.

"You've heard of us, I see."

Tim sat on the far bench, puffing lazily away. He had his rifle on his lap, the barrel pointed casually at Hadley. He didn't seem overly concerned with a misfire.

"I have," Hadley said.

Isobel leaned closer, steeling herself for what she was about to say, no matter how much it sickened her. "I believe you— that you didn't know Ella was fifteen. My husband and I are separated by twenty years or so. Age is only a number when minds connect."

Hadley licked his lips. "It's true. Madge introduced us."

"Madge Ryan?"

Hadley nodded. "I met her at the Olympia. Nice girl, but she… the man living with her drunk of a mother is a real piece of work. I was helping her get on her feet."

I bet you were, Isobel thought, but she held her tongue. She needed his trust. Silence wasn't her style. She didn't have Riot's patience. When he looked at a person, he was calm, as if he had all the time in the world. On the flip side, as Riot had informed her, she had daggers for eyes.

So she tried a different tactic. "You were helping Madge?"

"She ran away from home months ago. I helped her get a place to stay, and find work."

"Did you rent her a house?"

Hadley shook his head. "It wasn't like that. I wasn't…" He

trailed off. "Maybe at first, but I only fronted her some money. I found her a lodging house and helped her get settled."

"Then you met Ella?"

"Ella was different. She was vibrant, innocent, but headstrong. And sharp. Madge was already world-weary. I wasn't the first man to know her."

Isobel put on a pleasant, listening sort of face, while her fist curled at her side. No, you weren't the first man to take advantage of Madge, Isobel thought. But you did. And how old would Madge have been when Charles Hadley 'helped her out'? Fourteen? "Did your lady friend, Miss King, know about the girls?"

"Of course not. Look, Jessica and me aren't married. But I planned to do right by Ella. The house was only a first step."

"A first step?"

"I was going to marry her."

Hadley looked drained. He slumped against the seat, his eyes hard.

"Did you tell anyone about the house you rented for her?"

"Not a word," Hadley said. "I was careful. I know... I knew how it would look, her and me, and Jessica has a temper on her."

Isobel would have a temper on her if she discovered Riot was courting teenagers.

"Jessica would've brained her in a heartbeat. I have no doubt about that. But I didn't say a word to her, and I left no evidence. I was careful."

"You were careful?" Isobel asked.

Hadley nodded. "The mustache, the clothing, even my name. All I can figure is someone followed us from the Popular. But then I don't even know how you managed to find me." There was a question there, but Isobel ignored it.

"Someone? Who?" she pressed.

"Ella's brother maybe. She said she didn't tell Lewis the

address, but I'm not so sure. He's so strict, so controlling. She was close to snapping under the pressure he put on her."

"Was he hurting her?"

"He's slapped her before."

Isobel circled back around. "So you did meet Ella at the Popular that Saturday?"

"As I said, we were careful. We exchanged notes at the library, never actually talking there. But we'd slip them into books and whatnot, then checked out what the other had returned. The ad was another way. A signal."

"To do what?"

"That it was time. That I had everything ready for her," Hadley said.

A used bed and secondhand bedding. Classy. Isobel shoved that thought aside, and put on a sympathetic face. "That seems like an awful lot of subterfuge."

"Her brother and mother are strict. Ella was distraught when her mother told her she couldn't associate with Madge anymore. The two of them started the notes in the library books thing long before I came along."

"Why did you resort to the ad? Why not continue with the notes?"

"We found out the notes were disappearing—some of the ones we left for each other. We kept them cryptic, but I wager the librarians were tossing them in the rubbish bins. The ad was my idea. I figured if her mother believed she was working for a family, she wouldn't question why Ella was gone so much."

"What happened at the Popular?"

"Nothing. I met Ella outside. She asked for the address of the house I rented, then she went off to give her mother an excuse. But she must have told Lewis. That's all I can figure, or…" He trailed off.

"Or?"

"Ella used to watch a girl—the daughter of her mother's attorney. Ella didn't like the man. He made her uncomfortable. He was always deep into his cups when he was home."

"How would Mr. Grant have known where Ella went?"

Hadley shook his head. "I have no idea. Maybe she telephoned Ruby, the little girl, to let her know where she could be found."

Isobel sat back and considered. Did she believe him? Everything he'd told her was plausible, but unlikely. A last ditch effort to escape the noose. She wished Riot were here—that man could spot a lie from a saint.

There was the matter of the cards and adverts found inside the house. Lewis worked for the very company that owned the house, and Oliver Grant was also in the neighborhood. Maybe the operator had been mistaken and someone did answer the call Ella placed to Menke's after speaking with her brother. But why would Oliver Grant kill Ella? Had she threatened to expose something he did to her?

No, this was likely a last, desperate attempt by Hadley to go free. She needed some kind of confirmation. "Where is Madge Ryan?"

"I don't know. I haven't seen her for weeks. Ella said she got better accommodations."

"Where?"

"I can't remember if she told me or not. But Ella did say Madge found better employment."

"Doing what?"

"I didn't ask."

"What happened after you left the Popular? I need details, Charles."

The man ran a hand through his hair, handcuffs clinking with the movement. "After she made the telephone call, I took her to the Golden Gate Cafe. We walked through the park afterwards, then we went to the house on Sutter Street. Ella was tired, so I left her there with a promise that I'd return first thing."

"Did you have sex with her?"

Charles blinked, and shifted in his seat. "No. Of course not."

"You're lying," Isobel stated.

"We... got cozy."

"Speak plainly," she ordered. "I'm not encumbered by propriety."

Hadley glanced at Tim, who puffed on his pipe, looking uninterested in the whole affair. Isobel knew better. The old man could spring up like a jack-in-the-box in a blink.

"I showed Ella... a few things. That intimacy could be... pleasurable for her. But I left. I didn't want to move too quickly."

Isobel swallowed down her disgust. Ella might have been willing, but Hadley's deliberate seduction of the girl made her skin crawl. "And Sunday morning?"

Hadley gave a small smile. "Ella was rested, and... more than eager. Afterwards, she drifted off to sleep, so I left to get her some breakfast." He paled. "When I returned she was dead."

"Where did you buy breakfast?"

"At a bakery down the way. *Amelie's*. The French lady there will remember me."

"How did you find Ella?"

"I told you. Dead," he bit out the word.

"You said the other day that you folded her hands and put a sheet over her."

"Of course. I couldn't leave her like..."

"Like how?"

"She was all askew. Her legs, and... it was like she had been kicking. I didn't like the thought of leaving her like that, so I straightened her out, and folded her hands and legs."

"The cloth she was clutching?"

"After we… were intimate, she fell asleep with it between her legs. It was like that in her hand when I came back, so I left it."

"And the flask?"

"It was mine. Ella had had some the night before. Then I finished it off and tossed it on the floor. I figured they might think her death was an accident, or she killed herself."

"What did you burn?"

Hadley looked confused. "Burn?"

"Let me see your kerchief."

Hadley dug in his pocket and brought out a dirty one he had used to mop his face. He held it out, but Isobel only studied it from afar. It was silk, borderless, and his initials were stitched in a corner. Nothing like the one Riot had found partially burned in the house.

HOME SWEET HOME

TIRED, SORE, AND LOOKING FORWARD TO A BATH, ISOBEL climbed the stairs to her bedroom. She and Tim had handed Charles Hadley over to Inspector Coleman at the police station and filled out a heap of paperwork. The detective was impressed. On leaving, they walked through an army of reporters shouting for answers, but she owed the story to Cara Sharpe.

And now, late in the evening, she turned her key in the lock and opened the door.

Her room was empty.

"Riot?" she called through the bathroom door.

No answer. His fedora was gone.

Worried, she checked Sarah's room, then Jin's, but they were gone, too. A knot untwisted in her stomach. Riot had likely taken them on an outing, one that didn't involve guns, disgruntled agents, or assassins. She hoped, at any rate.

She turned on the taps, shed her clothing, and sank into a hot bath, wincing at the bruises covering her skin. It had been years since she'd fallen off a horse. With a sigh, she closed her eyes, and let the water carry away her worries.

A door opened, and she jerked awake in the water. Riot poked his head inside; his face had returned to its normal proportions, but the skin around his eyes and nose had turned a dark green. Plaster covered cuts on his forehead and his lips were still split, but his eyes were clearer.

She beckoned him closer with a smile, and he bent to kiss her lips.

"This is the only body of water I'll ever be able to rescue you from."

She snorted. Then pulled on his tie to kiss him again.

"Where were you?" she asked.

"Sarah and Jin decided I needed fresh air, so they took me for a snail-paced walk. I take it you found Hadley?" he asked as his eyes roved downwards. He was definitely feeling better. "You're covered in bruises."

"I did. And not all of me." Isobel hoisted herself out of the tub, and he pulled her to him. "I'll get you wet."

"I don't care."

"You have another week of bed rest."

Isobel grinned at the sound he made and draped her arms around his neck, pressing her hips against his. His immediate physical response was reassuring.

"Your eyes are clearer," she whispered.

"For the most part. Ewan's been here to check on me every day. My head still hurts." His palms were warm, and they caressed her back, strong and sure, until he hit a bruise and she winced.

Riot pulled back, reaching for a towel.

As Isobel padded out of the bathroom, she ran the towel over her hair, and brought him up to speed with a concise summary.

"Seems straightforward enough," he said when she fell silent.

"It was. I suppose." Isobel finished cinching her robe, and curled up in Ravenwood's throne-like chair.

"Do you believe Hadley?"

Riot sat across from her in shirtsleeves. His hair was tousled, collar undone, his forearms exposed, and his feet were bare. Riot wasn't a tall man, but his feet didn't suffer for it. He looked tired. And she noted he had removed his spectacles as soon as possible, still shying away from light.

"Inspector Coleman certainly seems satisfied."

"But you aren't," he noted.

"What do you think?"

Riot rubbed a hand through his hair. "I wish I could say."

For a moment, he looked so very vulnerable. Lost even. Isobel uncurled herself and knelt in front of him. She saw fear in his eyes.

"You're not well, are you?"

"Let's just say I'm not minding the bed rest as much as I should," he admitted.

"I shouldn't have left you."

"Stop it. I'm not telling you for sympathy. Only…" He searched for the word, grasping at emptiness.

"For honesty's sake?"

Riot nodded.

She took his hands in hers, and kissed them. "Dr. Wise said two weeks. At *least*. You still have another one to go. Give it time, Riot, and don't force things."

"I'm afraid I was a proper grouch with you before you left."

"Yes, you were. And I'll be sure to return the favor a hundred times over."

Riot rested his forehead against hers. She closed her eyes, savoring the moment. "There's something I need to tell you," he whispered. "And you'd best be sitting down for it."

Isobel's eyes snapped open. She leaned back.

"First of all," he said. "Jin is fine."

The way he said it made the room spin.

"What happened?" Isobel asked slowly.

NO BOUNDS

Monday, October 29, 1900

Isobel sat in the library reading. It was quiet. Far quieter than it had been in Ravenwood Manor the past few days. She tried not to think of her daughter, but it was difficult.

The moment Riot had finished telling her about Jin, Isobel lost it. She had marched upstairs and given the child a proper chewing out.

"Don't you *ever* do anything like that again. Do you understand me?"

Jin stood defiant.

"I did a lot of things as a child, but I *never* tried to kill anyone."

"I avenged my parents!" Jin screamed.

"You nearly got yourself killed!"

The conversation had deteriorated from there, until Riot dragged himself all the way up to the attic. He nearly fell over at the top of the stairs.

Isobel still wasn't sure whether it had been an act or not, but he managed to halt their heated argument.

Flustered at her own outburst, Isobel pulled Jin into a fierce hug that likely pained her injured shoulder, told her in no uncertain terms that she loved her, and then banished her to the attic for the rest of her life. For good measure, she took the rope ladder down.

All in all, it could have gone worse. At least that's what she told herself.

Isobel pressed her palms to her eyes. Maybe if she forced her eyeballs into her skull, she'd be able to focus.

The last days had been a series of blunders. Irritable and combative, she had confronted Lewis Fletcher at his sister's own funeral.

"Did you lie?"

"What?"

"About the address. The false one your sister gave?"

It was a crisp and sunny day, entirely at odds with the somber mood of the funeral. Reporters swarmed, the public was there to show support for the family, and Isobel accused Lewis of murder. At least she had pulled him away from prying ears first.

"I told you the truth," he said earnestly, his eyes red from emotion.

"No, you didn't. You *knew* where Ella was because she told you on the telephone. You needed the support of the Masonic Temple's Board of Relief. If Ella was caught with a man, your family's reputation would be stained, and they would withdraw financial support."

"Are you accusing me of strangling my own sister?" he hissed.

Isobel held his eyes. "Why else would you ask us to drop the case before her murderer was caught?"

Lewis took a breath, and unclenched his fists. "Miss Amsel, I appreciate what you did. You found Ella, and you caught her murderer. Why are you defending him? I'm the one who hired you. And I would *never* leave my sister there in a house to rot. Not even for a day!" The last was a shout that attracted curious stares, and found its way into the newspapers.

Lewis had stormed away, leaving Isobel standing alone next to Ella's grave.

"Bel," Riot whispered, touching her arm. "What was that about?"

Isobel met his eyes. "The pieces don't fit."

"I think they fit perfectly."

But she shook her head. "Why would Hadley go to all that trouble to set her up as a mistress? He rented the house for six months."

"Then you believe his story?"

Isobel clenched her jaw. "I don't want to. But, yes. I do." And if she was correct, she had handed over an innocent man to hang. Hadley was a predator of young, naive girls to be sure, but he was no murderer.

So now she sat reading in the library, her stomach twisting over her next blunder.

Questioning Oliver Grant had gotten her nowhere, so she had lurked in a park with Watson on a leash until little Ruby Grant came along with her childminder. Isobel had smiled and used Watson to strike up a conversation with the girl. Watson played his part admirably, and eventually Isobel worked the conversation around to Ella Spencer.

Bright, inquisitive, and sad about her friend, Ruby swore she had not picked up the telephone in Menke's Grocery. Isobel pressed the child on the matter, and eventually her questioning had reduced little Ruby to tears—all for a scoundrel's claim of innocence. She felt absolutely predatory.

Isobel looked down at her book, and the single note tucked between the pages. *Hamlet.*

She thought of Mack, caught up in some vendetta that wasn't his doing. Of the rage that simmered in Monty for years, rage that had driven him to try to kill the man who'd been almost a brother to him. And she thought about Mack's funeral. The Scottish Pipers who had come out in force, their bagpipes moaning in the Bone Orchard. Entire sporting clubs, boxers and coaches, along with every newspaper reporter in the city came to pay their respects to the fallen Scotsman.

Monty had been there, standing off to the side with his boxing club. He looked the worse for wear: one bloodshot eye, angry bruises and a crooked nose, and holding himself just so. Riot had given almost as good as he got. But that was a small consolation.

Riot and Monty locked eyes, then the big man had smirked and turned to his friends.

After the funeral, Isobel watched Tim walk over to the ex-agent. How many years had they worked together, she wondered? How many times had they saved each other's life? She tensed to charge, sure that Tim would shoot the man in broad daylight or pick a fight with the entire club. But nothing so dramatic happened. Tim offered a hand and the two shook, then stood and chatted amiably for a time.

"What the hell is he doing?" Isobel whispered to Riot.

"Monty didn't kill me when he had the chance," Riot said again. "He could have. But he didn't."

"He killed Mack," she growled. The nerve of Monty, showing up at Mack's funeral.

Riot gripped her arm. "Bel, let's go. Let it lie."

Vengeance. For Mack. For Riot's brush with death, and for every day of pain since. For his throbbing skull and sluggish thoughts and slurred words. And for all the fear Monty had caused her. It was a tempting path.

Hate, hurt, and pain—a recipe for murder.

How far would she go?

Isobel looked up as the door opened. A girl walked into the

library. Red-haired and smiling, she gave a little wave to the librarian and went straight to a favored desk.

Isobel glanced again at the note tucked in the pages. Cryptic, but only to those without context. She waited until the girl settled herself.

The library was full this time of night. Two readers sat nearby at separate tables, but deep in their books. Isobel took her copy of *Hamlet* over to the table and pulled up a chair beside the girl.

"Hello, Madge," she said.

The girl looked up, startled.

"I'm Isobel Amsel. I'm surprised you weren't at your friend's funeral."

Madge Ryan had rich auburn hair and green eyes. She was young, but world-wise, as Isobel had been at that age. Her skin was pale and freckled, and her cheekbones showed signs of malnutrition.

"I... I said goodbye to her at the morgue when I went by." She had a soft voice, nearly timid. "You're the one who found her, aren't you? The one in all the newspapers."

Cara Sharpe had gotten her exclusive, and San Francisco ate it up—the City couldn't resist a rebellious woman mired in scandal who solved murders.

"I am."

"I'm glad you found her." Madge's eyes looked down to her book. "The thought of her in that room... I didn't go to the funeral because her mother never cared for me, but I wanted to."

"I understand. I wanted to make sure you were all right. I worried that Hadley had done something to you, too."

The girl's shoulders slumped. "I introduced them." She sniffled and reached for a handkerchief.

Isobel put a comforting hand on her back. "I'm glad you're

alive. But did…" she hesitated, glancing around. "Did he harm you, Madge? Did he seduce you?"

The girl nodded in her handkerchief, tears welling in those captivating eyes. "I thought he was a friend. He acted like one. He helped me leave my mother and… that horrid man who moved in with us."

"Eric Harrison, the man living with your mother?"

Madge nodded. "Charlie was kind. He was different. He got me a room and… what was one more man?" She glanced around quickly, but the men nearby, absorbed in their reading, didn't seem to hear.

Isobel felt a pang of sympathy. "And he helped you get work, too."

Madge nodded. "At a department store."

"I heard you've found a new job."

"I did. I was able to get a reference."

"Where do you work now?" But Isobel already knew the answer. She just needed it confirmed.

"At a telephone company," Madge said.

"But Hadley lost interest in you before that, didn't he?"

That pale skin. So unforgiving. The slightest change in emotion caused pink to spread over Madge's freckles. "He never promised to marry me. I just wanted out of my mother's house."

"I'm sure you've read the newspapers about me. I'm not what you call a good girl either," Isobel confided.

Madge offered a small smile. "I gathered that much."

"Once you were settled, Hadley took away his financial support, didn't he?"

"I was working…"

"But you weren't expecting it."

"No," she admitted. "He started spending all his time with Ella."

"Seems you lost two friends at once."

Madge sighed. "I did. Why do you care?"

Isobel leaned forward. "Hadley's trial will be coming up in the next few weeks. I need you to testify against him. For Ella's sake."

The girl's eyes widened. "I'll lose my employment. I work under a different name. If they put my photograph in the papers…"

"The judge might accept a signed testimony, under the circumstances. Would you do that for Ella? I want to see Hadley hang for her murder."

Madge pressed her lips together, then nodded. Isobel went to the librarian's desk and retrieved some paper and a pencil, then slid it over to the girl. Madge began to write. When it was done, she passed it back to Isobel, who studied the handwriting.

"Thank you. Although I was hoping you'd include what you said to Ella before she died."

Madge blinked. "I didn't talk with Ella before she died," she said quickly.

"I think you did."

Isobel opened *Hamlet* to the end of Act IV, where Ophelia is found dead. And where Isobel had found the note. A note that Ella Spencer had refused to acknowledge, and so she left it in place as a message for her friend.

Don't do it. You'll end up like Ophelia.

Madge stiffened.

"You two had a falling out over Hadley. She stole him from you."

Madge was shaking her head. "I don't know what you mean. I've never seen that note."

Isobel tapped her signed statement. "It's your handwriting. And it was your idea to start passing notes inside books, wasn't it? You did it with Hadley, didn't you, as a kind of flirtation game?"

Madge looked like a cornered rabbit.

"And then when Ella was forbidden from associating with you, you introduced her to the idea, but she began the same thing with Hadley. And that's why their notes started to go missing. You were intercepting the messages."

"You're mad." Madge started to rise, but Isobel clamped a hand on her wrist.

"Considering the circumstances and your age, a judge may be lenient if you come clean."

"So what if I wrote that note? You don't have any proof," she hissed.

Isobel nodded to the kerchief in Madge's hand. Plain, cheap, with a single line of stitching around the corner. Nothing at all like something Hadley would have. Or Ella, who had a mother. But exactly the kind of thing a poor girl fending for herself would carry. "One of your handkerchiefs was found burned in the house where Ella died, and I suspect that if you roll up your sleeves I'll find fading scratches along your forearm."

Madge glared in silence.

"Before Ella went off with Hadley, she made two telephone calls from a Western Union office. One to her brother, and the other to Menke's Grocery. No one picked up the line there. But she didn't expect anyone to. She talked to the telephone operator. You."

Madge sat down, hard. "She said she wanted us to still be friends. She told me where he was taking her, so I could visit. I was furious," she whispered faintly.

"Hadley promised to marry her."

Madge nodded, dabbing at her eyes. "I was stained. Already ruined. And when I saw that house, so big for only two people... but perfect for a family... Ella *had* a home. She had people who cared about her, a family who cared enough to not want her out at night. I had no one but Hadley… and she took him from me!" The final outburst attracted notice.

"I understand, Madge," Isobel lied softly. "Did you go around to the house Sunday morning?"

"I *knew* he'd be there, so I let myself in the back. I heard what they were doing. And he was making all the same sweet promises to her that he whispered in my ear, too. I was *so* angry… I wanted Charlie to pay, and I knew he'd be blamed for her death, so I choked Ella after he left."

"While she was sleeping?" Isobel asked.

Madge gave a jerking nod.

"That's brilliant," Isobel said, impressed. "You nearly pulled it off."

A light entered Madge's eyes. Pride. "I did, didn't I?"

Isobel tapped *Hamlet*. "You did, but you ruined your life and those who loved you in the process."

"No one ever loved me."

"Ella did."

Madge tilted her chin up. "*Revenge should have no bounds*," she quoted.

But the pride went right out of her eyes when Isobel nodded to the two men sitting nearby. Detective Inspector Coleman clamped iron around the girl's wrists, and Isobel watched them take her away. Madge didn't utter a word.

"*The rest is silence*," Isobel whispered.

48

THE SNITCH

Sarah knocked at the bottom of the attic stairs. It was a silly thing to do. She doubted Jin could hear anyone knocking there, but maybe that was the point—if Jin didn't hear a knock, she needn't grant entrance.

"I don't think she'll help us," Tobias said. "Ain't she supposed to be resting?"

"She's likely bored out of her mind."

"What happened anyway?"

Never one to lie, Sarah kept her mouth shut. She didn't know the details, but her room was under the attic, and she had heard the shouting match between Jin and Isobel, along with more swearing than Sarah knew existed. She still wasn't sure about some of the words and their meanings.

Eavesdropping was a stairway to Hell, her gramma always said, but it had been impossible *not* to hear.

"Come on," Sarah said, opening the door.

Tobias blanched. "I'm not going."

"Why are you so afraid of her?"

Tobias gave her a look.

"Fine." Sarah tiptoed up the stairs, and poked her head up

to look through the railing slats into the attic room. Jin wasn't there, but the hatch to the roof was open.

"Jin?" she called up.

"What?"

"Can I come in?"

"You are already in."

"I'm coming up."

Sarah climbed the ladder and poked her head through the hatch. Jin lay on her stomach on the flat part of the roof. It was a tower like gothic design with a short iron railing around the access hatch. Sarah didn't like heights, and she didn't like the tower top.

Jin had her spyglass out and propped awkwardly on a rolled-up coat to account for her injured arm. She was scanning the surrounding homes.

"Are you all right?"

"I am alive."

Sarah thought about that answer. She couldn't tell if Jin thought that was a good thing or a bad thing.

Jin closed her spyglass, and turned to look at Sarah. "Who is Justice?"

"Who?"

"The man you sent to help me."

"Oh." Sarah retreated down the ladder.

Despite her arm in a sling, Jin simply dropped to the floorboards. She landed like a cat, eyes narrowing.

Sarah crossed her arms. "I'm not intimidated by you."

That brought Jin up short. She tilted her head. "What do you mean?"

"I mean you don't scare me."

"I am not trying to scare you."

Sarah frowned. "Really?"

Jin fiddled with her spyglass. "I do not mean to," she said quietly. "Not always."

Sarah shifted. She hadn't expected that. "I was worried about you, so I asked my friend to help. And before you get angry at Grimm, I bullied him into telling me what happened."

"I do not think Grimm can be bullied."

"No," Sarah relented. "I don't think so either."

"Who is your friend?" To appear less threatening, Jin sat on the floor, crossing her legs. She didn't ease herself down like most people, she just plopped in place, her legs bending like some kind of rubber pretzel.

Sarah sat down too, folding her legs in a more ladylike manner. "I can't tell you about him because I'm sworn to secrecy. I made a promise. But he saved me when those men came to my uncle's house. I was staying with him during the trial. You can trust him."

Jin considered this. Sarah expected demands, but the girl seemed to accept her silence.

"What happened?" Sarah asked.

"I tried to kill the man who slaughtered my parents."

Sarah choked. "Did you?" she whispered.

Jin shook her head. "Justice did."

Sarah blew out a breath. "Don't tell anyone that. He could get in trouble."

"I am not stupid. I am trusting you."

Sarah swallowed down her shock. "Thank you. I never had a sister, Jin. And I know you don't like me, but… I don't think sisters have to like each other to be friends."

Jin studied her. Sarah felt like she was being dissected, bit by bit. It was the same when Isobel looked at her. Adopted mother and daughter weren't related by blood, but the pair were like two peas in a pod. Or more like two knives from the same maker.

"A sister is more than a friend," Jin finally said. "I never had anyone kick someone for me."

Sarah blushed. "I'd do it again, too."

The edges of Jin's lips twitched upwards. With her scars, the gesture looked nearly painful.

"Can I hug you?" Sarah asked.

"No."

Sarah did anyway, which left Jin grumbling. "You're a lot like a grumpy cat."

"Thank you."

Only Jin would think that was a compliment. "Look, Tobias and I need your help."

"With what?"

"We've been trying to figure out who wrote that awful article in the newspaper. He's waiting downstairs."

Jin called him up, and the three sat on the rug, while they brought Jin up to speed.

"I went down to the *Call*, and they wouldn't tell me a thing. We've followed everyone," Sarah continued and began listing lodgers. "Mrs. Clarke calls on the neighbors, goes to church, and to charity events. I don't think she's wealthy, and that article puts her reputation in danger."

"But she's old. Old people don't care about their reputations," Tobias argued. "And who else *could* it be?"

"I don't know, Tobias!" Sarah said, frustrated. "I thought you were convinced it was Mr. Dougal?"

"You said it wasn't him."

"I did not."

"Did, too."

"Well, it might be him," Sarah said.

"And you want me to break into his room?" Jin asked.

"Yes!" Tobias said.

"No," Sarah said. "Well, I don't know. What do you think?"

"Why does it matter who wrote the article?" Jin asked.

"Do you like having a snitch in your own house?" Sarah asked.

"I just found out two snitches are spying on me."

Sarah turned a warm shade of pink.

But before she could think of an excuse, Jin rose smoothly. "I know who it is."

"*You do?*" Tobias and Sarah asked as one.

"It is no one in this house. The boarders are family. They are tied together, whether they like each other or not." Jin gave Sarah a pointed look, then motioned the two to follow.

She tucked her spyglass into a pocket, and climbed up the ladder.

Tobias looked to Sarah. "She's gonna push us off. I just know it."

Sarah rolled her eyes, and followed. When she got to the top, she stayed on her hands and knees, only to freeze a full two feet from the short iron rail.

"You will not fall," Jin assured.

"I don't think I can move."

Tobias popped out of the hatch, and walked straight to the edge to peer over the side. He whistled low. "You got the best room in the house, Jin."

"Yes. Stay low. I do not want anyone to see us."

"Who'd see us up here?" Tobias asked.

Jin got on her stomach and extended her spyglass. "Be careful with it, please. It is a family heirloom. Isobel will kill you if you break it."

Tobias's eyes went wide. He waved it on to Sarah.

Jin pointed at a neighbor's house. "The third floor window. On the right."

"It's an office," Sarah said.

"Yes."

"And…" Sarah sucked in a breath. "There's a telescope!"

"A big one? To look at stars?" The boy fairly vibrated with excitement. He loved stars. Sarah handed over the spyglass.

"That's it! That's the one I saw in the Sears catalogue! But ma said it was too expensive."

"You could save for it," Sarah suggested.

"I could. But I need another thirty dollars. I only have that coin we got from the treasure chest."

Jin made a sound of frustration. "Do you not see?"

"I see it," Tobias said. "What about it?"

Jin took back her spyglass. "The window with the telescope faces Miss Dupree's patio and French doors."

"Oh, Lord," Sarah muttered. "The man is spying on Miss Dupree!"

"But why would he write that article?" Tobias asked.

"His wife caught him," Jin said.

"How do you know that?" Sarah asked.

"They were arguing the other day." Jin told them about the woman who dumped wine in her husband's lap.

"So the wife wrote it?" Tobias asked.

Jin nodded.

"How'd she know about all that other stuff?" Tobias asked.

Jin's thin brows drew together.

"Mrs. Clarke!" Sarah said, snapping her fingers. "She makes social calls on the neighbors. I don't think she'd write an article like that, but I wager she gossips up a storm."

"Hmmhmm," Tobias said. "I told you so. You know how churchy ladies are, they gossip like the devil."

"That is not true, Tobias."

"Is too."

"They're not supposed to," Sarah said. "And you specifically told me it wasn't her just a few weeks ago."

"Did not."

"Did so."

"I said it was her today," he defended.

While Sarah and Tobias argued, Jin slipped back down the ladder, and the other two eventually followed.

"So are we going to knock on the door and give them what for?" Tobias asked.

"No…" Sarah tapped her lips.

"We will tell Atticus," Jin said.

Sarah started shaking her head. "No we won't. He's hurt. He's supposed to be resting."

"I promised Isobel I would ask before doing anything dangerous."

Sarah looked dubious. "That leaves a whole heap of wiggle room."

"I know. I will save the wiggle room for something important."

―――――――――

ATTICUS RIOT GRIPPED THE RAILING AS HE LIMPED UP THE steps to his neighbor's house. He had never met them. He vaguely recalled a complaint the Gibsons had issued against Ravenwood—for attracting undesirables into the neighborhood—when the detective was consulting from his study. But other than that single complaint the Gibsons had kept away from their eccentric neighbor.

Riot grimaced at the irony. Ordinarily, he didn't need a gentleman's stick, but he would have liked one now. The loss of Ravenwood's stick and pocket watch stung worse than the beating. Seeing Monty at the funeral had been a final blow.

But Riot was a gracious loser. In some things.

He banged the knocker against its plate.

Women's voices cut off inside. "I wonder who that could be."

A face peered out of a window, then a few moments later, the door opened. "Can I help you, sir?"

He tipped his hat. "I'm afraid we haven't met. I'm Atticus Riot, your neighbor."

The woman was in her forties. Brown hair streaked with gray, pulled up in the latest Gibson Girl fashion. She looked at him with shrewd, intelligent eyes, before making a decision. "Alice Gibson."

Riot shook her offered hand. "I believe Mrs. Clarke is also here."

This caused a reaction. She blinked in surprise. "Why, yes. Were you wanting to speak with her?"

"With both of you, actually."

"My husband isn't home…"

"That's for the best."

Mrs. Gibson hesitated, then opened the door to allow him entrance. He nodded to Mrs. Clarke, who responded with a flustered greeting.

"Mr. Riot. Why I hardly see you at the house. Only glimpses. I think we've only met briefly once in passing, and here you are now."

"I'm afraid it's not a coincidence," he said without prompt. "Do sit down, Mrs. Gibson. We have matters to discuss."

The women eyed his bruises, as he removed his hat. They sat together on the same sofa, and he took a seat opposite.

"I'm sure you're both aware of a certain newspaper article that was published in the *Call* some weeks ago."

"It was dreadful," Mrs. Clarke said. She leaned forward. "What I can't understand is why you haven't evicted that… tart."

A muscle in Riot's jaw twitched. His head still ached, and his patience was on the short side. "I'm a reasonable man, Mrs. Clarke. What my lodgers do is their own business, unless it affects my family. Whoever wrote those lies hurt us all. Wouldn't you agree?"

"Yes, of course," Mrs. Clarke said.

Riot looked to Mrs. Gibson, and let silence needle her.

Confronted with his stare, the woman leaned back, as if

trying to escape him. Slowly, Mrs. Clarke turned her head, eyes widening.

"There's a telescope in your husband's study, isn't there, Mrs. Gibson?"

"Yes," she said faintly.

Riot reached inside his coat and brought out a sheaf of papers. He didn't hand them over. Not yet. "Your husband is spying on Miss Dupree, isn't he?"

Mrs. Gibson gave a slight nod.

"You found out and confronted him, but he didn't stop, did he? It angered you so much that you poured a glass of wine in his lap the other day."

Her mouth fell open slightly. "How did you…"

"That doesn't matter. What matters is what you did before that."

"Alice?" Mrs. Clarke said.

Mrs. Gibson broke. "I was only trying to get her out of that house! I didn't think… I thought if I wrote the article, then Mr. Riot would evict her and George would stop…" Her mouth twisted in distaste. "He's always watching her."

"Why didn't you tell me?" Mrs. Clarke asked.

"I knew you were in a precarious situation." Mrs. Gibson looked pleadingly at Riot. "And it's disgusting."

"Have you witnessed any scandalous activity?" Riot asked.

"No. But I've heard—" she cut off.

Riot waited, staring at Mrs. Clarke. "You heard what?"

Mrs. Clarke placed a hand to her throat.

"You've been gossiping, haven't you?" he asked his lodger.

"Only with friends."

Riot continued to wait. With each moment the women grew more flustered until they turned… on each other.

"I confided in you in the strictest of confidence!" Mrs. Clarke exclaimed.

He let the ensuing argument flare. When both women were

red in the face and had turned their backs on one another, he decided it was time to play his final card.

"As I said, I'm a reasonable man. I'm willing to forget all this if you publicly admit it was nothing but idle gossip and retract your statements. I've drafted a letter of apology for you."

He handed that over.

"I can't possibly do that," Mrs. Gibson said.

"Why?"

"It's…"

"Embarrassing?"

She blushed.

"Imagine the stain you brought on my household."

"But most of that *is* true. Miss Dupree is an immoral woman," Mrs. Clarke said.

"Do you have proof?"

"I… it's easy to see. You two were very friendly at one point."

"I am a friendly fellow."

Mrs. Clarke huffed. "I know seduction when I see it."

"Then I'll be forced to evict you, Mrs. Clarke. And I'll have this published." He handed over another piece of paper. This was one of Sarah's sketches—a cartoon of sorts. Of what was clearly Mr. and Mrs. Gibson. A cartoonish portrayal of his peeping through the telescope and Mrs. Gibson hitting him over the head with a Bible.

Mrs. Gibson paled. "We'll be the laughing stock of San Francisco society."

Riot gave her a slight smile. "Send in that redacted statement and I'll keep this picture to myself."

"Are you blackmailing me, Mr. Riot?"

"No, I'm offering you a deal, Mrs. Gibson. I'll also put a trellis up between our properties to block the patio and French doors. And I'll take your husband's telescope off your hands.

You can have this drawing in its place."

"Alice…" Mrs. Clarke warned.

Riot knew when he had a winning hand. This was one of them. He was soon limping home with a telescope under his arm, which he promptly handed over to Tobias, who nearly fainted with delight.

49

A FAMILY RING

Saturday, November 3, 1900

ISOBEL WAS HAVING SECOND THOUGHTS. NOT BECAUSE THE children had hung off the side of the Mount Tamalpais Scenic Railroad car, or even because Sarah, Tobias, and Jin had bounced between bickering and screeching during the sail across the bay, the railway journey up the mountain, and finally the ride down the gravity car from the top. No, she was having second thoughts because of Riot.

The outing had seemed a good idea, but he wasn't entirely recovered. His pack seemed to weigh him down, and he lagged behind as the children darted up the trail, their camping packs bouncing on their backs.

"If you drop dead I'll never forgive myself," she warned.

"I've been resting for nearly three weeks, Bel. It's only my sedentary life catching up with me."

"I could carry your pack."

"You could. But you know I won't stand for it."

Besides, she had one of her own, and she was carrying most of their camping supplies.

"I could wrestle it from you and run ahead."

Riot chuckled. "The children would be highly entertained."

She let him keep the pack, but stayed by his side.

For the first time in hours, Isobel realized she was surrounded by a deep silence. The children had ceased their bickering, and were not laughing or making any sound. "Did they get lost already?" she searched the foliage.

Riot gave a slight shake of his head.

Then she spotted them in the emerald green, with ferns as tall as their heads and red trees that reached for the sky. Vibrant smells of damp earth permeated her senses. It was the smell of life, fresh and changing, yet ancient and timeless.

Jin, Sarah, and Tobias stood at the base of a majestic redwood. All three craned their necks to stare, jaws hanging open.

Riot removed his hat, and joined the children. He craned his neck back to gaze at its height with a boyish look of wonder, and Isobel smiled, her doubts falling away. This would be a good place to drop dead, she decided, under the silent sentinels of time.

Jin reached out a tentative hand to touch the soft, furry bark, then she pressed her ear to the tree.

"What are you doing?" Sarah whispered.

"Listening to it breathe."

Puzzled, Tobias did the same. And even Riot pressed his ear to the tree. Isobel had grown up with the giant trees. She had run under their canopies as a child and played in their ferns. The forest *did* breathe. She would swear by it.

Shrugging off her pack, she sat down and tugged her boots off, then lay down at the tree's base and pressed her bare feet up against the trunk. When she looked up its dizzying height, she felt like she was falling.

"That one over there has a cave!" Tobias darted off, and

Sarah followed.

Leaves rustled, and soon Riot and Jin joined her on the forest carpet.

"Why are parts of the bark black? Is it dying?" Jin asked.

"It's from a fire. And no, I think it's just fine. That's an old wound."

"It's so big," Jin whispered.

"These are a smaller subspecies of the giant Sequoia farther up north," Isobel said.

"There are *bigger* trees?"

Beside her, Riot folded his hands on his stomach. He had taken off his spectacles, and his eyes were closed. He was listening to the trees, and he looked to be at peace for the first time in a long while.

There was something timeless about the forest—primordial, with twining mists and giant ferns whose every surface glistened with moisture. And the quiet. It was deep and still under the canopy. Isobel never walked through the redwoods without feeling like she was in the presence of something greater than herself. Of time itself. It was hard not to feel like an ant crawling through the dirt.

"There are larger trees," she whispered. "But these are... special."

Jin was lying next to her. She turned her head to study Isobel. "Why?"

"They're thousands of years old," Isobel whispered. "Hundreds of feet tall, but the roots only go down six feet or so." Isobel raised her hands over their faces, intertwining her fingers. "The roots spread out just beneath the ground, intertwining for support. So even when one tree is hollowed out by fire, it will still grow strong. Naturalists call it a family ring."

Jin was quiet for a time. "Are you still mad at me?" she finally asked.

Isobel reached for the girl's hand. "I'm terrified I'll lose you."

Jin's hand tightened around hers. "Would you have done the same thing?"

Isobel took a deep, shaky breath. "I haven't lived your life. I don't honestly know, but I understand why you tried to kill Maa Min."

Jin's fingers strayed to the tattered leather bracelet around Isobel's wrist. It had been a gift from Jin when Isobel was in a bad place. It had belonged to Jin's mother.

Isobel looked at her daughter. "Do you feel better?"

Jin shook her head. "No," she said. Then paused. "Yes?" Confusion twisted her features. "When I think of Maa Min, there is only a hollow feeling. I do not feel peace."

"You never buried your parents," Riot murmured.

As soon as he said it, Jin's eyes dimmed. "I do not know what happened to their bodies."

Isobel held up their interlaced hands. "We have your mother's bracelet."

Jin stared, struck, her lips trembling. Then she nodded.

They hiked deep into the forest, where the trees were thick and the light of the sun never touched the moss-covered ground. Jin chose a spot by a stream dyed red from the bark. She stood in a ring of trees facing an ancient one in the center, its trunk scorched by fires and marred by axes—in silence so deep it drowned out the stream.

While Tobias and Sarah stood quietly nearby, Isobel and Riot helped Jin dig a hole at the base, until their hands turned red from the earth. When Jin was satisfied, Isobel carefully untied the tattered bracelet, and handed it to the girl.

For a moment, Jin hesitated. And that would have been fine. No one would pressure her to bury the only thing she had left of her mother. Then Jin sank to her knees, and placed the bracelet in the grave.

Jin pressed her forehead to the earth, and inhaled the

scents of life and death, the cycle of decay and rebirth. "Good-bye, bahba and mahma," she whispered.

As Jin's small body shook with grief, Isobel and Riot helped her push the dirt back, their tears mingling with the earth.

Eventually, she stilled, and Tobias brought over a pile of rocks. He made a circle around the freshly churned grave. Sarah brought a flower, then pulled Jin into a hug. And Riot took out a five dollar bill. He put a match to it, scattering the ashes over the grave.

"For their afterlife," he said in Cantonese. It was supposed to be fake money, but they were improvising. He kissed the top of Jin's head, whispered his love in her ear, and moved out of the family ring with the other two children.

Isobel knelt in the dirt, wiping her nose with a kerchief. "Sometimes I think it was easier when I refused to let myself feel anything."

Jin was staring at the grave. She looked like a puppet whose strings had been cut. "Do you believe in an afterlife?"

Isobel sighed. "I don't know, Jin. Most days I think it's just a nice dream. But then…" She sat back, leaning against the ancient old tree to fiddle with her wedding ring. The rings separated, forming a miniature model of the universe that she could hold in her hand. "When I come to a place like this, I'm reminded how very small I am. And I think, what do I know?"

Jin leaned against her shoulder. "I like it here."

"We can visit them whenever you like."

"Will you come with me?"

Isobel put an arm around her and tucked her in close. "Of course I will."

"My father and mother were tailors. They made costumes, and fought against hatchet men."

"What were their names?"

Jin told her, and then more—a torrent of small memories that lit up her eyes and filled the quiet with sunshine.

50

LOOSE ENDS

Tim was strangely still. He didn't rock. He didn't smoke. His pipe was cold and sitting in his pocket as he leaned against a wall in an upper story warehouse, watching the street below through a hole in a broken pane.

Across the street, a man came out of a boxing club. It wasn't a fancy Olympic club sort of place, with their hot baths and soft towels. This was a rough place—the sort that trained thugs. And that suited Tim just fine. He raised his rifle and drew a bead on the man below. He'd recognize that mustache and stride anywhere.

Montgomery Johnson stopped to light a cigarette. The man had fading bruises and a sheen of sweat on his skin. An early morning fog misted him as he took in the chill air.

Tim settled into the rifle that was close to a stranger to him. It wasn't his favorite; this was one he had picked up through the years. Maybe he'd got it secondhand, or off an outlaw, or even at a pawnshop. Tim couldn't recall when or where, which was precisely why he collected his arsenal of discarded weapons. They came in handy every once in awhile.

His finger rested on the trigger, the sight on Monty's head, between his eyes. His finger caressed the trigger for a moment before pausing.

Why hadn't Monty killed A.J.? It would've been simple enough to drag A.J. outside and brain him one final time. A.J. was already rubbing shoulders with death. Monty could have blamed it on thieves, or coated him in whiskey and made it look like he drowned in his own vomit. There were heaps of ways to kill a man and walk away scot-free.

Of course, Monty nearly *had* killed A.J. He had used him for a punching bag, and left him to freeze with his face buried in muck. Monty was a coward, Tim decided. He had left things to chance so he wouldn't be bothered by conscience, and that didn't set well with Tim, who was never one to leave a loose end.

"Ashes to ashes; dust to dust. You should've played fair, boy." Tim eased down on the trigger. A shot rang out, and Monty dropped to the street.

Tim calmly wiped down the rifle and tossed it out a back window into Mission Creek, then strode out to get a drink at a saloon run by an old gal who didn't have much use for clocks.

CONNECT WITH AUTHOR

If you enjoyed Where Cowards Tread, and would like to see
more of Bel and Riot, please consider leaving a review.
Reviews help authors keep writing.

Keep up to date with the latest news, releases, and giveaways.
It's quick and easy and spam free.
Sign up at www.sabrinaflynn.com/news

Now available:
Book 8 of Ravenwood Mysteries
Beyond the Pale

AFTERWORD

You've probably noticed by now, dear reader, that I tend to leave a few loose threads in every book. Life doesn't always tie everything up in nice little neat knots that get resolved in a timely manner. So never fear... any loose ends left in this book will be tied up, eventually. I'm a huge fan of overarching stories. But I'm sure you've figured that out by now.

———

This story is based on a case that "thrilled city and state" in 1902 San Francisco—the disappearance of Nora Fuller. Most of the details surrounding the case were taken straight from the *Morning Call*: the ad in the wanted section (word for word), the rendezvous at the Popular, and even Bennett's description. Nora did, in fact, telephone her brother, and either she gave him the wrong address, or the man she was meeting did. Either way, a real estate agent found her body some thirty days later in the back room on the top floor of the Sutter Street house, exactly as described in the book. The police detective who responded and the coroner both declared it either a suicide or death by natural causes. It wasn't until the press got a hold of the story and raised such a ruckus over it that the police were forced to investigate further. Of course, this is all according to the *Morning Call*. Reporters tended to toot their own horns and took every chance to highlight their own superiority over the police force. But based on later articles that talked about the competence of the police detective who took over the case, I tend to think that the original reporting was accurate.

A deluge of clues and tips followed, many of which are included in the story, including the sketch of Nora Fuller being choked to death. Although the police did eventually identify a man they believed to be the killer, he was never caught and brought to justice. Reports of his whereabouts were still being discussed in papers as late as 1908.

So many aspects of this century-old case remind me of modern day predatory behavior, including the social media stalking of young women. It seems this story could very well appear in a newspaper today. And sadly, as it was with the case of Nora Fuller, so few perpetrators are ever brought to justice.

WHAT ELSE MIGHT YOU BE WONDERING ABOUT? THERE'S ALWAYS so much… The Committee of Vigilance is factual. In 1851, Albert Bernard de Russailh wrote the following about San Francisco's newly formed police force:

"As for the police, I have only one thing to say. The police force is largely made up of ex-bandits, and naturally the members are interested above all in saving their old friends from punishment. Policemen here are quite as much to be feared as the robbers; if they know you have money, they will be the first to knock you on the head. You pay them well to watch over your house, and they set it on fire. In short, I think that all the people concerned with justice or the police are in league with the criminals. The

city is in a hopeless chaos, and many years must pass before order can be established. In a country where so many races are mingled, a severe and inflexible justice is desirable, which would govern with an iron hand."

Citizens and everyday merchants were forced to take matters into their own hands at times to combat roving gangs and outlaws who were fond of setting the city on fire. San Francisco was nearly burned to the ground numerous times before the great earthquake and fire of 1906. The city had lots of practice with rebuilding. And the first Chief of Police, James F. Curtis elected in 1856, was in fact a former member of the San Francisco Committee of Vigilance.

While the SFPD had a rocky start, they really got their stuff together in later years. In the early 1900s they were known for being one of the pioneering forces for modern law enforcement. But who knows, maybe that was partly due to Bel and Riot's influence…

ACKNOWLEDGEMENTS

Most acknowledgements at the end of a book are full of gratitude to everyone who helped a writer finish their book. I'm going to do things a bit differently for this one. It's still an acknowledgement. Just maybe not one of gratitude. So here goes: to Gus Gus, for eating my office wall, $300 worth of shoes, my dining room chairs, my basil, mint and rosemary plants, a rotten snake egg (Yay, vet bills!), wild onions (and subsequent poisoning), countless socks, an art glove, logs, frogs, innumerable papers, my chocolate, and too many plastic toys to count. You added a month of writing to this book.

It's amazing you're not dead (for so many reasons).

And I will acknowledge a few others—not, I hope, for eating odd things. Thank you to my beta-readers: Alice Wright, Erin Bright, Rich Lovin, and Chaparral Hilliard. Your feedback was much appreciated! To my creative editor, Merrily Taylor—you are the only one who I'm brave enough to send a first draft to! And to my line editor, Tom Welch—your attention to detail leaves me in awe. Thank you so much! And please don't eat anything odd from now to my next book. I don't know what I'd do without you!

ABOUT THE AUTHOR

Sabrina Flynn is the author of **Ravenwood Mysteries** set in Victorian San Francisco. When she's not exploring the seedy alleyways of the Barbary Coast, she dabbles in fantasy and steampunk, and has a habit of throwing herself into wild oceans and gator-infested lakes.

Although she's currently lost in South Carolina, she's lived most of her life in perpetual fog and sunshine with a rock troll and two crazy imps. She spent her youth trailing after insanity, jumping off bridges, climbing towers, and riding down waterfalls in barrels. After spending fifteen years wrestling giant hounds and battling pint-sized tigers, she now travels everywhere via watery portals leading to anywhere.

You can connect with her at any of the social media platforms below or at www.sabrinaflynn.com

GLOSSARY

Avó - grandma in Portuguese

Bai! - a Cantonese expression for when something bad happens (close to the English expression, 'shit')

Bahba - Dad

Banker - a horse racing bet where the bettor believes their selection is certain to win

Bong 幫 - help

Boo how doy - Hatchet Man - a hired tong soldier or assassin

Capper - a person who is on the lookout for possible clients for attorneys

Chi Gum Shing 紫禁城 - Forbidden Palace

Chinese Six Companies - benevolent organizations formed to help the Chinese travel to and from China, to take care of the sick and the starving, and to return corpses to China for burial.

Chun Hung - a poster that puts a price on someone's head

Dang dang - Wait!

Digging into your Levis - searching for cash

Din Gau 癲狗 - Rabid Dog

Dressed for death - dressed in one's best

Faan tung 飯桶 - rice bucket or worthless

Fahn Quai - White Devil

Fan Kwei - Foreign Devil

Graft - practices, especially bribery, used to secure illicit gains in politics or business; corruption.

Hei Lok Lau - House of Joy - traditional name for brothels at that time

Hei san la nei, chap chung! 起身呀你個雜種！- Wake up, you bastard!

Highbinders - general term for criminals

Kedging - to warp or pull (a ship) along by hauling on the cable of an anchor that has been carried out a ways from the ship and dropped.

King chak - the police

Lo Mo - foster mother

Mien tzu - a severe loss of face

Mui Tsai - little Chinese girls who were sold into domestic households. They were often burdened with heavy labor and endured severe physical punishments.

Nei tai - you, look

Neta - Portuguese for granddaughter

Ngor bon nei - I help you

No sabe - Spanish for 'doesn't know' or 'I don't understand'. I came across a historical reference to a Chinese man using this phrase in a newspaper article. I don't know if it was common, but it is a simple, easy to say phrase that English speakers understood.

Pak Siu Lui - White Little Bud

Sau pan po - 'Long-life Boards' - coffin Shop

Si Fu - the Master

Siu wai daan 小壞蛋 - Little Rotten Eggs - an insult that implies one was hatched rather than born, and therefore has no mother. The inclusion of 'little' in the insult softens it slightly.

Slungshot - a maritime tool consisting of a weight or "shot" affixed to the end of a long cord, often by being wound into the center of a knot called a "monkey's fist." It is used to cast a line from one location to another, often a mooring line. This was also a popular makeshift (and deadly) weapon in the Barbary Coast.

Sock Nika Tow - Chop Your Head Off - a very bad insult

Wai Daan 壞蛋 - Rotten Egg

Wai Yan 壞男人 - Bad Men

Wu Lei Ching 狐狸精 - Fox Spirit

Wun Dan - Cracked Egg

Wun... ah Mei - Find Mei

Yiu! 妖! - a *slightly* less offensive version of the English 'F-word'.

Made in the USA
Las Vegas, NV
19 April 2022

47689527R00256